STORMY'S THUNDER

Satan's Devils MC - Utah Chapter #2

COPYRIGHT

Published 2021 by Trish Haill Associates

Copyright © Manda Mellett

All rights reserved. This book or any portion thereof may not be reproduced or used in any manner whatsoever without the express written permission of the author except for the use of brief quotations in a book reviews.

www.mandamellett.com

Disclaimer

This is a work of fiction. Names, characters, businesses, places, events and incidents are either the products of the author's imagination or used in a fictitious manner. Any resemblance to actual persons, living or dead, or actual events is purely coincidental.

Warning

This book is dark in places and contains content of a sexual, abusive and violent nature. It may not be suitable for persons under the age of 18.

PRODUCTION ACKNOWLEDGMENTS

Cover Design by Wicked Smart Designs

Edited and formatted by Maggie Kern @ Ms.K Edits

Proof reading by Melanie Darrow

Photographer: Golden Czermak of Furious Fotog

Model: Nick Bennett

SATAN'S DEVILS MC

1
———

*S*wift…

"If you two are getting down to fuck, will you get a fuckin' room?" Bolt sneers good humouredly as he walks into the clubroom, his eyes rolling as he catches my eye.

Lying relaxed on my man's lap, my cheek resting against his chest, I'm too lazy to do much more than give Bolt a two-fingered salute.

"Are you claiming victory or giving him the equivalent of a finger," Honor asks, his brow furrowed. "I can never tell."

It's my turn to roll my eyes. Yeah, I'm bilingual when it comes to non-verbal swearing, as they well know. Being from the UK, I'm more used to the British version, honed to a fine art during my military days.

The altercation has attracted attention. Duty, passing a beer to Honor, stares and shakes his head. "Never thought I'd see the day when you went soft, Swift."

There's nothing about me that's soft, as well he knows. His comment causes me to growl. "Want to find out just how fuckin' soft I am?"

"I'm not soft." Road's chest vibrates beneath me. "And definitely won't be unless you stop wriggling."

"Jeez, they are going to start going at it in a moment."

Now Piston gets a V sign with my palm facing inward directed toward him. Just in case he doesn't understand it, I jerk my middle finger toward him as well.

Road chuckles. Lazily, I remind him, "If we hadn't had patched you in, I was going to ask Prez to make you a sweet butt."

"Ah, but you'd have been the only one to use me, so I doubt I'd have had a problem with that." His lips curve at the corners. "Fact is, I'd probably enjoy it. Nothing to do but lie around waiting on your command."

"Don't be too certain," Preacher, the sergeant-at-arms, drawls lazily. "Any port in a storm and all that. Sweet butts can't refuse a patched member."

"You want my ass?" Road snorts.

Preacher grins widely. "Nah. Not me, Brother, but last week at the party, I saw the way Grinch was looking at you. He did seem quite focused on your backside."

Unfortunately, I'd just taken a mouthful of beer and now it spits out of my mouth, all over me and the body I'm lying on. Bolt chucks over a box of tissues and we take a few moments wiping the mess up. I take the opportunity of rolling my arse over my man's cock as I do.

He winces and grabs me tighter. "Vixen," he says into my ear. "You're going to pay for that."

I hope I do. One thing my old man's certainly got going for him is how he can use his cock. Mmm mmm. I think it's almost time we call it a night and go back to our room. He's definitely hard and my knickers are definitely on the damp side. Glancing over my shoulder, I see him grinning at me and smirking. It's hard to know why I held out for so long, kidding myself I wasn't attracted to him. I'd been so wrong. Road's my soulmate, the other half of me. We've now been together for two months, and our relationship is only growing stronger.

A paw at my leg tries to get my attention. "Someone's feeling neglected." Grinning, I stretch out my hand, stroking the head of App, my hearing dog, gently pulling at his silky ears. *Road and App.* They've both brought something into my life. I realise I've become more relaxed since they've been around. They've brought out a side of me that's human. It's not gone unnoticed. Glancing around at my brothers, I know that I'm really accepted and no longer feel the need to prove myself. They're happy to take me as I am. Maybe they always did, but I hadn't allowed myself to see it. I can be a woman in love and still be a badass.

"Will you get me another drink, babe?" Road asks. "I'd get it myself, but you're weighing me down." He winks.

I'm too comfortable where I am, and there's an easier way to get the job done without me moving. "Prospect," I yell. "Two beers."

"Coming right up," Gears calls back.

He'll be quick about it too, if he wants to patch in. I watch as he hurriedly snaps the tops off two bottles, and comes across the room at a run with one in each hand. It won't be long until he's joining us around the table, but as a good prospect, he's showing no impatience or signs he's getting fed up with being at our beck and call while he's waiting.

I'm stretching out the three remaining fingers of my right hand ready to receive mine, the beer tantalisingly within reach when there's a loud roar of an engine, then a crash which shakes the clubroom. Instead of landing in my grasp, the bottle slips from Gears' hand.

"What the fuck?" Thor, the VP roars, already on his feet.

I've gone from prone to upright in one second flat. Road, just as fast, is on his feet behind me, his gun already in his hand. Thor waves us on ahead to the stairwell as we're closest to the door and already in motion. I slide my own weapon out. Behind us there's a thundering of feet, as well as the whirr of the elevator moving. Before I exit the door, a glance shows Thor's got everything in order as he makes quick hand signals choosing Gears, Piston and Rascal to stay back. Immediately they take up positions ready to take out any visitors who shouldn't be here, while the rest follow Road and me down the stairs.

Flying down them two at a time, I'm in the lead as we enter the reception area. Immediately I note Brute, who should be manning the desk, is nowhere to be seen. Holding my weapon in the ready-to-fire position, I scan the area, but see nothing or anybody.

"What you got?" Thor hisses with one hand on the bannister as he jumps the final few steps.

"Here!" Brute calls from outside the building. "Need help!"

Suspicious, expecting a trap, I call back, "Stat report?"

"You need to fuckin' see this," he replies fast in a tense voice.

I glance at Road, who raises his chin back. Like me, he's assessed Brute's not acting as if he is in any danger, instead his tone sounds incredulous.

Still prepared to be wrong, I signal my instruction to Road, and Thor, who's now beside him, to cover me as I go to the door. I ease my way through the turnstile-like affair, turning sideways to make myself less of a target.

Once outside, my eyes scan right and left, then to the front again as I check the perimeter until I assess there's no visible threat. I let my gaze fall on the prospect crouched next to something on the ground.

What the fuck?

Brute is kneeling next to a motorcycle that's obviously crashed into the building, lying on its side with the front wheel still turning. There, prone on the ground beside it is the person who must have been riding it. Brute glances up, relief flooding over his face as he sees help has arrived.

Still holding my pistol at the ready, I sink into a crouch. When I feel a tap on my shoulder, I look up to find Thor giving me a sharp nod. Jerking my head, I see the brothers are piling out of the building and taking defensive positions. Knowing they're surrounding me, I holster my gun.

"What you got?" I ask the prospect.

"I don't know if he's fuckin' breathing." Brute's hands are hovering over the body as if he doesn't know what to touch.

"Let me look," I direct, and the prospect slides out of the way.

From behind and above, I hear Thor snap out instructions, "Check the perimeter, make sure he's alone. Bolt, check the bike for explosives." I'm not the only one thinking the injured man could be a distraction.

Is he playing possum?

Knowing Thor will have my back if he is, I lean forward and place my fingers to the pulse in the neck of the man who's so still. I'm not surprised that Brute thinks he could be dead. As I feel the very faint beat, I know he's still alive, but possibly not for much longer. The pulse is weak, bradycardic. Still measuring the beats, I examine the body. It's twisted, broken. Some of it no doubt from the crash, but with my expert eyes I see there are too many injuries to have only just happened. In the light spilling out from the clubhouse behind, it's clear some of the bruises on the man's face are yellowing. His jaw is swollen, and one eye's firmly shut, the other only just open and blood's obscuring his features. This man has been badly beaten.

"Bike's clean." Bolt reassures me we're not at risk of being blown up in an explosion. "He breathing?"

"Barely."

"Need a bus?"

I make another assessment. Could we call in our friendly doc and have him check over the intruder? It's apparent that the answer is no, this man's hanging onto life by a thread. "Yeah." If any man ever did, this one needs serious medical attention. That's if we want to keep him alive and find out what the hell has disturbed our evening.

Is he a messenger bringing something to tell us, or, maybe, he's the message itself? But he's not one of us, though I only know that because we're all present and accounted for. This man is a stranger. With his facial injuries and his body lying so crooked, it's hard to tell if he's tall or short. Even if I'd met him before, I'd have difficulty making an identification.

"Recognise him?" Thor asks, sinking to his haunches by my side with his knees cracking nosily. He certainly does not, as he starts searching gingerly through his pockets. He brings out a driver's licence.

The denial I was about to voice fades from my lips when something catches my eye. My breath hitches and reaching out, I peel back the collar of the injured man's jacket, recognising a jagged lightning tat. "God-fucking-dammit. It's fucking Stormy!"

"You sure?" Thor sounds incredulous as he rocks back. "*Stormy?*"

"I'm sure. See that tat? That's his."

"Jesus H Christ."

"*Stormy?*" Bolt roars. "He dead or dying?"

I stand. Honestly, if I was going to try to do anything like stem the blood flow, I'd be hard pressed to know where to start. As it is, my own hands are already bloody. I wipe them off on my jeans. "Almost the first, probably the last," I reply.

"You think we should move him?" Preacher asks, looking dubiously down at the body.

"Nah." Thor rises to his feet. "He's smashed up pretty bad. We'll wait for the paramedics to get here." He glares down. "If we want to find out what the fuck's going on, we'll just have to hope they can patch him up and get him talking."

The way Stormy's looking though, I wouldn't waste betting any money he's going to make it.

The VP glances down at the licence he holds in his hand. "He's travelling undercover. This says he's Jeremiah Briggs."

"Stolen?" Prez having just arrived, steps up and asks. "Are you certain," he glances dubiously down at the body, "that it's really him?"

"Nah, not stolen. And yeah, it's Stormy. The photo is of him." Thor hands it to Snatcher. "It's a good fake."

Fuck it, Stormy. Why come back like this? One thing I don't like is mysteries, well, when I can't solve them that is. If he dies right here and now, I doubt we'll ever get to the bottom of where he's been or who beat him so badly. Two months ago he'd walked out on the club, leaving his cut behind. We've been searching since then and have never found the hint of a trail leading to him.

Everyone is here now, all standing around. Rascal kneels, but makes the same assessment as I did. We might know first aid, but fuck, where do we start with a man injured within an inch of his life? Blood is flowing from multiple wounds and staining the concrete.

I roll my neck back. Catching Road's eye, I shake my head. *Why did this have to happen, and how?*

Stormy's never been a favourite of mine. Most of the time when he was here, I ignored him, and it's safe to say there were more than a few times I actively hated him. Though he is, *was* a brother, I'd have given my life for his, but in his case, I wouldn't have done so gladly. Stormy was an objectionable ass. There had been nothing, in my view, to redeem him.

He nearly lost the club its charter.

Accepting there's nothing I can do now, I go to Road and lean into him, feeling his arm come supportively around me, while in my head I go back in time to that meeting with Drummer, the prez of the mother chapter of the Satan's Devils, and three other prezes of the club. Of course it sticks in my memory, it was also the meeting where it was accepted that I, as a female of exceptional calibre, would be allowed to be a full member. It had been touch and go at first. I'd spent a soul-destroying half-hour thinking I was going to be kicked out.

I'd then been relieved that it had been decided Stormy's crimes were all his and not sanctioned by the Utah chapter. His punishment? Well, that might have been my suggestion. I thought he deserved to be hit where it hurts. Drummer had quickly agreed to my proposal. Stormy was to be busted back down to prospect for six months and was to receive a beat-down. But instead of waiting to take his punishment for the wrongs he had done to the Satan's Devils, Stormy had run. In doing so, he'd committed the major offence of disrespecting his cut and leaving it behind.

As enforcer, I'd wanted him dead. Such disregard to his brothers could mean he was a danger to the club. But others were more understanding and prepared to give him space and time to get his head around his sentence. They were convinced that he'd return and do his penance like a man.

However, as days, then weeks passed with no sign, those periods of seven days had all added up until finally they became a month, and that quickly became two. We had to face that we'd harboured a coward within our ranks.

Of course we'd tried to locate him, but even with all the technical skills at our disposal, no trace of him could be found. I'd started to side with those who thought him dead already, his bike run off the road, his body waiting to be discovered.

Bolt held out that he'd left the country.

Stormy might have been gone, his absence an embarrass-ment to the club, but that wasn't all. The Utah chapter itself was on probation, and that we failed to locate one of our own was met with suspicion. Snatcher, our prez, had had his work cut out convincing Drummer we weren't lying, and we weren't giving shelter to a man who disrespected the Satan's Devils' patch.

Goddamn it, Stormy. You've got to wake up and give us answers, or else Drummer could dissolve our chapter.

As I tense, Road tightens his arms around me.

The sound of distant sirens pulls me out of my reverie. It spurs Pip to step forward. Until two months back, he was our prez, now he's just a consultant. But he's as sharp as a tack. When he speaks, we listen.

"Snatch," he puts his hand on Prez's arm, "buy us some time. He's got ID, go with that. No one needs to know he's back until we know what we're dealing with."

"And if he dies?" Snatcher asks, turning to stare at the man whose place he'd taken. "You know there's a good chance Drummer will take away our charter if Stormy doesn't come back. He doesn't believe that with all our technical skills we can't find him."

Pip stares, his eyes narrowing. "Just asking for some time, Prez." There's no irony in the way he gives Snatcher the title. "Fuck knows where Stormy's been or what he's been up to, but if he's bringing trouble on the club, it will buy us time to decide how to deal with it."

Time's running out for Snatcher to make a decision. On my part, I think coming clean is best—send Stormy to the hospital, then contact Drummer and tell him he's come back. But Pip's spent his life shrouded in the shadows. Mistrust and suspicion taints the air that he breathes, and he still holds sway with the prez.

Snatcher heaves a reluctant sigh. "We'll play it your way for now, Pip."

An engine cuts out next to us and the siren is switched off. As brothers step back, clearing the way to the injured man, we let the paramedics do their work.

"I've got a weak pulse," one says.

"He's bradycardic."

I could have told you that.

The first one gets a line in and starts a drip going. "Let's load him up." His eyes take in all us bystanders. "I'm not sure we can save him, but we'll get him in fast."

"We'll follow you. You taking him to Memorial?"

The paramedic confirms to Snatcher that they are. Once the doors of the ambulance close, the sirens restart, and it disappears away from the clubhouse.

Christ. I lean into Road. If we were ever to see Stormy again, I'd imagined him coming back, striding in nonchalantly in his arrogant way. He'd have taken his punishment like a man. I had personal experience that he wasn't afraid of pain. I was convinced he'd have walked back in under his own steam. Or not, in which case we'd have never seen him again.

What I didn't dream of was seeing him back like this, a man so close to death it's hard to see how he manages to keep breathing.

I don't know what to think or how to feel. From the looks around me, I'm not the only one. He's one of our own, but he's not. He chose to leave us, leave his precious cut behind. It's he who'd abandoned us. But as Snatcher steps toward his bike, something draws us all to mount up as well and to follow to where Stormy's been taken.

Maybe it's just because we live on information and data, and right now, we've got none. The burning questions are why he came back in the way that he has, and who has beaten him? On my part, I want him to live so that I can get answers. Once I know, I'll happily kill him myself.

Thor, as VP, rides beside Snatcher. As enforcer, I take my place right behind them and alongside Preacher. The other brothers sort themselves out with Road, as road captain, taking his place at the end of the column.

When we arrive, we pull up and park, taking over half a dozen parking slots.

It's a Thursday, but the emergency room is busy. Thor tilts his head toward Prez. When he gets a chin lift in return, he takes the lead. I watch him disappear through the glass doors and step up to the reception desk. After a moment, he comes back.

"He made it here, still breathing. They're working on him now. There's a family room they said we could use."

As we walk in I glance around noticing that quite a few chairs have been quickly vacated, with injured people and their friends shifting themselves up to make space, everyone eyeing us suspiciously. I'm not surprised, we're all wearing our cuts, and no one wants to mess with the Satan's Devils. I almost hear the collective sigh of relief as we're directed to the room the receptionist had mentioned.

"They're not going to tell us shit," Duty points out. "We're not fuckin' relatives."

"He hasn't got any." Friends and relatives were the first people we'd checked out when trying to locate him. It had been a dead end. Stormy, it seemed, had none of either.

"Er…" Thor shifts guiltily with a sideways glance toward me. "He has."

Honor takes a seat and stretches out his long legs. "So who's playing his brother. Or is Pip gonna be his dad?"

"Neither." Thor gives a quick grin. "I told them Swift's his wife."

"Jeez." I roll my eyes. "Go for the fuckin' obvious, why don't you?" I might not have a dick, but I'm a brother just like any one of them.

"Let's hope he doesn't have amnesia," Piston snorts. When curious eyes go to him, he elaborates, "If he has and he's told Swift's his woman, he might want to make good on that."

"He'll be fuckin' dead for certain if he puts his hands near her," Road growls, a possessive arm wrapping around me. I place my hand onto my man's chest. When he looks down, I just level a stare at him, making him hastily backtrack. "Or Swift will just take care of him herself."

"You bet, lover," I say softly.

The door to the room opens. Snatcher, who'd been waiting outside for Pip to park his cage, now enters with him. Prez takes a deep breath, then asks, "He still in the land of the living?"

"For now," his VP tells him.

The next few minutes are taken up with different conversations, all trying to make sense of what's happened tonight. It's futile as we go around in circles. All anyone knows is that Stormy appeared out of nowhere and crashed into the front of the clubhouse.

"Well, at least he's back," Pip says quietly.

"It will take the heat off, that's for sure, *when* I update Drummer." Prez seems uncertain whether we're taking the correct action by not coming clean immediately.

Pip shrugs. "And who's to say he's not been beaten by another chapter?"

Pip had been our prez for ten years, though has shit going against him that prevents him legitimately wearing a Satan's Devils' cut. Not in our eyes, but in the view of the other chapters. The regulations are strict—if a member can't ride, he has to turn in his patch. We'd known that, of course, which was why Snatcher had always been the outward face of the Utah club, something Drummer had seen as betrayal and another reason to mistrust us. One thing though, Pip should find that easy to understand, as he himself doesn't trust easily. He doesn't even trust the other Satan's Devils chapters.

"If he's dead, it won't matter," Thor says reasonably. "If he lives, well, we'll be able to find shit out. Fuck it..." He pauses and looks around at everyone. "He may have left behind his cut, but he's ours to punish, it's up to no one else. I'm kind of with Pip here."

It's a difficult call. We're already in enough trouble with the mother chapter. But what if Pip's right, and another Satan's Devil took our retribution? Glancing around, it's clear I'm not the only one who's angry at the suggestion.

It's my man who tries to bring the heat in the room down, getting to his feet and asking, "Anyone want a drink? Guess we're going to have a long fuckin' wait."

It appears everyone does. Honor and Cowboy volunteer to go with him, returning juggling cardboard boxes containing sodas, coffees, and an assortment of sugars and creamers. No tea on offer, though. I make do with a bottle of water.

By the time the first coffee is drunk, the door again opens. This time, in steps Grinch, Goofy and Mystic—our three old-timers who live at our old clubhouse and maintain the outward face of the Satan's Devils MC, Utah chapter.

After going through it all again, and after another round of drinks, we settle back. There are a few conversations, but most of us are lost in our heads of what the fuck has happened to Stormy, and will he survive to tell us? My mind keeps circling back to his arrival being a forewarning of trouble heading to the club. I hate the not knowing.

A few hours pass before the door opens again. This time it's by a man wearing a stethoscope around his neck.

"Mrs Briggs?"

Road jabs me in the side.

"Yeah, that's me." I'd forgotten I was supposed to be Stormy's wife and hadn't recognised the name we'd booked him in under. I try to put a suitably concerned expression on my face. Unfortunately, tears for Stormy are beyond me. "How is he?"

The doctor eyes me as I stand, but I can't read his face. He looks weary. "He's alive." He indicates the door and is presumably suggesting that I should step out into the corridor.

I indicate Thor, ready to explain I need someone with me to hear the news about my *husband*, but I didn't have to worry, it seems as an almost-widow, I don't need to explain.

He doesn't take us far, just a few steps outside. There, he leans a hand against the wall. "I'm afraid your husband is in a bad way. Do you know what happened to him?"

"I don't," I admit. "He crashed into the clubhouse, that's all I, or anyone knows."

The doctor looks down before once again meeting my eyes. "He's taken quite a beating, not all of it as a result of the crash. We're still trying to assess all the internal injuries. I had to mend a tear on one of his kidneys. We think we've stopped the bleeding, for now, anyway. He's got four broken ribs—one punctured his lung." He pauses for a moment. "You say he rode his bike?"

I nod.

He shakes his head. "Impossible. Not with those injuries. There's a contusion on his head that could have come from the crash, and the broken left femur, but not much else was caused by him coming off a motorcycle. His right radius is broken and has a fractured collarbone." He eyes Thor, then me, as though assessing how much to say. "He wouldn't have been able to ride."

"Nevertheless," I harden my voice, "he did."

A disbelieving sigh comes. "Some of his injuries are consistent with torture. He's got burns all over his body, a severe concussion, and one of his eardrums is ruptured."

"Would it be easier to tell us what isn't broken?" Thor states drily.

I shoot Thor a warning look. "Is he going to make it, Doc?" I don't need to fake sounding anxious. *Goddamn it, Stormy. You've got to wake up. I need answers.*

"I'm trying my best." His eyes seem to home in on Thor's VP patch. "I'm going to need to report this."

Thor straightens his back. "Cops won't be interested. He's a member of a one-percenter club."

"Mrs Briggs?"

"I'd prefer you didn't," I tell him. "I-I just want him better."

"Doc?"

It's Pip who comes out of the waiting room. Taking hold of the doctor by the elbow, he leads him away to have a low conversation. Strain as I might, I can't hear what they're saying. A glance at Thor reveals it's not my deafness, but that they're speaking so low. He also looks mystified.

When the doctor comes back, he seems resigned. "While he's alive, I won't report this. But if he dies…"

He'll have to report a suspicious death. Pip raises his chin at me, and I realise he's done his best. Last thing we need is cops prying into our business.

"Mrs Briggs, all we can do is pray for now, and hope there's nothing we're missing. Your husband, I'm afraid, is in a very poor state. We think we've caught everything life-threatening, but with such a severe loss of blood, and his overall condition, a lot has to depend on his will to survive."

"I'm his wife," I tell the doctor, realising I'm not showing any normal emotion of a distraught partner. "But we've been estranged recently. I can't tell you where he's been or what he's done over the past few weeks. I need you to get him well, doc, so I can kill him myself for causing me all this worry."

As Thor sucks in air beside me, the doctor smiles. "You know, you're not the first wife to have said that to me." His hand lands on my shoulder and he squeezes it. Luckily, he removes it before I follow through on my impulse to break his finger. "I'll keep you updated."

"Can I see him?"

"He's in ICU right now. When he's more stabilised, hopeful-ly." After his parting comment, the doctor walks away.

When we return to the waiting room, Thor sums it up

succinctly. "Stormy's a fuckin' mess. He may or may not make it. Seems like he's got an arm and a leg that aren't injured, and he didn't say anything about his liver. But everything else, well it's broken, damaged or bleeding." He pauses, then adds, "He's been tortured, and it didn't just happen today."

Stunned faces greet us. "Knew it was bad," Bolt murmurs.

"Should have stayed and taken his fuckin' beatdown," Cowboy observes. "He brought this on himself."

As the comments fly around, I cross the room and retake my seat beside Road. All I can think is Stormy can't escape me. I'll pray for him to come back to good health, but only so I can beat answers out of him.

If he lives, I'll make him wish he'd died.

He almost lost us our charter. And if Snatcher doesn't overrule Pip and inform Drummer, there's a chance his actions still might.

2

———————

Twelve years ago

Stormy…

"He was interested. I could tell." My father, all but skipping on the spot, is wearing a look on his face that's not one I can ever remember seeing before. "Well done, Son." He slaps my back hard. "This is all I ever wanted for you, you know?" For the first time in my life, I realise my old man's fucking proud of me. It's just a shame I couldn't give a damn. Too little, too late. And for the wrong fucking reason.

Around us the stands are emptying. Spectators, some elated, some with disappointed looks on their faces, depending on which team they've been supporting, gather their things and start leaving. A space clears in the vicinity of me and my dad.

"Don't fuck this up," he continues, reverting to form as his face darkens. "I haven't given you eighteen years of my life for you to fuck this up now. You hear me, Son?"

I hear his words and understand them only too well. A blind man would be hard pushed to miss the way his body has started to vibrate, or that his hands are fisted at his sides. It's been a while now since he'd used those fists on my face, my back, my ribs, hell, any part of my body I was fool enough to allow within range. But he won't hit me today, or for the rest of the time I'm living under his roof. If it's done nothing else, today has given me a certain level of immunity. Even if he could still take me on, he wouldn't want to upset my chances of getting a sports scholarship to one of the major colleges.

His dream, not mine.

He's groomed me to be a football star every day of my miserable life, his focus trained on nothing but me being picked up to play in a major league, his belief that he'd ride on my coattails, and any money earned would be used to take him out of the trailer park and set him up for life. It was why he'd bothered to keep me around after my mom had walked out.

He'd never bothered to ask me what I wanted, had never given me a choice. As the fruit of his loins, I was his. I belonged to him. I owed him, and one day, it was assumed, I'd gladly repay the debt. *Like fuck.*

I'd been undersized for my age until I turned fourteen, but that hadn't stopped him pushing me on. Other kids might have liked that their parents, or parent in my case, came to every game, hell, often turned up at practice as well. But not me. If he thought I hadn't tried, my reward would be a backhander when I got home, often adding to the punishment a scrawny kid like me had already received on the field. Had it spurred me on? Sure, but not for the reasons he believed.

Football practice, physical training, all gave me the opportunity for the fitness regime I needed to follow my own dreams.

I'd been sixteen when I matched his six-foot-two height, and in the last couple of years I had gained two inches more. Now a match for him, the unspoken threat in my eyes triggers his sense of self-preservation and prevents him throwing so many punches at me. But then, he no longer thinks he has a need. In his mind, he's achieved what he'd set out to.

My plan has been thought out over years of lying in my small bed in the filthy trailer I'm ashamed to call home. Do I feel guilty that I'm lying to him, if only by omission, leading him on? Fuck no. A pro-football player life is not for me. But it dovetailed nicely with what I wanted for myself and had given me time to plan and to get all my ducks in a line.

So I continue to lead him on, pushing aside the thought I'd rather celebrate with my teammates who are still on a high after winning the game. "Coach has already spoken to me. The scout's interested," I confirm. That's the truth, though personally I hold only fleeting pleasure in the achievement.

"This is a cause for celebration." He slaps me between my shoulder blades again, a blow that would have sent me staggering just a few years back. Now, I don't move, instead, I relish how he shakes out his hand.

His celebration not mine. Tonight he'll go out, talking me up with his friends, boasting how he's going to have a football player son. He'll come home drunk, as he always does. Or rather, he'll call me to bring him home. In the meantime, I'll be expected to hang around waiting for him. I owe him, you see. Owe him for every minute of my miserable life.

A social life of my own? I never dared to have one. If I stayed out with friends, he'd come and drag me home. That the trailer wasn't a complete hovel was all down to me and had nothing to do with him, but I never wanted to take anyone back there. He was a complete and utter disgusting slob, and I'd be on edge, waiting for him to lash out even at a visitor to our home.

He's the only parent I've known. Oh, I had a mom, once. I turn away from him, pretending to watch my teammates gathering their stuff, amped by our overwhelming success tonight, but in my mind, I've gone back in time. I'm that six-year-old returning home from school.

"Where's Mom?"

"Gone."

My brow had furrowed. Gone? Gone where? The shops? To see a friend? His tone had rung warning bells causing a feeling of dread to grow inside. Gone forever? Unthinkable. She couldn't leave me alone with him. She wouldn't, would she? "Where's she gone? When will she be back?"

The look on his face was one of pleasure. "She's gone for good. Fuck her sorry ass. Now it's just you and me, Son." He eyes me for a moment, his brows turning down. "Don't you dare fuckin' cry. Men don't cry."

I wasn't a man, I was a young boy. I couldn't help the way my bottom lip quivered, nor the tear that rolled from my eye. Mom had tried to stop him hurting me, got in the way of his fists more than once, taking my punishment on herself. Even then at my tender years, I'd hated it.

I got a fist in my face then. "Men don't fuckin' cry," he repeats. "I'll make you a fuckin' man if it's the last thing I do."

His blow, so strong, had laid me out on the floor. I lay, stunned, trying to process Mom had left. But surely, I'd see her again?

I never had. No calls, no visits. No birthday cards or presents at Christmas. The one person who'd made my life bearable had disappeared off the face of the earth. Did I hate her? I didn't know. She'd abandoned me, yes, but was now hopefully out of range of his ire. *Safe.* It had been my childhood dream to find out where she disappeared to and to go join her. Until those fists met my flesh time after time. That was when all a son's love had died for the woman who gave him life. *How could she have left me with him?* She should have taken me. She would have if she'd loved me.

He'd never divulged where she'd gone. As I grew older, I never bothered to search. She'd known what my future would be, yet she still chose to walk out.

"Drive me home, Son."

Yes, this was my life. Nothing more than his taxi driver. He'd lost his licence when driving drunk, got it back for a time, then lost it again. A never-ending cycle.

I always knew I was a commodity to him. He had no love for me, never showed affection. I was a means to an end, his meal ticket for the future. It made me bitter, and in turn, I used him as well, only waiting until I turned eighteen, then I'd start to put my plan into action. Soon I'd be able to fulfil the vow to never see him again.

Suppressing a sigh at his demand, I should have known by now it would have been useless to make plans for tonight. They'd be fucked, just as they always are. I suppose I'd expected he might cut me some slack if I'd played well, and as it turns out, I couldn't have done better. Expect my dad to show some decency or give me a reward? Stupid. It's more likely that hell will freeze over.

I seethe, inwardly, but nevertheless agree. Right now I'm dependent on having a roof over my head as my plans come together. Am I using him? Yeah, but I have no regrets about it. He's used me every day of my sorry fucking life.

"Just give me five minutes, and I'll take you home." Shielding my eyes from the setting sun, I see an arm raised in a wave.

"Now, Son."

I breathe in and hold my breath, knowing I have to give in or suffer the consequences of going home with him in one of his more cantankerous moods. While nowadays it's more me evading his fists, or catching a raised hand and preventing it connecting, there's always the risk my rage would match his own. Being arrested for assault or murder would not help me attain my future.

Resigning myself to texting the girl who's waiting for me instead, I take out my phone as I walk alongside him. Keeping a few paces behind, I call up her number.

"Finn?"

"Sorry, babe. I've got to take the old man home. Can't make it tonight."

"Can you drop him off and come back later? I can wait."

I eye the way my father is stumbling and know the next few hours will be spent taking him out to meet his friends, then collecting him when he becomes too belligerent for even them to deal with. Once back at the trailer, he'll insist I hang around, waiting on him to keep yet more beer in his hand then, finally, helping him into bed before or even after he passes out. Subsequently I'll be cleaning up the vomit that's invariably present, maybe even having to change his bed after he's pissed himself. I've had a lot of practice.

"Nah, not tonight."

There's a silence on the end of the phone and then come the words that aren't entirely unexpected. "Well, you call me when you've got *time*, and maybe I won't be busy myself."

"Babe..." But she's already gone.

Fuck my life.

Telling myself I've just got to hang on for a few more months, I take Dad home like a dutiful son, take him out, bring him back, pander to him, then when he's eventually asleep and, as expected, after I've cleaned up both him and the carpet, go to bed myself.

I'm woken by the sound of crashing—not an unusual occurrence. Dragging myself out of bed, I emerge to see what damage has been done. He's tried to make himself a coffee but dropped it because of his shaking hands. I clean up the mess, then start returning to my bedroom.

"I'm hungry. Cook me something."

I would argue, tell him to do it himself, the words on the tip of my tongue, but I swallow them with a reminder it's too important that I have a base for the next few months. Biting my tongue, I cook him bacon and eggs, knowing most of it will go to waste, especially as he washes it down with his first beer of the day.

"What are you doing today?" he queries, a calculated look in his eyes. He'll have a list of chores a mile long if I allow him to get started.

"Training," I tell him, knowing those chores will immediately lessen in importance.

His eyes gleam. That's something of which he approves. Wobbling, he stands, the action making him fart loudly. "You're a good boy," he tells me in passing, burping a lungful of sour breath in my face. "Going to get that scholarship, I know you will."

If I do, I'm not going to take it, but my excuse gets me out of the house, and training isn't a lie.

First, I drive to the beach. I've lived in southern California for all of my life, and swimming has always been one of my favourite pastimes and a way to escape. In the water I feel weightless and free, though doing it solely for pleasure stopped when I first set on my dream. Now I follow a punishing schedule, trying to put in at least a mile, timing myself to improve my performance as this is what will hopefully get me on the rung of the ladder to the next stage in my life. Back on the beach, I do push-ups and sit-ups, working until my muscles scream. Now I run a circuit I've estimated is a mile and a half while trying to beat my best, grinning when I shave off another second. After that, I dive back into the ocean to cool myself off this time, floating on my back and focusing my mind on the dream that's within tasting distance.

I've always excelled academically, fuck knows how. It wasn't in the genes my dad passed onto me, and I have to suspect those had come from my mom. She was intelligent enough to get out, even though she'd left me behind. Did she think I was turning into my old man? It's a fear that's always lurked in my mind during the intervening years, spurring me on not to be like him, in any way, shape or form while battling the fear nature might always win out.

Days pass, and I begin to grow excited. Dad sees the gleam in my eyes and thinks it's because of my football future. I don't tell him it's not. When the day I've been waiting for arrives, I sneak out of the trailer before he awakes.

I'd signed on the dotted line some weeks back and passed the background test as I'd always kept my nose clean. Now I'm taking the Armed Services Vocational Attitude Battery, a punishing series of tests. I emerge triumphant with a score in the high 80s and get my Navy contract. But that isn't what I'm aiming for.

It's coincidental, but when I get home elated about my marks, Dad is waving an envelope at me which he's already opened, of course. It's the offer of a football scholarship. He wants me to sign right there and then, even going so far as to offer a pen to me. I brush him off with a comment about first reading what I'm signing up for.

I bide my time. The Physical Screening Test is fast approaching, and this will be when I see whether all my training has paid off. I pass with flying colours, and that night return home with the SEAL contract in my hand. I hadn't had a moment's hesitation when putting my signature to that.

The second PST I conquer just as well as the first, and hell, I've never been so pleased in my life to receive my instructions to go to bootcamp in Illinois.

"The fuck?" my dad asks, as he sees me packing my meagre belongings into a rucksack. "Where the hell are you going?"

"I'm joining the Navy." Already I don't want to admit what arm of the services I've actually qualified for, wary even now of it coming back to bite me if Dad goes around spouting it off.

"You-you're fuckin' what?" His face goes red. "You're not throwing your fuckin' life away. You're going to be a football player."

"Nah, that's your dream, Dad. Not mine."

"You ungrateful bastard!" he roars.

Deciding I'll allow him just one, I brace, but for once he's not drunk, and his punch snaps my head back. I no longer need his address or a roof to lay my head under, I'm moving on. I flex my muscles and crowd toward him, my hands wrapping around his fists.

"No more, Dad. It finishes now. I'm going, and you can't stop me."

"I'm your father. You can't leave me. You've got the scholarship…"

Being my father is a title he's never earned. Nothing he can say will dissuade me. I toss him away from me, making sure he lands on the couch.

I don't bother to argue. "Goodbye."

I get into my car and drive away without one glance in my rearview. I'm never going back. That was a vow I kept.

3

____

Seven years ago

S
tormy…

I'm back in the sandpit again. Squinting, I take the shades out of my pocket and put them on as I walk away from the briefing. I listened, of course, but where I'm sent doesn't bother me that much. I'm used to having no say in what mission I'm sent on. Whatever it is, I'll do my best. I'm serving my country. This is my life and it's everything I'd ever hoped it would be, though it can never be described as easy.

I sink to my ass, take out a bottle and drink some water, idly staring at the base bustling around me as I find my mind drifting back to how I got to where I am today.

It was hard fucking work, but all those years back, I made it through training, formed friends in BUD/S—good men who had my back as I'd had theirs. I achieved my dream and became a SEAL. But I didn't stop there, continuing training in whatever opportunity came my way, specialising in explosives and obtaining college credits in computer science. I'm also the best damn sniper on the team, aided by my steady hand, good co-ordination and the way my brain has no problem calculating wind speed and distance. I make the most of all the chances given to me, knowing I'll pay it all back in spades as I've no desire other than being part of the teams so long as I'm physically fit enough or still alive. I'm a lifer. I can think of no other way I'd prefer to spend my days on this earth.

I'm proud to be one of the best, working with the best, always striving for the highest accolades in anything I do. Not for public recognition of course, there's no chance of that, but for the sense of a job well done, and the knowledge that we've all come through. As part of the teams, I've worked ops all around the world, essentially living the life I've always dreamed.

I might not get the thanks, cheers or praise, or the adulation and money that would come from being a professional football player but I don't give a fuck about that.

On a rare occasion, I might think back to where I've come from, but never with regret that I'd embarked on the wrong path. I didn't come from a happy home, but as it's turned out, I've found a far better one instead.

A few months back I was transferred to a new team to take the place of a man who hadn't re-upped. While I've worked on a number of continents, I've done a few tours in Afghanistan, and my fluency in Dari and Pashto, the two main languages of the region, was the main reason I was chosen. I'd learned as a challenge to myself, finding learning the alien tongue not too dissimilar to my first attempts to speak to a computer in program code.

To date, this deployment has been fairly easy, though we're working behind enemy lines. The op is helping to train the Afghans so hopefully, in time, they can take on the battle themselves. That I can talk to them in their own language smooths much of the way.

I'm still learning the strengths of my new team, never being one to take men at face value. That they're also SEALs means I don't have to question the inherent trust we're all on the same side. But as to each individual, well, I can't help reserving judgement. In my eyes, a man has to prove himself. I'll have their six, and know they'll have mine, but a designation means shit until you've got the measure of a man through experience. A therapist would say my distrust stems back to my dad. He was my parent, but nothing he did earned the title he wore.

If I've got the reputation of being standoffish, then I don't give a damn. I'll be cautious until I've reason not to be and dislike joining new teams for that reason. That said, I'm slowly coming to appreciate the strengths of my new team members. They're a good bunch of men, and I've discovered I like them.

Take Pooh, named because he looks just like a teddy bear, well, I've reached the stage to believe he's a real friend of mine. We couldn't be more different in background—he's still got parents who are as proud as fuck of how he earns a living, together with a wife and a new baby born just a few weeks ago. Me? I'm very much single, and happy to remain so.

Buster was harder to get to know. Unlike Pooh, he keeps his personal shit to himself. I've learned as much from his interactions with others as I have from the actual man. He prefers hand-to-hand combat, hence picking up his handle. We'd been ambushed a week or so back, and he hadn't hesitated to have my back. It was that incident that solidified my admiration for him.

Tailor? He's the unofficial leader of our group, the oldest and most experienced. The origin of his name is a bit blurred. Sure, he's great with a needle and thread, including in the absence of the platoon's combat medic happy to stitch up a wound, but the shortened version Tail works as well, as chasing it is one of his specialities. He's an open book, never keeping anything back, and always ready with his booming laugh. He kind of adopted me and while my natural instinct was to resent it, I tend to gravitate toward him.

No one knows why Gun got his name, the story's been lost in the mists of time. But he's a crack sniper, almost as good as myself. And Slice, well, his wet work is to be admired, and a silent death has been delivered many a time.

Years back when I'd joined my first team, I'd just been Finn, appropriately kept because of scuba diving. By the time I joined this unit, everyone was using my new handle, my reputation for being impatient with anyone not giving one hundred percent or issuing some bullshit command just to keep us on our toes had preceded me. When faced with a fuckup, the storm clouds came rolling in, covering my expressive face and betraying me. Apparently, they knew when to step back as my features would grow dark. At that point, I became Storm, or Stormy.

When you're named, you're stuck with it whether you like it or not. Sometimes in the dead of night the name gives me pause. Am I more like my old man than I'd like? On too short a fuse and liable to lose my temper? It's a notion I prefer to dismiss. I don't get angry for no reason, nor use my fists when I'm in a rage, or not often. Instead, words are my weapon of choice. I'm adept at leaving no one in any doubt as to what I'm thinking.

Truth is, I don't suffer fools gladly. Luckily, in the platoon of my fellow elite SEALs, we haven't many of those.

Never once did I regret not following my father's dreams instead of my own. I had more excitement in my life, and more than that, my life had a purpose. I wasn't entertaining wannabe experts sitting in the stands, I've amassed no fortune, though the pay for a SEAL isn't bad. The life I live has me fulfilled. I'm wired for this, far more than I would have been as a football player. Receiving the Navy SEAL Trident pin had been the proudest day of my life.

"Any questions from the briefing?" Lieutenant Commander Smythe stops by my side. I jump to my feet. "No, Sir."

Smythe's new. A week or so back, he replaced our previous task unit leader who'd taken a bullet to his leg. I'm still feeling him out, but so far I'm not impressed, and at times have silently questioned how he'd ever made the grade. Sure, the words out of his mouth sounded right, but he didn't have the mental agility which I admire. Once a plan's in place, he seems slow to change it up as the situation demands.

I've kept my thoughts to myself, but tonight, as our team leader walks off, I leave my reminiscing behind and go over to join my team, reaching them just as Pooh brings the very same thing up.

His eyes stare in the direction Smythe disappeared. "I worry he won't bend if it's necessary."

As I nod my agreement, Gun shows he disagrees.

"See? There's something to be said for sticking to your, well, guns." He grins self-deprecatingly. "I'd rather know what I'm heading into and what I'm doing, then have someone constantly changing it about. Smythe is someone I respect."

"Patton was better," I observe, referencing our previous leader. "I trusted him."

"You trust your own fuckin' self," Buster observes without malice, and with a grin. "Sometimes I don't think you trust us."

"Getting there," I tell him, honestly.

"Oh, we pass, do we?" Tailor tosses in with a smirk.

"Guess we're honoured," Slice chuckles. "We all know how high your standards are."

"Stormy's standards have saved many lives," Pooh puts in to support me. "I, for one, am fuckin' glad he's with us."

"Hear fuckin' hear." Tailor adds his endorsement, then changes the subject without giving me time to get embarrassed. Praise from him is praise indeed. "Anyway, good news, after the op tomorrow, we should be heading back Stateside." He pauses to light a cigarette. "What are you guys doing when we go back on leave? What do you have planned?"

It's the normal shit, the discussion just a way to pass time. I listen but don't offer anything. My contribution would only consist of finding a place to get drunk and a willing woman or two to fuck. Slice and Buster will be visiting family, Pooh, his wife and the son he hasn't yet seen in the flesh. Gun's a loner like me and states he'll just go with the flow. Tailor will be returning to his on/off girlfriend. I gather from what he's been saying, the tumultuous relationship's on again now.

I listen, nodding in all the right places. I've no home other than the accommodation I have on base, and no family anymore. Without me there, Dad had taken up driving once more and wrapped his car around a lamppost a year back. Did I feel guilty? Hell no. He'd have done the same whether I'd been a football player or SEAL. Even Stateside, I wouldn't have been there to chauffeur him around.

My lack of remorse hadn't worried me, and I hadn't bothered to ask for leave to attend the funeral.

Sometimes I feel adrift, having no roots, no one apart from the men around me to grieve were I to die in this forsaken desert overseas. No one, other than them, would give a fuck if I wasn't around. My job is my life, my mistress the country which depends on me. Though sometimes I do wonder what I'm missing, as I had when I looked at the photos of his newborn son Pooh proudly showed around. Having a baby hasn't softened him, in fact, I'd say it's made him more determined to make the world a safer place for him and his family.

Does having something to live for make everything more worthwhile? I can't see that. Having a son meant fuck all to Dad. It would have been better for me if he'd never procreated. Maybe it's best to be unencumbered with distractions or to make commitments it's not inside me to make. The fear of exactly what I might have inherited from my sperm donor raises its head again. My other parent's contribution wasn't particularly admirable, she'd walked out when the going got tough.

Conversation carries on around me, but I've descended into

a sombre mood. With murmured 'goodnights' I take myself off to grab a few hours' sleep.

I'd been a football star at high school, my virginity lost long ago to one of the cheerleaders. *What was her name? Dana? Dinah?* Something like that. And while it hadn't been my intention for it to have become a one-night stand, it had been around the time my dad had lost his licence to drive and I had gained mine. The threat that he'd kick me out if I didn't toe the line curtailed my social life so he could have his. I'd made the sacrifice, driven by the fear of not being able to complete the education I needed to become a SEAL if I was made homeless.

Maybe I'd have run from a relationship anyway. Maybe my frustration with him had been tinged with relief. What did I know about women? The only female who'd been in my life had been my mother, and she hadn't cared enough to stick around or even stay in touch. Now, at thirty years old, I think I've got so set in my ways, I'd find it hard to share a home with anyone.

Of course I'm a sexual beast and my urges don't go unsatisfied. I've fucked, tens, probably hundreds of women. Though I might not have gotten close enough to anyone to admit I'm a SEAL, the fact I've got a Navy uniform is enough to get many a female into bed. I don't see the harm in it as long as I make the expectations clear from the start. It's more a rest from my hand for the night which is damn all I get when I'm on a tour.

But Pooh's rightful excitement at seeing his family makes my future seem lonely. In the darkness, I shake my head. I probably wouldn't know what to do with a woman if I found one—apart from the obvious that is.

As I lay my head on the pillow, I don't dwell on the mission ahead or in wondering what I'll do with my time on leave. Instead, I switch off fast. Like many enlisted men, I've learned to take the opportunity of downtime when it occurs. My thoughts never keep me awake for long.

The next morning I awake one hundred percent focused on

the task ahead, attending our final briefing just to hear a confirmation of what we already know.

Instead of training the indigenous forces, today we've got an op of our own. I can already feel the excitement churning inside me. Seated around the table in a makeshift conference room, we go over the plan one more time.

I may not have a lot of time for Lieutenant Commander Smythe, but I do pay attention. The town we're heading for was once slap-bang in the middle of the war zone. There's barely a building left standing, all residents moved out long ago. But satellite images have shown activity in a broken-down warehouse that once stood proud.

While the area has been relatively quiet, trucks have been coming in under the cover of darkness and dropping off loads. Advance intel from one of the local forces is the deliveries have consisted of weapons, explosives and mines. We can't know what they intend to be used for, but something definitely is planned. Our op is to get in and blow that damn armoury up before the Taliban have a chance to plant said mines and take a chunk of our force out.

Any tangos we find will be interrogated and hopefully provide the explanation for the build-up of what's supposed to be an impressive-sized munitions dump. That's the reason we're not just launching a ballistic missile and taking the whole thing out.

"We'll go in at 2300 hours. I'll stay in the bird and monitor operations. You'll rappel down, landing on the roof, here." Smythe points to a diagram.

"Stormy. You and Pooh will make your way down to what we've been told is the store." Smythe indicates it out. "That's our target, the munitions. Pooh, you cover Stormy while he's setting the explosives. You've got twenty minutes, no more, okay? This is a quick in and out."

I raise my chin. Nothing unusual.

"You want me to do an inventory so we know what they have stored there?"

"No point," Smythe replies. "Just blow the fucking thing up."

I suppress rolling my eyes. If we knew exactly what they'd gathered it could provide intel as to what they're planning. But Smythe's got his orders—blow the darn thing up. Sometimes I wonder whether he's even got a brain.

The man himself is continuing, "Tailor, Slice. You'll give cover to Stormy and Pooh. Make sure they have a clear route out of there. Gun, Buster, you're to go through floor by floor and take out or preferably capture any tangos. We want at least one alive, okay? Everyone, keep your eyes open, that building's already unstable."

I think we've all got it now, but Smythe wants us to have it memorised word for word. I focus on him, but in my mind, I'm already going over how I'll be playing my part, and precisely what explosives I'll need to take with me.

"At 23:20, the bird will return for you. At 23:21 I'll be pressing that detonator, so make sure you're all clear." Smythe finishes up. "Any questions?"

We have none. It's straightforward enough, the unknowns being how many tangos we'll encounter. I'll be relying on Tailor, Gun, Slice and Buster to clear my path and allow me the space to do my job. Pooh raises his chin at me and gives a slight nod. It's far from the first time we've worked together.

I'm more than happy to blow that place sky-high, particularly knowing I'll be obliterating hated mines. I've seen only too often what they can do to a body, civilian or soldier alike.

Meeting adjourned, we start to prepare, equipping ourselves with all the best in technology Uncle Sam can supply. Even after all these years, this moment makes me proud to be part of the US military.

While flying in any type of aircraft is not my favourite pastime, jumping out is actually the part I don't mind. Flying means I need to trust in the pilot's expertise, when parachuting, or as today, rappelling down, the control is all mine. All my nerves flee as the target comes into sight, and the countdown to exit begins.

"Go!"

I don't hesitate when it's my turn. Anticipation, the thrill I live for fills me as the wind rushes past. Landing within seconds, I tilt my head, letting go of the tether and listening for sounds as my five teammates land around me. Above us, the helicopter lifts away, flying off to a safe distance.

As the sounds of the rotating blades fade, using gestures clearly seen via our night goggles, we begin to spread out. Pooh and I follow Tailor and Slice to the stairwell, our task to descend as fast as we can, our two companions clearing the way in front of us. Above me, I can hear Gun and Buster beginning their search on each of the floors.

Tailor pauses. *Tango ahead,* he signals. His M4A1 leads the way, a burst of fire taking the tango down. No chance to take a prisoner here, it was kill or be killed instead.

We descend floor by floor. Just one more to go, and I'm feeling twitchy, expecting to have found more human obstacles in our way. It's too quiet. There's only the occasional burst of gunfire above me. We soon reach the basement where the weapons are stored.

Tailor's voice sounds through my headphones, mimicking my concern. "It's too fuckin' quiet. But do what you have to do, we'll watch your backs."

Pooh's already doing his task. He's completed one circuit, checking for anyone hidden. He opens his mic. "No one here. No other entrances or exits. We'll be okay here, Tail."

Tailor's eyes find mine. It's so damn empty it feels like a trap, but Pooh appears to be right. So I give him a sharp nod, then he and Slice disappear the same way we'd arrived.

Wasting no time, I set about placing the explosives while

Pooh busies himself opening boxes and crates. I grin. Guess he had the sense to do a quick inventory after all. When they blow up, Smythe won't know they were closed or open. Through my headphones I can hear repeated calls of *all clear*.

Turning off my mic, I say to Pooh, "I hope they leave someone alive. Else we'll have no one to question."

No one would criticise anyone for shooting back if they were in the line of fire, but there has to be one who'll surrender rather than die.

"Three dead tangos," I hear Tailor report. "No one still breathing."

"Shit." Smythe's plans have gone out the window and he doesn't sound happy. "Sitrep, Stormy."

"Setting the explosives now," I say through my now open mic.

Pooh motions me over. Like I did just now, he cuts off the comms for a moment. "I don't fuckin' like this. Under these guns is straw. The mines too. This isn't some large armoury, there's hardly any shit here at all."

I grimace and speak quietly as I give Smythe the update. "Got a few mines. Nothing of the amount we were led to believe."

After a moment, there's a sharply drawn in breath. "You're not there to do a fucking inventory."

"Kind of hard to miss." Pooh shakes his head at me, making me grin.

Smythe's unable to argue. Tailor comes back with an explanation, and it's one none of us like. "Fuck. They might have already planted them. Or moved them on."

"Not for us to worry about. Complete the mission," Smythe says. "Set the explosive."

"Copy that."

"We could leave it," Tailor resists. "Stay here and watch for anyone coming back."

"Our mission is to destroy whatever there is." Smythe is adamant.

Smythe's reply makes me roll my eyes. I'm with Tailor, something's off.

"The bird's returning. You've got five minutes to get yourselves back to the roof," Smythe reminds us.

"Copy that," Tailor resignedly confirms.

Having no option, I set the explosive and arm it. The control is up with Smythe who'll set off the detonation remotely.

"Over here," Pooh says quietly, waving me too him. He's just moved a box and has found a trap door.

Signalling I'll take the lead, I sink down, listening carefully but I can hear no sounds from below. My arm reaches forward, pulling the ring to lift it up. Pulling open the door, I duck back for cover as soon as it's wide. Pooh's gun appears over my shoulder, but our night vision goggles reveal nothing inside.

Still hypervigilant, I drop through, my SIG Sauer P226 held at the ready as I scan my surroundings. It's basically a single room with an alcove off to one side. I step forward to the small opening. Perhaps here's where I'll find the real store of weapons. I start to approach the alcove when I hear a low child-like cry which is immediately cut off.

"Trap," Pooh says quietly. "Gotta be, man."

Could it be? It could be a recording left playing, but is the doubt I feel worth it? "I'm going to check it out."

"Storm—"

"Head for the extraction point, I'll catch up."

"Fuck that. You're staying to check, you need someone to watch your back."

I've still got an open mic and my words weren't heard by Pooh alone. "Stormy, Pooh, get back here *now*. Tailor, Slice, Buster and Gun are waiting to leave." Smythe sounds impatient. "That's an order, Stormy. The bird's on its way to pick you up. Soon as it's here, we're taking off."

Mentally, I flip him off. It may be nothing, but I'm not leaving here without investigating the sound. When this place blows, it will take most, if not all, of this warehouse. There could be someone here that we could question.

"We got another escape route?" Pooh asks.

"One floor up at ground level. You should be able to get out." It's dependable Tailor who's clearly consulting the plans.

I hear Smythe start to protest, but I ignore him.

"We've got two minutes," Pooh tells me. "Let's do this."

Signalling to Pooh to be quiet, I listen again, then step in the direction I'd heard the sound. The back of the alcove is piled with rubbish. With Pooh aiming directly inside, I start clearing that shit out.

"Get back here *now.*" Smythe's angry voice sounds in my ear. "Repeat. Stormy, leave it the fuck alone. You and Pooh get your asses up top."

Though no one can see, I feel my eyes roll. There's nothing to stop us delaying the explosion until we're certain there's no one here. But that's Smythe. His explosion will go off at the allotted time, even if we haven't fully completed the mission. He'll proudly state the time in his report.

"We've got this. We'll take the street exit." I catch Pooh's eye and see him give me a sharp nod. He's a good man. If he thought I was wrong, he'd argue, but it's clear he doesn't.

I move planks, rubble, sacks and then... *Oh fuck.* There, squeezed inside and tightly bound on the floor, are two girls. One appears to be in her late teens, another, a child possibly young enough to be her daughter.

At that moment, I think I know what this is. A setup, an elaborate hit. Just a few mines and guns left to draw us in, to carry out a death sentence on these girls. Instantly, I wonder why they're important.

"Abort the mission," I say fast into my mic. "I've got two girls."

"Locals or ours?"

"Locals," I confirm.

"Leave them. Get out of there, Storm."

"Fuck that," I reply.

Pooh's already got his knife out and is undoing the ropes that have them bound.

"It's likely a fucking trap. They've probably got explosives strapped to them or a grenade hidden in their clothes. You've got no time to search them. Get the fuck out!" Smythe's ranting.

But Pooh's got them free. He motions to me, indicating he's checked and there's nothing on them. Like me, he can't leave them to die.

We've got no time to argue, no time to explain. I scoop the youngster up into my arms throwing just one sentence back at the older girl. "It's dangerous," I tell her in her own language. "We've got to get out of here now."

My sense of urgency gets through to her.

I ascend the stairs, the crying kid in my arms. The teenager is right behind me, followed by Pooh.

"Stormy," the voice in my ear growls.

"Give us time to get free."

"They'll slow you down. Leave them. Get out of their now. We've got reports of tangos. The bird has to lift off. You want to lose your whole fucking team?"

I don't, but escape is only seconds away.

"I'm detonating now," Smythe warns me.

"For fuck's sake, give us two minutes." It's all we need.

I spy the door to the street. Carrying my burden, I run as fast as I've ever run in my life, kicking the door open and exiting. We're not clear yet, that building's going to blow sky-high. I know, I set the fucking explosive and I don't fuck up.

"One minute. We've got incoming fire."

I heard the shot. It sounded like a pistol rather than a rifle, but I can hear the jitters in Smythe's voice.

One minute should get us clear. I don't look around, just register the two pairs of feet running behind, then the cry followed by Pooh's voice.

"Come on, love. Get to your feet."

She won't understand him, but the tone is calming and gentle. Looking back, I see him trying to help the teenager up.

"One more minute, Smythe." But he doesn't acknowledge he's heard me.

Pooh sweeps the teenager into his arms, then runs as though the Devil himself is chasing him.

A loud blast, the heat of which I feel on my back, sweeps me off of my feet. I roll, protecting the kid I'm holding, glancing back in time to see the older girl sailing through the air as Pooh has thrown her. She gets to her feet and starts running again, collapsing next to us.

Pooh. Fuck it. *Pooh.* Pooh, unlike the girl, isn't moving. He'd taken the brunt of the blast, a block of masonry lying next to him.

"Pooh's down. We need a combat medic here fast."

"We'll send a team back for you." Smythe's voice is uncannily calm as I hear the rotors of the helicopter flying away. "Watch your back, tangos might be approaching."

4

———

*S*wift…

"Any news?" Pip stands as I enter the clubroom.

Shaking my head, I throw myself on one of the couches. Gears heads over with a beer already in his hand. Taking it, I stare at it for a moment, then close my eyes. I'm physically tired and utterly fatigued of this charade. I'd agreed to this farce of pretending I was Stormy's spouse as a way of getting updates on his condition. I just hadn't expected it to go on so long. He's clinging onto life despite everything.

Over the past week I've spent hours sitting by the side of a man in a coma pretending I care. The additional lie, that we were estranged, only takes my less than sympathetic approach so far. I'd be thought less than human to have no compassion for the man I was supposed to have once promised to love until death.

A dip in the couch and a familiar scent tells me it's Road who's sat beside me. Leaning in close, he asks, "How are you holding up?" Carefully he places App in my lap, and automatically I begin to stroke the spaniel's fur. It has a calming effect.

With my free hand, I take Road's and squeeze his fingers. With him, I don't need to pretend. He doesn't make me feel any less strong if I give into human weakness.

"I'm exhausted," I reply, equally quietly. I may not like the man lying in the hospital bed, but it's hard to watch a man more dead than alive and feel no sympathy, nor wonder why he's fighting so hard to stay alive. It would be easier for him to give up and breathe his last breath.

Placing his hand over the back of my head, Road pulls me into him. Resting my cheek against the chest of the man I actually love, I breathe in deeply. With the rest of my brothers I can joke that this is just one more mission, and I'll approach it with the dedication and emotional detachment such a task deserves. With Road, I can allow him to see this isn't a normal anything.

At first, I'd half expected I was there to ensure that Stormy wasn't pretending, acting an Oscar-winning role to give himself a chance to heal so he could make good and escape while we weren't looking. But as time has passed, it's obvious he isn't faking.

"He coded last night," I tell Road, still with my voice lowered. Fuck, but that had been hard watching the doctors and nurses rushing around trying to save him, keeping air flowing into his lungs before, at last, the defibrillator paddles had shocked him back into the land of the living. It had taken a while. Too fucking long. For a moment, I'd thought we'd lost him. Even so, the doctor expressed concern that yet another bleed on the brain might have caused cerebral damage. Once he's again stabilised, they'll run more tests on him.

I need him alive, able to speak and think normally. How else would I question him? That's the only reason I was rooting for him to survive—he needs to provide answers about who had beaten him so badly. Was it simply he'd finally upset the wrong person, or was it something more? Was it just him who was the target, or was someone gunning for the club?

"You want another beer before church?"

I shake my head and pull myself away from my man, feeling stronger now. He always has a calming influence on me. "I'm fine."

Road tilts my head toward him, examining my face carefully, and slowly that gorgeous smile of his appears. "Yes, you are."

He's been my rock since the moment Stormy first crashed into the building, listening to me rant about the loss of my opportunity to punish Stormy for the risks he brought down on the club. Simply being there when sitting with Stormy had drained the life out of me, but never once has he complained I'd been spending more time with another man than with him. Road's got one hundred percent faith in me. It's not that he's not got it in him to be jealous, he just trusts me completely. His stance makes it easier, and I know I'd be the same if our roles were reversed. Not for the first time I thank the stars that aligned to bring him to me.

Now he's standing, holding out his hand. "Come on." He jerks his head to indicate the clubroom's emptying.

Once I'd have waved off his help, but Road's taught me I can use his strength, as I can give mine to him. So I take his hand and allow him to pull me to my feet.

"App." I tap my leg. The spaniel jumps off the couch and comes to my side. Our little trio proceeds to the lower floor to take our places in church—a meeting where we'll likely just go around in circles again.

Everyone's here, including Grinch, Mystic and Goofy, so all chairs are occupied today. Stormy's seat was removed the day he disappeared. Not only because he'd left, but because before he'd walked out, he'd been busted back down to prospect. If he survives and returns, he'll have to earn the right to sit around the table once again. That's if I don't kill him first, and believe me, that's an option depending on what he has to say for himself.

Prez is at the head of the table. I go to sit by the side of the VP, leaving Road to take his place in the middle of the ranks. I nod at Rascal, our treasurer, sitting opposite and raise my chin at Preacher seated at Prez's right hand. At the far end of the table sits Pip, who's role is only advisory now, and as such, he lacks voting rights.

Snatcher bangs the gavel and we all sit forward. "Stormy?" He poses his question to me.

I rub my temples and sigh, then give them the update I'd just given Road. It takes a moment for the news to sink in.

"Brain damage?" Honor's eyes have gone wide.

I raise my chin. "Possible, according to the doctor. Maybe even probable."

"It might make him pleasanter to be around." Duty nudges his friend.

"He could do with a fuckin' personality transplant," Grinch offers.

"He wasn't always that way," Mystic puts in, casting his eye around the table. "Sure, he was always a grumpy ass, had no patience if anything wasn't done right, but he was a team player, until he went nomad."

Prez nods as though that's given him his cue. "I know there's not a lot of love left for Stormy. Christ knows, he brought enough trouble down on our heads. All but lost us the fuckin' charter." He pauses but doesn't add the thought that's uppermost in all our thoughts. *He still might.* Shaking his head, he continues, "Then he compounded that by running away." He waits a beat for that to sink in. "But he was, *is*, a member. Patched or prospect, he's one of ours."

The VP starts to voice what Snatcher had avoided. "Are we going to discuss what hiding him now means to us? What fuckin' loyalty do we have to him? Didn't he lose all respect by running? We're running a risk hiding his presence from Drummer."

"He's still part of the club," Snatcher confirms. "We never voted him out. It was in the cards, but he wasn't declared out bad."

"Technicalities," Cowboy says. "We all knew he was out. There's no way back in."

"But not officially," Prez states firmly. "Drummer suggested we give him three months before declaring anything which makes him still club." I'm opening my mouth to give him my thoughts which are along the same lines as Cowboy's, but he holds up his hand. "I think we're in danger of missing shit by being blinded by the events that happened a couple of months back."

Watching him, I think Snatcher's grown back into the role he'd held for years before Pip took over the club. Maybe he learned from working with him, or maybe it's no longer having the mafia on his back, an enemy that once proved too great for him. But he has a new authority about him that makes me consider what he said.

"What's on your mind, Prez?" I ask.

"Forget it's Stormy," Snatcher demands, his dark eyes scanning all the faces looking his way. "Focus on it being a member who's been beaten so bad he's still at risk of losing his life. Consider a man so desperate to return to the club, that he broke the laws of physics in doing so. It shouldn't have been medically possible for his ass to ride in the state he was in, so what the fuck drives a man in that condition to come back?"

There's a moment of silence as we all readjust our thinking.

"He came back," Honor repeats, now looking thoughtful. "He was hurt, and yet he returned to us."

Us. The people who were prepared to give him a beating. I frown slightly. Snatcher's right to point out the desperation of Stormy's actions. He must have had a good reason.

"Could he have meant to return shortly after he left? Could he have been held somewhere and by someone against his will?"

Duty ponders aloud. "We found fuck-all trace of him. Maybe that's why?"

"No," my rebuttal comes fast. "I've questioned the doctors carefully. There's some evidence of dehydration, and some of his injuries predate his crash, but a few days at most, not months. Though he's pale now, he still has the signs of a healthy tan. He doesn't look like a man who's been held prisoner since the time he left. He's been somewhere else in the meantime."

Prez glances around the table. "We agreed to hide his identity until we knew whether he was going to live. We still don't know what we're dealing with, but that decision could have ramifications for the club, so it needs to be discussed. What I can't overlook is Stormy cheated death to come back to us, and the question is... why? Did he have a message for us? Was he sending us a warning?"

Pip raises his hand. "Playing Devil's advocate, why not tell Drummer he's here, and draw a line under that? Stormy dies, well, that's the end of it. He lives, and his future is ours to decide. Either out bad, or you do as agreed, a beatdown," he pauses for the scoffs and some mirthless chuckles to die down as if one more punch wouldn't matter to Stormy, "and then he prospects for six months."

"Pip's raised good points." Snatcher gives the man his due. "But this is our fuckin' club. We tell Drummer, the likely result is that the other chapters will be all over us. Dealing with them would distract us. What if Stormy's return was a warning? If we take our eye off the ball, we might miss something coming." He pauses and takes a deep breath. "I ask again, what brought Stormy back? With luck, he'll wake up and tell us, but if he doesn't, we need to find out ourselves. I don't want to be distracted running in circles just to prove loyalty to Drummer."

"Whoa!" Road raises both his hands. "I'm Utah, I think I've fuckin' proven that, but I can't have you cast Drummer as the bogeyman. He'd bend over backwards to help this chapter, unless he feels he's being slighted. Keeping secrets is the quickest way to get on his wrong side. You already know that."

"Not doubting your loyalty, Brother," Prez says fast. "Just saying Drummer gave us three months. I think we still have time. If someone tried to kill Stormy, what happens if it becomes common knowledge he's still alive? Especially if they're coming for the club, and not just the man himself. Can you honestly say you trust every man in every chapter to keep that titbit to themselves?"

Damn it. I'd been so wrapped up in resenting Stormy, I hadn't thought of that. It's quite possible that knowing they've failed Stormy, and by extension us, could be in danger if they want to take him and finish the job. What do I know of the members in the other chapters? These Utah men I know will have my back, but there's at least fifty more I know nothing about except they've earned the right to wear a Satan's Devils patch. Prez is right. How do we know we can trust them?

"If he's got a warning for the club, I agree we need to hear it." Thor's jaw is set. "Or, if he can't tell us, then we need to discover what it fuckin' is."

"Where's he been?" Knowing Thor's right, I now try to engage my head. "Why did he leave? We'd given up on him, but he did return. What was he doing, and who did he cross?"

"Good questions, Swift," Pip comments, but not condescendingly. "Though again, if I was representing the Devil, I'd query whether it could be that he knew he was already a dead man and returned to the only family he had."

Does he have no one else? That's more than sad. Even I have my parents, though they're in another country. I drum my fingers against the table. Although others assure me he wasn't always such an ass, I have only known him in his recent reincarnation. "What do we know about Stormy? I was only patched in two years ago and didn't get to know the man. He was already a nomad when I joined." All I saw of him was a man I instantly didn't like.

Pip waggles his fingers. When Prez jerks his chin toward him, he begins. "I can answer that quite simply. No, he was not always an ass, or not a complete one. He doesn't have family and totally bought into that aspect of the club. It fulfilled a need inside him. I won't disagree that he could be hard, and unyielding at times, but there was never any doubt that we could trust him."

"He was a good brother," Honor observes. "He took a break for personal reasons. When he came back, it was as a changed man. From that point on, he was on a very short fuse."

"You could fuckin' say that," Grinch says with feeling. He jerks his head toward the men sitting at his side. "Mystic, Goofy and I got the brunt of that."

"I thought he just needed time," Prez states, looking weary. "When it didn't get better, I agreed with Pip that sending him out as a nomad was better for our mental health. To say he'd become fuckin' difficult to deal with is an understatement."

There are nods of agreement with that, and a heartfelt, "Amen, Brother," from Grinch.

Pip clears his throat, indicating he's more to add. "When Stormy joined the club, I obviously investigated his background and history. It was up to him how much he generally shared."

There's an unspoken rule that we don't go digging in member's personal business—not once they're past the prospecting stage. Someone like myself, being brought to the table after him, wouldn't be privy to the reasons Stormy had for joining, and he, himself, had deigned not to share them.

Snatcher's watching Pip carefully. "I think you know more than anyone, Pip. All I know is the headline. Stormy was a SEAL, and he lost the right to call himself that when he was dishonourably discharged."

That's news to me. My eyes go to the man seated opposite Snatcher, and I'm not the only one to have a creased brow.

Pip shrugs. "I was recommended to Stormy, but the recommendation went both ways. It's no secret he already came with his handle attached. The man was known for his temper, but only when justified. Let's just say, he exposed weaknesses in his commanding officer, weaknesses which couldn't entirely be covered up. He couldn't be allowed to escape punishment, but a full court martial would have exposed too much. He was kicked out but didn't serve time in the brig."

I wince, understanding how proud SEALs are of being able to claim an alliance to that elite body, even when they no longer served. It must have killed Stormy to be unable to claim a connection anymore. But I do have a question. "Was he right to do what he did to get kicked out?"

Pip raises and lowers his chin. "Yes. The lieutenant commander he served with was removed from active duty. But he kept his designation, even received a shoreside promotion after a while."

"Enough to send any man off the rails," Goofy observes.

Pip grins. "When he first came here, he was more miserable than angry. He thought his life was completely fucked, but instead, he found a place he could fit in. Here, with us, he settled. Until, as you say, he took time out. The changes weren't immediately obvious when he first returned. He'd always been something of an asshole, but it got worse." He looks down at his hands, his cheeks reddening slightly. "I suppose I ought to admit the reason he gave me for wanting some personal time was a heap of shit. He said it was because his mom was dying—his mom who'd walked out when he was six and with whom he'd had no contact with since. I was suspicious, but hey, I wasn't going to pry. He'd been a good brother. If he needed time out, he could take it."

"And you let him get away without an explanation?"

Snatcher bangs the table angrily. "And you didn't think to tell me, your VP at that time?"

While embarrassed he's had to admit his failing, Pip doesn't look contrite. "He was wound up, distraught about something. It could have been woman troubles for all I knew. No, I didn't call him out. I mistakenly thought he'd sort it and then come back. He kept in touch, that's all I could ask."

"Jesus." Prez breathes the word out. His eyes flare at his former prez.

What's done is done. Sure, I think Pip was wrong, but what's the point going through all that now? "And when he came back, worse than before, that was when you decided to let him go nomad," I state.

Again, Pip's shoulders rise and lower. "Stormy's got fuckin' skills. It was either lose them or send him out where he wasn't going to upset the balance of the club. Yeah, it was my decision. I thought eventually he'd work it out of his system."

"But he never did," Snatcher observes, still sounding angry. "In fact, out on his own, he grew worse. His lack of trust in us, his brothers, led to him acting rogue and nearly losing us our charter." His knuckles wrap the table edge, and he leans forward. "I want to know every fuckin' thing about Stormy. Pip, do you know details of how he showed this commanding officer up?"

Pip pauses for a moment before shaking his head. For a moment I wonder whether he's holding back anything, but this is *Pip*, the ex-prez, so I accept his words at face value when he informs us. "Only the bare details. He disobeyed an order. An order that shouldn't have been made. Stormy was under a non-disclosure agreement. I couldn't get further than that. Well, to be honest, I didn't bother."

My brow furrows. That's not like Pip. Normally if he hits a roadblock, it's like a red rag to a bull. I wonder what he's not saying. I notice Snatcher's not totally buying it either, if I go by his expression.

"Well," Duty nods at Honor, "start digging, Prez."

"Do that," Snatcher snaps. "I want to know everything about Stormy down to the brand of fucking underwear he prefers. We need to know where he went four years back, where he went two months ago, and every fuckin' step he's since taken."

"We've already tried," I point out. "We've busted our butts trying to track him down, but he disappeared into thin air."

"Using an alias we didn't know about." Honor sends a crooked grin my way. "We assumed if he took a different name, he'd have left a trace of pulling together a new identity. I've already discovered Jeremiah Briggs came into being years back. Now we know of it, we'll get further."

"Or, at least, can track back who issued that ID as a place to start," Duty suggests. "It was a professional job. One has to wonder why he bothered with it."

Preacher enters the conversation. "Whether or not Stormy's roused a hornet's nest that will cause blowback on the club, we can't ignore the possibility. I want everyone to be on their guard. No riding alone and take fuckin' precautions. Those living outside the club might want to stay close for now."

I exchange a glance with Road. We've just got settled into living in my house, enjoying the privacy. He shrugs and sends a look back that I interpret as it's best to be safe for now. I grin slightly as he touches his lips, easy to see it's a suggestion I'll have to be quiet. *Me?* His groans of satisfaction could wake the dead. Or so I've found when I've left my hearing aids on.

Rascal catches my eye, and my face immediately straightens. "Just make sure, Swift, when the asshole wakes up, that you don't immediately kill him. We need him to talk."

Prez also casts his gaze my way. "For now, Stormy is still a member of this club, and as such, if he's been wronged, it's revenge we'll be seeking."

I raise my chin. Message received. I'll use kid gloves until we know the truth of the situation. After that, all bets are off.

If Stormy's again brought trouble to the club, nothing will save him. He'd be better off dying before he comes around.

5

Seven years ago

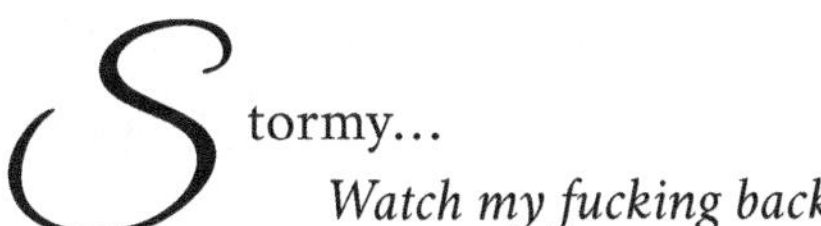

tormy…

Watch my fucking back?

I've got two hysterical girls and a man down. And, apparently, tangos approaching.

My eardrums are ringing with the aftermath of the explosion. Added to the tinnitus there are the crashes and groans as the building continues to come down, sending up billowing clouds of dust that render even my night vision goggles useless.

I can hear no shots. *Were the tangos somehow hidden in the building?* If so, they'd be dead.

What's certain is, unless the girls' rescue was all for nothing, I have to get them to safety. I stand, still holding the youngster. "Come with me," I say in the local dialect.

The older teenager gets to her feet. She's visibly shaking, turning to look first at the body lying only feet away, and then at the destroyed warehouse. Her jaw drops and her eyes go blank. I don't need to have more than a passing acquaintance

53

with psychology to know she's realising she and her sister would have been blown to bits had we not gotten them out.

"Stay with me," I snap. She'll have time to process later. "We've got to find somewhere safe." If the enemy's approaching, we're sitting ducks out in the open.

Thinking she'll follow me if I take the younger girl with me, I spy a half-demolished building opposite. Running across, I move some planks and lower the youngster inside. As suspected, her mom or whatever she is has come with her.

"Wait here. I need to check my teammate."

Pushing her in, I pull the wood back over the hole to hide them. With my head pivoting as I check out directions in a similar way I would for oncoming traffic on a busy city street, I run back to Pooh.

I already knew it would be too late, and no help on this earth would save him. The cinder block had smashed in the back of his skull, his brains leaking out onto the pavement. Those eyes which now will never set sight on his baby son stare up at me, unseeing.

My comms are fucked, I realise as I go to give a status report, so I take Pooh's headset off him. Strangely enough, his is still working. Quickly I use it to replace my own, then regret the action, having to tune out Smythe screaming insults at me for having gotten Pooh killed. I am tempted to rip the darn thing off as I scoop up his body, cradling him in my arms.

Why hadn't it been me? No one would have cared. Instead, Pooh leaves a widow and a fatherless kid. Devastated by the needless death, I try to focus on the two girls. They have a chance of life, years they wouldn't have had if we hadn't stayed back to free them. My life would have been worth giving if it saved theirs. My biggest regret is it's not Pooh taking care of them instead of me, my envisioned distress of his wife and the child who'd never meet him, is a constant pain I can't shake off.

At last I pull myself together enough to update my status. "Pooh's dead. We need recovery."

Smythe's anger again makes me want to dispense with the headphones. There's nothing he can say that will berate me more than I'm already beating up myself.

"I hope it was fuckin' worth it," he screams at me, then, fractionally more calmly says, "There's a unit heading your way."

"ETA?" I'm proud of how my voice only shakes slightly.

"Two hours. They're on wheels and may have to clear a path. Not losing more men tonight because of you not being able to follow an order. Losing comms now. We're heading out of range."

Not having him shouting in my head is one thing I won't miss.

I concentrate on my immediate problem. Should I leave Pooh lying here or carry him to where the girls are hidden? But that would mean subjecting them to the sight of the body of the man who saved them.

Even though I know in this world they're probably too familiar with the sight of dead bodies, I can do no more with Pooh now. "I'm sorry, man," I tell him inadequately, as I close his sightless eyes and leave him.

Returning to the place where I'd stashed the girls, I pull myself inside, covering us all behind our makeshift barricade. Smythe seemed convinced there are tangos in the area. A small number I could take out myself, a whole fucking Taliban army drawn by the explosion? No way. While I'm not averse right now to committing suicide, these girls have to live to make Pooh's sacrifice worthwhile. So, I'll stay hidden with them, only showing myself as a last resort to protect them. I settle down to wait.

"What are your names?" I ask, thankful I speak their language. Even so I have to wait a few moments for their shock to subside enough for them to speak to me. "Hey, don't worry.

We'll get out of this. I'll protect you." I wait patiently. "My name's Stormy," I try, hoping the humanisation of myself will help them.

Patience pays off. Kids, particularly in this region, are resilient. They have to be. As the night quiets around us with only a few final death cries as the bombed building gives up its fight, the older one starts to speak to me, and slowly their story comes out.

They're sisters. They were kidnapped, taken off the street, and secured in the building. They were told to stay quiet, else US soldiers would find them and *goddamn it* rape them before killing them. The older girl had obviously obeyed, the younger, so scared, had cried out. It was that cry I heard, and that one which had saved them. I question them but can't unravel the mystery of why they were taken. Had someone known about our mission? Had this been premeditated murder? I can't understand. That, surely, is unlikely. They're just kids, one the teenager I'd previously thought, she's eighteen and called Nazia. The younger one is older than I'd expected, a small nine-year-old named Marjan. Neither had answers for me.

Time passes slowly. At last I hear an engine, and making a gap through the planks, see a truck full of men I recognise—SEALs from another unit. Easing myself from my hiding place, I approach cautiously, eyes scanning around me expecting an ambush.

"Where are they from?" The large man I know is called Haystack hisses as he spies the girls who follow me out. He's as vigilant as me.

As are his team members who are reverently recovering Pooh's body.

I tell him what I've gotten out of them so far. When I finish, I spit on the ground. "A message to the friendlies I suspect. Though whether they knew it was a death sentence, I've no idea."

Haystack shakes his head. "You saved the girls, but while I hate to say this, I'd rather Pooh was fuckin' alive. He was a good fucking man."

I'd have both if I could.

"Hey, Stormy. Where did you put the girls?"

As if my nightmare isn't ready to give up on me, I turn to point them out, only to find they've slipped away. Jesus Christ. Now I've nothing to show for my actions and can only pray they know their way to safety.

That the finger's pointed firmly at me—all the blame for Pooh's death—doesn't stop when I finally get back to camp, and my team is waiting for me.

"Fuck it, Stormy." Buster shakes his head, his hands bunched into fists and the way he's vibrating suggests he's only one step away from letting them fly at me. "Pooh's fuckin' dead."

I round on him. "You think I don't know that?" But fuck, how could we leave those kids there?

"Whoa." Tailor steps between us, poking his finger in Buster's chest. "Pooh wouldn't have walked away. He's got... had... a thing about protecting kids. Smythe shouldn't have pressed that fuckin' detonator. It's a wonder any of them are alive."

"Smythe was following orders," Gun snarls. "If you'd done that, Pooh wouldn't be dead."

Slice stays silent, but the look on his face says everything. Despite how Tailor had phrased it, Gun's right. All the blame sits with me.

"What the fuck, Stormy?" Smythe approaches, his face red with rage. "You'll be court martialled for this. I issued a clear instruction. You and Pooh were to get out of there."

"And cause a fuckin' international incident?" I'm enraged. "You know who would have killed those kids? Us. US soldiers. We'd have gotten the blame."

"And now I've got a SEAL dead. And that's on your head. You've done it now, Stormy."

Tailor's hand grabs my arm and pulls me to him. "Leave it, Stormy. This is a fuckin' mess. Let the dust settle, then we can talk about it calmly."

"What do you propose to do about them? You lost the darn kids as well. No fucking witnesses to question."

I shrug out of Tailor's hold and send a disdainful look Smythe's way. Yeah, he could never think fast on his feet. "They were scared kids," I spit at him. "They knew nothing more than what they told me."

Tailor's the voice of calm again. "We should be able to find their father. Find what shit he's in."

"Or not," Smythe remarks. His eyes darken, signalling promise as he adds, "Who the fuck cares about two enemy brats? This is the end for you, Stormy."

Is it? Is this how I end? A court martial? A death sentence? But honestly, I don't give a damn what happens to me. I care more that Pooh won't meet his son or hold his wife again. I close my eyes, it doesn't help. The nightmare is still there when I open them. The only thing that makes sense of Pooh's death is that the girls are alive. Fuck this world. Fuck people who can torture and kill in this way. And fuck Smythe. If it wasn't for him, Pooh wouldn't be dead.

I know, at the least, I'm staring the loss of my Trident in the face. Whichever way I look at it, it doesn't matter where blame sits, I disobeyed an order, and now a teammate is dead. It shouldn't have happened this way.

Knowing I can offer no acceptable, to Smythe at least, justification, I let myself go numb, barely conscious of anything going on, deaf to the muted conversation around me.

I remain so as I'm packed on the earliest transport headed Stateside, and don't emerge outside my head until two weeks later when I'm at the Admiral's Mast, slightly bemused, but only vaguely intrigued as to why I didn't find myself in a court martial.

There's a lawyer by my side, but I hadn't briefed him. Still, he's seems to have the bare bones of the details. Someone else must have told him.

I've barely spoken at all since that last mission, just hidden myself away. Pooh's death, so unnecessary, had hit me hard. I've come to terms with the fact that the person who should take responsibility will get off scot-free, while I, a poor grunt, takes the blame.

"Are you going to say anything in your defence?" the admiral asks me directly.

I'm starting to form a negative response when the lawyer shifts at my side. I stretch out my smartly attired hand, literally waving him down. I suppose, if anyone's to say anything on my behalf, it should be me.

"Sir, I disobeyed a direct order." My words are clipped.

"As a result of which, a fellow SEAL died."

I can't stop my eyes closing momentarily in pain. Then in a strong voice, I reply, "Yes, Sir."

"That's it? No justification? No excuses? No pointing fingers elsewhere?"

"No, Sir."

Admiral Hillier confers with the squadron commander. I know what the outcome will be and am resigned. I'll be sent for court martial, then will serve time under lock and key. Doesn't much matter. Unlike Pooh, I'll be alive.

I bide my time, hands behind my back, spine ramrod straight, and feet slightly apart as I wait for my expected sentence to be announced. I stare at the Stars and Stripes hanging behind the men who hold my fate in their hands, thinking how hard I'd worked to become a Navy SEAL and how much this was my dream. I'd planned to stay in the service for life, and now it's all been taken away from me.

The admiral's loud sigh brings my attention back to his desk. "You don't make it easy for us. With no plea for clemency, no justification uttered in your defence, I have no option but to remove you of your Trident. Furthermore, you will be dishonourably discharged."

That's it?

It could have been worse. Much worse. Would it have gone better had I pointed the finger at the right man? Or, would that have counted against me? It depends whether he'd got his story in first. Nothing would bring Pooh back to his family. I'd gotten off lightly.

So what could I say? "Yes, Sir. Thank you, Sir."

As the lawyer gathers up his papers, I stand stunned, realising it wasn't just Pooh who'd lost his life that day. It would have been kinder to kill me as well. Would I go back and change it? Would I leave those kids to die?

No, I wouldn't even if I had the chance. I can hang onto the hope that they have their life, even though I feel I've lost mine.

In a daze, I exit the room to find my team waiting for me. I hadn't expected to see them.

"Well?" Buster asks.

"I'm out."

"They've punished the wrong fuckin' man," Tailor tells me, his voice overly loud. Probably unfortunate as the admiral and commander are walking past.

Surprisingly, the admiral holds back. After examining my face for a moment, then shaking his head, he takes a note out of his pocket and passes it to me. I take it and put it away without opening it.

"You should have spoken up."

"Would it have made a difference, Sir?" I can't see how it could have.

He shakes his head. "Maybe not. I'm sorry to lose you,

Palmer. But contact the name on that card, Phillip Hound. He could have a place for you."

A place for me. Nothing could replace what I've lost.

"Beer?" Tailor asks half-heartedly when the admiral's walked off.

Maybe in time I'll catch up with them as old friends, but not now. Now I've got to lick my wounds, pack my stuff, and leave my Navy accommodation behind. *What will I do now?* I'm a SEAL no more. What else will fill this hole inside me? I'm a complete failure. For the first time in my life, I regret being alone.

I slide my hand into the pocket of my smart pants, knowing I'm entitled to wear the uniform no more. My fingers find the paper I'd just placed there. Could the admiral have handed me a lifeline? I can't see it, having convinced myself that none exist. But what harm could a phone call do? What have I got to lose? Contact this Hound chap or try to exist in the civvy world. What reputable employment could there be for a man dishonourably discharged? Is there a use for my computer skills and explosives knowledge, or someone who wants to employ a sniper?

Let's face it. I'll probably end up washing cars or sleeping on the streets when my savings run out.

I endure the back slaps, the well wishes, the grumblings from Gun about what new man will take my place on the team now. Buster tells me I'm an ass, but an ass they've become used to. Slice just shakes my hand and hopes I'll have good luck. After insincere promises to meet up when they're next Stateside are exchanged, I watch the men who've had my back over the past few months walk out of my life.

Feeling gutted, I walk out.

I have to find a new place to live, somewhere at least to store the few belongings I've collected over the years, or maybe I'll just leave everything behind.

Before I make any decision, I need to get drunk. Very drunk. It turns out to be one of the things at which I excel.

I survive the next few days half in an alcoholic haze and half with the resultant hangovers. On the fourth day, I exit the cheap motel where I'd holed up and decide I need to find my own space, as even cheap soon starts to get expensive. But where should I live? Here, in San Diego?

Apart from the training I've undertaken to become a SEAL, I've lived my whole life in California. My first impulse is to stay. The climate is good. It's why the state has become so damn popular. But popular also means high prices, as I find when I look for an apartment at a reasonable rent—I'm not successful. I don't want to go through my savings too fast. Anything in the price range I can afford is not the type of accommodation I have in mind.

What comes first? Job, or a place to lay my head? Well, the latter for sure. Most reputable employers would want a permanent address, or something better than a shady motel. *Most reputable employers wouldn't want a man who can hack into anything, blow shit up, kill a man at three-quarters of a mile with a single shot, or dole out death by his bare hands in ways they can't even imagine.*

Yeah, I mentally scoff, *twelve years as a SEAL hasn't exactly prepared me for civilian life.*

Having vacated my last night lodgings and leaving my meagre possessions in the car, I walk to the nearby park, needing to clear my head of yesterday's hangover. Sitting on a bench, I've got my head in my hands wondering how my life has become so fucked up when my phone rings.

"Finn Palmer." I'm not Stormy anymore.

Except, it seems to the man who's called me, I still am. "Stormy? Just wanted to call. Our leave's been cut short. Before we're wheels up to get back to the sand pit, I was wondering how you are?"

Hungover? Lost? Missing my team? I settle for, "I'm okay."

Tailor pauses as if recognising the lie in my words, but not certain whether to challenge me. Thankfully, he doesn't. "I needed to let you know some shit before we headed out. Smythe was out of line, we all agree. Well," he pauses for a second, "Gun's been speaking up for him, but you know how Gun likes to be."

I suppose it's nice that at least some people have my back, and yeah, I'm well aware that Gun can take the opposite view just to cause an argument.

"You heard the rumours about Smythe?"

"That he's in line for a fuckin' promotion?" I growl. I had heard. One more tour and he'll be taken out of the firing line. I suppose it means he won't be able to fuck up again. But still, it hurts. I'd had the whole fucking book thrown at me.

"At least he'll be Stateside." Tailor sounds like he's happy about that. "Hey, I wanted to say, I've got your bike in storage."

It's on the tip of my tongue to tell him to sell it, then I rethink. I love riding my Harley, driving my car not so much. Though a car is more useful, it's at least a place where I can sleep if I need to, but of the two, I'd prefer to have my bike. Crazy, perhaps.

"Thanks, man. Can you leave the key with Tanya?" Tanya being his long-suffering girlfriend.

"Sure. I've already done that."

"I'll come pick it up when I can."

"You got anything settled?"

"Not yet," I admit. "I'm considering my options." To be truthful, considering what options I don't have.

Another pause, then, "You called the number the Admiral gave you yet?"

I shake my head, then realise he needs words. "Not yet."

"I would," he says, decisively. "You don't know what's there for you unless you try."

I suppose he's right. "I'll think about it." Even now, I'm hesitant to commit myself.

"We'll get together when we're next on leave."

"Sure." I try to inject enthusiasm into my voice, but I'm not sure it worked.

"You should have spoken up."

"You know how shit works."

He sighs. "Yeah, I do. Take care, man. Watch your back."

My own back, as no one will be there to have my six. Christ. Twelve years I've been used to someone being behind and beside me. That will take some getting used to.

Ending the call with my instruction for them all to stay safe, I look around. It's early still, but bright blue skies are overhead, and the day is already warming up. Moms and their kids are emerging to get some time on the play equipment before the day gets too hot.

My eyes are focused on a little girl, about the age of Marjan who's the reason I'm here and not flying out with them. If I had my time, I'd do it all over again. *She's alive.* But my thoughts are tempered as usual by the anger that Pooh had died. Apart from the guilt that he's dead, it's compounded that I haven't gone to see his wife. Haven't been in contact with her at all. However much I know it's the expected thing to have done, I'm wallowing under the weight of my culpability. *If I'd obeyed, Pooh would still be alive.*

If I'd followed orders, those children would have died.

Would his wife agree the lives of two kids in a faraway land are worth more than the feel of her husband's arms encompassing both her and his child? She would not.

He never got to meet his son.

I like to think I'm a strong man, but I've no strength for thoughts like that. It destroys me every time. I've been stripped of my rank, turned out of my job. Nothing shouts guilt louder than that.

The park is filling up. A man, rough looking, sitting on his own is attracting attention. It reminds me I haven't shaved for days. I've barely remembered to shower.

I've got to do something.

Seeing no other option, I take out from my pocket the crumpled piece of paper that the admiral had given me what seems like a lifetime ago. After a moment's hesitation, I think *fuck it* and place the call.

"You got Pip."

"Er, Phillip Hound?"

"That's me." He sounds cautious.

"My name is Finn Palmer. Admiral Hillier suggested I give you a call."

"Stormy?"

I purse my lips. Seems my contact wasn't unexpected.

"That's me." It's my turn to be wary now.

His voice lightens, and I believe I can hear amusement. "I hear you're in need of employment."

I am, but I don't deny or confirm it.

"I may have something to suit. Can you find your way to Utah?"

Utah? A landlocked state. Not the best locale for a sea-loving SEAL, but perhaps, as I'm that no more, a change might suit me.

I've wasted days wallowing in self-pity. The idea of having a direction in which to head, a destination to aim for even if the job isn't one I'd want to take, makes me feel lighter. I don't hesitate to say yes. "I've got to settle up a few things here. I can be there at the end of the week."

"I'll text you the address. Friday, at eleven am?"

"I'll be there."

He ends the call almost abruptly.

6

———

*S*wift…

Another week has passed. There's been no change in Stormy, though the doctor is hopeful he's stabilised to some extent.

Another church, this time without Grinch, Goofy and Mystic.

Snatcher bangs the gavel as I reach down to stroke App's head, bringing my attention back to the prez as he kicks off the meeting.

Prez brushes his hand down his face. "We've been alerted by his security that there's been suspicious activity around the family of a senator in Ohio."

"As in what?" Cowboy asks.

"There have been sightings of the same men more times than to be coincidence. Or that's their gut feeling."

"Hasn't he got enough security?" Bolt queries. "His own bodyguards can't handle that?"

"They've been clocked, that's their worry. Would appreciate some new bodies going to check it out."

Piston glares. "Isn't that what the cops and feds are for?"

"Isn't this where we earn our money?" Snatcher retorts. He stares Piston down for a moment, then relents. "Look, I know we want to keep hands on deck to investigate our own problems. We've been lucky and had it quiet for a while, but I'm not about to turn work down. Especially where kids are involved."

"If you need me to go, I'll volunteer." Road holds up his hand.

"Me too," Rascal offers.

Prez raises his chin at the two who've spoken. "Four should be enough. So, if it's not too much of an imposition, Piston, are you okay to go?"

Piston sighs dramatically. "Yeah. I don't mind."

"I'm presuming you'll want me with the plane."

Preacher assumes right and also gets a chin lift. A few more details are thrashed out, then Snatcher looks at me. "Swift. How's Stormy?"

"Stable. For now."

"Any sign of him coming round?"

I shrug. "It's up to him. The doctors are weaning him off the shit that keeps him in a coma."

"Who the fuck beat him up?" Rascal throws the question out there, but his head moves in a negative way as though he's not expecting an answer. We've been searching but haven't found out anything further. Even knowing the identity Stormy had been using hasn't moved our investigation along. Without a trace of where he'd been and what he'd been doing, we're stumped.

"Whoever it was, wanted him dead." Preacher frowns. "Even a beatdown from us wouldn't have left him with wounds like that."

"Did he escape, or did they let him go?" I wonder aloud. "It's a fucking miracle he managed to make it back. Talk about running on fumes, he had nothing left in his tank."

"Did he upset someone recently, or does it go far back?" Prez asks, not seeming confident he's going to be given an answer.

But Pip raps the table causing Snatcher's eyes to go his way. "I'm looking into that. We've agreed Stormy changed four years back. Has he been hiding from something since then? Did his past finally catch up?" He's yet another who poses a question that no one can address. "He might have upset someone in the months he's been gone, or it's linked to an event from years ago. I decided to start there. I've spoken to the admiral who recommended Stormy to me." Pip pauses, and seems to gather exactly what he wants to say. "Seems that order Stormy disobeyed caused the death of Pooh, another SEAL."

"Christ," I breathe. That's about as bad a crime as you can get.

The ex-prez looks sharply at me. "That he wasn't court-martialled and that he had the Admiral's support suggests there's more to it."

Nodding sharply, I acknowledge there's truth in that. I'll reserve judgement until I know all the facts.

Now Pip continues, "The Admiral did tell me that Stormy's old team was killed in action, all except one member. And that man, Gun, never forgave Stormy for Pooh's death. He was pretty vocal about it at the time. Oh, Swift, Admiral Hillier asks you to give his wishes for a full recovery to Stormy."

I acknowledge the aside—I'll pass on the message but doubt Stormy will be able to hear me—and ask, "You think this Gun could have held a grudge for, what, seven years, then came across Stormy…?" My sympathies lie with this Gun if he had evidence against Stormy. No one forgets a fallen team member, though waiting seven years for revenge seems extreme. Unless Pooh had been a very close friend.

"It's unlikely I know." Pip scoffs at the idea he'd just proposed. "But any lead at the moment could be one to follow. Gun's the first name I've found who could have a hard-on for our boy."

"Was Gun close to the man who was killed?" I test out my theory.

"I have no idea," Pip admits.

"Know which unit he's with?" Snatcher prompts.

"No." Pip's brow creases. "Hillier mentioned he's moved on and left active duty, coincidentally just before the time that Stormy had a break from the club."

"Got a government name and recent location for this fucker?" Honor asks, his eyes sharp and interested.

Pip shakes his head. "Gun is a Jeffrey Morgan, but so far I know nothing more than that. I will say Hillier laughed when I asked whether he might be holding a grudge. *What for?* was his answer. Sure, they were all upset when a team member died, but to hold onto that seven years later?" I nod, Pip's just voiced my thoughts.

Duty sighs. "Sounds like we're going to be hacking into the Navy records. This man's the only lead we've got."

"You think this is a path worth exploring, Pip?" Snatcher challenges.

It's interesting, and not the first time I've noticed a change in dynamics. A few months ago, Pip would have said jump and, as his VP, Snatcher would have asked how high.

Pip briefly closes his eyes. "Stormy's always had a temper, but he knew how to rein that shit in. He wouldn't have gotten through his prospecting time if he couldn't control himself. All I can say is he became the man he is now after he took time out."

"We've been over this. He didn't become an asshole until he got back. That was unlikely to be connected to losing his dear old mom." Thor's looking thoughtful. "You say the whole team with the exception of Gun were lost? That shit can hit a man hard. Does that timing fit?"

Thor's right. It can.

Pip shakes his head. "It was about the same time. I suppose he must have learned of it, but he never said. Even if his friends' deaths upset him, I can't see how it's linked to the current situation." He pauses, then states carefully, "Someone did their best to kill Stormy. Who, or why is a mystery. We can't discount it's connected to the club and not to his past in the Navy."

"Because he was a lone biker on the road? Could it be as simple as that?" Piston wonders aloud.

"His choice," Snatcher states. "Stormy's been nomad too long. It was his choice not to have a team at his back. Who knows who he could have upset when he was out there on his own? Stormy didn't trust anyone."

"Demon and Lost would have reason to seek revenge." I grimace as I put the hard truth out there.

Prez's eyes snap to me. "You think they could have come across him?" He scratches his nose, then continues, "Possible, maybe. Maybe Utah's not the only chapter to keep secrets."

"We're fucked," Thor states. "We can't ask them or Drummer, without revealing we've found him."

"All the more reason to keep his presence secret," Piston drops in. "They might want to finish what they started."

"Well, that's what we're fuckin' doing, isn't it? Adding to the list of his enemies. I agree, Demon and Lost should be at the top." Prez rubs his hand over his forehead.

Jeez. I hadn't wanted to start anything. Pointing fingers at the Colorado and San Diego clubs sounds serious. But like Snatcher, now it's come into my head, I can't discount it.

Pip's scowling. "I never sanctioned what Stormy did. You know that. Stormy took their kills all by himself. Trust and Stormy definitely parted company along the way."

"Did he trust you?" Snatcher asks.

"I gave him his chance. He wasn't just introduced to me, he was recommended. I cut him slack as I was well aware of the kind of man he was, once you got under the prickly exterior. Obviously he didn't trust me enough. I only found out he didn't trust the other chapters after he took Major and Alder out."

"For which he nearly brought down the club," Snatcher reminds him. "I don't care what personal shit he had going on, he doesn't get a pass due to that."

Pip's lips curve slightly. "Which is why you're the best man for that seat, Snatch."

"Hard as fuckin' nails is our Prez," Thor chuckles.

Snatcher looks down at his hands as though he doesn't know whether he's been given a compliment or not. When he looks up, he shakes his head. "So, we've got Gun on the list but still don't fuckin' know whether Stormy's absence a few years back had anything to do with him being a SEAL. Or whether Gun had such a close relationship with the SEAL who died that he's seeking revenge seven years later. Now we've added Lost and Demon, who, I'd suggest, are equally unlikely."

"Or Red," Preacher says. "He wasn't impressed with Stormy. Maybe Stormy took a trip to Vegas and his luck ran out."

Snatcher bangs his hand on the table. "Before we start accusing other chapters, let's focus on Stormy's past. I want Gun looked into."

"We'll get onto it." Honor nods at Duty.

"You going back to the hospital today, Swift?"

Giving myself a mental shake at the change of subject, I raise my chin toward Bolt. "Got to. He's having another brain scan today. After that, we'll know more."

"Has he even got a fuckin' brain?" Piston widens his eyes. "Or is the scan to prove he doesn't?"

Bolt, sitting next to him, slaps him around the back of his head.

"What are they looking for?" Thor asks, trying to get the conversation back on track.

I shrug. "What's keeping him out of it, I suppose. Another bleed perhaps."

Preacher slams both fists down. "After everything, Stormy

could die with his fuckin' secrets intact, or survive without being able to speak of them."

I grimace, knowing he's right. We might never get to the heart of Stormy's issues or know who left him for dead.

"Okay," Snatcher picks up the gavel, "Piston, Rascal, Road and Preacher, you get ready to fly to Ohio. Swift, you get back to the hospital and play your part of the grief-stricken spouse."

"Prez?" Snatcher raises his chin at Road. "We still keeping this from Drummer?"

Thor snorts. "Seems like we've dug ourselves a hole. Two weeks back we thought Stormy would recover or die, not leave us stuck in limbo like this. What the fuck can we say now to Drummer? Especially if there's a chance another chapter could be involved."

Prez wipes his hand over his face. "Drummer gave him three months. There's two weeks left. Two weeks to pray we get some answers."

Pip's fingers drum on the tabletop. "We'll just put our thinking hats on. We'll come up with something to satisfy Drummer. If we need to that is."

I just wish I had his confidence. Drummer chills even me. He's not a man to cross.

"In the meantime, we'll get going." Preacher looks down at his phone. "Mystic's at the airfield. He says the plane is ready and fuelled. Half an hour enough to get your shit together?"

Road, Piston and Rascal raise their chins to him.

As Snatcher declares the meeting is at an end, I glance down the table at Road and nod. We stand together, and I walk behind him deep in thought as we go to our room, App trotting along by my side.

Before I met Road, I'd only one weakness, and that's that I'm deaf. Now he's added one more, a deep-down fear that I can't dislodge, that he'll go off on a mission and not return. It's not the first time, and it won't be the last, but each time he goes, it seems worse than before. I wish I was going too, then I could watch his back and make sure nothing creeps up on him unawares.

Was this the reason I kept to casual liaisons before I met him?

I'd always thought it was having kids that would make you weak, but I never expected to feel the same way about a man. Now I wonder how I'd survive were anything to happen to him. How would I go on without him by my side?

I'm Swift. I can cope with anything. But the loss of my soulmate? Would I even have a reason to live anymore? Of course I would, but I'd be half a woman doing it. I'd end up as bitter as Stormy. It makes me wonder whether Stormy lost someone close. That would explain his behaviour. That teammate of his, Pooh? Surely that couldn't be it.

Road presents his keycard to the lock, and when it flashes green, he pushes open the door. As soon as I enter, shutting the rest of the world out, he pushes me back against the wood, his mouth crashing down on mine.

I give in to the temptation of ravishing his mouth, of our lips, tongues and teeth melding together, trying to get a sufficient amount of his taste to tide me over the days when he'll be gone.

Eventually, he pulls back, his eyes darkened with desire, focused on mine. As if he can read what's going through my head, his hand smooths down my face.

"I'll be back," he promises. "I won't take risks. Preach, Piston and Rascal are all good brothers, babe. They'll have my six, and I'll have theirs. I'll be back." His tone firms on the final words.

"I know you will," I tell him, injecting confidence in my voice.

"Unless the fuckin' plane crashes," he adds, contradicting what he said before.

His words make me grin. "Arse." I punch his arm. "Preacher

knows how to fly." Road's not a fan of being in the air, preferring to keep his feet firmly on the ground.

"Swift," he starts, then stops. His hair flies almost whipping me in the face as he shakes his head.

"Go on."

"I'm worried about you. Worried about what might be coming for the club."

For a split second, I wonder whether being a couple is worth it. Both partners concerned about the other when they're apart. But the benefits outweigh the risks.

"I'll be fine, Road. You worry about yourself."

His face splits into a smile. "You do the same. At least you've got App."

This won't be the first time we've been separated, but now I've got App, my hearing dog. I can remove my hearing aids at night without being worried. App would wake me should there be an alarm going off or an intruder invading our house.

"Do you need to get anything from home?"

"Nah." He glances around. "A spare pair of jeans, a couple of t-shirts and I'll be good. I've got those here." As he speaks, he turns and picks up his duffel, throwing in the items he'd mentioned, then going to the bathroom and getting some of his shit from there.

"Time for a quickie?" I bat my eyelashes, my unlikely feminine gesture making him snort.

"Sorry, babe. But hold that thought. I'll be back before you know it." He does, however, have time for another kiss. Finally, he opens the door, and leaves.

I don't go to see him off or make a big thing of him going. That's not who I am. My worry I'll keep to myself and not let it show.

Straightening my shoulders, I walk to the closet. Selecting some appropriate hospital visiting clothes, I put my cut neatly on the back of a chair and change out of my fatigues. It's then I notice App sitting, looking longingly toward the closed door.

Going to him, I sink to my knees and bury my face in his fur. "He'll be back," I tell my dog firmly, wondering whether I'm trying to convince him or myself.

Picking up App's lead, I go to the elevator and descend to the ground floor. Brute's seated behind the reception desk today. Clipping the leash onto App's collar, I hand it to the prospect. The hospital is one place they prefer me not to take my service dog, and the prospects are used to watching him for me. He already has a bed and toys set up under the desk.

Taking the keys to one of the club's SUV off the board, I get on my way. I've foregone the bike, wanting to appear as the concerned wife, and not a member of an MC.

I know my way to ICU by heart now and am greeted like an old friend by the nurses.

"How is he today?" It's my usual question, and I get the usual response. *No change.*

"Mrs Briggs? The doc says he'll be round to speak to you later."

I thank the nurse, knowing there's no point in questioning her further. I head for Stormy's room.

With an expert eye, I view the machines monitoring his vitals. As the nurse said, there appears to be no change. The ventilator moves up and down as it forces air into his lungs. His heart is still beating in an even rhythm, and his blood pressure is slightly high but looks steady.

I take my normal seat by the side of the bed and draw my Kindle out of the deep pocket of my coat. I settle down for an engaging read about modern warfare. It might not be to everyone's taste, but it's right up my alley.

"Karen?"

The doctor's voice catches me unawares. *Christ, I'm losing my touch.* Annoyed with myself, I look up to the medic with whom I'm now on first-name terms, or him with me at least.

"How is he, Doc?"

"Good news. The bleed on the brain has ceased, and the swelling is going down."

"He's still in a coma."

He nods at my observation. "He is. I know you're going to ask me for how long, but to that I can't give an answer."

I frown. "So it could be hours, days, weeks or years?"

He glances at me sympathetically. But he's seen me here enough and knows he doesn't need to mince his words. Sometimes I wonder if he thinks I'm hovering around just to pick up money that may have been left to me.

"I really can't say when."

Or if, I think to myself, knowing there's a chance that Stormy will never wake up.

When I return to the club, there's a buzz about it. *Has something happened to Road?*

"Swift?" My name is called almost immediately.

"Prez." I approach him cautiously, fear rolling in my gut.

"Something's come up. San Diego has a problem. Nasty shit. A porn ring involving kids."

Glaring, I spit out, "We going to help?" Porn and kids are two words which should never go together. Shit like that needs to be stopped.

"Yeah. You and Bolt head down there, okay? Honor and Duty will be working the back end."

There's nothing I want more than to break up that type of shit. "What about Stormy?"

"Tell the doc you've got to go out of town. Give him my number for emergencies. Tell him I'm your big brother or something and get him to keep me in the loop if Stormy wakes up."

"Want me to feel out Lost about Stormy?" I refer back to the decision in church.

Prez presses his finger and thumb to the bridge of his nose. "Not outright. If they've nothing to hide, or even if they want to pull the wool over our eyes, they'll be the ones to mention him. They'll be fuckin' cocky as hell if they think they've solved our problem. Just see how it goes, okay? Listen and learn." His look shoots a warning at me. "Whatever you gleam, report it back. Don't go acting on your own initiative. Can't see it putting us in Drummer's good books if you use thumb screws on one of the San Diego members."

I stab at him with my finger. "You spoil all my fun, Prez."

"We're flying commercial." Bolt strides up. "We've got tickets booked. Red-eye flight."

Of course we are. Preacher's taken the plane. Just my luck.

As I listen to Bolt giving me the details, I get my head in gear for our visit to San Diego. At least it's a change from sitting by a near-dead man's side, and a chance to find out if his condition has anything to do with our Californian brothers.

7

———————

Seven years ago

Stormy...

Friday only gives me two days. Checking Google, I see I'll have a five-hundred-mile journey to reach Utah, and luckily, being summer, good weather is expected most of the way.

I'd been so focused on achieving my dream lifetime career that now it's been cut short, and in such an ignominious way, my head's still trying to catch up with what is my new reality. Disgraced, shamed, a man for whom the world has no place. Maybe a long ride, wind therapy and seeing the pavement disappearing beneath my wheels might go some way to getting shit in my head straighter. Give me some time to work out whether I'll be able to move forward, and what direction my life could take. Up until now, I've found it impossible to think of a future that holds anything worthwhile. *Up until now, I've spent most of the time drunk*, I remind myself.

I drive to Tailor's house and after speaking to his girlfriend, leave my car in the parking lot, and get my bike out of his storage. There's nothing to keep me here, so I decide I might as well get on the road and take my time with the journey. Decision made, I stop only to top off my oil and gas, and then take one last look back at San Diego. Snorting to myself when I realise I've no goodbyes to say. I've no ties, no loving family and not even friends to wish me good luck. The ones I have are back overseas. I feel empty, lost. Could Utah have something to fill this hole inside me?

I doubt it. Nevertheless, I press start, kick down into first and head out of the city.

I'd like to say that a burden is gradually lifted from me as I put miles between myself and the naval base, but I'd be lying. Each mile that passes makes me more homesick, and resentful of all that I lost.

Should I have spoken up? Put blame where it was warranted? No, that wouldn't have saved me. I disobeyed a direct order, nothing to absolve me from that. Sifting through maybes and what-ifs isn't going to do anything to alter the position I'm in now. I'm like a piece of driftwood, with no direction to head in, and no idea where I'm going to end up. Except almost certainly washed up.

After about four hours of riding, I stop, dismount the bike and stretch. It's been more than a minute since I rode so long in one go, so my ass is definitely feeling it.

After booking into a cheap motel, I find somewhere to eat, shoving food into my mouth mechanically, with no more pleasure than when I topped off my tank. Like my bike, it's just fuel for the journey ahead.

I sleep, well, no I don't. I lie on the bed trying to stop my overactive brain from thinking about what my ex-teammates are doing. Eventually, with the thought that I've never felt so lonely in my life rattling around my brain, I force myself to switch off and finally sleep.

Waking early, I get on with the final stage of my journey. When I near the city I'm headed to, I pull off, checking the directions.

Eventually I find the address. It's a steel and glass three-storey building on the outskirts of an industrial estate with nothing to tell me about the kind of business they're about. Apart from a street number, there's no name on the door. Curious, I bring my bike to a halt and park up in a visitor bay. Putting my aviators away, I swing my leg over the seat and take the key from the engine, studying the building in front of me for a moment. There's nothing about the exterior which gives away what goes on inside.

Some secret organisation?

I snort.

Oh well, I haven't ridden more than six hours just to turn back without finding out. Best go inside and see what this is about.

The doors are the revolving type, so I step inside and they automatically begin to move, depositing me in a reception area with a man seated behind a desk. He comes as a surprise. Not that I'm sexist and think a woman should be sitting there, but it's the fact that though he's smartly dressed, he can't quite hide the tats which go up to his neck and cover his hands. He's got a beard, his hair hits his shoulders, and he's well built. My first thought is that he's an ex-serviceman who's been given a pity role.

If they take on vets, that might explain why I'm here. But if that's the case, then I hope there's something better planned for me. With my moods, a good receptionist is something I'll never be and not what anybody would want.

Although I've clocked he knows I've arrived, he continues to tap at his computer for a few seconds before looking up, a quizzical expression on his face.

"I'm here to see Philip Hound."

A raise of his chin confirms I'm in the right place. "And you are?"

"Finn Palmer."

He consults his screen, then stands. "I need to pat you down."

I grit my teeth, wondering why he'd assume I'm armed. I hold out my arms and am subjected to a thorough pat down, not amateurish at all. *Ex-military police?* Quite possible. He easily finds my knife in my boot. Then, to my disgust, he confiscates my phone.

"I might need that." I hold out my hand to take it back.

His face is set and determined. "If you want to meet Pip, then your phone stays here. You can get it when you go. Or, you can take your phone and leave now." His manner suggests whichever I decide wouldn't bother him.

For a moment, I'm considering saying *fuck it* and going back home. Two things stop me. I haven't got a fucking home, and while I can spare the time wasted on the journey, I've come all this way and don't want to back out now. I think I've already decided there's unlikely to be anything here for me, but do I really want to walk away for the sake of the loss of my phone for half an hour?

"It better be here when I get back," I growl.

He rolls his eyes. "I'm not going to steal your phone, man." After he puts it pointedly into a drawer and turns a key, he straightens again. "Follow me."

I don't have any other option, so I trail in his wake as I'm led on down a hallway with industrial carpet underfoot, passing and ignoring an elevator that obviously would go to the upper floors—more offices, perhaps? I wait as he knocks on a door, pausing for the permission to enter, then one pace behind him, I step inside.

"Finn Palmer to see you."

Looking around the receptionist's shoulder, I see a man seated behind a large desk.

"Show him in." The man gets to his feet and stretches out his hand. "Stormy, it's good to meet you."

I'd be remiss to avoid his greeting, so I reach out my hand to take his, clasping it hard enough to be a test which he passes—his grip is as firm as my own. "Philip Hound, I presume?" He hadn't introduced himself. When he nods, I correct him, "I just go by Finn, or Palmer now."

His eyes narrow. "I'm Philip Hound. And as for who you are, that's for me to decide," comes his puzzling statement. "Take a seat."

He waves me to the chair placed in front of the desk. It's at this point I realise, as the receptionist is being thanked and dismissed, that he's not the only one there. When he sees I've spied the man leaning against the wall, this time he does perform the introduction.

"This is Snatcher. My VP."

So Hound is the president of whatever this company is. I nod toward Snatcher, then, as I'm automatically turning to face Hound again, my eyes snap back to what they'd registered before my brain had a chance to analyse what they'd seen. Snatcher, a weather-worn, battle-scarred man, is wearing a leather vest. On it, there's a patch reading VP. It's not something a company executive would wear. I start to get a bad feeling.

Halfway through seating myself, I reverse my action and straighten. "What is this?" I demand. "Who are you?"

Hound's lips curve, but only slightly. "We're the Utah chapter of the Satan's Devils MC."

The Satan's Devils MC? Hell, to the no. Most people have heard of that infamous gang. There's even a chapter based in San Diego—thugs riding around on motorbikes scaring women and kids. Even I, a man who can look after myself, tended to keep well clear. If I was out for a ride on my own bike, I didn't usually stop, however desperate I was for refreshment, if there were multiple Harleys being guarded by a man with a prospect patch. They're one-percenters, that I know. San Diego has long had a reputation for running guns and drugs, and probably any other racket they can extort money from. I wouldn't put murder beyond them.

"I'm wasting your time." I turn to go.

The click of a gun cocking draws my eye, it's pointed straight at me. No wonder the prospect checked to see if I was armed.

I was a SEAL. I begin to prepare, readying myself to call all my unarmed combat skills into play. Working out angles and how fast I could get the drop on the man holding the gun, I've no doubt I can take him.

"Why don't you sit and hear what we have to say?" Hound seems totally unconcerned, either at my reaction or the fact his VP literally has me in his sights.

Without removing my eyes from the threat, I refuse, "You've got nothing to offer me."

"Well now, that's a fuckin' shame. You see, you're exactly what I need."

Ignoring him, I make a subtle move toward the VP, but he's watching me carefully and fractionally adjusts his stance. This is no untrained man. I assess him, wondering what skills he'll betray that I'll need to be wary of.

"Sit," the VP commands. "There's no danger to you here. All we're asking is a few moments of your time."

"You stopped being friendly when you pulled your weapon on me." I'm in no mood to have a conversation at gunpoint.

Hound heaves a sigh. "You're a sniper, Stormy. A fuckin' good one at that. Studied computer science, and you're an explosives expert. You've done numerous tours in Afghanistan and other countries, and before your discharge, you were on rotation for SEAL Team Six."

What the fuck? "I was never on Team Six." Is it true I was actually considered? Fuck, what a chance I'd blown. To be called up for that elite team is any SEAL's dream. I shove the idea back down. If I was, there's no way this man could have known. He's blowing smoke up my ass for some reason.

"No," Hound agrees with a grimace. "Your career was fucked up too soon."

I snort. I can't argue with that. "So I'm a fuckup. Doesn't mean I'm like the rest of the dropouts who run with an MC."

Now Hound laughs. "If you were, I certainly wouldn't be interested in you."

He might not be truthful about SEAL Team Six, but his previous statements echo through my head. He's sure got a rundown of the things in which I specialised. "Who gave you the information about me?" If my voice snaps, I won't apologise for it.

"Gave?" he chuckles. "Admiral Hillier gave me your name. My boys did the rest."

"You have my military record?" I'm incensed. Hanging by my sides, my hands clench.

"I… obtained it… yes. I like to know who I'm bringing into my team."

There's a security breach somewhere, but now's not the time to assess what it means for my future, nor what I can do to prevent it happening again, though you can bet I'll be looking into that later. I concentrate on what Hound's just said instead. "Team?" I scoff. "Your criminal crew, you mean."

"Will you sit the fuck down?" Snatcher suddenly thunders, clearly losing patience. "Listen and learn, asshole."

So I'm an asshole, am I? Talk about how to get a man on your side. I'm not impressed. If it wasn't for that gun facing me, I'd already be out the door.

"What have you got to lose?" Hound asks in a more reasonable tone. "I can't force you to join the MC, but give me a few moments of your time, and you might find I've got something you need."

I very much doubt it. But we're at an impasse. They don't intend to let me go without me hearing what they have to say. Will they let me go at all if I say no? Again, I eye the door, the VP has positioned himself in the way, but even if I take him down, what would I find were I to escape? A bunch of other thugs waiting for me?

"If I'm not interested, I'll be free to leave?"

"Sure."

Since Pooh died and my discharge, I haven't had much to live for. I consider my chances and believe them to be good. I could probably take the VP, get his gun, shoot Hound—assuming he too isn't armed—and make my escape. If the rest of the outlaw club were waiting for me, well, I'd go down in a blaze of glory. At least I wouldn't have nightmares about Pooh anymore. Maybe I'd end up sharing a beer with him in the after-life. Not that I believed in such things, and if I did, I'd probably be headed in a different direction. Pooh was a good man, far better than me.

A few more seconds tick by, then, I do sit, folding my arms across my chest.

Hound slides a file my way, keeping his hand on top for a few seconds. When he pushes it the final inch and moves his fingers away, I wonder whether I'll find an inventory of guns, or details of the movement of drugs inside. If I do, once I'm out of here, if I'm still alive, I'll make sure I get the information into the right hands.

Opening the file, however, I find it doesn't hold what I expect. Instead, the first page is press cuttings of a case that was in the news—the kidnapping of the daughter of a CEO of a major company. I remembered hearing about it on the news. She'd been returned, unharmed, extracted by the feds I'd assumed.

Why have they shown it to me? There's only one answer that occurs to me. "You want me to kidnap her again?"

Snatcher snorts. "It was fuckin' hard enough for us to get her back the first time."

My brow creases. "You're trying to get me to believe you rescued her?"

Neither man agrees nor disagrees. I start flicking through the file. One by one, kidnap and extortion cases emerge. A few where the kidnap was thwarted, some, like the first case, where the kidnappee was returned unharmed.

When I reach the end, Hound starts, "I run this MC. We ride motorcycles and live life free, just like the rest of the Satan's Devils Chapters. We run an auto-shop and fix cars and bikes. We live outside the law, but that doesn't mean we're criminals. You join us? You'll be joining a team. We can give you a place to live and a reason to stay alive."

That hasn't told me a lot, nor why the admiral pointed me their way. Had he thought I was already a lost cause? Perhaps I should tamp down my disquiet for now and find out more. "You want me, why?"

"Whether I want you or not is to be decided. You've got skills I can use, there's no doubt about that, but we don't take just anyone in. You don't walk in and start working with us. First, you have to prove yourself. You'd prospect for two years."

Fuck that. I've proved myself worthy of wearing the Trident which should be more than enough. I've done my time. "Not interested." I close the file, pushing it back across the table.

"Afraid of hard work?" Snatcher sneers. "In that case you're probably right. You wouldn't be a good fit for us."

"No harm no foul." Hound gives a smile so lacking in warmth I'm hard pushed not to shiver. "We're offering you a chance to fight these types of crimes, but if it doesn't interest you, you best be on your way now."

Fight crimes? Not commit them? It seems unbelievable, but a strange reluctance has me hesitating to get to my feet. He notices. "I presume you've got other options, of course you would—a SEAL like yourself."

"I'm not a SEAL," I spit out through gritted teeth. It's the truth, but the truth often hurts.

The man in front of me sighs. "You would be to us. Obviously, not in name, but I can offer you work that uses the skills and training you have."

"I can kill a man with my bare hands." I remind them just what I'm trained for. "Blow up buildings."

"And make computer systems jump through hoops. Clearly you're in high demand." I don't know why Hound shakes his head. Is he disappointed?

The image of me washing cars for a living comes into mind. If I walked out now, that might be all I can find. If I stay here, I might have to clean the member's bikes, but hell, is there really much difference? I've always counted myself as an upright member of society, doing more than most to protect America and her way of life. I loved and served my country.

What have I got to show for that? Would anyone notice if I continued to walk the right side of the line? Is that a kernel of excitement I feel inside thinking about crossing over to the wild side, just to give it a try?

"If," I start. "If I prospected and found I didn't like it, would I be able to walk away?"

"Of course," Snatcher remarks from behind me. "Prospecting works both ways. Obviously you won't know our inner workings from the start. That way if we part company, you've no knowledge to bring us down."

"So I wouldn't know where the bodies are buried?"

"Exactly." Hound exchanges an amused grin with his VP.

Criminal activities aside, I can see the logic in that. I lean forward, resting my head in my hands. I'm homeless, and my job prospects, at least for employment I actually want, are limited to none. Once again Hound seems to read my mind.

"Board, lodging, and some dollars in your pocket. That's what we offer. And, something to give you a purpose in life."

In truth, the money doesn't have to be much, just enough to prevent me having to dip into my savings. But a purpose? That's certainly a good carrot to toss my way.

"I'll be straight with you, Stormy. We get results that others can't. Not saying we always toe the line, and sometimes darn stomp right over it, but it's always for a good cause, never bad."

If I can believe him, it's tempting. But it doesn't tally with what I thought I knew about the Satan's Devils MC.

"You already ride a bike," the VP states.

"Rode up here on my own Harley," I confirm, not bothering to ask him about how he knows. Nothing, it would seem, is a secret. I raise my eyes to the man seated the other side of the table.

For a moment, neither he nor his VP speaks, giving me time to work it out in my head. "You have other members who are vets?"

Hound nods. "The majority."

So my first thought about the receptionist had been right. I've got doubts, heaps of them, but also there's a feeling there could be something here for me. I'm still not completely sure what I'm going to say when I at last open my mouth.

"Mr Hound," I address him politely. "I'm willing to relocate and give it a try. But two things, first I'm not committing to anything, not until I know what goes on in your club. Second, if there are things I'm uncomfortable with, then I'll walk away."

"Fair enough. And no need to stand on formality. The name's Pip, or Prez to you now." Hound, or more rightly Pip, stands and holds out his hand. "I presume you need to return to San Diego and collect your stuff. We'll be ready whenever you are."

8

———

Four years ago

*S*tormy…

Stretching out my long legs, I take the offered beer out of the left hand of Bolt, one of our newer prospects. His right is a prothesis, one of the standard ones, obvious as fuck and limited as to how much it will do. Unbeknownst to him, there have been conversations around the table of sourcing one of the new experimental high-tech versions for him. Pip, who I've learned can achieve almost anything, of course knows a man who has a prototype he'd like to have tried out.

At a cost of course, something like that doesn't come cheap.

I'm always cautious when anyone new is around, but Bolt seems to be okay. He's just completed the first year of his prospecting time, and already he's a sure bet to be brought to the table in twelve or so months. Soon, he'll move on from proving himself as a brother in an MC and start to learn what the Utah chapter needs. I reckon he'll sail through. I should know. I was patched in just a year back.

Even restricted to being one-handed, Bolt can hold his own, and I've seen him use his prosthesis like a club. Of course, it hadn't been much good after that and needed to be replaced. I wonder whether he'd be more careful with a high-end model. Still, that's in the future for now. No point investing the dollars until we're sure he'll patch into the club.

Prospecting for Utah is hard and there's no guarantee anyone will pass it. My time's not so far in the past that I can't remember.

I'd come here full of doubt, emotions festering inside me, dragging me down. I thought life as I knew it was over, but I discovered it hadn't yet begun. Like Bolt now, during my first year I'd had to prove I was loyal to the club. It was a loyalty that I was able to easily give as it turned out. My doubts and fears that the club was filled with criminals had soon been laid to rest. In fact, it was quite the opposite. It was full of honourable men, either discarded like I had been or disillusioned with trying to set the world to rights in their previous employment. Honor and Duty were ex-cops, many others, were vets like me. The one thing linking us all was a desire to be part of a team, and the knowledge that we were making a difference in people's lives. Whether it was extracting a kidnaped person, preventing them from being taken in the first place, or helping those abused escape their circumstances and setting them up with a new life, in between missions we earned our daily bread doing other work. I split my time between doing vehicle maintenance and taking my turn in the comms room—a place filled with so much tech even the National Security Agency would be envious.

Even though I'd had enough hazing when I first joined the Navy, I'd found it hard to plaster a smile on my face when doing every fucking thing I was asked when I first prospected for the Devils, often given meaningless tasks for equally pointless reasons. Grinch had tried the left-handed wrench ploy on me, but I hadn't fallen for that. The request for Tartan paint had me scratching my head for a while before telling Mystic he was full of shit. But I'd persevered. My second year? Well, that was when I was honed to become the type of member this club required. It was then my commitment to the club began to pay dividends and they started to involve me on their missions. I've never looked back.

I might not have been asked to blow shit up, but I had at last been allowed to put their extensive computer systems to the test. While it irked me to stay back while others walked into danger, I played the support role, providing information to those at the front line so they could do what they did best, more than once, saving their bacon.

It had taught me not only was I once again part of a team, I was valued. When it came time for the vote, I was patched in.

Prospecting does indeed work both ways. Not only does the club learn to trust the new recruit, the newbie, in that case me, learned where they fit. It had elevated my lonely existence to being part of something again, something I could be proud of. A member of an elite force which no one knew existed. Just like when I was a SEAL, I took pride in that, uncaring, just as I'd had then, that it would be lacking in public appreciation.

I watch as Bolt jumps to attention when Pip walks into the room, offering him his favoured whisky immediately. Yeah, that kid is going to do well. I grin. His smile is genuine, and not faked like mine had so often been.

My phone rings. Taking it out of my pocket, I frown. The caller is Tailor. It's been a while since I'd heard from him. My old team had eventually taken the hint—that part of my life was behind me—and had ceased the invites to meet up whenever they were on US soil. At first it had been because I hadn't wanted to be reminded of what I'd lost, then, as my place in the MC had been defined, I'd realised I hadn't wanted to go back, even if the chance had been there.

While Pip ran a tight ship, there was always room to manoeuvre. He trusted the calls made by the men on the ground, something I valued. In all the years I've been here, I haven't fucked up, though I had gone against our agreed plans, but never without reason. My judgement was respected, and in return, I respected that of my new team members.

When I finally answer the call, I soon wish I'd followed my first instinct to reject it.

"Stormy."

"Well I did call your fucking number," Tailor responds.

"Hold on a moment. Let me go somewhere quieter." And private. I don't speak about my past and don't want brothers overhearing. Once I've taken the stairs two steps at a time and have arrived outside, I speak again, "Long time, Tailor." It's been three years.

"Yeah." The one word hangs in the air for a moment. "Look, Stormy. I don't know if I'm doing right contacting you, but intel's come in and it's not fuckin' good."

"Tell me." I glance up at the sky. Clouds are sweeping over, and in front of me a raindrop falls. As I listen to Tailor, my mood becomes darker than the weather.

Pooh shouldn't have died, but I'd comforted myself that at least the children he sacrificed himself for had a chance of a good life. Of course I couldn't know what had happened to them, but when they came into my mind, I imagined them safe and back in the bosom of their family.

What I could never have imagined was the horrific story that Tailor was telling me. I sink to the pavement, my phone still grasped in my hand, uncaring that my ass is getting wet on the damp ground.

"A fuckin' suicide bomber?" I repeat, hoping to fuck I'd misheard.

According to Tailor, Nazia, one of the girls I'd rescued who'd be what, twenty-one or so now? Well, she'd walked into a busy marketplace frequented by US forces with a bomb strapped around her. That it hadn't gone off was a matter of chance. Obviously, she'd been arrested.

"You sure it's her?"

"There's no doubt."

"What did the interrogator get out of her?"

I hear a deep sigh. "That's why I'm calling you, and why we knew who she was. All she'd say was 'I did it for Stormy.' She wouldn't say another fuckin' word." Tailor's voice sounds cold. "They tried to tell her you weren't available. I don't know if they thought about getting in touch but then she was found dead."

"So she wanted to die." It's just lucky she hadn't taken US soldiers with her. *But why?* Why hurt the people who'd saved her life? When that failed, she'd topped herself. *And why mention me?* Could it be she'd never gotten over that night?

"How was she radicalised?"

"She might have always been, Stormy."

"Back then she wouldn't have volunteered to have been blown up. I fuckin' knew it, Tail. She was fuckin' terrified. She'd tried to stay hidden." Christ. Pooh sacrificed his life so other soldiers could die. What in the meantime had changed her mind? I'd have expected she'd steer clear of explosives forever.

"Look, Storm." Tailor breaks into my thoughts. "Whatever you're thinking, we all understand. Maybe it's that that's giving me doubts."

"Doubts?" I almost shout. "What fuckin' doubts could you have? She owed us a debt, yet apparently hated us."

"Her death doesn't make sense."

What?

He fills the silence. "She was useful alive, she still had things to tell us. You know we aren't fuckin' careless, we know people we catch are dedicated and promised glory in the fuckin' afterlife, though perhaps seventy odd virgins wasn't appropriate in her case. She was watched, man, carefully. Fact is, she was stopped from talking, and I'm not convinced it was by her own hand."

"What?" That puts a different complexion on it. "But she was going to blow herself up. That's a death wish for certain."

"I don't know, man. I've seen the footage from when she was arrested. She was shocked, but when I replayed it, I thought I saw relief. You know how it is, women are forced into this position. We can't discount that's what happened to her. Nor that someone got to her."

"She must have been guarded by US military," I state.

This time he lets the pause hang out before replying, "Exactly. She was."

"I don't understand."

"I won't kid you, Stormy, but I don't either. But there's a coincidence I don't like. She mentioned your name, that's how we knew her identity. *Who* she is, is the fuckin' talk of the town, and you know who's over here putting in an appearance?" I don't, so I stay quiet. "Fuckin' *Commander* Smythe. Of course he got his promotion as a desk jockey but that doesn't stop him from throwing his weight around."

"He connected the dots?"

"Oh yeah. Your name and Pooh's is everywhere. And he's getting mileage from saying the kids should have been left to die the first time."

"Bastard!" I roar, suppressing my instinct to throw the phone, trying to think calmly. What would I have felt if Nazia's suicide bomb had exploded? Nazia's still dead, sure, but if she'd succeeded there could have been many more. Soldiers and innocents. For a moment I don't know what to think. At least part of me sympathises with Smythe. *If I'd left the kids there, Pooh would be alive, I'd still be a SEAL...*

"Something smells, Stormy. I don't know what. I don't even know why I'm calling you." *Because you wanted to share shit around? Bring me down?* "I just... I don't know what you're doing now, man. But you used to be able to find shit out. If someone got to Nazia while she was in custody…"

What he's saying is, it had to be one of us, and that he wants me to find out. Could I?

"Do you know what's happened to the other girl, Marjan?"

When he tells me he's got no fucking idea, I realise I'd like to know. But what can I do? "I'm not on the ground, Tailor." But as I say that, my mind's whirring on whether I could find a way to touch down in the sandpit I'd thought I'd left far behind, as a civilian of course. I'd have no authority, and no one with me.

"Yeah. I know that."

"I can look into it from here, but that's all I think I can do for now."

"All I can ask, isn't it?"

"I don't like Smythe being around."

"You and me both. But he won't be here long. He's just with a politician checking up on the troops."

I really don't like the coincidence he was there at the right time. "Keep in touch, Tailor. If you find out any more—"

"I'll let you know."

"Watch your backs." With that, I end the call. It's only when he's off the line, I realise I didn't ask about the rest of the team. But then, his contact hadn't been social.

It just goes to show a blast from the past isn't necessarily rainbows and sunshine. For the last few years, I've managed to put what happened behind me. Of course I'll never stop regretting Pooh's death, nor that I lost my career. But I've gained a new one, and more than that, a family, the likes of which I've never experienced before.

But Tailor's phone call has caused me to blame myself all over again. Nazia, apparently so fuckin' dirty, means her staying alive meant Pooh's death was in vain. Damn it to fucking hell.

What can I do? Sure, I can hack into almost any database, but what would I be able to find out?

I could ask my brothers for help.

Which would mean coming clean and telling them my secrets, and in this case, I'd come off the worse. How could they ever trust me knowing my error of judgement let Pooh die in order to save someone who'd take US soldiers with her to her grave?

I thought I was doing the right thing. The only saving grace had been that she and her sister had lived another day, albeit in Nazia's case, hers were numbered. She, at least, hadn't ended up living a good life.

Pooh died. Those kids lived. Well, now there's only one of them hopefully alive. *Shit.*

I return to the clubhouse, not because I want company, but I need a drink like I need my next breath. Unfortunately, as I reach the bar, I'm not the only one there.

"You okay, Stormy?"

"Yeah, Prez." I've never been the life and soul of the party, but even I know I've gone unusually quiet, trying to sort out crap in my head. One drink, then I'll get down to the comms room and start searching around for any information I can find.

Smythe's in Afghanistan. I don't like coincidences.

I could go back.

It's the worst possible time. Smythe would call for a lynching party, using what's happened to heap more blame on my head.

I sip my bourbon. I could do it. No one needs to know that I'm there. I speak the language and had gotten on with some of the local guys who we had trained. Maybe I could come at this from two ways, by mining data, and talking to people on the ground. If I could find out Nazia was coerced, that she was left no choice, it would at least settle something inside me. The bomb she was wearing hadn't exploded, why not? She was in custody, but she died. Again, why?

So many fucking questions and not enough answers.

Pip had absorbed my answer to his innocent enquiry. Now I

elaborate my response. "Actually, I'm not okay. Something personal has come up, Pip."

"Anything we can help with?" If this was a situation occurring in the US, I might have asked him. But the team only works on national soil, none of our missions take us out of the country.

So I shake my head. "Nah. This is down to me. I might need some time off." If I take some personal time away from the MC, I can go by myself. Not that I have any expectation of being able to do anything, but it's better than staying here and regretting decisions I'd made in the past.

Pooh's death can't be meaningless. I have to find something to balance that out.

Someone must know what's happened to her, and that someone is likely to be her sister. I'll have to find her. And if she's deep in crap as well, extricate her.

Still casually leaning against the bar with one foot propped on the rail, Pip, while I've been lost in my head, has had his attention caught by a joke Rascal is telling. He laughs loudly at the punch line. I wait until he glances at me again. He reads my expression immediately.

"Want to talk in my office?"

"Yeah." I trail after him as he leads me there.

"What's up?" He barely gives me time to sit down.

I've had minutes to come up with a story I think would work, just as long as no one investigated. But why should they? I'm a trusted member of the MC and have my patch to prove it.

"It's my mom," I tell my prez, lying through my teeth. "Look, you should know I'm not close to her, haven't seen her in years. But I just got a call to tell me she's had a heart attack. It doesn't look good. I'm going to need some time to be with her before it's too late to make amends." I cross my fingers hoping he doesn't know I haven't heard from her since I was six.

Pip stares as though he can see right through me. He taps his fingers on the desk. "Never took you for a dutiful son, Stormy."

"Didn't have much of an incentive. Mom's not a good mother. But," I shrug, "perhaps it's because I need closure if she's going to die."

"Closure," he repeats. "Yeah, I can see that. Sure. You want to bring this to the table?"

"I kind of got the impression time is of the essence," I tell him, hating that I'm lying through my teeth, but knowing the truth would open a can of worms I'd rather keep closed. I've never been one to air my dirty laundry in public. Even Pip knows just the headlines about why I'm no longer a SEAL, or that's all he's revealed to me.

"Urgent, huh? You leaving tonight?"

"I think I have to."

He sighs. "Well, I'll update everyone tomorrow. You take what time you need, Stormy. I know losing family is always hard, even if you're estranged from them. I hope you find what you're looking for."

So do I. Thanking him, I turn and walk out. Forgoing finishing the drink I'd promised myself, I head straight for my room. There, I pack a small bag with only the essentials a man who likes to travel light requires and add my laptop. After lifting the bottom of a drawer, I extract the documents I had hidden there. Having taken one last glance around what's been my home for the past three years, wondering when, if ever, I'll see it again, I walk out.

Giving absolutely no thought to my mom who could already be rotting in her grave for all I care, I ride to Salt Lake City, park my bike in storage, then head to the airport. I board a plane, my fake passport in the name of Jeremiah Briggs causing no issues. After changing a few flights, I arrive halfway across the world.

It's hot, dusty. I breathe in the air I last inhaled into my lungs when I was a serving Navy SEAL. I'm a white American, I stand out. Heading to a bazaar, I purchase some local clothing, and change in the hotel room I'd booked for the night. With my head covered, my swarthy complexion, though paler than the locals, allows me to blend in more easily. I also hook myself up with a trader who deals in more illicit items and purchase a couple of handguns and knives.

I'm on my own here, but that's alright. While I've no one to have my back, conversely, I'm not responsible for keeping anyone alive, or letting them die, which is probably more to the point.

At first my voice sounds rusty as I try out the language I've not spoken for years, but my ears soon become attuned to hearing it, and once again, I'm fast communicating like a native.

Now disguised I rent a jeep and find a different and more suitable hotel that's run down and where they're unlikely to ask questions. Ignoring the less than savoury smells in the room I'm given, I settle down and open my laptop. At first, I wade through local articles, finding information in the public domain. My reading of Dari is rusty, but the unfamiliar characters soon begin to form intelligible shapes and before too long, I'm reading it fluently.

The story, reported from different angles, reveals nothing more than what Tailor had already told me.

For the next four weeks, I live as an Afghan, trying to blend in. I visit the haunts where I know the locals go and am lucky enough to meet up with one of the men I'd previously trained. He's a dour, serious man, with an attitude much like my own. His drive is to make his country safe. We'd clicked during the training all those years ago.

Sure, at first, he's suspicious, knowing I've no official posi-tion anymore, but again, like me, he doesn't like mysteries. After I've got him onside, he does try to help me, but what he finds out brings forth more questions than answers. Marjan, the girl I'd wanted to find, has disappeared off the face of the earth.

"Should I talk to the family?"

Sharmeer considers my question carefully. "I don't think it would help. After the affair with Nazia, one of my men made contact. They wouldn't even talk to us which means they won't give you the time of day."

"She's only twelve years old," I tell him. "They must be worried sick about her."

He shoots me a look. "Or protecting her to keep her alive."

Is he right? Could Nazia have agreed to do what she did to keep her safe? That would make some kind of sense. The girls had been close, I'd witnessed that, but that was three years ago.

"One thing, that suicide bomb was unusual." When I raise my eyes, he shrugs, then continues, "Your forces are retreating, going home to the US. We have far fewer US soldiers deployed here now. If anything, if that bomb had taken out US personnel, it would have increased the presence, not lessened it. You trained us, Stormy. You know we can take over the peace-keeping role, and your lot moving out would lower the tension. So why risk the likes of you coming back?"

He's made a good point. That just adds to my long list of questions that after twenty-eight days, I'm still no closer to finding answers for. Did Nazia really commit suicide or did someone manage to get inside the prison cell and kill her to keep her quiet? And if the latter, why? Where is Marjan? Is she safe or even alive? Nazia wouldn't have been able to build a bomb, so who gave it to her and why? Who wanted to upset the fragile newly found stability of the region? So many damn questions. It's frustrating as hell.

What's worse, I've seen Smythe in the distance, and my original intention to get close to some of the base personnel has to be forgotten. He'd eviscerate me were he to know I was around, and I'd risk anyone previously willing to speak to me clamming up.

Oh how I wish Afghanistan was more like the US, with access to CCTV footage and all the technology back home I'd have at my disposal. I'm restricted to using the only tools at hand, but one man, a foreigner at that, walking around and asking questions, was never going to get far.

I'd told Tailor not to expect much. In that, I didn't disappoint him.

Pip has contacted me a couple of times, remaining in ignorance that I am no longer in the same country as him due to the rerouting I'd put in place for my phone signal. I brushed him off with a *mom's doing well, but she's not out of the woods yet.* Time is fast coming when I have to head home or give up another chunk of my life for the girls I'd once rescued. I was a SEAL, now I'm a Satan's Devil. If I didn't have that, I can't see a future ahead of me.

Daily, a rage burns inside me until I have to accept, I could spend a year here and not find anything out. It's best to go home, however frustrating I find that.

As I head back to the airport, swapping my Afghan robes for my American t-shirt and jeans, I hate to admit I was a failure. But try as I might, I can't locate Marjan. It's like looking for a needle in a haystack.

My run of bad luck, in that things don't go my way, has clearly not come to an end as my plane's delayed. I roll my eyes at the announcement. Over the past few weeks I've checked in with Tailor and kept him updated with my lack of findings. We hadn't bothered to meet. There was too much risk my presence would get back to Smythe and that was bound to cause issues. With time to kill, I decide on one last call, even though I've got nothing to tell him. I'd tried my best—it wasn't good enough. One man wasn't enough to find answers.

The phone rings out. I don't leave a message and am not disturbed. He's probably been called out on an op.

I sit in the lounge, waiting for my flight to be announced, idly watching the local news on the monitor. When four familiar faces and two I don't know fill the screen, I rise to my feet, cursing my ability to read the Arabic script, wishing I could remain in blissful ignorance. Quickly, I take out my phone and google. *The news has to be wrong.*

Jesus. My worst fears when I first saw their picture is confirmed as the correct interpretation. Tailor, Buster, Slice, Gun and the two team members who'd taken my place and Pooh's are all dead, their transit being taken out by a terrorist explosion.

My brain refuses to process the information. *How could they be gone?* Tailor? I only spoke to him yesterday. One of them, perhaps, taken out by a mine, but all six at once? It had been a goddamn rocket fired at the vehicle in which they were travelling.

But the vehicle was armoured. They knew the territory. They're SEALs for fuck's sake. They knew to remain alert to threats. What could have happened to them?

If I'd still been part of the unit maybe I'd be dead along with them.

If I'd been part of the unit, I'd have assessed the intelligence, maybe picked up on warning...

But I hadn't been. All because I disobeyed an order from a superior whose brain wasn't worth shit. I'm alive. They're dead. I'm the last surviving member of my team.

I'm unable to process it.

I hadn't stayed in close contact with them for my own reasons. Had never asked whether my replacement was solid. I hadn't bothered to ask Tailor anything personal, like whether he was still with Tanya, or whether he was single, let alone the rest of the men who'd been as close to me as brothers.

But Gun, Slice, Buster and Tailor still held a place deep in my soul. Now they're gone. Worse, I'd been in the very same country on a wild goose chase. *If I'd been part of the team...*

I'd lost them once when I was tossed out of the platoon. Now their loss is permanent.

Tailor, Slice, Gun and Buster are dead.

I'd failed in my mission to find the girl.

Could things get worse?

9

———————

Four years ago

Stormy…

I came back to the States a changed man, and not for the better.

Still lying to Pip, I stayed away for another month, unable to get things straight in my head. Nothing made sense. Nothing. I'm ashamed to admit, I resorted once again to getting drunk, only to find that didn't solve problems. No answers come from the bottom of a bottle, all alcohol brings is a raging hangover.

I had to return to the Devils, I could do nothing else. Not only was I a disgraced ex-SEAL, the intervening years I've spent with a one-percenter motorcycle club would be unlikely to provide me with a good reference on a résumé should I try to attempt to do anything else.

I sobered up and began avoiding the escape offered by alcohol. When Pip next phoned, I was able to think rationally, and recognised that his more probing questions revealed an impatience with me.

I knew it was past time to return. I also thought I was strong enough and would be able to compartmentalise shit and pick up where I'd left off. I thought I could slot right back in with my MC family, that just going back to the familiar would make everything right.

As it turns out, I was very fucking wrong. I no sooner walked into the club when instead of seeing my laughing, smiling brothers around me, I see their dead faces superimposed over those of my old teammates. They greet me warmly, welcoming me home, but all I hear are their anguished cries as they lie dying, and all because something I'd done went tits up.

I'm a coward. I don't want to be there to witness their deaths, don't want to be responsible.

It isn't that I'm afraid of dying, far from it. I welcome it. I've already lived more than my time. I should have died with Pooh or instead of him. But if I was going to leave this earth, I didn't want to drag anyone down to hell with me. I'd made a call, it had been wrong. If I'd still been a SEAL, maybe my team would be alive. I stand in the doorway to the clubroom, then swiftly turn on my heels bumping into Pip.

One look at my face is all it takes, and he beckons me to follow him. When we get to his office, he directs me to a seat.

"How's your mom?" Pip enquires, his eyes softening.

"She died."

He gives me a sharp look that I can read nothing into, then shakes his head. "I'm sorry, Brother."

I shrug. "End of a chapter, that's all." That book had closed years back, though hopefully Prez doesn't know that. My mom could be still breathing, but nothing would make me seek her out. In the same way that she hadn't bothered about me, I couldn't care less about her.

"Well, it will be good to have you back around the table."

I'm caught in a dilemma. If I turn around and go, I'll be back at square one—with no home and no purpose. That would have me staring at the bottom of a bottle very fast, and maybe into the barrel of my gun. On the other hand, how can I stay? *Maybe I just need time.*

Or, maybe again, I'm wrong.

It's the first church after my return that shows me, and my MC brothers, how I've changed. I don't mean to, but I can't filter the words coming out of my mouth. Almost from the word go, I'm behaving like an ass, even when I don't mean to. I can't seem to stop the sentences which have just one intention and effect, that of pushing people away. Deep down, I know I'm avoiding them getting too close, trying to stop them from meaning more to me than they do already.

I snipe at suggestions, shoot holes in plans. It's clear at first they put my asshole behaviour down to the fictional death of my mom, though I try to get them off that topic fast. Every time she's mentioned, I watch and listen with care, but no one seems to have tried to track me down or disprove my story.

Pip gives me two weeks during which I manage to piss off just about everybody before calling me into his office.

"What's your fuckin' problem, Stormy? You're acting like you don't want to be part of the MC anymore."

I clasp my hands together, having nothing much to offer. "I kind of got used to being on my own in California." It's a lame excuse, but the best I can come up with.

"Well." Pip sits back, crossing his arms over his chest. "I guess it's hard losing a parent. You handing in your patch?"

The suggestion put so starkly shocks me. Such harsh definitive words makes me realise that's the last thing I want. What am I if I'm not a Devil? Hastily, I try to think of something which won't be so dire, but will see me away from the club where I don't feel responsibility for my brothers.

"I kind of want to work on my own for now." My eyes rise, and I see his gesture for me to carry on. "I was thinking nomad. I could still work for the club, reporting directly to you, Prez."

His fingers drum on the desk. "Stormy, that's the last thing I fuckin' want. But I'm not sure I can argue. You're upsetting the team. Everyone's either pissed with you, or talking about the last thing you've done or who, this time, you've upset. It's not only in church I've seen it, but whenever brothers try to talk to you, you're more likely to snap their heads off. Whatever's crawled up your ass, Stormy, I want it gone. It's no fun walking on eggshells around you." He sighs. "Nomad? Well, that gets you out of everyone's hair. But can I trust you?"

The more I think on it, the more it's what I want. Just like my visit to Afghanistan, I'd be on my own, not having to carry anyone else. "You can trust me, Prez. I'll go where you send me. Work on whatever you want. Use me as a scout to get advance information on missions, if that would be useful. As one man, I can go where a team can't. I can still hook into the databases and use the systems. I can dig out information and shit for you, maybe even keep an eye out for jobs."

His lips purse. "I can't have you upsetting everyone, Stormy. If it wasn't for your personal issues and the shit with your mom, then maybe I'd take your patch myself. But perhaps some time out will help get your head on straight."

Thinking I've got what I want, I start to thank him, but he brushes my appreciation off.

"I'll be watching you, Stormy. You might not be here, but I still want you to play nice. You do every fuckin' thing I tell you, or I *will* have your patch. Are we clear?"

"Crystal."

For the first time in weeks, maybe in months, I leave the room feeling lighter.

I just hadn't taken much account of the saying, *be careful what you wish for.*

The feeling of freedom was amazing. I was elated to be out on my own, not having to look over my shoulder to make sure no one had fallen by the wayside, nor having to watch the back of a brother in front. I still had accountability to Prez and the MC, but I was under no obligation other than to do things my way.

It was perfection. Just what I needed. Pip sent me work, I did it. If it was information needed, I got it. A reconnaissance job? No problem. A hit to take out a child molester, well, Pip called me and I got it done. To track someone of interest to the club? Well, get in touch. Give me a problem that needs investigating? Just ask.

I had no base, simply moved around the country, going to where my club needed me. I was living the life and enjoying it, all under the pretence that at heart I remained a Devil.

Did I miss my brothers? At first, I had. It had taken longer than I'd thought it would to not turn around and expect to find someone there. But as time moved on, I thought I was better, faster, more capable on my own.

My mental outlook started changing. I couldn't say when, but now that I no longer had a team relying on me, I started to believe I couldn't rely on them. Pip was the constant, my only contact with the club. It was he I took orders from and he I'd report to when a mission was done. I often wondered whether he discussed my missions in church, or whether he used me as a resource of his own. Either way, it didn't bother me. I still paid my dues to the club and received payment into my bank account each month. I also still wore my cut, albeit with a nomad patch on the back.

I was happy, I thought. No one depended on me, and I had no one to depend upon. Bliss. The only mistakes I could make were my own, and the sole person to suffer was me.

Imperceptibly at first, I was beginning to keep more and more to myself. I was still taking missions from Pip and fulfilling them, but not so regularly updating him. I started to follow my own leads. It wasn't something that happened overnight, it was years in the making. Maybe I'd been too long on the road, maybe solitude wasn't actually good for me. In my mind I was settled, content, and as far as I was concerned, I was doing no wrong.

Becoming aware of a snake called Major, I began to keep my own records of what he was doing. I'd located him in Vegas and quickly found any air he breathed was a waste. I'm not naïve, what Major had been doing was fulfilling a need for the most deviant of men and that need would remain whether or not he was there to provide it. But taking him out was a good start.

He'd taken women, held them captive, then provided them to men whose desires went way beyond vanilla sex, and way out of the realm of kinky. You wanted to choke a woman to death? Well, for a fee, Major would provide her, then dispose of the remains with no questions asked. Brand her with a hot iron burning her flesh? Whip her until she bled? If you had the money, Major would let you take your choice.

He was evil, no other word for it.

How had he survived so long? Because he'd made so much money and had such powerful friends, he was untouchable.

A resourceful girl had escaped, along with a teenager and had made her way to Colorado. One of Major's faults was that he didn't like to lose, and he was determined to get them back. I knew this, I'd been watching him carefully, infiltrating his security systems, his computers, and even, in disguise, one of his parties.

I knew he was going to make the attempt to retrieve them, even though they were miles away and under the protection of the Satan's Devils MC chapter in Pueblo.

Maybe the old me would have done things differently, but I'd gone from being grateful for having no one beside me, to actively being suspicious of everyone else. I could have approached the Colorado chapter as a nomad from the same club, but that notion had never occurred to me. The most I did was drop anonymous hints to their tech guy. That's when I made my only slipup when I failed to adequately hide my location, but I thought I would get away with it. I put any concerns aside, any errors would fall only on me. If I had fucked up, I owned it and would deal.

I knew Major would catch up with Shayla Yonovich and young Esme, it was only a matter of time. He'd be out of Vegas, away from his base which was protected like a fortress, and I'd have my chance to take him out.

I tracked his movements, predicted where he'd be and when. When I knew all that, I seized my chance. Perched in my sniper's nest high on a roof far away from proceedings, I staked out the Satan's Devil's Colorado clubhouse. I didn't care about sleeping, eating or anything else. I stayed still, unseen, watching for the opportunity. I *knew* Major would turn up—I'd been studying the man long enough.

When he did, I took my shot. One bullet and he was dead. I'd even grinned at the looks on the faces of my Colorado brothers, expressions of shock, confusion and fury.

I'd drawn a firm line under the affair. Major had money, he was drowning in it. I couldn't trust that the Colorado club wouldn't accept payment to send Shayla Yonovich back into his clutches, worse, bring them into his fold either as customers or suppliers of more women. What did I know of the brothers I'd never ridden with, even though we bore the same patch on our backs? I didn't even consider it. I took that excuse for a man out without a second thought. I couldn't take the risk he could buy them.

This time Pip and I are having a rare face-to-face. I ride to meet him. He'd driven to a convenient halfway point. He even has a beer waiting for me.

I reach over the table and shake his hand, then sit opposite him.

"Stormy," he admonishes lightly, "you could have left it to them."

A rebuke, sure, but only a gentle one. I often thought Pip and I were on the same page. "Nah, Pip. I did what I needed to do. Couldn't risk that motherfucker walking free."

He raises his whisky, takes a sip, and asks, "You think he might have cut a deal with them?"

I shake my head, putting my beer bottle to my mouth and swallowing. "Who knows what people will do if the price is right?"

Pip snorts. "You don't trust many people, do you?"

"Nah," I agree. "I trust me and my rifle. Oh, and you." When did I start being so suspicious of people's motives? It's hard to say. Sometime over the past four years it had slowly crept up on me.

"I feel honoured." He grins. "Oh, and I have another job for you."

"Someone else in the same business?"

"Trafficking this time." He chucks a folder across to me.

Opening it, I skim through it. "Ah," I exclaim after a moment. "This will have me crossing state boundaries again."

"Why do you think I've given it to you, Stormy? You're a loner, you get itchy feet staying in one place too long."

"And I live to remove scum from this earth."

"That you do." He chuckles softly. "Wish I could have seen their faces when Major hit the ground. They have no fuckin' idea who took him out. Their mysterious contact has disappeared as well."

I give him a sheepish look. "Sorry about that."

"Fuckin' schoolboy error, forgetting to cloak your IP address."

"It won't happen again," I promise.

"See that it doesn't."

"I know the score, Pip. What we do only works if we keep underground."

Underground. So far under the radar I'm certain he doesn't

even update his club. I'm sure of it. While I wouldn't want to return to Utah and justify myself around the table, Pip never even asks. It doesn't bother me. Why talk to brothers I no longer have faith in?

Me, myself and my gun. That's how I like it.

10

*S*tormy…

The case Pip had handed me had so many strings it had me burning the midnight oil to figure it out. Once I had, I'd had to have a whisky myself. This one involved not one, but two chapters of the Satan's Devils. I was going to pitch myself against brothers flying the same colours again. Maybe I could have brought them onside, worked with them openly, but that wasn't my style. Everything in my psyche told me to work alone, anonymously from the outside.

Alder Cantor had his hand in many dirty pies. He trafficked innocent victims over the border to be sold into a life of horror. But his trucks didn't return empty, he brought migrants back—men, women and children expecting to start a new life in the US. Instead, they found themselves slaves.

For that alone, he needed to be stopped. But this time, he'd taken a victim who was vital to get back. He'd kidnapped a State governor's daughter as a favour to the cartel.

I'd been tracking him across the country, but he hadn't stayed in business by being stupid, and I'd lost all trace of him. I knew his destination though, it was the Mexican border.

Alder also didn't like loose ends, and there was one big one that was about to start unravelling. It involved a young man, Connor, who was supposed to be dead and who had relocated from Colorado to San Diego under the witness protection program. His mother, Patsy, from whom he'd been estranged for a while, had decided to accompany him.

The woman's husband, and father of her son, though dead, had been Alder's business partner. That alone had made warning hairs stand proud on my neck.

Patsy also had a daughter who was the old lady of one of the members of the Colorado Satan's Devils. Though when Patsy entered the Witness Protection program with her son, she knew all contact with her daughter must stop. I knew she was going to slip up. A mother will never abandon her child. Except for mine. But from what I read about Patsy, she was a completely different sort.

Bait to attract Alder? Maybe.

The San Diego club was told to watch out for them, but not to get close. When I found danger was approaching the woman and her son, I decided to use them as pawns. San Diego thought they had a technical expert, hell, he's still in kindergarten as far as I'm concerned. They weren't even aware there was a threat.

I'm not averse to using people, and I needed to keep the woman and her son alive while I figured everything out. I couldn't provide a personal protection detail, so I enlisted their help by sending anonymous messages direct to their tech expert, Token's, screen.

Sure, they tried to discover who was sending them, but this time I made no rookie mistakes. It had the desired effect, Patsy and Connor were taken to the safety of the Satan's Devils San Diego compound. Now they were protected, I had time to sort the rest of the mess.

Damn, they're klutzes at this, I impatiently thought. *They think*

Alder knows Connor's still in the land of the living. Worried they were focusing their attention in the wrong direction, I sent more clues, and sit back chuckling as they worked it out.

I stayed close, close enough to see Patsy making a break for it. I followed, aided by the tracker I'd had the forethought to place on her car. I got close enough to send up a drone when she pulled off and parked, watching after her while Lost and his crew chased to catch up.

My hand had hovered near an immobilising device, ready to take out her engine should she start driving again. My problem was it would take out all the vehicles in the rest area, so I was loath to do that except as a last resort.

I hadn't had to. They'd retrieved her.

San Diego had, after my prompting, done their work well. I admit to being impressed when they located the tunnel Alder used to get his cargo under the Mexican border.

Knowing what he was transporting this time, I knew the man himself would turn up. Again, I was in place to take the shot. A perfectly executed bullet went straight into his forehead.

Man, I could get used to this. I laughed as I once again saw confusion and anger on the San Diego members' faces. But while I'd used them, unbeknownst working under my instruction, I didn't trust them. Alder could pay his way out of anything, and those brothers? What did I know of the type of men they were?

This time, full of the success of my mission, I'd updated Pip with a phone call. This time, he wasn't so lenient.

"I'm calling you back, Stormy."

Er, fucking no to that. "I did what had to be done, Pip."

A sigh loaded with exasperation comes down the phone. "No, you fuckin' didn't. You had a task—"

"Which I completed," I say, ire in my voice. "The governor's daughter is back with her family. I hung around. The police collected her from the hospital." I shake my head though. Fuck knows what damage had been done to that young girl. But at least she hadn't been taken over the border and sold.

"I gave you the task."

"I got it done. Lost and his crew were already all over it. We lost track of her coming across the country, but I knew where she was going to end up. They had the manpower, I just helped them along."

"Without them, we would never have gotten the coordinates."

"Which we had to decipher for them." I sigh to myself, not understanding why Pip's all over this.

"You really can't tell, can you?" His voice sounds clipped. "They're Satan's Devils, Stormy."

I let the pause draw out, then complain, "I pointed them in all the right directions."

"You're making a habit of this—"

"I made the kill."

He snorts. "And left them frustrated as hell. You're doing it too often. And enjoying it too much."

Can't argue with his last point. I grin as I come up with an excuse. "There was a chance they might cut a deal with Alder."

"No there wasn't." Pip's frustration comes down the line. "Two hits. Two clubs. How long until someone puts this together?"

"They needed my help."

"Sure, they needed *our* help. And we gave it to them. But they should have been allowed to take Alder out themselves. You're running the risk of exposing us."

"I'm not," I protest, loudly. "I was nowhere close. I knew I could make the shot, and I did."

"Not questioning your fuckin' ability. I question your method. Lost will be going crazy. It was his hit, not yours. No point arguing, Stormy. One time, I gave you the benefit of the doubt. Not doing that again. You're coming back to the nest."

"I don't play well with others," I growl.

"Too fuckin' bad. You're going to get your ass home."

I slam down the phone.

I could walk away. Carry on doing what I can. I don't need anyone, let alone the Utah club.

You wouldn't even have Pip.

Would that bother me? Hell no. I can survive on my own. I've been doing it for four years.

I could go anywhere.

It's strange, but it's only when you're cast adrift that you start to analyse yourself.

I'm a man used to following orders. I *like* being able to complete missions in the way that I want, but I also like to have direction. Not having Pip? Becoming nothing more than a mercenary doesn't sound attractive at all. For a start, I'd have to start charging for my services, which would mean emerging from the shadows. I wouldn't have the resources of the Utah club which I tap into. Of course, I could get my own setup, but that takes time, money, and a base.

Slowly, I realise I'm fucked.

I'm angry. Why did Pip have to call me back? Why did he have to upset what I've become used to. I *am* a loner, I'd told the truth. I no longer see myself as a member of a team.

Lying back on the bed in my hotel room, I start to come up with a plan. I'll return to Utah, make myself as obnoxious as possible. Or, in the darkness my lips curve, in other words, be myself. It won't be long before I'm sent back out.

My opportunity to show my true self comes as soon as I step into the Utah club. Though I'd been gone three years, the building's the same, and Bolt has been patched in which wasn't unexpected. There are three new prospects in various stages of completing their time, Gears, Brute and Igor. But the new fully patched member? Well, she took me by surprise and not a pleasant one at that.

I thought the club had started taking in sweet butts when I first saw her. My dick perked up—she was a good-looking bitch, an athletic figure without any softness or noticeable curves, but hell, I could put up with that. But when she turned, she showed me the patches on the back of her cut.

For a moment, I didn't breathe, rubbing my eyes and checking my eyesight, but when I looked back, she was still wearing our colours. A full member? Fuck no. Not on my fucking watch.

I'm greeted warmly, given back slaps galore, but I've only one thought on my mind, how fast I can get her on her back. Either in bed, or laid out, I don't much care which. I'll show them they've lost their fucking minds.

"You think you can wear that patch, little girl?" I make a beeline for her. "Well, I'm back. And I ain't soft, not like my fuckin' brothers." I turn my head, letting them all see my glare.

She eyes me up and down, and sneers. "Well, *little boy*, whatcha planning on doing about it?"

"I'll put you in your fuckin' place."

"Storm—"

"Fuck off, Pip. This is between me and…" I toss her a look dripping with disdain. "Her."

"Hold my beer." She turns and passes her drink to Bolt. "Don't drink any, this won't take long."

No it fucking won't… *Fuck! How the fuck did I get here?*

I'm lying on my back, my jaw pounding with pain, and as for my stomach… My lungs don't work. When I at last manage a gasp of breath, I open my eyes, looking up suspiciously, wondering if Thor has taken her place, but all I see is the woman calmly taking her beer back from Bolt. She hasn't even broken a sweat.

She glances down at me with complete disinterest. "The name's Swift. I'd say nice to meet you, but somehow I can't."

She'd taken me by surprise, that's all. Next time, she won't. Accepting Preacher's hand, I let him pull me to my feet. I point to my eyes, then to hers. "You and I aren't finished, *doll.*"

"Stormy," Pip growls, "Swift..."

This time I'm ready, but my God, this woman's got moves. I hold my own for about five seconds, successfully evading her blows, but not landing any of my own. It's not chivalry or that I'm programmed not to hit a woman. Well, I am, but not when it's *her.* The only result is that I'm on the floor *yet again.*

Fuck.

"I tried warning you," Pip says casually.

From that point on it's war. *I hate her.* Women have no place in an MC, and I'll make it my job to persuade her of that particular truth.

I must be tired, out of practice. I've hidden behind my rifle for too long. One good thing about returning to the club, there's always someone willing to spar. A few bouts in the ring with Thor will sort me out. Next time, I'll take her.

I'd love to say I settle back into the old routine, but I don't. I'd love to say I find my place back around the table, but everything about the club irritates me. I don't want to be here.

I don't want to let them back in.

No, that's not it.

You'd have people you care about who you could lose.

No, I won't. Caring about people only brings hurt.

I hate being here. Surely, it's only a matter of time until Pip comes to his senses and realises I'm a more productive member of the club if I'm out on the road on my own. The Utah patch hangs heavy on my cut. I long to replace it with Nomad once more.

Only a matter of time.

I'm still waiting when a stranger turns up at the club, bold as brass walking straight into church, interrupting our meeting. He's from the mother chapter in Tucson, and it's blindingly obvious he's been sent here to spy on the Utah club.

While I don't want to be based at the clubhouse, I'm proud of my patch with the Utah rocker. If the club loses its Satan's Devils' charter, which we will, if Drummer, the prez of the mother chapter, finds out how we actually run this club, I'll be stuffed along with my brothers. Easiest solution? Kill the fucker, stop any leaks stone dead. We wouldn't even get blamed. Roadrunner came here alone. Everyone knows men riding without company are prone to meet accidents on the road. Very prone. The thought makes me grin.

My preferred way out is obviously shared, but I'm probably the one who's most vocal. I'm also in the minority.

To my disgust, the conversation proceeds in a different direction. Why are they even discussing bringing him into the club? Roadrunner's got nothing to offer—he has no military experience—all he fucking knows is how to ride a bike. It's clear as the fucking nose on your face, he'll never fit in here. But I've said my piece. All I can do is listen and watch as they make a mess of things.

What comes next makes me snort a laugh—perhaps it's a good punishment of a sort. They've teamed him up with Swift. Good luck with that. He might keep his life, but his balls are in serious danger. Roadrunner's not going to make the grade in this chapter, and Swift won't take prisoners. Maybe Road has been given a death sentence. I'll just wait for the fireworks, it should be a good laugh.

But it turns out no one finds anything amusing when Swift gets kidnapped. Hell, I might hate the bitch, but however I feel about it, she wears our patch. And would you fucking believe it? It's actually Road that ends up rescuing her. She's soon back, not undamaged as she's missing a fucking finger, but she's still breathing. It could have been worse.

What's more surprising, instead of seeing Road as an imposter, someone who shouldn't have stepped foot in the club, they've done more than team up together. He's tamed the bitch, or maybe she's tamed him. Whatever, quickly they pass the friendship stage and become lovers.

This club is fucked up. Who needs members fondling each other at the table?

Jesus H Christ.

"Pip?" I walk into his office. "This isn't fuckin' working. I need my nomad patch back." Before I go stark raving mad.

"Not getting it." He doesn't even look up, just continues shuffling some paperwork on his desk.

"Prez—"

"Stormy! I said fuckin' no." This time he does shift his attention. "I need you close. I can't afford to have you—" He breaks off. His eyes shoot to the door, aware, just as I've become myself, of a commotion outside. "What the fuck?"

When he stands, I'm right there with him.

When he comes to an abrupt halt, I'm there sucking in air beside him.

I might never have met the man, but have no problem immediately recognising who our visitor is. I know it's bad fucking news, and exactly what Pip had been trying to avoid. Drummer, the mother chapter fucking prez, and his top team have come all the way from Tucson.

Immediately I suspect Road, but apparently he did nothing to warn him, but given Drummer's renowned sixth sense, it was that non-warning which caused an alert all was not right in the Utah club. Not right for Drummer that is, perfect for us.

It's not just Drummer we have to worry about, he summons the prezes of the other Satan's Devils chapters—Red, from Vegas, Lost from San Diego and Demon from Colorado. Our fate is to be discussed and decided. Fuck. Two out of the four will have no reason to love me when what I've done comes to light.

As Pip had thought and I'd dismissed because as always, I knew better, I fucked up by taking the hits from San Diego and Colorado.

Just like all those years back at the admiral's mast, I'm going to be busted out of the life that I love. I might not want to sit around the table with the club members, but losing my patch? Not even being nomad? How can I live with that?

Should I sacrifice myself? Give up my patch to save my brothers? Or, hang on for the course. I decide to wait and see what transpires in one of the most serious meetings I've ever attended in my life. The admiral's mast was easy compared to this.

I sit, my whole body tense, wondering whether I'll be able to justify myself.

The first item on the agenda is Swift. I almost feel sorry for her. I might not like her, but it's clear she's found something here she was looking for, and I don't mean her relationship with Road. Like me, though more honourably, she lost her military career, but discovered her place here. Now she's going to lose it. If I can't save myself, maybe I can put in a word for her.

I try to speak, but Thor gets in first with his fist to my stomach. I wait a moment before I attempt it again. Leaning away from the enforcer, I open my mouth. I almost surprise myself with the words that come out.

"Swift is as good, if not better, than any fuckin' man around this table. Me fuckin' included. I have no problem riding beside her. Hell, half the time I forget she's any different to anyone else." I might not have said that a few days ago, but she's impressed me. Maybe it was how she dealt with being kidnapped.

They toss it around for a while, and the outcome is, Swift stays in the club. If it wasn't against my character, I'd give her a thumbs up.

Pip, though, he's not so lucky. He is the reason the club keeps what it does under wraps, and what seals the deal against him? Well, though he's well balanced on his prosthetics, his two fake legs mean he can't ride a bike. Pip's out, but to be retained as a consultant, and Snatcher steps back into the top spot.

This meeting is tiring, and I suppose I'm still to be discussed. There's another delay when Swift is voted in as fucking enforcer.

I suppose she's got the skills, but hell. As if a female member isn't bad enough, but as enforcer? That's a fucking joke, isn't it? But it seems it's not.

When proceedings move on, the expected heat comes down on me. Yeah, seems they didn't like me taking the kill shots for them.

It's Lost, who speaks first. "Your excuse, as I understand it, is that you didn't fuckin' trust us to interrogate our captives. You fuckin' thought both Demon and I would see the lure of lucrative deals instead. What the hell do you fuckin' take us for?"

I have to defend myself. My hand crashes down onto the table. "I don't know you," I yell. "Yeah, it was unlikely, but Major and Alder were experts at twisting things to suit themselves. If enough money was on the table, you might have been tempted. I had the shots, so I took them. Problem solved."

"You took the shots because it was a fuckin' challenge." Drummer's correction thunders down the table. "I don't buy your suspicions for a fuckin' moment. You were showing off. What the fuck is your problem, Stormy?"

"I ain't got a problem," I say sullenly.

"From where I'm sitting, you have," Drummer snarls.

Blade, the Tucson enforcer, offers to extract answers from me. I want to curl my fingers around beckoning then backing it up with the words, *bring it on.* But I stay silent.

Drummer looks like he's seriously considering Blade's offer

for a second, but shakes his head. "No, he deserves to have his patch taken and sent out in bad standing."

The blood drains from my face. "You-you're sending me out bad?" I swallow hard. This, I did not expect. Take my patch, yeah. But to be prevented joining another club and being a target for any biker to take a shot at me? They'd do better to kill me instead.

I sit stunned, oblivious to the words continuing to fly around me. When Swift opens her mouth, I wonder whether she's going to throw me to the wolves. I wouldn't blame her, I've never tried to be friendly.

"Stormy's got issues. Fuck knows what they are, but though he doesn't always show it, he lives for the club. He needs us, but I think he's forgotten how much. You say he shouldn't be a member, well, I agree with that." I'm full on glaring at her by this point. "Why not bounce him back down to prospect? Give him six months. Let him reprove his loyalty to the brotherhood. Let him remember what it's like to be one for all and not all for one. If he can't do it and fails to regain our trust, he's out."

Prospect? I got by last time, but again? No, I can't do that. How can I prove trust and loyalty when I have none left? I don't fucking trust myself.

There's another punishment loaded on top. A beatdown. Yeah, I can cope with that. That holds no worries for me. A bit of pain might be what I deserve, but to lose my patch and replace it with one that reads *Prospect?* Hell to the no for that.

But my fate has been decided.

"Right. Prospect." Drummer jerks his chin toward and pointedly at the door. "Leave us. Prospects are not allowed in church." Drummer's smirk broadens as he reminds me.

Taken by surprise, I open my mouth then snap it back shut, knowing they won't listen to anything I say. While multiple pairs of narrowed eyes stare at me, slowly I place my palms on the tabletop and push myself to my feet. Throwing an especially vicious glare toward Swift, I move to the door, open it and step out, slamming it loudly behind me.

I keep on walking. As I pass by reception, I take off my cut and throw it down on the floor to Brute's astonishment. The look on my face stops him from asking any questions. I go straight out to my bike with only the clothes I'm wearing and take off.

11

Cat…

"How are your mom and dad?"

Weston sneers. "Same as fuckin' always."

"You've seen them?"

My cousin's face tells me he has. I turn away, busying my hands making coffee. His disgruntlement shows he's probably tried to tap them for money, but whatever they once had, had gone into his hands long ago. I love my aunt and uncle. Their son? Not so much. If he's here to try to get me to finance whatever hairbrained scheme he's come up with now, I won't be giving him anything.

"You able to go back to wrestling?" He was about to turn pro before he went inside. He's still big, but my assessing eyes tell me he's not as muscular as he was before. *Still formidable,* I remind myself. When he comes out and says what he wants, I'll have to let him down gently. That I'm a woman and a relative won't stop him from using his fists. I shudder but try to suppress it. I've felt those hands on me many times while we were growing up.

"Nah. I got a job."

That surprises me. I pause with the coffee pot in my hand. "That sounds good. Doing what?" I wonder if it's something his probation officer had arranged for him.

"Mind your fuckin' business."

Turning back to my task, I roll my eyes. A movement out of the window catches my eye, and I see Star kicking up his heels and tearing around his paddock. *Crazy horse,* my lips curve as he distracts me from my unwelcome visitor. *Wonder what he's seen now.* Which reminds me, I've got to go to the store and get some winter feed. Won't be too long before I need it.

Caspar, my, well my mom's white German Shepard who I've adopted comes to sit by my side, looking up hopefully, in case I get out cookies and drop a few crumbs. He's going to be out of luck. I'll give Weston a coffee, but nothing else, and hope it's not too long before he realises he's not welcome and leaves.

I finish the coffee, pass him his cup, pushing sugar and creamer over. I note I was right, he's clearly not in training now, not if the way he takes three spoonfuls of sweetener is anything to go by.

Having prepared his drink to his liking, he pushes the cup to one side. I just wish he'd hurry up and drink it. He's so big, he makes the house seem small.

"I bet you miss your parents," he observes, glancing around. "You haven't done much with the place."

They've only been gone a few months. Well, that's not strictly true. Dad had died twelve months back having gotten the worst of an argument with some of the farm machinery. He'd bled out before anyone found him. Mom, well, I came back to visit for the funeral and ended up having to stay. The obstinate woman hadn't previously told me, but she was battling with cervical cancer, having missed out on her pap smears. By the time it was diagnosed, it was almost too late. Maybe even then she would have had a chance if she'd been willing to fight, but the loss of my father seemed to sap her will to live. I was their only daughter, and a nurse with a job in the city. Although oncology wasn't my speciality, I could care for her, and alone, she certainly needed that. So I took the only path open to me. I swapped providing care to strangers to nursing her. She'd died just four months past.

Since her death, I've been stuck in limbo. *I miss them.* I still haven't come to terms with their loss.

There was no will, and I was an only child so the farm had come to me. I could have sold the place and gone back to the city, but I felt close to them here, and something was stopping me from moving on. Again I gaze out of the window. The bulk of the land we'd sold off to neighbouring farmers while Mom had still been alive. It was too much for an invalid and a nurse to keep going. But the paddocks I kept for Star, my childhood pony now retired, though the way he kicks up his heels belies it, along with the barn and the chickens.

I hadn't consciously made my home here, I couldn't afford to stay long term for a start. The upkeep while having no job makes it impossible. I've always known I would have to move on, but while I still had some savings, I couldn't find the impetus to leave. It was like I was abandoning my parents somehow. This farmhouse had been in my family since my great-grandfather had built it. *I'm the last of the line.* As normal, the thought saddens me.

"You going to sell it?" Weston asks me, as though he can read my mind.

Suspicious of his motives, he's not entitled to anything of mine, I turn back to him. "I'm not sure. I suppose so, eventually."

The gleam in his eyes suggests he's wondering how he could work me coming into money to his own advantage. I suppress a shiver. I don't need to know that he'd spent the last few years inside to know he's not a decent human being. Growing up, we'd been thrown together, and he was an absolute bully.

I stop being polite and ask him directly, "Why are you here, Weston?"

There's a shifty look in his eyes. "Can't a cousin come to see one of his only remaining relatives?"

I shrug. "We've never been close."

"Well, maybe that should change. I'm a different man now, after..." His voice trails off, but his expression becomes bitter.

He must be alluding to going inside. Sure, he's changed, *like hell*. He's just like the proverbial leopard and nothing will alter his spots.

"Hey," he gentles his voice, "it's been years, Catherine. I thought it would be good for us to catch up. My parents asked how you were doing. It made me realise I haven't seen you for a long time. Why don't I take you out for dinner?"

I doubt his parents would have expected him to come and see me. My parents—once Weston's cruelty to me, his younger cousin, had become apparent—had kept us apart. My aunt and uncle were alright, though even at my mom's funeral, had refused to meet my eye. *They knew. They'd seen the bruises.* Huh, I think I'd been his first punching bag.

I've got red hair and to my shame, the volatile temper that it's known for going with it, but today I'm working hard keeping that under wraps. I don't dare do anything he might think threatening, even raise my voice. I know my limitations. He's too big for me to throw out. A gun, taser or pepper spray would be handy right now, but I don't possess anything of the sort. Agreeing to go to dinner with him is last on my list of things I'd like to do, but the attractive point about his statement is he'd no longer be here in my house. Once I lock up, I'll refuse to let him back inside.

"Come on," he cajoles, and winks—a gesture totally at odds with what I know of his character. "Brook's Diner is still open, isn't it?"

While I've no desire to eat with him, at least one of my aims would be satisfied—he wouldn't be breathing my air. Brook's is always crowded, so I won't be alone with him. *Maybe the sheriff or his deputy would be eating there. Or someone who'd be suspicious seeing us together, and check that I was alright.*

"That's a great idea." I try to sound enthusiastic. And, as it's just a mom-and-pop place, I don't need to leave him alone while I get dressed, what I'm wearing now would do. While there's not a lot for him to steal here, I don't want him rummaging through my things. "I can come as I am."

"You can drive," he tells me.

"Why don't you follow me?" After we've eaten he can take off to wherever he's living afterward.

His face darkens, sending a shiver through me, making my self-preservation instinct kick in. Nope, I don't want to upset him. I learned that as a child. Weston's fists can be pretty persuasive.

"I came by cab," he informs me. "Ain't got no transport."

I bite my tongue. When you're a scrap of a thing like myself, you don't tell an ex-professional wrestler he can take a hike, or summon another taxi to take him back to whatever rock he'd crawled out of.

The sooner we get to eat, the faster he'll be gone. I don't delay, pausing only to check Caspar's water bowl is topped up. After patting my mom's faithful dog on the head and telling him to be a good boy, I pick up the keys to my father's truck.

I'm not convinced this is wise, but can't see what other choice I have. "Let's go then."

Swigging back the remnants of his coffee, Weston looks at me and smirks, as though he realises why I'm being so compliant, that even after all these years, I know he's a threat. Flexing his muscles, he lumbers over and snatches the keys out of my hand. "I'll drive."

Under my breath I count to ten. He wouldn't hurt me like he had when I was a child, would he? My arm still aches in cold weather from where he'd deliberately broken it. But I don't want to test my theory. The vibes I'm getting from this man are not friendly.

He wants something. But what? I wish he'd just come out with it.

The truck's big, but Weston still looks ridiculous as he pushes the seat back as far as it can go, and I lean into the passenger side so his muscular arm doesn't touch me when he puts it into gear.

Luckily, Brook's Diner is only a couple of miles down the road, so I grit my teeth and don't comment when he drives too fast. *Maybe we'll get pulled over and I can tell the cop he's kidnapping me.*

But I have no such luck. We arrive, park, and walk inside. Once seated, we're given menus. Wanting to keep a clear head, I refuse the alcoholic drink he offers to buy me, sticking to soda. Weston does the opposite, and he's on his second beer by the time we've ordered.

He goes for steak, while I basically point at a chicken salad. With no appetite under the circumstances, I can't manage much more.

He spends his time leering at the other customers. When he pays attention to me, he smirks, an expression I long to wipe off his face. It's as if he knows something I don't.

As I sit, I'm wondering how soon I can get rid of him. Maybe when the meals over I can drop him somewhere instead of taking him home. *He's got my keys.* Would an excuse I left my wallet in the car work? I could take off and leave him here. Or, I could say I've got to take a bathroom break and disappear.

A voice breaks into my thoughts.

"Hey, Cat. We don't often see you." Rosa, a waitress I've spoken to on a few occasions, stops by my side.

When my mom was dying, I spent all my time with her. I've only recently started to venture out of the house. Most of my childhood friends have moved away, like me, preferring city life. I vaguely remember Rosa from school, but she was a year or two ahead.

Seeing her eyes flicking warily at my companion and not wanting her to think I've poor taste in men, I sigh. "Rosa, this is my cousin, Weston."

Weston raises his eyes from her boobs, and gives a sly smile as they settle on her face. I don't miss Rosa's slight shudder, though good waitress as she is, she covers it quickly.

"That's nice. You could do with some family around you."

I probably could, but Weston isn't the one that I want. For a second I need to suppress my sadness that my parents have gone.

"Can I get you anything else?"

"Another beer," Weston says, tapping the table.

He's going to get drunk if he doesn't watch out. I narrow my eyes, choking back the comment that normally I'd make. I can't afford to make him angry. What do I know? Man his size could have hollow legs. *Maybe he'll drink so much I can sneak off and speak to Rosa?* She could ring the cops. As he's an ex-convict they would be on my side, wouldn't they?

With a plan in mind, I decide to follow it. Our meal is done, his plate cleared, mine barely touched. I pick up my bag.

"Where are you going?"

"To the bathroom."

"Woman, you can hold it. You're five minutes from home. You're still as fuckin' weak as you were when you were a child."

I could plea that I can't, but I feel my lips set stubbornly. *I'll show you weak.* He's challenged me, and you don't do that with a red-headed woman.

With another of his smirks, he pushes the bill my way. Picking my battles, I roll my eyes and pay. It's not much, but more than I wanted to waste on him. Hopefully, now he's fed, he'll leave me alone.

"Shall I call you a taxi?" I offer, a little sweetly. See? I can be a thoughtful cousin.

His eyes suddenly sharpen. "What the fuck for? I'm coming back with you. I'm staying at your place tonight."

Oh no you're not. "Weston." I start to protest, quickly looking around, but Rosa must be on a break, and there's no one I know here. It would take too long to explain why I'd prefer my relative arrested than return to my home, and God knows what he'd do while I was doing so. He'd smash the place up, starting with myself. I might have a temper, but it's nothing compared to his when roused. "Weston," I start again in a hiss. "It wouldn't be right. I'm a single woman."

"Fuck, woman, I'm not going to jump your bones, am I? We're family." His look is one of disgust. "And you're not my type. I prefer my women more curvy."

I would tell him living in a house of death doesn't do much to help keep weight on, but why bother.

His body is tense, and he makes an effort to calm himself. His sympathetic smile he plants on his face looks forced. "Look, Catherine, I know we didn't always see eye to eye. But my mom was right. You're wasting away rattling around in that house. Just let me keep you company tonight. You've got a spare bedroom, yes? Tomorrow, I promise, I'll be out of your way. Maybe we can watch a film and catch up or something? It's not good for you to be alone."

He's trying to sound sincere. With every bone in my body shouting out I mustn't do this, so far, he's done nothing to hurt me tonight. Maybe prison has changed him, and maybe, for once, it wouldn't be so bad to have some company. I've lost everyone else. Possibly the most valid reason is, now he's fixed himself to me like a limpet, I'm not sure how to shift him. Sighing, I capitulate. "One night, okay? Just tonight."

"All I want, little Cuz. Got somewhere to be tomorrow."

"Your new job?"

He nods enthusiastically. "Yeah, that's right."

This time, he lets me drive, while he settles back with his head against the headrest, but his eyes stay open, as if he's checking the road. All of my senses tell me what I'm doing is wrong, but I'm stuck in a hole I can't get out of. Still, I take him back home.

He's not drunk as it turns out. Maybe tipsy, but not that much while six beers would have had me under the table. The amount he'd drunk had made me hopeful at first, that if I showed him straight to the spare bedroom, he'll just crash, but no, instead he prowls around the house, coming to a halt in front of my PC.

"You got an Airbnb account?"

What? Flustered, I answer truthfully, "Sure. Not that I've used it in forever."

"Need you to book me a place to stay. Some of my friends and I are going fishing in Utah."

"Book it yourself." I shake my head at the imposition.

His hands form fists. In a remembered childhood response, I take a step back. With a shudder, he comes back to himself. "Thing is, Cuz, I'm not long out of the pen. I ain't got a permanent address. Those bastards check. You book it for us, I'll pay you back."

I doubt I'll see the money again, but I'm starting to think he's showing his true colours, and if I anger him, he'll retaliate.

I long to refuse, but this is Weston. There was a reason for him coming here, is this it? "If I do this, you'll go?"

"Yeah. It's for this coming weekend, so I've got to be there." He winks. "Need to get myself some rods. I'll leave in the morning."

"I thought you had a job to go to."

His face tightens as though he doesn't like me questioning him, but then he shrugs. "I start next week. Can't a man have some fun first?"

Should I? Book a place for him to stay? It might leave me short of a few dollars, but if that's all he wants, wouldn't it be worth it? Undecided, I bow my head, rubbing at my temples. I don't trust him at all.

"Do you know where you're going?" I'm starting to think this is going to be a long night. The last time I booked a vacation rental for myself and a girlfriend, we spent days checking all the properties out before deciding which appealed most.

I'm to be pleasantly surprised. He opens his wallet and pulls out a scrap of paper. "This one."

Right. I turn on the PC, pull out my desk chair and sit down. It takes me a while to remember my login details, but at last I'm in. I search for the location he's chosen. The price makes my eyes water. He might have told me he'd pay me back, but I'm likely to end up paying for an expensive fishing trip for him and his friends. *It'll be worth it, he'll be gone.*

I go through the screens, put in the information, soon it's all booked. I close my eyes briefly, sending up a silent prayer that good to his word, in the morning he'll be gone. He should. It's Tuesday now, and the cabin is booked from Thursday and all the way over in Utah.

I don't bother asking how he'll be getting there, worried he'd tap me for airfare as well.

"Thanks, Catherine. I knew I could rely on you. Now, I'm off to bed."

Grateful he's forgoing the aforementioned film and social evening, I remember I'm an, albeit reluctant, hostess and start to stand. "The guest room—"

"I know where it is. I've stayed before."

Has he? I couldn't see my parents giving him accommodation, but it must have been while I was working away, and before my dad had died. I don't worry my head about it, just feel the relief as he stomps his way up the stairs.

Idly, I stroke Caspar's head. "You know," I tell my beloved

dog quietly, "if you were any kind of guard dog he wouldn't have gotten into this house." Caspar wags his tail. Yeah. He must have missed that training session in puppy school.

I let Caspar out and let him back in once he's done his business, make sure the windows are closed and the door is locked and finally take myself off to bed.

There are snores coming from the guestroom. Even so, I wish there was a lock on my bedroom, then laugh at myself. I might not trust him, but he's my cousin. Any danger is not to my virtue, even Weston wouldn't do that. It takes time, though, until I drop into an uneasy sleep.

It's still dark when I'm rudely awoken. One minute I'm sleeping, the next I'm flying through the air, or, more accurately, being carried by Weston.

"Let go of me!" I scream, beating at him with my hands. Of course, my puny attempts to get free don't work.

Caspar's almost non-existent protective instinct suddenly comes to the fore. I hear him barking and feel him leaping, followed by a yelp, and the sound of a body falling down the stairs. After that there's a whine that's followed by more barking.

"Fuckin' mutt bit me."

Good. But I'm scared. "Don't hurt him, Weston. You're frightening him." And me.

"Keep quiet, bitch, and I might let your dog live."

Might?

"What are you doing?" I scream, punching as hard as I can, but my fists bounce off his muscles hurting me rather than him.

He kicks open the door to the cellar, taking me down. While I was sleeping, he'd obviously gotten himself prepared. There's a thin blanket on the floor. I struggle, not understanding what he's going to do but knowing I'm not going to like it. As if fed up with me fighting back he hits me, putting the force of his wrestling experience behind it, and I know no more.

I wake up, my head throbbing. My hands are handcuffed in front of me, a chain connecting them that's padlocked to an iron support. There are a couple of bottles of water lying beside me, a bucket and, what looks like the contents of my pantry he's raided—a few bags of chips, a loaf of bread, some cheese, and a box of cereal.

I hear his footsteps on the stairs. *I'd thought he'd left.*

"Now you be a good girl. I'll only be gone a few days, then I'll be back to free you."

"Weston, please. Let me go. Why are you doing this?"

"Why? Because you know where I'll be. Can't let that info get out, Catherine. But don't worry, you'll be fine. I'll be back before you know it."

"I won't tell anyone about your fishing trip. You can't leave me!" I'm screaming now.

"Can't I?" He smirks, his finger resting on the switch of the overhead light. "You just watch." He leaves me in the dark.

Those are his last words before he thumps back up the stairs.

I scream, plead and beg long after he's probably left the house. I cry out until I'm hoarse, but no one comes.

I may be twenty-five years old, but I'm scared of being in the dark, scared of him forgetting to return, scared of dying alone. My parents' farmhouse is isolated and set well back from the road. It's privacy a danger now, however much noise I make, there's no one likely to hear.

I can't stay here until Weston decides to come back, I simply can't. Why did I even let him inside? I almost curse that my parents had brought me up to be polite. I should have told him to get lost when he'd turned up at my door, or found some way to call the police, or had asked Rosa at the restaurant to summon help.

I'm already cold. The farmhouse is old. This root cellar was ideal for storing stuff before refrigerators became common place, keeping whatever was here cool all year. I've been left with a thin fraying blanket and am wearing nothing more than a tank top and sleep pants.

I've cried out for Caspar, hoping he'll be able to throw himself at the door and open it. I need him for his body warmth and comfort if nothing else.

What will happen to him? He'll be locked in the house without food or water. At least Star won't starve, he's still got enough in his pasture, and water in his trough. That has to last, but for how long for? I'd booked that cabin for a week. Who's going to feed the hens?

Once I've worried about my animals, I worry about myself. The meagre rations he left me are not going to feed me for days. One maybe, not seven.

Gradually the room lightens a little as daylight comes, providing just a sliver of brightness under the door.

Fear of the dark won't kill me, I repeat to myself. But my heart beats so fast I think maybe it can. Why, oh why did I have to be a fan of horror films? My mind seems to be running through every one, conjuring up horrors which could be hidden in the corners. I berate myself. The horror was Weston, and he's been and gone.

Now my survival depends on him coming back.

No. I can't give up. I have to get free by myself. I tug on the chain, it doesn't budge, but the tugging makes the cuffs dig in. In no time, my wrists become bloody. *The padlock.* Being unable to see anything in the dim light, I move my hand around the floor, hoping to find something which I could use to pick the lock, dismissing the thought I've no relevant skills even if I could find a loose nail.

Frustrated, I scream once again.

I end up screaming until I'm exhausted and hoarse in the vain hope that someone will hear. I'm not expecting anything, but maybe there'll be a delivery I've forgotten.

"Help!" I bellow as loudly as I can. "I'm stuck, down here!"

Was this how my father had felt? Trapped under his upturned tractor, the weight pushing his face into the mud, his life blood slowly leaking out of his body. I'd tried to avoid thinking about that before, how he must have screamed for assistance which never came. The thought so horrific, I'd tried to block it out of my mind, preferring to imagine him lying unconscious rather than hurting and fully aware that unless help arrived soon, he was dying.

Maybe he'd been lucky, it had been minutes or an hour for him, not days like me.

I try to stay calm, but it's impossible. Redoubling my efforts has the same result, *I can't get out.*

Weston will come back. He promised me.

Can I last?

I fall into a fitful doze. When I awake, I try again to escape with no more effect than it had before. My meagre supplies won't last long. I know I have to ration my food. I nibble on a piece of bread and a small portion of cheese, but it does nothing to ease the hunger gnawing at my gut. A few chips? Sure, but no more. I've got to eek this out.

The day goes slowly, but all too fast the slither of light disappears. It's night, a time to sleep, but I'm too cold. I'm also stiff and sore. I can sit up, lie down, and crouch, but I can't fully stand.

The second day brings horrors afresh, the first being forced to use the bucket for what Weston had obviously put it there for. When I reach out my hand for a packet of chips, it moves away from me, rustling across the floor.

Rats.

I scream so long I make myself sick, vomiting up little more than bile as my stomach's so empty. *Rats.* I might be an animal lover, but I hate those rodents. My mind goes to something worse. *What if there are snakes?*

"Caspar!" I scream, over and over. He might not be able to help get me free, but he can keep away the critters.

Spiders. Oh, shit. I'm a total wimp. I don't like nature at all.

I curl up into a ball and sob, wondering if I'll get out of here with my mental state intact.

I try to make what he left me last, but after the rats invaded while I was asleep, all I've got is water. I feel so cold, perversely I'm hot. I grow more and more scared, nightmares of being eaten alive jolt me awake, and when I do drop off, I'm more unconscious than sleeping.

Frantically I struggle hoping somehow I'll loosen the chains. I hurt, I ignore it, and go back to struggling again. In the end, the pain shoots through me making me think I may have broken my wrist or at the very least badly sprained it.

And still, no one comes.

I lose all notion of whether it's day or night, or how many sunrises there have been since Weston imprisoned me.

How long does it take to go insane? I think I'm about to find out. Unless, I die first.

12

───────

*S*tormy...

My shoulders feel light and empty without the heavy weight of the cut I've worn for the past seven years. But there's no going back, only forward. I've burned my bridges.

I need to move fast.

Working at lightning speed, my brain issues instructions to my body almost without conscious thought. I might not have my colours, but I had the foresight to bring my wallet with me. I risk stopping in town, thinking they wouldn't have sent out a lynching party yet, suspecting I've ridden off in a pique and will return once I've cooled down.

I ditch my phone, buy a burner, and a top-of-the-line laptop. I visit the bank I use, open my safe deposit box and collect my fake passport and papers I'd left there for safekeeping when I went nomad. Next, I go to a second bank and transfer all my money into the account under the Jeremiah Briggs identity that I last used four years ago. My pre-emptive strike entirely necessary, I wouldn't put it past the club trying to freeze my accounts when I don't turn up.

When I don't turn up, I'll be out bad for certain.

I could go back. *After that fucking meeting? No way.*

All I can do is get the hell out of Dodge.

For no particular reason, I ride north. Miles fly past. After a couple of hours, I cease keeping an eye on the road behind me. Continuing along the same route, I stop only for gas and fuel for myself, before getting on the move again. For almost twenty hours, I ride, or until I know I can't go on anymore. When I halt, I'm unaware of what state I'm in, mentally or in actuality.

Entering the motel room, I collapse fully clothed on the bed, falling asleep immediately.

I wake as sunlight comes in through the curtains. For a moment, I wonder where I am and how I got here, and why I'm not back in my room at the clubhouse. As the events of yesterday come flooding back. I lie, hands behind my head, thinking.

The brothers won't understand. I'll have left them believing I'm a coward and that I ran to avoid my punishment.

I did not.

I might have been riding blindly yesterday, not caring where the road was taking me, but in my head, thoughts were whirring. Things that should have become clear years ago, only coming into clarity now.

Nazia trying to blow herself up, Marjan's disappearance… No, it starts before that with Pooh's death. A senseless act caused by Smythe's panic, which didn't absolve me. I was guilty as fuck, but how could I have left those kids to die?

Then came Nazia's unexplained death and my inability to find her sister, followed immediately by the news that my whole team had died. Loss and failure, failure and loss, cycles of my life on repeat.

A therapist would probably tell me I'd been struggling since, and maybe they'd be right. My actions hadn't been rational, though my reasoning appeared sound. I thought I was being sensible, not wanting to put myself in the position of losing brothers again or being responsible for them, but instead it all got twisted in my head.

With sudden clarity, I understand. It wasn't that I didn't trust them, I didn't trust myself.

And fuck, I was right not to. Look what a fuckup I made of things. Drummer could have decided to take our charter because of what I'd done. But perhaps it wasn't just me to blame. It had been Pip's desire for secrecy which upset Drummer most, but that had only given me enough rope to hang myself. I took distrust to the fucking limits and stretched it further. Pip's desire to fly under the radar might have provided the envelope, but I'd written the letter, outwardly showing my disdain for men wearing the same patch as myself, simply because they belonged to another chapter.

As the sun starts to rise in the sky, I admit everything at last. I hadn't run because I was a coward. I'd run because I was ashamed.

The punishment doled out would have done nothing to assuage that. A beatdown would have been painful, but I'd have survived. Six months prospecting would have been hard no doubt, but it wouldn't have wiped the slate clean. I let my chapter and all of the Satan's Devils down. There weren't sufficient amends I could make.

The devil on my shoulder reminds me I wasn't the only one to bring Drummer's wrath down onto the club. That honour's all Pip's. He patched in Swift which stretched the Satan's Devils' rules almost, but as it turned out, not quite to a breaking point. Pip was the prez who couldn't ride, that little fact which blew every regulation out of the water. He was the one who'd stepped in and taken over the club, for good reasons, but ones which primarily served his own purpose. He was my enabler, I couldn't forget that.

But Utah had become something admirable, it gave purpose

to all our lives. It had saved me from disappearing down a hole of my own despair. And I rewarded them how?

There's no denying I personally insulted two of the chapters of the club, and by association, Drummer and the mother chapter. That was the straw with potential to break the camel's back. As it is, Snatcher is hanging on to his charter by his fingernails now. Drummer will be watching very carefully.

I haven't left forever, in my heart I know that. I will return. But I'm not going back empty-handed. I need something to make them trust I have their interests at heart and that I deserve a chance to prospect for them again. It won't wipe the slate clean, but maybe it'll make their acceptance of me, and mine of them, easier.

For now, the Satan's Devils Utah will have to ride on without me.

They're hanging on by a thread, Drummer will be all over them like a rash. And one thing they don't need is something coming along and catching them on their blind side.

I might be arrogant, but I've remembered something they've overlooked during the last couple of days with the mayhem of Drummer's arrival, and that's that while Swift's captors have all been dealt with and the reason behind her kidnap had all been to do with Pip and his past, there remains one thing which makes it a matter that's not yet a closed book.

There's a risk that though the kidnappers are dead, there could be someone else involved who's still very much alive. If there's one, there may be others, and Pip might do well not to stop looking over his shoulder.

It's a small lead, but one worth investigating.

Swift was kidnapped and held in a vacation rental, and an unknown woman had made the booking. Maybe under duress, maybe she was part of the team. Maybe it wasn't a she. It could have been Saul Kincaid or one of his cohorts registering under a fake name. But Airbnb do run rudimentary checks. To my mind, something would have needed to be set up to prove the woman who rented the place had at least at some point had an existence that would pass scrutiny. Who is she, and what risk remains to the club?

It may be something, it may be nothing, but I could check it out. If I found anything, I could eliminate any remaining risk. Only then will I return to my club and take my punishment, at least I'd have something to prove my allegiance.

It shouldn't take long. I sit up, realising I hadn't undressed, and feeling the loss of the one garment I should be wearing. I roll my shoulders promising myself it won't be long until I wear my cut again. Albeit, I muse wistfully, with a prospect patch. The sentence has been passed, I have to accept it.

Now I'm fully awake and plans consolidated in my head, my stomach growls loudly. It's an inconvenience, but I have to eat. I shower, dress again in yesterday's clothes. Despite knowing it's not there, I automatically reach for my cut, when my hand hits air I let the pain pass through me. I pick up my saddlebags and stride to the restaurant located next door.

Even without my cut, my appearance screams *biker* and *stay away from me.* I'm not bothered, it means no one will bother me. I walk to a corner table, sit with my back to the wall, and take out my laptop. I give a cursory glance at the menu, then start to work.

When the waitress appears, I order coffee—black, no sugar—and the food that will set me up for the day, when she's left me in peace I settle to concentrate.

Always hoping I'd be sent out on the road as a nomad once again, I'd used my time wisely while I was in Utah, leaving myself a back door into their systems. My brothers might be good, but I'm their equal if not better, and they'll never know I've been in and used the resources they have. I log in with the full confidence I've disappeared off the grid and that they'll never find me.

The online booking site gives me no problems, and soon I have a name—*Catherine Beeswick*—and an address. It's in Kentucky. With a huff at myself, I remember I don't actually know where I laid my head last night, and have to glance at the address on the menu to find out. It seems I'm in Minnesota, well, fancy that. Googling it's another nine hundred miles to bring me close to her. It'll be another long ride, twelve or thirteen hours give or take and depending how hard I push it. Right now my ass wishes Preacher would turn up with his fucking plane, but there's no point wishing for resources I no longer have. Kentucky's a fucking long way from Utah. If my brothers are looking for me, I'll have time to find answers. Only a lunatic would have ridden so far.

As my drink appears, I take a long swig of the hot coffee, thinking as I swallow. *Why Kentucky? Where did Kincaid come from? Has he links to the state?* I can't recall. Though Pip had told us the story of Dengra's daughter being groomed and kidnapped by Kincaid's twin brother, I don't think he'd said where it happened. Oh well, no point dwelling on that now. I can hardly call Pip and ask him. Doing so risks giving my location away, and the club will move heaven and earth to find me. I'll be on their most wanted list now.

Did Kincaid come halfway across the country to kidnap Swift for revenge? Or, is he more local, and Catherine Beeswick either doesn't exist, or is just someone he could call on to do him a favour? I suppose it doesn't stretch the imagination too far to think that she might be just a casual acquaintance. *What's her connection with him?*

Hey, could you book a rental for me? I haven't access to the internet right now.

Plausible, perhaps. This could be a wild goose chase, but if so, which Saul Kincaid does Catherine know? The one who ended up in jail, or the one with the doctored CV that got him admitted to Dengra's residence and access to his daughter and her baby son, allowing him to play the role of loving uncle until the child had sadly passed away.

Whether I'm already pursuing a lost cause, having a destination satisfies the need inside for direction, even though it's me determining my fate now. I'll finish up here, find somewhere to buy some new clothes—t-shirts and underwear at least—and a tube of toothpaste then head to Kentucky. I'll arrive under the cover of darkness, just right for scoping a place out.

I'm no stranger to long journeys, but even so, another full day's riding when my ass is still sore isn't the most attractive option. Maybe that's why I begin to have second thoughts. Saul Kincaid had managed to come up with a background that hid his time in the pen and made him out to be an upstanding citizen. It's possible that he either had data skills himself, or had access to someone who could provide them. If so, it would be child's play to hack into a random person's account and make a booking. That makes sense, Saul wouldn't have wanted to make it in his name. All he needed to have done was to cloak the email address and get all correspondence sent to himself.

Going to Kentucky could be a complete waste of time. Catherine Beeswick might never have known her account had been hacked. Or, said woman never existed in the first place. The more I think, the more either option seems likely.

Damn. What do I do now? Go back to the club with my tail between my legs? Fuck that. I promised myself I'd only return if I had something to give. I'd still have to take my punishment like a man, but I'd have proof I have the best interests of the club at heart. Without anything to offer, I'm just a sore loser.

Ruefully, I throw sufficient dollars on the table, stand and stretch, pick up my saddlebags and head out to my bike. Maybe I'm just searching for an excuse, but to do what? An excuse to return to my club, or an excuse to go miles out of my way and speak with a woman who probably has nothing to offer?

My hands itch to straighten the non-existent cut on my

back. As I bring my arms back to my sides, I realise I've never run from anything in my life. But yesterday, I did. Today, I've calmed down. I admit I was riled most at the thought of being a prospect again, not the promised beatdown. What would I have suggested if another member had put the club in such a dangerous position? Losing them the charter, I'd have opted to kill them.

My crimes are serious, I know that. Now compounded by running, even now I could have been declared out bad.

Fuck.

I'm a man who doesn't like prevaricating or staying still. If this fails, maybe I'd be safer to go into hiding or leave the country. For now though, I'll stick to my initial plan. Swinging my leg over the saddle, I get on my bike, shift into first, and point the front wheel in the direction of Kentucky.

I'm a biker. I enjoy the long ride, despite the small detail that my ass is aching, and a long soak in the tub sounds increasingly attractive. I lock the throttle to give my hand a rest, stretch my fingers, placing them on my knee for a while, rolling my neck to get the kinks out as the miles pass. When the sun dips in the sky, I've still got a long way to travel.

Why am I doing this?

Christ, I don't know. It's just something I feel I've got to try, even if it proves only a process of elimination. I grow more convinced that what I'm going to find is a decent middle-aged woman in her bed sleeping, dreaming innocent dreams with no idea her identity has been used.

Well, it would cross the mysterious woman off the list, I suppose. A bone to offer the club, a small one. One which shouldn't have necessitated a journey to Kentucky to find out.

Unless dear Catherine's up to her neck in this shit. If she is, she'll soon wish she wasn't. I start to hope that's the case and consider how best to get information out of her. Swift might be the enforcer, but never fear, I've a few interrogation techniques of my own.

I'm stiff, every muscle hurts as I near the town limits of the place where she resides. By now the moon has risen in the night sky. Over the miles, I've refined the details of my plan. I'll check out the house, talk to Catherine if she's still up. If she's innocent, I'll go find the nearest motel for the night. Right now a park bench would do—anything that would allow me to stretch out. If she's not, well, we'll both be in for a long night.

Ah, there it is now. The house isn't set in a town, instead it stands on its own, surrounded by a decent sized piece of land. In the pasture I can see a horse, sleeping with one of its back hooves bent in a posture of total relaxation. I envy it. But of course, the noise of my engine wakes it fast and it scatters, going from standing to snorting and tossing its head.

Switching off my engine, I coast the final few yards, noticing the house is in darkness.

When I last checked, it was only nearing twenty-three hundred hours, perhaps she goes to bed early? But if she's got livestock, maybe it's understandable. This does look like a farmhouse.

Maybe I won't knock, maybe there's a barn and I could find some hay and hole up for the night, and wait to confront Ms Beeswick in the morning.

I know my racing mind won't let me relax, not when I've travelled so far to solve this mystery. I've spent many a wakeless night when I was protecting my country. One disturbed night for her is nothing in comparison.

Sure, I'm an asshole, but I'm going to be waking her up, and I won't take no for an answer.

Husband, boyfriend? Lover, brother or son? They won't get in my way, I've got questions to ask. The sooner I have what I want, the sooner I'll be out of the house and on my way, hopefully with information to satisfy my club.

Dismounting, I take my gun out of the hidden holder on the bike. Looking around, I see and hear no threat, so I go to slide it inside my cut. When the weapon meets air, I sigh, and place it instead in the waistband of my jeans. Putting my hands on my knees, I breathe in deeply, then kicking out my legs, I shake them, first the right followed by the left. I roll my shoulders and ease back my head. *Fuck but I'm sore.*

Right. I'm ready. Approaching the front door, I bang on it, sighting a doorbell I ring that too.

No answer.

Whoever's home, they sleep like the dead. I could be anyone, a burglar or murderer.

After knocking and banging once more, I step back, and make my way around the house. The curtains aren't drawn, my flashlight beam illuminates a pleasant enough interior, comfortable furnishings in the living room, a kitchen with elderly but clean and serviceable appliances, everything put away except for two cups left out on the countertop.

Can't mark her down for leaving out cups. Everything else is tidy. I'm just about to turn away when my light falls on something else. I move in closer, cupping my eyes against the reflection of the moon behind me. There's a smashed plate on the floor. Surely someone as house proud as this homeowner would have cleared that up before going to bed?

Hairs rise on the back of my neck, and I slide out my gun, feeling it's comfortable weight in my hand.

It could well be nothing. Maybe she's not here and went out in a rush, and will clear that up on her return.

Or, maybe, she's had a home invasion.

Coincidence? I don't believe in them.

But Kincaid, Hughes, McGregor and Dean are dead.

What if someone else was working with them? That would make sense. It might not just be me she's a loose thread for. If she made the booking for them, she'd have known at least one of their names, maybe even what they were doing.

I hesitate only to consider the best way to proceed. *I need to get into that house.* Walking around the perimeter once more, I check for any signs of a security system. The most I can see is a Ring doorbell at the front, so I head back to the kitchen and the rear door. Taking out my small toolkit I always carry, I make short work of the lock, and soon, soundlessly, I'm pushing open that door.

Using the skills I learned as a SEAL, I proceed stealthily into the house. On first inspection it reveals nothing more than I'd already learned from looking in through the windows. Every few steps I wait and listen. There's no sound other than a buzzing of flies. Maybe there was food on the plate I saw smashed?

I round the kitchen island carefully, stopping when my foot touches something soft. I drop to my haunches and direct the beam of my flashlight. *Shit.* I can tell the dog is long dead, cold and stiff to the touch. *Bastard.* My jaw clenches. While I've never had a dog myself—it has been more a matter of convenience than inclination—we had dogs on the teams. I admired them a lot. This poor fucking thing's been stabbed and is lying in a pool of blood. Uselessly I swat the flies away, then rise once again, frowning down at the animal. By my estimation it's been dead for days.

What happened here? Where's Catherine Beeswick? Whatever's gone down, it's clear it happened some time ago and the trail has gone cold.

I was right to come here, but I hadn't gotten here soon enough. Has Catherine been kidnapped like Swift? Or killed like her dog and been buried somewhere? Or, is her body still here?

My hands clench at my sides, knowing I have to check upstairs and make sure the woman's not lying dead in her bed.

Or see if there's a sign of a struggle which would prove she was abducted. If so, I've a feeling it's got something to do with Kincaid. But what, why and how, given that the man himself is dead? Those are questions I have no answer for.

With a heavy heart, and every expectation I'll find a body, I climb the stairs. I remain quiet and vigilant, but am fairly certain whoever caused trouble in this house isn't here now.

The first bedroom I come to appears to be the master. The bed's unmade, but apart from that, there's no sign of any trouble. Inspecting the laundry basket, I see it's full of dirty clothes, just as could be expected.

She's neat. Tidy. If she left of her own volition, she'd have made the bed.

I try the remaining two bedrooms. One, like the master has sheets lying in disarray, but there's no other sign of anything. *Maybe she's not such a good housekeeper. Maybe the downstairs is tidy in case visitors turn up.*

But what about the dog? Who leaves their house with a dog, dead or alive, lying on the kitchen floor?

Damn. I wish Honor or Duty were here. As ex-cops, they might be able to see things I'm missing. But I can hardly give them a call. I don't even know if Catherine or this mystery has anything to do with the club, except for that Airbnb booking. And even with all the questions here in this house, it's still in the cards she had nothing to do with Kincaid who might have unbeknownst to her used her name and address.

Returning downstairs, I go to the dining area and notice a desk with a computer on it. I start opening drawers and pulling correspondence out, putting it all in a pile I'll go through in a moment. I reach for the switch to bring the computer to life, when something, an instinct, makes me turn, and I notice a hitherto unseen door under the stairs.

The hairs on the back of my neck tingle. A closet? I don't leave anything unsearched, and certainly not a hiding place where someone could be waiting to sneak up on me. I go to check, but when I open it, find some old stone steps. Yes. This is an old farmhouse, it probably leads to a root cellar. *Maybe there's something down there?*

Whether there is or not, I need to take a look.

I take out my flashlight again, holding it in one hand and my gun in the other. It could be my imagination, but some sixth sense warns me I'm not alone.

Silent, not switching my light on, I inch my way down, stopping when I come to the bottom. I pause, holding my breath, but I can hear nothing at all. My hand, feeling the wall, touches a light switch.

Holding my Glock out in front of me, I flick the switch. A single bulb provides little illumination. Now using my flashlight as well, I let the beam shine into the corners, almost completing a circuit before pulling it back. An unpleasant odour hits me, making me reel back. It smells like something had crawled in here and died. I shiver slightly, like many cellars it's dark and dank, the sun doesn't permeate down here.

There's a bundle of old clothes. Or, is it? Stepping closer, I see there's also a wig, dirty and dishevelled.

Wait. That's no fucking wig. In two strides I'm across the space, falling to my knees. My light reveals a body of a woman. *Well,* I rock back on my heels. *I've found her.* Or so I presume.

I'm too late.

Damn it. Reaching out my hand, I gently brush the auburn hair off her face, touching her skin as I do.

She's cold, but not icy, and soft, her skin is yielding.

My eyes widen, and I move my fingers to her atrio venous pulse, holding them there for a second, not breathing myself.

There's a weak beat.

She's alive.

Barely.

13

*S*tormy...

   I've found Catherine Beeswick, or that's who I assume this is, and she's breathing but in a bad way.

   I'm a bastard, everyone knows that. I've been an asshole all my life. What I should do is call 911 and get paramedics here to help, but in my head I see them whisking her away, and me losing any right to question her and find out what she knows. So the decision is easy, I'm keeping her here and will do what I can to care for her myself.

   Quickly I check her out to see what I'm dealing with. She's so fucking cold. How long has she been this way? She's probably dehydrated and depending on how long she's been left, starved. There are empty bags around her, but no food. If she was left any, it's run out by now. A rustle in the corner gets my gun back in my hand... *Fucking rat.* I turn back to her again. *Or the food was stolen by rodents.*

   I examine her more closely. There are no visible wounds that I can see, but maybe there's more under her clothes, not that she's wearing much. When I pry the too-thin blanket away, she's in shorts and a tank, as though she was dressed for sleeping. *Fuck, could she have been abused?*

She's not the old woman I'd expected given the décor in the house. She's younger than me by quite a few years, but that's as far as my disimpassioned thoughts go. If I'm going to get questions answered, I've got to ensure she stays breathing.

The padlock keeping her chained was clearly beyond her, given that her nails are broken and bleeding, but is child's play for me to release. As I get her free, I run through triage and treatment in my head.

Warm her up. That's the first thing she needs.

Gently lifting her in my arms, I carry her up the stairs, and then up the second set that leads to the bedrooms above. I lay her on the bed in the master suite before searching for what I need. Finding an old claw-footed tub in the main bathroom, I turn on the taps, pleased when I test the temperature that hot water flows. Using my hand, I make sure it's warm, but not scalding, and return to the bedroom.

Her clothes are soiled, but hell, I've seen worse. Clinically, I ease the blanket off of her, quickly stripping her out of her meagre amount of clothing. Soon she's back in my arms, and I carry her to the tub.

Gently, I ease her down in the water, keeping one arm around her shoulders to keep her from going under. With my free hand, I start massaging her arms.

When the water cools, I run some more hot in, slowly raising the temperature. I could do with a thermal blanket, but all I've got is this and that will have to be enough.

If she doesn't stir soon, I'll need to call in the experts. Fuck, I hope it doesn't come to that. I want my chance to talk to her.

While I'm working on raising her core temperature, with a dispassionate eye, I run my eyes over her, noting the rawness around her wrists, and the way one is lying, swollen. Broken or badly strained is my diagnosis. Her skin is dull, dehydrated. Her ribs show, but she's been imprisoned for fuck knows how long without food.

Slowly her skin begins to lose that bluish complexion, going white, then slowly morphing into pink. Testing the water, I check it's not too warm—by my judgement, it's just right. *Do I know what I'm doing?* I should call for help.

But I never trust others to do what I can myself. *I got this.* Haven't I?

Jeez, I hope that I have as I gently brush some strands of red hair off her face, wishing she'd open her eyes. *What colour are they?* Fuck, what does it matter? I'm here for info.

Lifting my hand and drying it, I slide my phone out of my pocket. I can't estimate how long it's been since I found her, but I'll give it another half hour. If she doesn't stir when that time has passed, I'll dial 911. While I hate to admit it, I've no idea what she's been through or for how long. Saving her might be beyond me. Fuck, even if I get her to come round, she might still need expert help. All I need is her conscious enough to answer my questions, after which I'll gladly let the professionals take her. At least now she's naked, I can see no other injuries, no bruising or wounds that would suggest sexual abuse. Of course, the bulk of those would be internal.

I still. *Was that a murmur? Wasn't her mouth closed?* Almost without breathing myself, I stare at her chest, watching it rise and fall. Is it wishful thinking, or is the movement getting stronger?

Suddenly and so fast it makes me startle, her eyes open wide. Water sloshes as she screams and tries to cover herself.

Green, I notice with strange satisfaction—the colour of her eyes is a vivid green.

"Wh-who?" "Wh-who are you?" she tries again. Her whole body is violently trembling. It could be shivers that she's still cold, but more likely from terror. Her voice is croaky, her throat dry and probably misused from futile screaming.

"Hush," I say fast, trying to find words to calm her. "I'm not here to hurt you. I'm just warming you up. You were so fuckin' cold, I couldn't think of anything else." Except calling for paramedics. Yeah, maybe I should have done that.

Her pain-filled eyes flutter wildly, one of her hands covers her breasts, and the other her mound. I'm tempted to roll my eyes. No matter that she's half dead, her modesty is more important than her health. Just like a fucking woman. Would a man first think of covering his dick? I think not. Though if he was as cold as her, he wouldn't have much worth hiding.

As her terrified eyes stare at my face, I try to gentle my voice, or at least, speak less gruffly. "Let's get you out of here." When I reach for her, she feebly tries to push me away, but she's too weak to make anything more than a token effort.

Ignoring that I'm getting wet, I reach my arms around her, pulling her slender form into my arms. Balancing her against my shoulder, I grab hold of a towel, wrapping it around her.

"I…" she croaks.

"Hey, stop. I'm trying to look after you. You're cold and dehydrated." *And fuck knows what else.* "Let's get you settled on your bed, then I'll go and get you some water, okay? I needed to get you warm first."

She starts to wriggle, and her lower half, slippery with water, escapes my hold. She tries to take her weight, but her legs, unused for fuck knows how long don't hold her. Again, I sweep her up into my arms, getting a firmer grip this time, and take her into the bedroom. There, I sweep her dirty clothing and soiled blanket off the comforter and lay her down. I rub her limbs to get her dry and cover her up.

I feel her sigh of relief now her body's no longer revealed to me.

"Stay here," I instruct, though I doubt she can move far. "I'll be back with some water."

Knowing how adrenaline and shock can quickly overcome a

person, I waste no time. Taking the stairs fast and entering the kitchen, I grab a bottle of water, then, opening cupboards, find a can of soup which I open. Tracking down a bowl, I heat it in the microwave and grab a spoon.

I'm back with her within minutes.

"Let's sit you up." I move in close, perching on the bed so I can get my arm around her. Holding the water to her lips, I caution her to take it slow. "Don't drink too much, else you'll just throw up. Little and often, okay? You think you can manage some soup, sweetheart?"

She's compliant, half still out of it I believe, but it suits my purpose as I hold the spoon to her lips. She slurps some of the soup, some of it dribbling out of the side of her mouth, but I ignore that, more thankful when she gestures for more. Before she's finished, I pull it away.

"Let's see how that stays down first, okay?"

There's a little frown on her face, but I know the dangers of eating and drinking too fast. The mind wants more than the body can take.

I note she's got more colour in her face now. It brings out her freckles. "More water?" Her nod is a little more energetic. "Just a little. Small sips." When she appears to be sensible about it, I release my hold on the bottle. Nodding at her left wrist that she has avoided using, I ask, "Can I have a look at that?"

A shy up and down of her head grants me permission. She seems to have got the message I'm here to help. Gently, I take her arm, carefully supporting it. "Can you move your fingers?"

She tries, winces, but I'm pleased to note there's slight movement. "I don't think it's broken, but you've obviously wrenched it. Have you got a first aid kit? I can bandage it to support it."

Her eyes come to my face. "Who, who are you? Are you a friend of Weston's?" I clench my jaw seeing fear making her tense as she mentions the name.

"Weston?" The name triggers loud bells in my memory.

"Weston Hughes?" I can join the dots as well as the next man. "*Tiny?* Who is he to you?" Shit. She's involved in this right up to her neck.

My compassion starts to recede, until I remember the condition I found her in. And that anguish when she mentioned his name… *Don't jump to conclusions.*

"Who is he to you?" she counters. She's scared, but there's bravery in her challenge.

I wonder how to answer. Is he her boyfriend? I might not know anything about her, but she doesn't look the type who'd go for a man like him. He was responsible for chopping off Swift's finger with no more thought than swatting a fly. Everything I know about him suggests he's evil. She, I somehow think, is not. Trying to remain open minded—any woman can walk on the wild side, I suppose—I settle for, "I asked first."

There's only a moment's hesitation before she replies haughtily, "My cousin." She grimaces slightly. "Is it a joke that you call him Tiny?"

It is, he was a big fucker, the answer so obvious I don't provide it.

I suppose we can't choose our family, and I can't assign guilt just because they share blood. If he was the fucker who left her to die, their link didn't mean much to him. That's what I've got to ascertain now. While I prefer not asking leading questions, this time I'm direct. "He got anything to do with leaving you like this?"

She glances away. As gentle as I can be, I touch her chin, and move her face back. "Catherine?"

Again, her eyes widen. "How do you know my name?" An answer occurs to her and defeat fills her face. "Weston, of course. I presume he sent you. I suppose I should be glad he didn't forget about me."

Well, it wasn't a yes/no answer like it could have been. This time I'm the one with information. The fucker is dead, and whether he had any intention of returning to free her, the point is moot. Right now, I doubt it would do any good to explain I'm only here by happy circumstance. If I hadn't turned up, she'd have died chained like an animal. She'll realise that soon enough and will likely have nightmares about dying alone with only rats for company for a very long time.

"Catherine—" I start.

"Cat," she corrects. "No one ever uses my full name, except for *him*." There's a wealth of disgust in the way she refers to who I assume is her cousin.

"Cat," I repeat, happy to give in on the small things, while thinking with her striking green eyes how well the name suits her. "You want to tell me how you came to be chained in your fuckin' cellar?"

She closes her eyes, wincing again as though it hurts to remember. Suddenly her eyes come open again. "Caspar!" It's as though the name has just occurred to her. As I'm wondering how a fucking ghost fits in, she repeats it again, this time, urgently, "Caspar? Where is he? He should be here. God, he's had no food or water. How long has it been? Don't tell me Weston let him out, he could be anywhere by now."

I realise immediately she's talking about her fucking dog, the one which bled out over her kitchen floor, presumably, so frantic barking didn't alert anyone that anything was amiss. If Weston wasn't already six feet under, I'd kill him for that alone. I can't abide abuse to animals, nor am looking forward to being the one to tell her.

I'm an expert at hiding my thoughts, but not this time it would seem. Cat covers her mouth with her hand, her eyes start to water.

"Tell me. Tell me now," she begs, then adds more strongly, "Where's Caspar?"

I can't meet her eyes and look away.

Her good hand comes out, grasping my chin with a strength I didn't think in her state she'd possess. "Caspar?"

What can I do, but simply say, "I'm sorry."

"He starved?" Her voice is choked.

I can't lie. "I presume Weston killed him. I'm fuckin' sorry, Cat."

I barely get out of the way in time, as she vomits over the sheets, an agonised wail comes out of her mouth. "No, that's not true."

"Hey." I wipe her mouth with the edge of the sheet. "Hey." I'm fucking useless at this. Another man would be able to comfort her, but I can't find the words. I'm consumed by the need for revenge, but that's already been dealt. If I could, I'd go back, dig Weston up and kill him all over again, this time with my own bare hands.

I stand, turning my back on her. I don't know the story, but I can fill in the gaps between what she's said and what she hasn't. Weston left her here to suffer. Even if he hadn't been prevented, was he ever going to come back? Would he have left her to a lingering death? A glance back reminds me how much she's been through. The wounds on her wrists showing how much she fought to get free, but she hadn't a chance. And killing her dog? Fuck, just an animal, but he mattered.

Always a practical man, I let her weep for a moment, hating the way her weakened body is subjected to shakes and shudders. When I've given her enough time, I turn around, scooping the comforter along with her, and pick her up gently and place her in the chair by the wall.

"Clean sheets?" I ask when her sobs become less regular.

Incapable of speaking, she inclines her head. Interpreting she means the closet, I go over and pull a fresh set of bedding out, and get on to remaking her bed for her.

"I should... *hic*... be doing that... *hic*."

"Cat, you can barely stand." Otherwise ignoring her, I go

back to my task, cleaning up a spill of vomit she'd gotten on the floor. When I've finished, she's in my arms once again as it's the easiest way to move her. Business like, I notice she's far too thin for my liking. I like a woman with meat on her bones. I sense it's caused by more than however long she spent in the cellar. Does she starve herself to look fashionable? Is, or has she been ill?

Strangely, I find myself wanting to find answers.

I eye her, noting her pallor which looks improved now, but she could still do with some more colour. I might have found her unconscious, but I doubt she's had a proper sleep without worry since Weston left. Rats would keep the strongest of us awake.

"You rest up," I tell her, collecting the half-empty soup bowl. "Try to get some sleep. I'll be up later to see what you want to eat. You need to get your strength back up."

"Where are you going?"

"To do your laundry, for a start." I bundle the dirty bedding together. Seeing her looking nervous, I attempt a smile. "I'm not going to hurt you, or rob you, Cat. You can trust me on that."

There's a small nod. If I was here with an ulterior motive, I needn't have woken her up.

"Wait. Who are you, and why are you in my house? You never said what your relationship is to Weston."

"No relationship," I say fast. As to who I am? I'm conscious I'm still flying under the radar. Now, more than ever, I don't want to be dragged back to the club until I've got the answers I set out to seek. I can't be Stormy, nor Finn. Though it seems wrong to give her a fake identity, I give her the name I've been using along my journey. "I'm Jeremiah. Jeremiah Briggs."

"Army?" She weakly indicates the way I'd tucked the sheet in.

"Navy." I give her the minimum. "Former." I stare down at her for a moment. "I'll be up later; we'll talk more when you're stronger. Call me if you need anything." I swing on my heels to leave her.

"Jeremiah?" Hesitantly, she tries out my name. When I turn back, she's looking concerned, and her bottom lip is trembling. "I've a horse, chickens. Can you check on them? If they, if they… There's hay and chicken feed in the barn."

"I'll sort them out," I promise her. I can only hope Weston left them alone.

14

———

*S*tormy…

I couldn't let her see her beloved dog, I muse as I remove my shirt having found digging a hole in this unforgiving soil is hard work. Idiot that I am, I've chosen the spot carefully, under a tree. It's certainly not the easiest, nor my normal method either. Usually I'd be burying a body where it would never be found.

I even carefully carried the dog instead of dragging it. He'd clearly been a good friend to her, and worthy of respect.

Not your fault, boy. I reckon you died a good dog. Too good, perhaps, trying to protect your mistress.

Once I've replaced the earth on top, I fashion a cross out of two pieces of wood.

The half a dozen hens who hadn't made it, I throw in the trash, having checked that they're no good for the pot. Luckily, the bulk of them had survived, and are very grateful for some feed and fresh water. The pony? He'd looked after himself, thank fuck. I wouldn't want to be digging a hole for him.

I'd never had a dog growing up, or any kind of pet. I doubt it would have lasted long in our trailer. If I'd shown any affection for it, my dad would have seen it as something to taunt me with. On tours, I'd thrown a few scraps to some of the dogs hanging around our camps, but never had the urge to take one under my wing. It's just something I'd never thought about. The service dogs though, I'd known them not to bat an eye at being strapped to their master and parachuting out of a plane. To my mind, they were to be respected as fellow soldiers.

Was Caspar a guard dog as well as a pet? Well, that doesn't matter, nor that if he was, he failed in his task. At the end of the day, he'd been loved by Cat, and that's all that matters.

As I lean on my shovel, watching the sun dipping in the sky, I realise I've steered clear of letting anything get close to me in my life. Dad would have killed it, broken it, or fucked it up. Even women. I used them for sex, but never for anything more. I'm not a bastard about it, never leading them on. As a SEAL it wasn't hard to find a lady to put out for the night, my excuse being I couldn't get attached as I was going on tour. As a biker, well, the hangarounds at our parties were equally eager to get their itches scratched. Sure, some might dream to be an old lady, but I'd always kept them at arm's length. Sometimes there are benefits to being a moody fucker.

Am I even programmed to be a one-woman man? It's not as if I've had a good example to follow. A psychologist would probably tell me I have a deep-seated mistrust of women, having been abandoned by my mom. Did she think my dad would take care of me after she'd gone? She must have been crazy if she did. His abuse to her was probably why she'd walked out, fed up with black eyes, swollen jaws and bruises covering her torso. Or was that not the worst of it? Did she leave because I was an unlovable kid? Was that why she didn't maintain contact?

In my head I'd often pictured my mom with a new family, a

man who could give her everything she wanted. I'd have been okay with that, if only once she'd remembered she'd had a son. Shaking my head, I do what I normally do when I think of the mother I barely remember, confine her to the past where she belongs.

After I replace the shovel in the barn, I walk back into the house. It's charming, but again it strikes me how it's not to a young woman's taste. The PC on the desk is the only modern item here. I wonder what Cat's story is. Does it suit her to live in this way, or, has she just moved in? Is this place rented, or owned?

Spying some photographs on a wall, I walk over. My head tilts as I examine the evidence. The first is a photo taken, I would guess, sometime before the second World War. A couple in love, arms around each other, in front of this house. Moving on, the man disappears from the pictures, replaced by a boy, then the boy grows up himself. The pattern repeats until the final pictures show another man with more than a familial resemblance to the ones who had gone before, now with a young woman who looks a little like Cat. She's pregnant in one, holding the hand of a daughter in another. The kid's got red hair and green eyes.

That's Cat.

This must be her family's farm.

Where are her parents?

Something else to ask her. Except, it doesn't interest me. Not in the slightest. Snapping back to myself, I realise I've been lax. I've no answers to take back to Utah. I should press her, question her further. When I've got all the information that I can, I should let the authorities deal with her and hightail it back to the Satan's Devils.

Or would that cause trouble for the club? Does anyone know Weston's missing? If so, they might be interested if I turned up.

Would the cops get involved, and would, somehow, my curiosity means his dead trail might lead them to the club?

Whatever compassion for her I have, I need to suppress it, and give her no knowledge in return for her answers—questions for her, however, abound. Why did Tiny leave her tied up and helpless, and was he coming back for her? Am I projecting when I think she hates him, their only connection being that they're cousins? Am I judging her innocent when she's nothing but? Maybe she's up to her neck in this business.

He'd killed her dog.

Could she ever forgive him?

How the fuck should I know? Women, to me, are a mystery.

Going to the kitchen I find a well-stocked fridge and freezer and am happy to see there's meat. With Cat's affinity with animals, I'd hoped she wasn't a vegan. I'm hungry myself and am wondering what I can pull together when I hear a whimpering, followed by a scream from upstairs.

My gun's instantly in my hand. Carefully, I ascend, trying to keep to the sides to avoid the loose treads. Adopting a fighting stance, I leap through the doorway ready to shoot whoever's molesting her...

She's dreaming. No, it's a nightmare. The bed sheets are twisted around her, and she's thrashing, her hands warding something off.

It's such a pitiful sight, it twists my gut. Putting my gun down, I go straight over to her, sliding onto the bed and pulling her into my arms.

"You're alright. You're safe. I've got you." Just three short sentences repeated over and over.

Slowly she begins to still. Still half asleep, she burrows into me.

Is this the first time I've held a woman for anything other than during sex? I think it might be.

Suddenly she gasps. "I'm so sorry." She tries to get away from me. I raise my arms, letting her get free, then move off the bed and stand with my hands held up defensively so I don't intimidate her.

"Nothing to apologise for. I shouldn't have left you alone." Rookie mistake. She was bound to have bad dreams after her ordeal.

"Please, don't leave me." The dream's still got her in its grasp of terror. "Please, I was alone so long."

Fuck. She was. I run my hands over my skull, feeling out of my depth. "I won't leave you, Cat," I promise. "But I'd like to get some food going. You need something, and well, I haven't eaten in a while."

"I'll get up—"

"Nah," I say fast. "I'll do it. You just need to get your rest." I notice she blanches at this and change my mind. "Tell you what, how about I bring you downstairs? You can keep me company while I get something together." Her brow furrows, and her bottom lip trembles. "What's up?"

"C-C-Caspar."

"Darlin', I buried him, okay?" I washed the blood up as well. I knew it would do her no favours to have to deal with the days' old corpse of her pet. "He's under the apple tree. You can go say goodbye to him there when you're stronger."

Her chin drops to her chest. Her good hand wipes tears from her eyes. "I can't believe he's gone. I wish he was here."

I have nothing to say, so I try to stay practical. "Let's get you dressed, then we'll go downstairs. You got sweats or something comfy?"

She seems to still be thinking of her lost dog. I have to enquire again before she tells me, "In those drawers."

I open them. In the top one I find underwear and extract a clean pair of panties, choosing plain white and avoiding looking through the lace which another time might intrigue me. In a lower drawer, I find a t-shirt, and in the one below, some stretchy leggings.

I pass them to her.

"No bra?"

"Don't bother on my account. You need to be comfy." My shrug shows I'm thinking of her. It doesn't matter one way or another to me. It was only hours ago I'd held her naked in the tub, and in the condition she's in, she's not going to arouse me sexually. "I'll leave you. Give me a call when you're ready."

I stand sentry outside in the hall. After a moment, I hear some grunts and groans, and a muttered curse.

"You okay?" When she doesn't answer, I put my head around the door. She's managed to get her underwear on, but her leggings are stuck around her knees. As for the top, she's got her good arm in. Her face is wet with tears.

Weakness. That's what's making her cry.

"Hey, let me help." She squeals and tries to cover herself. I'm not put off. "Cat, I was holding you naked in the bath earlier, you've got nothing I haven't already seen." I didn't take advantage earlier, and I certainly won't now. I don't say the words, but they hang in the air.

Stepping back inside, I eye her clinically. "Lift your ass, and I'll pull these up." I bunch my hands in the material around her knees.

"I feel so goddamn weak," she complains with another sob, but she does as I suggest.

Eyeing her sleeve, I analyse the problem, and curl up the loose material, stretching it wide so she can put her injured arm through the cuff. Then it's a simple matter of pulling it the rest of the way up. Once she's decent, I lift her.

Her good hand clutches at me as though I'm going to drop her. I won't. She weighs barely anything at all. Still, I watch my step as I go down the staircase. At the bottom, I gently place her on the couch.

She struggles to get up.

"Stay there." My voice is firm. I wait a second, but the snap in my voice seems to have stunned her into compliance.

Confident she's going to obey me, I go back in the kitchen, opening more soup and heating it for her. Finding a tray, I place the bowl and spoon on it, add a fresh bottle of water, and take it back to her.

Her face lights up, then she frowns. "Why are you doing this for me?"

Why? Because I'm a bastard. Because what I should have done was call the paramedics so she could be cared for properly. But that would negate the reason I'm here. The reason is that I want to question her, to get to the bottom of what she knows and what's her involvement with Tiny.

While I still harbour suspicions that she might have been working with Tiny, it seems out of character. I'd more likely hazard a guess she's not part of his plot, that this is a loose thread that's not going to further unravel, but I need to be sure. While it's not much, it's information I can take back to Utah.

As I watch her lift the spoon to her mouth, I realise there's a part of me that doesn't want to go, and it's not because of the punishment I'm due to be facing.

Returning to the kitchen, I take two steaks out of the freezer, placing them into the microwave for defrosting. I lean on the counter, looking out into the paddock where her horse is grazing peacefully. It hits me that I've never had a chance to stop and slow down. It feels like I've been running forever.

When my mom left home, I slept with one eye open, always wary of my father's fists that could descend for no reason. Joining the Navy meant I was running to keep up, always trying to prove I was worthy of earning the Trident. On ops, as part of a team, there was little downtime, or not when you could switch off completely. Even shore leave had me making the most of the moments on familiar soil.

Joining the MC, prospecting, well, I couldn't be caught sleeping. Even as a patched member, there was always work to be done, even in between missions. I was pre-programmed never to be found wanting, of giving everything my all. It had once been the only way to keep my dad from hitting me.

Staring out of the window, it dawns on me—the peaceful scene is totally alien and sums up what's been missing from my life. Maybe I could stay for a while. I'll remove her name and details from the vacation booking so the Utah brothers don't come looking for her and find me. I'm off the radar, using a name they'll never discover. Time, space, a chance to switch off, maybe that's what I can find in Kentucky.

While I'm here, I can make one hundred percent certain any legacy Tiny left was buried with him. That assurance will be my currency for buying my way back in when I eventually return to the club. If, in the end, that's what I want.

Cat may not want me to stay.

A half-smile appears on my face. I'll just have to find a way to persuade her. That she hasn't requested me to contact a friend or family member suggests she, like me, is a loner. As such, maybe she'll see we should stick together.

When the microwave beeps, I turn the meat over, then go back to the living room and the woman on the couch. She's emptied the bowl completely and is now drinking the water, sipping it carefully, just like I'd suggested.

"I've got steaks out of the freezer. You think you'll be able to eat?"

"I'm full." She glances down at her bowl.

"It won't be ready for a while, you might be when it's done. Or is there something else you'd prefer?"

"Whatever's easiest," she tells me. When I bend and lift the tray from her lap, her eyes harden slightly. When she breathes in, the sustenance has made her stronger. "I asked you before, now I'll ask you again, Jeremiah. Why are you in my house?"

There's a spark in her green eyes that wasn't there earlier. Hmm, maybe she won't be a pushover.

Raising my chin, I acknowledge her but leave to deposit the tray in the kitchen. When I return and take the armchair, I sit back, balancing an ankle on the opposite knee and steeple my hands under my chin. My choice of seat has her narrowing her eyes, as if it once belonged to someone else.

15

*C*at…

What would have happened if Jeremiah hadn't turned up? Would I have died in the cellar? Hungry, cold, and paralysed with fear of being eaten alive by rats? I could still be there now if he hadn't arrived.

He'd stayed and he helped. But what do I know of him except he's ex-Navy? I might have a general respect for any man who's served, but I shouldn't be blinded by it. While it seems unlikely, unless he knew because Weston told him where I was, there's no other reason that he had stopped by the house. Unless it was with the intention of robbing a home, which appeared empty. I mustn't discount he's here for purposes which don't have my best interests in mind, despite how much he's helping me.

I watch him take the seat that was my father's. It's wrong seeing another man sitting there. Since his death, it's been left empty. But nothing is right about this stranger being in the house. He doesn't belong here, and definitely not in that chair.

The food, drink, and being warmed up, has made me feel stronger. How many hours ago was it he rescued me now? I've been sleeping or crying the whole time it would seem. Why has this stranger taken on the task of caring for me? Why, when by happenstance he found me, did he not go straight to the cops?

He should have taken me to the hospital, that's where I should be now. *I'd have hated that.* As a nurse I know there's not much else that could be done for me other than the tasks he's quite expertly performed. *Warmth, water to rehydrate, and food in small quantities.*

A doctor wouldn't have chased away my nightmares with his arms.

But who is he? And how did he find me?

He knows Weston. I'm being stupid if I look any further than that. Am I still trapped in the bad dream of my cousin's making? My gut tells me Jeremiah wouldn't be helping me if he were a danger to me. But what if my gut's wrong? I didn't trust Weston, but I never thought he'd leave me to die. The question remains, did he send Jeremiah here to rescue me? Was Weston held up and sent him instead? Did he not expect to leave me so long? Was my suffering an accident or by design?

I need answers.

Jeremiah seems to be taking a moment to come up with something to tell me. I try to prepare myself to hear lies and wonder whether he'll try to con me. Con men are successful simply because they're adept at covering their true nature. Is he trying to concoct a believable story right now?

He's been kind.

Why?

I'm not a woman who likes to feel weak, but being so help-less, unable to free myself, has knocked all the stuffing out of me. Now, for my preservation, I need to dig deep and find my strength again.

I didn't protest when he held me naked, or when he helped to dress me. In my fragile state, I trusted him.

Who is he? Jeremiah Briggs. A non-descript name. But not a non-descript person, no way. His face has a swarthy complexion, his eyes so dark they seem like mirrors into his soul. His rugged features are handsome, his body muscular and strong, I know. I wasn't that out of it when he carried me as if I was no weight at all. His hair makes him seem like two different people when viewed from one side or the other. One half is long, and the other shorn. Just fashion? Or is there a deeper meaning?

He's done everything right. He set me free, got me warm, fed me carefully as though he knows exactly what to do. But conversely, he did everything wrong. Why didn't he call professionals to help me?

He wants something, I know it.

He knows Weston. The thought won't leave my mind.

Can I trust a man who knows my evil cousin?

He buried my dog. But can I trust it wasn't him who killed Caspar? Evidence tells me I can. I hadn't heard Caspar barking or trying to get to me since Weston left me alone. Swallowing hard, I tamp down my sadness at the loss of my mom's faithful companion. There'll be time to grieve later.

"Well?" I prompt, realising he hasn't attempted to answer my question. When he doesn't immediately answer, I feel my red-headed temper flare. "For fuck's sake, tell me what's going on."

His fingers tap against his chin. "Before I answer *you*, I'd like to know why you booked Weston an Airbnb in Utah."

What? I pull my aching legs up under me. "It seems like you already know," I snap waspishly. I was already nervous about a connection between him and Weston. I'm doubly so now.

"I know your account was used to book the place, but as to how much you were involved, that's what you're going to tell me."

I am, am I? "And if I don't want to tell you?"

The look he shoots me sends a shiver down my spine. *He wouldn't have saved me just to hurt me, would he?* But hell, what do I know, particularly about men who could be friends with Weston? The trouble with having the famed red-hot temper means I sometimes speak first with later regret. I can't anger him, like Tiny, he's too big to fight, even if I were stronger. I tone it down.

"How do you know my cousin?" I ask directly. "Did you get to know him in prison?"

"Answer me," he snaps, then shakes his head, the rage that quickly entered his eyes dies, and he holds out his hands palms up. "Cat, look, you don't know me. Can you trust me when I say I never *knew* Weston?" He barks a short laugh. "And I've never been in prison. But Weston was involved in hurting someone… close to me. I've come here to find answers. The trail led to you and that booking of the fishing cabin."

I'm quiet for a moment. Weston hurt someone close to him? That in itself is believable. Heaven knows, he used to hurt me. Frowning down at my hands, I wish I could go back and change things. If only I hadn't given in to Weston. I should have known the fishing trip was nothing of the sort. But if I'd fought him, he'd have fought back, and he's so much bigger than me. But why don't I just tell him? I've done nothing wrong.

I take a breath and decide to come clean. Perhaps once he knows, he'll just leave. *That's what I want, isn't it?* "You already know Weston is my cousin. We never got along. He was always a bully. He was the kid that would pull the wings off of butterflies just for fun."

Jeremiah's face once again flushes, but this time I don't think his anger is directed at me. "He ever hurt you?" His words are clipped and he has the grace to look sheepish. "Before he locked you in a root cellar, that is."

I lower my head, for some reason ashamed of what my cousin had done to me, both recently and in the past. It's like admitting a weakness but I say, "Yes, he did. He's an only child like myself. His mom and dad, my aunt and uncle, are lovely. It was always a mystery how they went so wrong with their son. After Weston broke my arm, I didn't have much to do with him.

My parents didn't want me going over there, and he never came here, to our home."

"Is this your childhood home?" He looks around him, his chin tilted as though he's solving a mystery.

I blink rapidly. "Dad died a year ago. When I came home for the funeral, I found Mom had been keeping a secret from me. Cancer. I'm a nurse, so I stayed to help out. She died four months ago."

"I'm sorry."

I shrug off his comment. It's what everyone says, as though they've got something to apologise for. I focus on his face—his look of sympathy appears genuine at least. "I'd given up my job to look after her. I'm an only child, so the farm came to me. Not that there's much of it now, we sold off the bulk of the land after Dad was gone. We needed the money, and the upkeep was too much for us."

"So this is your home now?"

I shrug. "For now, yes. To be honest, I'm kind of in limbo. I'll need to find a job soon, but I'm just dealing with everything." I raise and lower my shoulders again. The burden of grief is too strong, its pull still holding me tightly. I wipe away a tear, one of the many I've cried since Mom had gone, and force myself to get onto the things he wants to know. "One night, Weston came to visit me. I thought he needed money, or to fuck with me, I don't know. I hadn't seen him in years—he'd been in jail. I didn't want him inside the house, but he's a big man, and there was little I could do about it." *What could I have done differently?* I ask myself. It's not as if I could have overpowered him and sent him away. "When he suggested he treat me to dinner, I wanted him out of the house, so it seemed like a good idea to go. He hadn't any transport, he'd arrived in a taxi."

"You own a car?"

I nod, waving my hand in the direction of the door. "Yeah. Well, I drive my dad's truck. It's outside."

He shakes his head. "It's not."

My fists clench. *Damn Weston.* "He must have stolen it." Ignoring what's possibly the least of what Weston had done, I continue, "After the meal, I thought I'd be dropping him somewhere, but instead he made me bring him back here." I shake my head. "Fuck knows how he persuaded me to let him stay the night." I want to justify myself. "Weston has a nasty temper, as I know only too well. He used to fight for a living, and I, well, I…" Now my hand gestures down at my body and my slender frame. "I knew I'd end up hurt if I refused. I was a coward."

"Not a coward, just fuckin' sensible. Even a soldier knows when to fight and when to retreat."

His words elicit my nod of gratitude toward him, his lack of judgement gives me the impetus to continue.

"It was at that point he asked me to book an Airbnb. He knew they run rudimentary checks, so couldn't book it himself. He told me he and his friends were going on a fishing trip."

"And you believed him?"

"I don't know," I say truthfully. "I guessed he couldn't afford to pay for it himself, but I just wanted him to leave. I didn't have much choice." I rub my arm where it had been broken so many years ago, coincidentally, just above where Jeremiah's expertly applied bandage sits now. "I know what he's capable of."

Jeremiah's eyes darken. "He'd have hurt you. He'd have forced you. You were right not to fight."

I give a little shudder. *Christ, I'm so weak.* I should have said no. "I just wanted him gone."

He digests that for a moment. "You know anything about these friends of his?"

I shake my head.

"Did you ask?"

This time I roll my eyes. "If you know anything about Weston, you'd know I wouldn't want anything to do with any friends of his. I didn't ask, and he didn't offer. I did what he asked to get him out of my house. Only," I bite my lip, "that didn't work."

Again he taps his fingers against his chin. "Instead of leaving, he chained you up."

I shudder, remembering how he'd taken me downstairs. "He'd gone to bed. It was hard sleeping while he was so near, but eventually I dropped off. He woke me… I couldn't fight him." To my dismay, tears prick in my eyes. "He's too big." His brow furrows as I add, "I don't understand why. I did what he asked. Why did he tie me up? And why kill Caspar?" The last comes out as a wail, and a tear falls.

Now he leans forward, putting both feet on the floor and clasping his hands between his knees. His eyes meet mine. "Because he didn't want you telling anyone where he was going. The reasons for what he did to your dog were probably twofold. One, he's a cruel motherfucker, and two, he didn't want his barking to draw attention to the house."

I wipe another tear away and take back control of the situation. "I know you said you didn't know him, but that begs the question, how did you know I was here? Did he send you to free me?" I sit, my body taut, as I wait for his answer. I examine his face, looking for any sign that I can't believe him.

"No," he admits. "I had no idea he left you here. The reason he rented the Airbnb was not a good one." He breaks off, and I see signs he's holding something back. He seems at war with himself, and his mouth works, then he finally tells me, "The place was used to hold someone they'd kidnapped." His brow immediately furrows, as if he's given me too much.

My hand covers my mouth. "God, no. If I knew—"

"If you knew, or guessed he was involved in anything criminal, there was nothing you could do without ending up hurt. But I'm presuming he didn't want you alerting the authorities, hence he chained you in the cellar."

My eyes close. That makes horrible sense. I open them and

look at him again. "Should I go to the authorities now? Tell them everything I know? Is the kidnap victim safe? Hell, what am I going to do if he comes back?" In some ways, I wish he hadn't told me.

"No authorities," he says fast, his eyes holding mine. "The situation has been… resolved. I can assure you he won't be back. It's over, Cat."

He sits forward, this time with his eyes closed, and his hands linked behind his head. He seems like a conflicted man.

I sense his pronouncement was final. "Is, is he dead?"

A pained look crosses his face. "Would it bother you if he was?"

If he was, it would explain why he'd left me so long that I'd become certain death would reach me before rescue. If he'd been alive, would he have returned and pretended to be a loving cousin—not that he ever been one, of course.

"Is he?" Strength is returning to me slowly, and now I've back some of my old spark. "I need to know. Weston's evil, always has been. If there's a chance he could come back, I'll need to know so I can take care."

"You knew what he was and still didn't." His eyes open and find mine once more.

It's a fair point. "I wasn't expecting him. Now, I am, I'll keep my daddy's shotgun close by me."

He snorts, the sound followed by a chuckle. It's the first time I've seen his face anywhere near relaxed. I decide to strike while the iron's hot and catch him unawares.

"Why did you come here? If you have nothing to do with Weston, and you had no clue what had happened to me, how come you're here?"

He sucks in air making his cheeks hollow. While I'm wondering whether I'll be able to trust the truth coming out of his mouth, he seems to come to a decision. "I shouldn't have told you as much as I have. But Cat, there's really no need to go to the authorities. That kidnapping was of a team member of mine. She was taken as a lure to target my boss. Weston and his co-conspirators were dealt with, and that's all I'm saying. But we knew a woman rented the cabin. I tracked you down as I wanted to know whether that was the end of it, or whether there was an ongoing plot with others involved."

"You thought I had something to do with it?" My eyes widen.

"I don't like loose ends."

"Do you trust that I'm not a criminal mastermind organising a kidnapping?"

His reaction isn't what I expect. I expect him to laugh or answer in a negative and produce handcuffs. Instead he says softly, "Sadly, I do."

"Sad?" It's at that moment I realise he looks defeated, as if all the wind's been taken out of his sails.

What did he expect to find? Me up to my neck in conspiracy and extortion? I'd laugh if it wasn't so serious.

"Well, now you've got your answer, I presume you'll be on your way." He's not like Weston, he's far too in control of himself. But that doesn't mean I'm comfortable with him being in my house. Like Weston, he makes the place seem small. Though in Weston's case it was his bulk, Jeremiah is just larger than life.

If I wasn't sore, hurting and, once again, as he'd predicted, hungry, I'd appreciate him as a man. But not for me. I suspect it would take a very experienced woman to handle Jeremiah Briggs, and not a shy, unassuming nurse such as myself.

I've been sneaking surreptitious glances at him, and now I find he's looking directly at me. As if he can read my mind, his lips curve in a smirk.

"Are you trying to get rid of me?"

"Well," *yes.* "Ungrateful as it sounds as you did rescue me, I'm safe now. There's no reason for you to stay."

"No reason?" He looks surprised. "Woman, you've been

chained, starved. You're dehydrated and scared. I'm not leaving you to deal with this alone. For a start, you'll need help around here until your wrist is better. I'm staying."

I can't work out why, nor know what my reaction is. On one hand, being alone will give me nightmares, but having him stay could make them worse. "You don't need to. I'll manage." It's me who's been looking after others for a long time now. First as a nurse to the general public, and then to a patient of one. No one's looked after me since I was a child. "And even if I do, why should it be you?"

"You got a support network?" he asks. "A man to come in and help?"

"I don't need help." I do, but I'm not going to admit it.

"I'm staying." He gets up and starts to walk away, but after a second comes back. He stands awkwardly, as if uncertain, his hands rake back through his hair. As he comes to a decision, he leans forward. "If you really want me to leave, I'll go."

He's made an abrupt U-turn. Now he's given me the choice, perversely I don't know what I want. He's the man who saved me. I'd lost consciousness, I know that. If the rats had started eating me alive, I couldn't have fought them off. I would have died if he hadn't found me. The way he's treated me since has been nothing but gentlemanly.

He hasn't behaved as a threat toward me.

Glancing outside, I see the world growing dark. I shudder, knowing I'm going to be scared to sleep, knowing I'll feel rats crawling all over me. Crazy as it sounds, I'd rather a stranger stay than be on my own.

If he'd looked at me with any sexual intent, if he'd copped a feel while he was dressing me, maybe I wouldn't be of the same opinion, but just as I thought, he was too much man for me. Not once has he indicated such an interest in any way. Not that I'd expect him to, he'd go for a different type of woman to me.

"Well, do you want me to leave?"

I attempt a smile, my first of today, and many days past. It feels rusty as though it's forced. "Did you say something about steak?"

I don't think he'd been expecting that. His lips curve and he snorts a laugh. "I did indeed."

16

———

Stormy…

I'd planned to stay, had been prepared to use my powers of persuasion, but when she told me about Tiny, I knew I had to distance myself from anything that fucker had done. So I took a chance and gave her the opportunity to kick me out. She didn't take it.

If you asked, I'd be unable to explain what drives me to want to be here in this rundown farmhouse in Kentucky. Sure, she needs help, but normally I'd leave someone else to provide it. Hell, I could have employed professional help if there'd been no one else. My desire to be close isn't because I'm horny for her. She'd been naked in my arms and my dick didn't so much as twitch.

She intrigues me though. There have been flashes of the mythical red-headed temper which is probably more down to her, and nothing to do with the colour of her hair. Still, it fits. I grin to myself—she's like a kitten spitting at a lion when she brings out those claws. If I need to stay low for a while, I've an idea that here, with her, I won't get bored.

That I don't want to bed her actually takes off some of the

pressure, giving me no reason to pretend to be something I'm not. With her, I can be myself—not that I'm completely sure who that is anymore. Finn Palmer who had his dreams stolen? A SEAL whose country comes first? A Devil with my pack behind me, or, just a man who needs to rediscover himself.

Fuck knows.

Later that night while Cat is resting watching some inane program on television, I get out my laptop, hacking into the booking website and deleting all records of the reservation she'd made. Having done so, a sense of relaxation comes over me. No trail now leads to her, or to me. *I'm safe here.*

My grand plan to return a hero holds no water now. What could I offer but a lame statement that all loose ends have been tied? Maybe I'd be given some kudos for using my absence to work for the club, but it was yet another trip not sanctioned. The result wouldn't be enough to stop me from being sent out bad.

Before I close my laptop down, I take a deep breath. *Isn't it better to know?* Before I have second thoughts, I hack into the systems, easily diving under layers of security, some of which I'd set up myself. Rascal's the treasurer, come secretary. While he takes only brief notes of the main decisions in church, something like me being declared out bad would be a major event to record. With shaking hands, I look through the minutes. Sure, I'm mentioned, but only with a reference to the search having started in earnest. For now, it seems they count me as part of the club.

It means I have time. But how much? There's no doubt their patience is finite. If I return, I'll have to throw myself on their mercy, which isn't like any version of Finn Palmer I know.

If I'm going to lose my patch, would I prefer to do it on my own terms? Just simply never go back?

It's a question I lock in a box at the back of my mind, and as each day passes, I take it out to examine less frequently. I become comfortable here. I become comfortable with her.

I get the impression that it's no bother for Cat having me here. I'd go so far as to say she enjoys the company. A week goes by, and my excuse she needs help becomes less relevant as her wrist improves, only giving her slight twinges now. The rings where the cuffs have bit in are fading, but she doesn't raise the subject of when I'm going to go.

I'd summed up her situation quickly. She needs to leave this mausoleum and start a new life, but her past is like an anchor dragging her down. I don't pretend to understand, blood family was a shackle I shrugged off long ago, but it matters to her. While she's waiting for the impetus to move on, I'll do what I can to make things easier for her. I'm not selfless, more self-serving. All the little jobs I find are keeping me occupied and giving her a reason to keep me around.

Another week passes. She often has a smile on her face and good food is putting some weight back on her slender frame. I begin looking at her with fresh eyes. Yesterday, when she bent down to look in the fridge, the sight of her heart shaped ass actually got my cock swelling. *Down, boy,* I'd told myself. *Don't fuck this up now.* It's not her I want, I've just not been laid for a while, and she's just a convenient hole. If I'm going to continue my peaceful interlude from life, I can't rock the boat.

"I've fixed the fence." Walking inside, I take a bottle of water out of the fridge, and hold it against my forehead. It's a warm day and I've been working hard. "I noticed a few shingles loose on the roof while I was out there. I'll get those done." I pause, realising I'm fucked as to how to collect new ones. My bike is great for getting from A to B, and for picking up a couple of days' worth of groceries, but no good for carting heavy shit around. The asshole Tiny had stolen her truck, and until now, finding it had been pushed to the back of my mind. Without transportation, she's dependent on me, which shows just how much I'm invested in hanging around.

"Just remember I didn't ask you to do any of this." Cat points her spatula at me with one of her easy smiles, and a flash of her brilliant green eyes.

"I know. But I'm here…" I shrug. This place has lacked a man's touch for a while now. I walk over to the stove and lean in. Something smells good. At least I'm getting fed well. "I'll go wash up." After we've eaten I'll get down to what I already should have been doing. But hell, it's been a breath of fresh air just concentrating on menial tasks and not doing anything that requires my brain working. I don't think I've had space like this since I was a child, maybe not since my mom upped and walked out.

She's still working her magic, tossing ingredients into a pot when I exit the shower. I watch her for a moment, relishing the fluidity in the way that she moves. My cock twitches, but I turn quickly away. She's not for me. She's not a one-night stand type of woman, and I'm not a hang around kind of man.

While I'm here though, I can be useful. Returning to the living room, I take my laptop out of my saddlebags and plug it in. The battery has run out, it's been that long since I used it. I wait until it's got enough charge to work, then cast my own spells, hacking again into the servers of the Satan's Devils MC back in Utah. I'm fully confident they'll never know that I've commandeered some of their resources.

First, I get into the database of the vehicle licensing department. She said she'd registered it in her name after his death, so I used that and the results of a casual enquiry about her birthdate. Those gave me the details of the truck I was seeking. It's an older Ford 150—that's a surprise, not what I expected.

Of course I could have just asked her, but if Tiny had taken the truck to Utah, I'd have to think carefully about how or whether I could retrieve it. I'm not ready to go back to my brothers just yet and showing my face in the state where they're based could lead them to me.

First, I narrow the search based on what Cat had told me, and what I already know. Tiny left here in the evening and ended up in Utah a day later. Either he had pedal to the metal all the way, or, he used another method. I go for the latter first and hack into the security cameras in the long-term parking at the airport.

It's there.

I get into their system and soon have the receipt for the truck downloaded onto my phone. It's already overdue for pickup. Her proof of ownership might have been sufficient for her to claim it, but this way we'll be in and out fast with no questions asked. We'll pay the extra few days parking, and she'll have her transport back with no one any the wiser.

Tiny no longer exists in this world, he won't be returning to claim it. *Thank fuck.* As always when I think on how I found her, my gut clenches with rage. *If I hadn't come calling, her body would be rotting in the cellar.*

If her cousin had lived, would he have come back to save her? He might if he could have been identified as the last person to have seen her—they'd eaten out that night. But he could well have toyed with the idea of just leaving her. A bully like him would probably enjoy thinking of her being tortured by those fucking rats. I tell her none of that though, not wanting her to dwell on the evil in the world.

Job done, I lean my head back. Cat's a good woman, and not weak at all, she's strong. She had to be to survive relatively unscathed from what her cousin had done to her, the only reminder she's not out the other side yet are those nightmares she still has. I don't think she's aware of how often I sneak into her room to soothe her, only retreating once she's in an easier sleep.

One of my first jobs had been to get rid of all the evidence of her imprisonment. Cat isn't going down to the cellar anytime soon. Strong woman or not, no one could blame her for that.

"Five minutes, Jeremiah."

"I'll be there," I call back.

I glance around the room I'm sitting in, once again struck by how the furnishings bind it to the past. Outside shows its age as well, and I'd quickly realised the task of keeping this place running is more than a one-woman job. It's a money pit in fact.

I've been helping her do it up, not just to make her life easier, but hoping I can drop some hints she's better off listing it on the market. Why does a single woman need a house this size? Not when the land's been sold off, and she's no viable income from it. The hens don't lay enough eggs for her to bring in more than a few dollars. And that horse is ancient, just living out his days in comfort.

I've heard the legend, if you save a life, you become responsible for it. Perhaps that's why I'm invested in her moving on. Sure, she's got happy memories here, but she can't live off those, especially not with Tiny's taint on them.

I don't deny the charm of the old farmhouse, just as I can't deny hers. Perhaps if things were different—if I were a different man—I'd stay around.

Linking my hands behind my head, I picture the disused barn. It would be a great place to restore motorcycles.

Vigorously, I shake my head, trying to clear those thoughts from it. I'm a soldier in need of a war, not a goddamn home-maker and mechanic. The best I could do is become a mercenary for hire, and I doubt Cat would think much of it.

My place is with the Satan's Devils MC, isn't it? While I have the laptop out, I frown, then delve back into the Utah servers again. There's another mention of me in the minutes.

Three months.

They've given me three months. Thirteen weeks. I'll be out bad if I'm not back by the time limit they've set.

They're actually generous, I wouldn't have given myself three hours. Still, at least I have a time frame. It's up to me what I do with it.

Tomorrow, we'll go get her truck. I'll sort her roof tiles out and when that task's done, I'll head off into the sunset. I've been here too long.

I need to find a woman to sink my cock into before it decides Cat's irresistible. There are limits to my self-control, and while I'd never force myself on her, I've caught little glances, odd smiles, and at times her face reddens for no reason that suggest if I turned on the charm, I've little doubt she'd respond. I think too much of her to take advantage.

Three months. Even if I stayed, my time with her is limited. That's if I want to reclaim my life.

Tomorrow's going to be interesting. To get to the airport, she'll have to ride on the back of my bike. That, in itself, doesn't worry me. I know some of my brothers are dead set against having anyone but their old lady riding behind them, but I've never subscribed to that notion, never expecting to land a woman of my own, and seeing my passenger seat as just a convenient mode of transport. Not that I've had anyone riding behind me before, but nah, I have nothing against the idea of it.

Except, this is Cat. Her breasts up against me, her arms around my waist? That could be one of the limits to my self-control I was just thinking about.

It really is time that I should go. I can't offer her a future, and she'd want nothing else.

"Dinner's ready!"

"Coming."

There's a formal table and six chairs in the dining room, but since the first night we've fallen into the routine of just using the stools at the counter. Cat knows her way about the kitchen and seems to enjoy cooking. I'm happy to eat whatever she serves up. She could rival Cowboy in some of her dishes, and her chili tonight is no exception. I don't feel guilty leaving the meal preparation to her. I'll clean up after, and work to my strengths getting the exterior of the house in order.

When I tell her I've found her truck and we can collect it the next day, she sighs with relief. "I thought that was gone."

"If it was, you could claim it on the insurance."

"I'd have had to have told them Weston had taken it, and as I can't contact him…"

I grimace. Yeah, that would have opened a can of worms. The Satan's Devils hadn't left any evidence of Tiny being in Utah, but a plane ticket would link him to that state. My brothers would prefer not to have attention brought to his disappearance. Now I'm glad I found the truck for more than one reason.

"You've told me no one else would contact me about the booking, but I'm still worried." Her lips press together. "Even if I don't have to worry about Weston, what if he's got friends who try to find him? If they knew he was here, they might come calling."

As far as I know, his friends, or more accurately accomplices, are dead. I doubt she's got reason to worry. But, what if she's right? Could I view staying here as providing protection? At least for the next couple of months before I have to make a decision.

Sure. A bodyguard with fantasies of getting into her bed. I sigh, unwilling to tempt the limits of my resistance.

Sometimes I wonder how I'd have treated her had I turned up to find her unharmed. Would I have suspected her of protecting her cousin? Probably. But the cards fell as they had, and the thought of anyone hurting her doesn't settle at all with me.

Should I go before I cause her pain, or stay and risk the consequences?

Replete with food, and with a beer in my hand, I settle back uncharacteristically and join her in watching a quiz on television. Arrogant, I'm certain I'll know more answers than her, but she surprises me with general knowledge that surpasses my own. When she yawns and says she'll go to bed, I say goodnight, assure her I'll lock up, and wait for her to finish in the bathroom before I go to the guest bedroom.

I've never not worked since I left home, except for that brief spell of unemployment when ejected from the SEALs, but even then I'd been searching for jobs suitable for a disgraced man. These past couple of weeks I've been content to let the world turn on its own, having no desire to look for trouble or even go searching for shit on the dark web. *It's a vacation,* I tell myself. And, like any vacation, I'll end up getting bored. *But not just yet.*

The next day is dry, the sun shining down as we set out for the airport. Cat's never been on a bike before but approaches it with something more akin to excitement than trepidation. If you're over twenty-one, you don't need to wear a helmet in this state, but being gentlemanly, I give her the one that I always carry with me anyway. Without me having to tell her, she's wearing jeans, a denim jacket and sensible boots.

Having given her basic instructions, she slides on behind me, her arms coming around my waist without being told. Immediately, her closeness affects me in ways it shouldn't. Trying to ignore the scent of her shampoo and the strand of hair that's escaped from her pony tail and which the breeze whips around my face, I kick up the stand. I allow myself a moment to get used to the extra weight—not that there's much to notice—then I engage first gear and smoothly move off. Her delighted shriek makes an uncharacteristic grin appear on my face.

The airport is an hour away, and I quickly get used to her being behind me. When we stop at a red light, I turn my head, but the question of whether she's doing okay dies on my lips. Her eyes sparkling, her mouth curved, give me all the answer I need. *She looks like she's exactly where she needs to be.*

Regret is what I feel as we pull to a stop and I park in a motorcycle designated parking slot. Maybe I can convince her to come for another ride with me, or maybe I shouldn't risk it. But for now the question is moot. She's got to get her truck.

She does so without any difficulty. I wait on the exit ramp until she comes into sight, and follow her on the return journey.

Thoughts are going through my head. If I'm to return to the Devils without further punishment other than the beatdown and prospect patch already decided, I should start to make my way back. Three months was the limit. It will go easier for me if I don't make them wait.

But something's been growing inside me that has me questioning whether returning is what I want. It's not the thought of prospecting all over again, it's the question that since losing my SEAL dream, I've never once asked myself… *What do I want?*

I worked my ass off to become a SEAL. Except on short periods of leave, I could never relax. On tours, I had people barking orders at me. Prospecting the first time was more of the same, then I threw my all into becoming a full member.

Then what had I done? I'd fucked up again. My carefully ordered world where I thought I made a difference had come tumbling around me. Could I ever get back to the man I was before I returned from Afghanistan for that last time, or would I get back and find the chip still firmly attached to my shoulder? The chip I'm barely aware of when I'm with her.

Is thirty-six too late to start over? To find my way in a citizen world? Could I marry and start a family?

Fuck. *Is that what I really want?*

With Cat I've had a glimpse of the man I could be were I to stop running from the demons chasing me.

I don't have an answer for myself by the time she pulls her truck onto the driveway and continues up to the house. I park alongside her.

That truck is a heap of trash, I think to myself. Hate to think of her driving around in it. Before I leave, I'll check it over, make sure it's safe at least.

Another excuse to delay the inevitable. Because one way or another, leaving is something I'll have to do, and sooner rather than later.

Noticing Cat hasn't got out of the truck, I go stand beside her door, my head tilted in question.

"We need food. I was going to head out to the store."

I pull open her door. "Move over."

"What?" *Uh-uh.* There's that sudden temper.

"I'm coming," I say calmly. There's no reason to, but I'm loath to part company with her, or be alone in a house that has nothing to do with me.

"I don't mind that," she says, her eyes flashing. "But it's my truck, I'll drive."

Normally I'd have no problem with that either, but I noticed the blue smoke coming from the rear and want a chance to assess how it runs. "Humour me, okay?"

She rolls her eyes but moves over.

I start the engine up, noticing it's firing unevenly. Shifting into first with an audible crunch, I pull out onto the road. "How long since you had this thing serviced?"

A sideways glance shows her looking down and fidgeting with her hands. "It's been a while," she admits at last. "It was my dad's. I flew down, so I just took over using it. Mom couldn't drive much by that time."

"You have your own car?"

"Had. Back in the city. But I sold it."

Her mom's medical costs were high, we've already talked about that. I guess she's avoiding the issue as she couldn't afford repairs. "I'll go over it when we get back, see what needs doing." Probably an oil change for a start, and a good look at the gearbox.

We'd had sun while riding the bike. Fortuitously, we're now

in a cage as the sky clouds over and a light drizzle mists the windshield. The wipers, unsurprisingly squeak and seem hesitant. Another thing on my list.

Cat sighs when I swear under my breath. "Look, I know it's a heap of shit, but I don't drive far."

Heap of fucking shit is right. I wonder if she'd accept a replacement from me, but why should she? We're little more than strangers who pass in the night. Soon I'll be leaving and that's the last she'll hear of me.

But as we drive up to the store she points out, I notice a tattoo parlour across the way. For the first time, I consider getting my Satan's Devils' backpatch tattoo blacked out. Once they declare me out bad, retaining it would be a death sentence.

That I even consider it astounds me. The idea of removing the sign of my allegiance to the Satan's Devils MC isn't welcome. But soon, unless I make contact or go back, it might be my only option.

It's my fault.

I ran. I left them. I should have taken my punishment and stayed.

17

———

*E*at…

I've had boyfriends before, I'm no innocent virgin. I even lived with a junior doctor for a few months before we both decided it didn't work. So it's not the first time I've been grocery shopping with someone, but this is a new experience for sure. The only times my boyfriend had come to the store, he'd moaned all the way around.

Shopping with Jeremiah is different. He's patient, more so than I expect, as I pick my way through the items that are discounted due to their short use by date. I ignore him adding packs of cookies into the cart, already aware he's got a sweet tooth, but when we get to the meat counter and he picks up a pack of two prime steaks, I slap his hand lightly.

"I can't afford those."

"I can." He grins. "I'll pay. How about I grill these later? Save you from cooking tonight."

I already know he cooks a mean steak, he'd found some that first day, ones I'd bought cheap and had in the bottom of the freezer.

The problem is, it all seems so normal, and it would be so easy to say yes. But I've no idea why he's staying with me.

I've no real objections, he saved my life after all and he's been good company. At night I still have nightmares, and when I wake, am comforted to know there's someone else in the house. On a couple of occasions I've woken to find him lying next to me. I pretend to be sleeping, not wanting to chase him away.

I can't discount all the repairs that he's doing either. I haven't failed to notice he cleared out the cellar so I wouldn't need to go down there. Even the thought of it sends shivers through me.

I was lonely before he arrived.

But do I want a houseguest for a period of undetermined time? That's what I can't get my head around.

He's a handsome man, way out of my league. It's not that I don't think I can scrub up well or hold my own with other women of my age, but there's just something about him. Just the way he moves is sexy and as for handling that bike? Hot as hell. The problem is he's fit and muscular, a man who grabs life with both hands and I'm just me. I know the kind of men I attract, and it's not someone with a bad boy image like him. Too much for me to handle? Well, yeah. Not that I'm likely to get a chance.

He takes over pushing the cart while I mechanically go through the things I need to get. Milk, bread, orange juice, salad and fruit while at the same time musing he's never shown the slightest bit of interest in me. Oh, we've talked. I've told him how I came to be back in Kentucky, but he's shared little of himself, other than he was in the Navy, but nothing about what he's done since. He could be a criminal for all I know, but I don't get that vibe.

There's been no tender touches, oh, you can't count that one where he's just accidently brushed my arm to pick up some beer —a touch that made my skin tingle, but had no effect on him at all.

He holds a bottle of wine, and I nod, though really it's a luxury I can't afford.

No, he's made no move on me at all, except for the early days when he carried me around because I was so weak. If I think hard, I can remember the feeling of his arms around me. *I'd like to feel them again.*

He's seen me naked.

He's shown no wish to repeat the experience.

So what does he want from me?

It's past time I asked. Suddenly I stop. "Why are you here, Jeremiah? How long are you staying?" Even his name seems wrong. He's not a Jerry, and Jeremiah doesn't roll off the tongue. *Who is he?*

One look at his face shows my direct question has taken him by surprise. He moves the cart to one side of the aisle, allowing people to pass. "You want me to leave?"

Do I? "I'm kind of getting used to you being around, but I don't know what you want. I'm not saying I'm not grateful you found and rescued me, but I don't know why you stayed." *There.* I've pushed it now. *He'll go.*

He stares at me, then shrugs. "I needed answers from you. It was a dead end. You weren't involved with Tiny's plan."

I'm suspicious he might think I'm withholding information that he still needs, but that doesn't make sense. Once I gave him answers about Weston, he'd backed off. He can't be stupid enough to think I was working with my cousin when he had left me for dead.

Or am I just feeling unsettled as I've a sexy-as-hell man living in my house, and to be honest, he's playing havoc with my libido, while not coming close enough to touch.

Is he gay?

I snort quietly. No, it's definitely not that. Unless my gaydar is very far out. "Why are you staying?" I ask again, then gesture at myself. "You clearly don't want anything from me. You've made it plain you only want to be a friend, so why are you so intent on playing house?"

A myriad of expressions cross his face. First his eyes narrow, then his brow creases. His lips press together as he looks down into the cart, his gaze landing on the steaks he'd just picked up. That's not all—there are his cookies, and the food I've selected is clearly for meals for the two of us.

Now his eyes widen, as if he hadn't noticed before.

"Fuck," he says softly. His hand hovers over the steaks as though he's going to put them back on the shelf.

No, I cry internally. *Why did I have to open my mouth?* I like him, perhaps a little too much. The last thing I wanted was to chase him away. I'd be lonely if he went, scared in case Weston returned—unlikely as I suspect he's dead—but it could be one of his friends. But it's not just a body I want living with me for protection. It's him. That ride on his bike today with my arms wrapped around him had made me feel things, need things I have no business wanting.

It's been growing on me for days—me fighting an attraction that it would be useless and embarrassing if I were to show it. But I've shown my cards. I harden myself, preparing to hear him dismiss me.

Suddenly his empty hand rises from the cart and wraps into my hair. He pushes me back against the shelves. Cans rattle as I scrabble for balance.

"You want my cock?" he hisses, getting right up into my face. "You want me to take you home, thrust into you and show you what a real man feels like? You want some biker loving, babe?"

He rides a bike. *Is he a biker?* He's not wearing one of those vest type things they wear on the television program I sometimes watch. But perhaps it just needs that engine throbbing between your thighs to be a performance enhancer of some sort. Biker or not, an inner sense tells me he wouldn't disappoint.

My mouth falls open, and I don't know how to respond. One way makes me sound needy, or worse, a slut. If I say no, I'm lying to myself.

"Do you want my cock, Cat?"

"Damn woman. If you don't, I do." A woman winks as she walks past, pretending to fan herself.

The reminder this conversation is happening in a totally inappropriate place has my cheeks flaring red, especially when another shopper rushes her two small children past, with a muttered, "You should be ashamed of yourselves."

Using his momentary distraction, I push him away, take the handle of the cart and start pushing my way down the aisle. No longer focused on shopping—if I've forgotten anything it will remain forgotten—I make my way toward the checkout, not bothering to see whether he's behind me. I'm a mess. Half of my brain is on the sudden change in him. Does he want a place to stay so badly that he'll sacrifice himself and do the country girl? Or, have I awoken a beast that was already mine for the taking? Last, but not least, have I got enough money in my account to pay for everything in the cart. *I should have left the steaks.*

My turn comes. Jeremiah pushes past me and starts bagging everything up. I can't, won't, meet his eyes. When it's time to pay, he pushes my hand holding my wallet away.

"I got this."

"No."

"Don't argue, Cat. Half of that stuff I'll eat anyway."

If you stay.

Having already been embarrassed today, I don't want a fight at the till. I bite my tongue and wait until we're outside. My temper grows until I can't hold it back. As he's loading the bags into the back of the truck, I grab hold of his arm.

"*I'm no whore,*" I hiss.

"Whoa!" He holds up his hands. "Where did that come from?"

I'm not even sure, but my finger pokes his chest anyway. "You said you'd fuck, but you bought that stuff. It was as if I was getting paid."

His eyes shutter. "Fuck." He brushes his hands through his hair. "We need to talk, Cat."

He doesn't want me. I suppose I've ended up with a mountain of food that will keep me going for a while. Not to mention the repaired fence and the hundreds of other little jobs he's done. Damn it. Feeling tears prick in my eyes, I start to turn away, realising how much I've gotten used to him just being there.

Why did I push? Why couldn't I have left things alone?

He opens the passenger door for me, and gestures inside. "Get in the truck. We'll talk at home."

My home, not his. Without argument, I climb up, fasten my seatbelt, and stare out of the window as he drives. Surreptitiously, I wipe a tear away, knowing it's just one more person who's going to leave. I'm feeling sorry for myself, and I don't like it. Instead, I try to make plans. I can't afford to stay in the house, it's time to move on. The reason I stay is for the ghosts, and now there will be one more. While I don't want to be disrespectful to my parents, I think it's him I might miss the most.

He might only have been here a couple of weeks, but I've gotten used to him being around. *What did I expect?* A man like him is hardly likely to fall for my limited charms.

He offered to give me a pity fuck. That's all it was. He didn't seem particularly enthused about it. If that's the price I'd have to pay to keep him around, then he can go. I've more respect for myself than that.

I force myself to analyse my life, accepting I'm a pitiful mess. I don't have a job. I don't have a man. For the past year I've had no life of my own. I've been existing when I should have moved on. I'll sell the house and go back to the city. It shouldn't take me long to get a new position, good nurses are always in demand. Perhaps, I'll try internet dating, I've been on my own far too long.

Positive thoughts, but ones with no joy. It will destroy me to leave my childhood home, the house that's been in my family for almost a century now.

Intellectually I know, bricks and mortar don't mean anything, it's the memories that are important to me. But it's still hard. It feels as though I'm turning my back on my family's legacy. If I was looking forward to a new start it would be easier, but I know I'm leaving behind everything I've ever known.

The truck stopping brings me out of my head. We're home. I sit awkwardly for a moment before clambering out.

He waves me off when I try to help with the bags, so I open the door, leave my purse on the side, and go into the kitchen. When he comes in and drops off the bags, I methodically start putting the groceries away.

"Leave those out. I'll cook them later." He points to the steaks.

They might be prime meat, but if he's preparing a goodbye meal, he could give me dry bread for all I'll be able to taste. *I don't want him to go.*

"Cat," he starts, leaning on the counter as I busy my hands opening cupboards and shifting stuff around. "Fuck, this is hard. You know nothing about me, and I don't want to lead you on."

I reach up to the top shelf to slide in the cans of tomatoes. His pronouncement gives me pause. *I don't know anything about him.* He's right. "Who are you? Are you even called Jeremiah?"

His eyes widen a little, but he gives me an honest answer, "No."

I can't berate him for lying to me, he's said almost nothing about himself at all. "I get why you came here, but not why you stayed."

He harrumphs. "And that's why it's difficult to explain it to you. I don't have the answer myself. Cat," his hand reaches out and takes one of mine as I lean over a bag, "you're a beautiful woman, and I would love to fuck you. But I'm not going to use you like that."

Now he's lying. He doesn't think of me that way at all. He's letting me down gently.

"Just go, if that's what you want. I'm grateful to you, Jeremiah, or whoever you are. But—"

"I don't know what the fuck I want to do," he interrupts. Letting me go, his hands brush back through his hair in that achingly familiar gesture of his. "I should go. But not because of you, but because it's something I should do." For a second, he meets my eyes, then he turns and starts to pace. "I've got another life waiting for me."

My hands find my hips. "You're married?" I spit out.

"Fuck no. Not that." His eyes widen in disbelief, after a pause, he gives a shuddering sigh. "You want to know who I am? Well, perhaps so do I. Perhaps this is the first time in my life I've a chance to find out."

My brow furrows. "You don't know who you are? Did you get a bump on your head or something?"

He snorts. "Nothing like that." He takes a few steps away. He stops pacing, comes back, and again takes my hand. "You want to know why I haven't made a move on you? Well, it's because you're not someone I can fuck and move on. And, babe, that's all I've ever done. I've never done this." He waves his hand around the house. "I've never had a relationship. Sex was a bodily function, nothing more than that. And no, before you ask, I haven't left a trail of broken hearts. I've never fucked a woman who didn't know the score, and that's why I hesitate with you."

"What is the score?" I bite my lip, unsure whether I want to know. Would I throw myself into his arms, desperate to know what it feels like to be his if only for one night?

His eyes, almost midnight black, focus on mine. "The score

is a night with my cock deep inside you. It might not even involve a bed. Then, I'd leave."

It's on the tip of my tongue to say at least I'd know what it felt like, but I'm worth more than that. However much I'd regret not taking the chance, I know being loved or however he wants to describe it, and left, would hurt me more. Like most women I know, I'd go into it with my eyes firmly shut, believing that I could change his mind. That one night would become two, and perhaps more after that, until he wouldn't want to go. But I don't have a magical pussy, even I admit that.

"My mom left me when I was six. One day she was there, one day she wasn't." His eyes glaze as he starts to think back. "My dad was… difficult. Fuck it, he was a mean drunk. I grew up evading his hands and fists."

My heart aches for him as a child, but he sees my compassion and brushes it off. "Dad wanted me to live the life he never had. When I showed promise in sports, he pushed me on. His dream was me becoming a pro football player. He had it all planned—I'd make my fortune, buy him a house and he wouldn't have to pretend to look for work anymore."

"But you weren't good enough?"

"I was," he states with a glimmer of pride. "I won a scholarship. But that was his dream, not mine. I admit I led him on, but I followed my own path. I signed up and became a SEAL. I had this idea that serving my country was more honourable than chasing a ball around a field."

A SEAL? Not just a Navy man like he'd originally said. "So, you're a hero?"

"Not now," he scoffs. "I fucked up. Another SEAL lost his life. I was discharged and lost everything I fuckin' worked for."

My mouth drops open. *He got a man killed?* "Was it a mistake?"

"Mistake?" He gives another of his characteristic snorts. "I disobeyed a direct order, but the real question is, should that order have been made?" He shakes his head. "I was focused, driven, Cat. All my life I worked hard to get what I wanted from life, and suddenly it was all lost. I'm not a good man. It affected my head. Maybe I'm more like my father than I thought, as it all got bottled up inside."

He turns and starts pacing again. "I grew up angry at my circumstances. I was kicked out of the SEALs and left enraged at what had occurred. I was given another chance, and I fucked that up as well. Yeah, Cat, I should leave. I should go back to where I've people waiting on me. But…" His voice trails off. Suddenly he's standing right in front of me, his hands resting on my arms. "It seems I've never had a moment of peace until I came here and met you."

Peace?

"Yeah." A small smile plays at his lips. "I came, sure, you were in trouble, so I stayed. I got hooked by your green eyes and luscious red hair." His fingers play with an errant curl that's escaped from my messy bun. "I don't know what to do with this, Cat. I don't know whether to stay or to run. All I can say is here, I feel no stress."

"Then stay," I say fast. "There's no reason for you to leave."

His eyes close, and he turns away. "But there is. There's a clock ticking and I can't leave it too late." He shudders. "If I don't return, I lose everything that makes me who I am. If I go, I lose you, and fuck, you're important to me. I'll be honest, I don't understand why."

18

───────

*S*tormy...

I've been running all my life, driven by ambition and the need to succeed, the desire to be the best. But life has knocked me back as though punishing me for my arrogance, placing me in situations I can do nothing about.

I haven't lied to Cat. Landing here was like slamming on the brakes. Over the past couple of weeks, I've been able to relax. Nothing's spurring me on, and those things that fired my temper have settled into the past.

Dad was an asshole, but I got out. Smythe fucked up my career. I saved those girls once; I couldn't save them again. My team was killed. Maybe I should have been with them, maybe I could have prevented the transport being blown up, or acted on intelligence and evaded that course. But the anger I'd been driven by has resolved with the knowledge I'm only one man. Saving Cat was like wiping the slate clean. Finding Cat was like coming home.

It's why I haven't made a move on her. She's not just a quick fuck. Giving her my cock would mean starting a relationship, and could I really commit? Is it fair to try? She doesn't even know my real name, even though I've disclosed the barebones of my past.

All I know is Cat is pushing buttons I never knew I had. I feel like a different person around her. She makes that burning inside disappear.

Rounding the counter, I go to stand beside her, curling my hand around the back of her neck. "I'm here if you want me. Can't make promises, but I won't run."

She raises an eyebrow. "If I want you?"

I tighten my grip, leaning in so she can feel the warmth of my breath on her skin. "If you want my cock."

She flushes. *She's not immune to me.* But I already knew that. Without sounding vain, I know when a woman wants me. It's giveaway signs,—nipples peaking when the room's anything but cold, a restlessness when we're sitting together on the couch—a lick of her lips, a squirming in her seat. I've known she's wanted me for days.

I've been fighting to resist. Well, that stops now.

Deciding actions are better than words, I take hold of her hand, and lead her away, tugging to get her to ascend the stairs.

I haven't been in her bedroom for days. Not since she recovered. Before that, I admit to being a creep, standing there watching her sleep, or on nights when she was most disturbed, slipping under the sheets and lying beside her, disappearing before she woke. Not that she'd been aware of that. SEALs can be stealthy when they need to be.

I've seen her naked before—the day when I rescued her and warmed her in the bath. I'd been a gentleman then, but I wouldn't be today.

I kick open her door, using the same foot to close it behind me once we're both inside. Pulling her around to face me, I rest both palms on her cheeks.

"I'm not romantic," I warn her. "I don't know how to do hearts and flowers. But by fuck, I'll make sure you enjoy this."

She swallows and then does it again.

"I may not be the type of man you want."

It's as if any resistance has fled. "I-I don't care."

It's all the permission I need. Shrugging aside the vestiges of civility, I plant my mouth on hers, nipping at her lips until she opens and lets me in. Fuck, she tastes as good as I'd hoped. Even kissing, her movements are less practised than other women I've been with, hundreds of nameless faces which I'd be hard pressed to remember. They were women who wanted a SEAL or a biker in their bed just for their cock as though who it was connected to didn't matter. Her pseudo innocence is more exciting than any polished move I've experienced before.

I might be controlling the kiss, but it's her who's devouring me. My cock hardens to the point it's almost painful.

She's eager, almost desperate, making me wonder why I haven't pushed her before. But hell, I was trying to do the right thing. Now, though, I'm going to be selfish and take something for me, hoping to fuck I don't hurt her in the process. I've been clear, I can't promise her anything when I don't know what I want for myself. I can only pray she's going into this with her eyes open.

Tearing my lips from hers, I gasp, "Clothes off." Releasing my hold on her arms, I allow her to step away.

She stares, her lip trembles, but I don't relent. If we're doing this, we're doing it my way. When I raise my eyebrow in challenge, she responds.

I wouldn't call it a striptease, it's more like ripping off a Band-Aid as she turns away and tears the shirt off over her head. Without pausing she wriggles out of those jeans, almost forgetting until the last moment to toe off her shoes.

"And the rest," I instruct when she's standing in a plain cotton bra and the least sexy panties I've ever seen. Even so, my cock's at full mast and I can't remember ever seeing a sight that was better.

A moment's hesitation, after which she straightens her shoulders and unclips the bra, slipping the straps down her arms. Next, she bends as she pushes those oversized panties down, inadvertently giving me a glorious view of her ass.

I've fucked women, biker bitches, beauty queens and once a low-budget film star. I never wanted for attention as a SEAL nor as a biker. Women preened themselves hoping for some attention from me. I'm not being arrogant, it's just how it was. Most nights I could take my pick of what I wanted the most.

Today, I'm limited to one choice, and I'll be fucked if she's not perfect. A small voice inside me tells me she's not what I'd have gone for in the past, but hell, I must have been crazy.

"Turn around," I say gruffy.

Her body moves as though she's sucking air down into her lungs, then, with arms over her breasts, she turns to face me. As I stare, she lowers her face, and drops her hands.

Her ass, as I've already noted, is heart shaped, her buttocks rounded with flesh I can grasp when I pound into her. Her breasts I see are full now they're out of their confines with nipples that harden under the caress from my eyes. Her stomach, now she's back to a proper diet, is slightly rounded, and her pubic hair is neatly trimmed allowing me to see, as I'd already guessed, she's a natural redhead.

"You're fuckin' perfect," I breathe. Her eyes come up to my face, and I'm driven to answer the unspoken question. "I don't lie, Cat. You're perfect to me."

"You're overdressed," she challenges.

"Yeah? Thing is, Cat, if I let my cock out to play, I'm not going to last long. First, I want to taste you and hear you scream as you come on my tongue." I do nonetheless rid myself of my t-shirt, ripping it over my head.

"I'm not perfect, you are," she tells me huskily, and hell her tongue comes out to lick her lips.

"On the bed, Cat." My tone is full of command. When she's settled with her head on the pillows, I add, "Spread your legs."

"What?"

"I want to see you."

"But…"

I cock an eyebrow at her, waiting until she obeys. Fuck me, even her cunt is pretty, and glistening I'm pleased to see. She clearly likes a man who takes charge in the bedroom, she's already turned on.

Her headboard is slatted, perfect if I had handcuffs on me. But I don't, so I bind her with words instead.

"Hands above your head, Cat. Hold on to the slats and don't let go."

Again a look of confusion, but she does what she's told. Raising her head so she can watch me stalk up the bed on my hands and knees, I wonder about blindfolding her and assaulting her senses unseen, but dismiss the idea, enjoying too much the sense of wonder in her green eyes.

As my intentions become clear, I question whether anyone's gone down on her before. If they have, I don't mind the competition. I've always strived to be the best I can in any endeavour I take on.

I'll make my Cat purr if it's the last thing I do.

Hungry for her taste, I can't wait any longer. I lower my mouth, using my tongue to lick her clit, then swiping it downward, delve into her cunt. My taste buds leap into action. She's so fucking sweet, it makes me salivate more, my juices mingling with hers.

"Jeremiah!"

How I wish it was my own name she's calling. Not that of a person who doesn't exist. But although I could correct her, I retain some semblance of sanity and resist. *What she doesn't know can't hurt her.*

I proceed to lick, suck and nip, using all the ammunition in my arsenal as I rouse her to fever pitch. Suddenly, I feel hands in my hair.

"What did I tell you?" I growl, stopping all activity.

A quick learner, her hands recede, and I pick up the pace once again. Through my hand on her stomach, I feel her muscles rippling, and her thighs unconsciously form a vice around my head, keeping me tight to her, but it's no problem, I'm happy like this.

Even more so when a keening sound comes out of her mouth. *She's close.* She goes taut, her body tight. Raising my eyes, I see her back bow off the bed as she comes with a scream.

I continue to lick and suck, bringing her down gently, then achieve my objective of sending her to the peak once again. Raising my face, I rest my chin on her mound, watching her lungs heaving, and that gorgeous flush on her face darkening her freckles, making them more obvious.

Now, at last, I ease myself up and free my dick. Reaching into my pocket for a condom, I open the packet and slide the latex on fast.

She still hasn't come back to herself fully as I raise myself onto my knees, lifting her legs and putting them over my shoulders.

Lining myself up, I push in with my dick. She's so tight, I wonder how long it's been, but I'm always up for a challenge. Slowly I work myself in as her mouth opens in an O of surprise.

A swivel of my hips moves my cock over her sweet spot.

"Jeremiah!" Her exclamation suggests no one's found that before. "Jeez, Jeremiah. Oh God…"

I'm quite enjoying her running commentary, at least it's showing me what works. But when she clamps down with her muscles, I'm groaning myself. "So fuckin' good, babe. Yeah, that's right."

"Jeremiah!"

I don't even hate the strange moniker coming out of her

mouth, it's me who's fucking her, and it's her who's making it hard for me to demonstrate my usual stamina. Normally, whether just vaginal or with clitoral stimulation, I like the woman to come a couple of times more before I let myself go. But with her, she's sorely challenging my control over my own body.

Thank fuck! All the signs are there. She's tightening, throttling my cock. I try to think of anything to keep from spilling inside her until she's gone first.

She's there!

I can't hold on any longer, as her body pulsates I'm with her, cum shooting up through my dick and flooding the condom. My hips jerk of their own volition as I come as hard as I can ever remember.

I hold myself still, relishing the feeling as her body shudders with aftershocks.

I feel I should apologise, that it was over so fast, but one glance at her face shows me there's no need. She's wearing a blissful satisfied smile, her cheeks showing dimples, her freckles pronounced as her breathing begins to slow. A low satiated rumble comes from her mouth.

I did it! I made my Cat fucking purr.

Reluctantly leaving the warmth of her cunt, I pull out, holding onto the condom, pulling it off and tying a knot in it. I drop it down by the side of the bed to deal with later, then roll onto my side, pulling her to me.

She turns to rest her cheek against my chest. I start to stroke her hair while analysing my feelings.

I've never wanted to cuddle after sex, normally politely dressing and showering, and casually handing the woman her clothes if she hasn't got the hint first. If I'm up for another round, I might offer a drink, but I don't hold her, not like I'm doing now. The relaxation that comes from the physical release normally dissipates fast, and I've a natural mistrust not to fall asleep with a stranger.

But Cat's not a stranger, and I could easily close my eyes and drop off. *It's different with her.*

Is it because we've become friends? Or is it more?

"Jeremiah—"

"Hush," I tell her, as her voice reverberates against my skin. "Give me a moment."

She might think I need time to recover, but that's not it. My body's trained to be ready to move fast, honed by my time as a SEAL when I could never relax with foes likely to come after me, a state of readiness I've never shaken off. No, I need time to think—what to admit to myself, and what to say to her.

Do I want to return to the Satan's Devils? If I don't, what does life hold for me? If I went back, could I take Cat with me? Would it be right to uproot her? But what's she got to stay for here?

Or, could I stay with her? Make a go of the farm, set up my own business. Would I be restless or content?

And, how much of the choice is hers? Hell, she might not even want me. Neither of us went into this making any promises.

19

*C*at…

I knew I was attracted to Jeremiah, and more than I've been to anyone before. It was why I hadn't protested when he'd suddenly changed and taken the decision out of my hands.

If this is just once, it's something I'll remember for the rest of my life. I've never been with a man like him before.

I suspected he'd be too much for me to handle, and he almost was. I nearly faltered when he'd told me to undress. I would have objected were it not for that dominance in his tone which I'd found myself obeying, while feeling scared that he wouldn't like the body I'd exposed.

He'd seen me before, but this time was different. When I was vulnerable I'd welcomed his indifference, this time I wanted him to like what he saw.

He'd described me as perfect.

Could it be that at last I'd found a man who didn't expect me to order salads, or cut my hair or wear different clothes. I hadn't adorned myself with makeup, had worn nothing more than what I normally do around the house. But it had been enough. His eagerness was the evidence.

And oh, the sex. I've never come so hard before, never been with a man so focused on my pleasure. So expert in his handling of my body.

He must have had practice.

Well, if all the women before had helped him acquire his expertise, I'm the one getting the benefit now. But for how long? That's the question.

"Cat, we should talk."

The words every woman dreads to hear, especially when she's found a man who can give her multiple orgasms.

"No, don't tense up. I'm wondering where we go from here." He sits up. I'm prepared for him to stand, to pull his t-shirt back on and to leave with a few words of goodbye. *He didn't even bother to get completely undressed.* Tears prick in the back of my eyes, but I'm determined they won't fall, not yet. I'll wait until he's gone.

I hardly dare breathe in case I sob, but as my eyes follow him, he doesn't move far. He perches on the edge of the bed, leans forward to remove his boots, and pushes his jeans down to the floor.

"What's that?"

His back is turned toward me. I sit up fast, hearing his intake of breath as I trace the large tattoo on his back.

His hand snakes out and grabs mine as I try to make sense of what I'm seeing. This isn't like the small lightning tattoo I've noticed on his neck before, this is the real deal. I might not be an expert in tattoos, but isn't it odd that he's got the insignia of a motorcycle club inked on his back? It's well done, but scary, showing the grim reaper holding a scythe hovering over three little demons, with the words, Satan's Devils MC beneath.

The question seems pointless, but still I ask, "Are you in a motorcycle club?"

He drops my hand and leaves his back turned toward me. "Yes. And no."

"You can't have it both ways," I snap.

He takes another deep breath. "I feel like I'm at a crossroads. I'm a member now, but I don't know if I want to stay one. I could go back, or forward, and for the life of me, I don't know which I fuckin' want."

"Can you leave the club, just like that?" My experience, okay, only gained from a television show, suggests he doesn't have a choice. Isn't it like a gang where you swear fidelity for life?

He huffs. "No. For a start, I'd need to get the tat blacked out."

It's so big, that would look awful, but I suppose it can't be disguised. "What happens if you don't?"

"If I don't go back and I keep the tat? They'll kill me, or someone would on their behalf."

Gasping sharply, I cover my mouth. "This club is serious? How the hell did you get mixed up in something like that?"

When he speaks next, I think he's ignoring me. "I should have another tat. Active SEALs don't advertise who they are, that's just inviting death. But a former SEAL gets a tat to show they've served. But I couldn't do that. I'm not a former SEAL. The Navy would prefer I'd never served. I could never wear their insignia with pride."

"So you joined an MC? An MC who'd kill you? Just to wear a tat?" That can't be it, surely?

He turns now. "Cat, I want you to understand. I wanted to be a SEAL until I died, but I didn't get that chance. I left, disgraced. No one wanted me, except the Satan's Devils MC." He puts his fingers on my lips. "Before you judge, listen to me?" His voice pleads in a way I've not heard from him before.

I nod, knowing I shouldn't rush to make judgement.

"The Satan's Devils MC has a number of chapters, but it was Utah who approached me. They, well, they call themselves bikers, live the lifestyle up to a point. But we do more than ride motorbikes. We're technical experts, and I fit right in with my computer skills. We ride in to right wrongs. If someone's been kidnapped, we extract them. If someone's under threat, we protect them. We've stopped sex trafficking rings, ended gun running trades."

My eyes widen. "You're the good guys? But isn't that like the FBI or something?"

He gives a quick grin. "Yeah, but sometimes our methods aren't legal. We're not bound by red tape."

"Like a modern day Robin Hood?"

His lips curve further. "I'd never say never, but we haven't robbed the rich to pay the poor as yet."

I try to work out whether to believe it's as good as it sounds. "So you're still working for your country, just not on the side of the law?"

"Something like that. Trying to put the world to rights and to keep it that way. Or, they are. Me, not so much. Not since I betrayed them."

"You…" I'm stunned. Jeremiah wouldn't betray anyone, would he? "You, betrayed them? How? Why?"

He lets out a loud sigh. "My name's not Jeremiah Briggs. I'm Finn Palmer." Finn. That suits him much better. But he hasn't finished his explanation. "And I go by the same handle I did in the SEALs. I'm known as Stormy. And babe, yes, before you try and figure it out, it's because I've got a short fuse."

But he's been immeasurably patient with me. My brow furrows. "I haven't seen that side of you."

"No." His lips press together. "Don't ask me why that is, but when I said I felt at peace here, what I meant was that with you, the anger driving me has gone."

"Is that a good thing?"

"It's not me," he says, his forehead creasing. "But I can't deny I like it. I've never been able to relax before, but with you, I don't look for ulterior motives. I trust you, Cat. And you have no fuckin' idea how rare that is." He pauses, closes his eyes for a second, then shakes his head. "I've never just seen a person and known instinctively they were trustworthy, not the way it was with you. I tried to fight it, tried to say you weren't exactly as you seemed, but I could never make myself believe it."

"You had proof," I point out. "I couldn't have chained myself in the cellar."

"It wasn't just the evidence of my eyes, babe." He reaches out and brushes hair off my face. "That was all you, which means I'm in a conundrum." I tilt my head until he explains. "I don't want to walk away from you. How can I? How can I leave something I might never find again? This isn't me. I don't cuddle after sex, I get up and go. But I couldn't leave you if a team of horses tried to drag me out of here." He pauses and gives a self-deprecating grin. "Part of the reason I tried to resist was half of me knew how this would end. With me, wanting to keep you."

Trying to lighten the moment, I wink. "I thought it was my body you couldn't resist."

He chuckles. "There's that too. Didn't even need the trial run, babe, to know you were going to be perfect."

I reach out my hand and touch his. "It was perfect. *You're* perfect. But what are you going to do?"

"That's what I'm wondering," he admits. "But for now, how about I prove it wasn't a fluke? After that we'll go cook those steaks."

"And talk later?" I don't want to be left hanging. Now he's let me in, I want to know everything about him and what makes him tick.

"Yeah." He pushes me back, his lean body pressing into mine, and his lips find my mouth. As his tongue pushes inside, I twist mine around it. He doesn't pull back or make like this is just a prologue to something else. As my hands curl into his hair, I can't remember enjoying a kiss quite so much.

I feel a hardness poking at my stomach, and his movements become more urgent as he rubs his cock against me. I can't help my hips pressing back.

"Someone's eager," he murmurs, his face still close to mine.

I think we both are, but I keep that response to myself.

"On your knees, give me that ass."

"My ass?"

That boyish grin appears once again. "Well, maybe not your ass right now, unless you're offering. But one day, I'll take you there."

I'm obviously too slow, as he manoeuvres me to where he wants. I hear a crinkling of a packet behind me, and a tersely asked question, "Are you still wet?" He finds the positive answer out for himself, and before I have time to think, he slams inside me.

It's a shock, making me gasp, but oh fuck, it's so damn sexy. His hands grasp my hips, pulling me tight in to him.

"You feel so fuckin' good," he gets out between pants.

"So do you!"

He releases my right hip. Suddenly I feel a slap of his palm on my flank. I startle, but arousal floods through me.

"I think you liked that." He does it again.

I want to protest, want to tell him I don't. I want to explain how nice ladies don't appreciate being spanked in the middle of lovemaking but hell, how can I do that when I feel my muscles start to tense?

"Yeah, my Cat likes that."

It seems that I do, and that my body isn't under my control anymore as his cock moves over my G-spot. He releases my other hip, his hands now doing a one-two motion, a slap one side followed by a second on the other.

I can't breathe as my orgasm starts to build, my muscles clench as everything tightens. I'm reaching… reaching…

He slaps both my buttocks at the same time and I scream.

"Christ, fuck, woman." His movements are jerky, his words gasped as he comes inside me. "Fuck, you take all my control."

I suppose I'm feeling quite pleased with myself. "Is that a bad thing, Jeremiah?"

He's rested his chin on my back, but now he raises his head. "Call me Finn," he says tersely. "I can't pretend with you, Cat."

Is it a good thing he's reclaiming his name? Or does he also want to reclaim his life? Where will that leave me?

I've kind of gotten used to having him here. Moving what we have to the physical level signals to me we could be building something good. But what if he's still planning to leave?

As his flaccid cock falls out, he deals with the condom in the same way as before, then rolls over onto his side. I turn so I can look at him, memorising his features as if preparing myself to losing him now.

Brushing back my hair with his hand, he sighs. "What's that look for?"

I breathe in deep. Should I let it ride, should I hide my fears? Should I steal another few hours, days or whatever we have left? But I'm not that girl. I don't bury my head in the sand. I'm the one who forced my mom to tell me what was wrong when she'd tried to hide her symptoms. Knowing means you can face what's ahead, even when it's something you'd prefer to avoid.

"You asked me to call you Finn. Are you taking back who you are? And what does that mean for me?"

He's silent so long I think I may have it right, but different words come out of his mouth. "I don't know how to do this, Cat. For the first time in my life, I want to stay in one place. I'm comfortable, content, and I don't know what to do with that. Of course, you might not want me around, and even if you do, we might not be able to make this work."

"I've got dreams too… Finn." His name sounds alien on my tongue, but also right. "I moved away to follow my career. I could have stayed closer, but I wanted to experience city life. I'd been a farm girl, grew up in a small community. I wanted to stretch my wings and branch out."

"Did you find what you wanted, before you came home?"

Shaking my head, I admit, "I couldn't find my place. There, I was a small fish in a big pond. Here, I'm still small fry, but the pond's just a puddle and offers nothing for me. I don't think I've ever found what I'm looking for."

"You ambitious, babe?"

"Not particularly, no. I want to pay my way in the world, that's why I became a nurse. I enjoy what I do, but it's not everything to me." I risk a look at him, knowing if I'm honest, I could turn him off. "I suppose I wanted what my parents had. A happy marriage, a baby or two."

His face has tightened and he grimaces. "I never thought I could offer a woman much. I didn't have a good example with my parents. Kids? Never been around them. While other chapters of the Satan's Devils are family orientated, that's not happened at the Utah club."

"You don't want children?"

"Cat," he props himself up on an elbow, leans over and clasps my chin, "before I met you, I'd have said I never wanted a relationship at all. Now I'm thinking how the fuck I can keep you. Kids? Can't say yes, can't say no." He winks. "The idea of a little girl with green eyes and red hair who's as sassy as her mom, well, that scares the shit out of me."

"And you think I'm not scared of a little boy with a hankering for odd hairstyles."

He full-on laughs now, rolling over on his back with his arm thrown up over his eyes. His body vibrates as he continues chuckling. "Guess we don't have to get it all sorted now."

"When do you need to decide whether to go back to your MC?"

His mirth disappears. "Babe. In their eyes I disrespected everything when I walked out. They think I ran, I didn't. I knew I fucked up and knew I needed to make retribution. What I should have done was contacted them immediately when I found out you were nothing to worry about. That would have put me in better stead."

"Why didn't you?"

Another glance comes my way. "First, I wanted you to be stronger. If I'd called them, I don't know that they trust me anymore. Preacher would have flown them out to talk to you themselves, and I wanted you able to deal with that."

"And they wouldn't trust you because you fucked up."

He winces at my statement. "I did worse than that. I flat out told them I didn't trust them. And that's the problem with going back. They might let me back in, but is there really a way to move on from that?"

"Why did you tell them that?"

He sits up, pulling up his legs and putting his arms around his knees. It gives me a perfect view of that tat on his back, a reminder of what he is. Not an honourable SEAL, but a member of a biker club. Men for whom lives and women are cheap. I should be running a mile, not talking about ways of making a future with him.

"I promised you steak. Let's go get the food ready, and we'll continue to talk."

"Am I asking too many questions?"

He half turns his head so he can see me out of the corner of his eye. "Your questions are making me look at the situation. That's not a bad thing if it focuses me on what I want. What you want too, Cat. Because one thing I'm becoming certain of, as long as I won't be dragging you down with me, I want you by my side, whatever we decide."

He moves off the bed and starts pulling up his jeans. Commando, I note as he tucks his dick into his pants. He picks up his t-shirt, and gathers my own clothes, handing them to me, minus my underwear.

"Er, I don't mind going braless, but I need panties."

He rolls his eyes, but bends, picks them up and passes them to me. Jeans without panties, *ew.*

"So," I start, putting my arms into my shirt, "you want a pros and cons discussion."

"Pros and cons?"

"Yeah, sort of like triage. What treatment if any do we offer? Will the patient get better without intervention, or is medication or surgery required?"

"Surgery in my case being going back to face the music."

I put my head through the neck of my shirt, then nod. "Sometimes doing nothing is the best route. Reassurance given that there's nothing seriously amiss."

"While still charging an arm and a leg for that advice." He chuckles, softening his words. He picks up the used condoms and takes them into the bathroom. Shortly after, I hear the toilet flushing and water running into the sink.

By the time he returns, I'm fully dressed. "You protected me," I observe, walking down the stairs. "Are your biker friends violent?"

"No." He sounds shocked. "But, babe. One of our members was the person kidnapped. She now has a finger missing. Weston chopped it off. She didn't get away unscathed. They'd have wanted answers about your involvement."

"A female biker? You have women members?" I didn't expect that. It makes me more sympathetic to them. Why, I'm not sure. Are females less likely to be criminals? Probably not.

He snorts. "Just the one, and there's no other like Swift, babe. She's one in a million. Not that I'd ever tell her this, but I admire the fuck out of her."

20

———————

Stormy…

Why did I never tell Swift I admired her? Why was I always such an ass? Another influence lingering on from my father—that women had a place in this world and being part of a man's wasn't it. Did I resent her?

Would I have resented any of my brothers who'd got into Delta Force? Hell no. I'd be fucking impressed, and she'd done the British equivalent of that.

Instead, I'd sniped at her. I don't credit myself with making her life miserable, she's far too strong. I'd been more like an annoying fly buzzing around her.

Maybe it's Cat's influence on me, really talking to a woman for probably the first time ever that's making me look at things differently.

As she starts pulling stuff out of the fridge to make a salad, I put my head into my hands, rubbing at my temples.

"I disobeyed an order I should never have been given, I've told you that. The outcome being a SEAL's life was lost, but civilians were saved."

She stops what she's doing and stares down at the lettuce as though inspecting it for bugs. "No one can win them all, Finn. That's what being a nurse taught me." Lines appear around her eyes. "Are you saying that the loss of a SEAL is worse than the loss of innocent lives?"

Probably to Uncle Sam considering the money spent training them, but in the scheme of things, the children saved were human beings. Until Nazia wasn't anymore.

"I'm fuckin' glad we got them out of there. Pooh shouldn't have died, there was no reason." Or no good one, except for Smythe panicking. "I lost my job, but at least I knew two girls were able to live their lives." Of course, there's only a slim chance of one of them being still alive. Marjan, too, could be dead.

"That didn't count for anything?"

"Only to me. They were right to throw the book at me. A man who can't obey commands can't be trusted."

She looks puzzled now. "But if it was the wrong command, surely there would have been mitigating circumstances?"

"I wasn't going to point fingers, Cat."

Another of those hard glances, followed by a shake of her head.

I continue my story. "I'd gotten back to a semi-good place. The club gave me something to live for. Until I got word something was up."

"What?" she prompts when I go quiet.

I slam my fist on the counter. "I think the whole thing was a setup. Something was wrong, bad, about the whole mission. What or why, I don't fuckin' know. Four years back, I found out the older girl became a suicide bomber. They managed to take her down and disarm her before she blew up herself and a lot of US service personnel. She was killed while she was held by the military police."

"Oh my God!" she cries out. "Why?"

"Again, I don't fuckin' know. The younger kid, she'd disappeared. It makes no fuckin' sense, Cat." She puts down her knife and comes to me. Automatically, I put my arm around her waist, holding her tight. Dropping my head, I breathe in her scent, using it to ground me. "The US troops were withdrawing, it was what the hostiles should have wanted. The area had become peaceful, so why stir it all up?"

Her head moves side by side, but not surprisingly, she has no answers for me.

"There's more. When I was on my way home, I found my old team had been killed. All six men, Cat. Four of them I would have counted as my best friends."

"Jer… Finn," she gasps, looking up into my face. "Finn…" As if realising words are inadequate, her hands cup my face. "I'm so sorry." She nibbles her lip. "Did you tell your club? Could they help you find some answers?"

I breathe out. "No. It happened in Afghanistan. The club only operates in the US. It's down to me, babe. I've looked, I've studied everything I could find. There are no answers to the questions I can't get out of my head. If I could go back and change things, would I choose to have Pooh alive and leave those kids to their death? Maybe, if I'd had a crystal ball, the answer would have been yes. Pooh and I might have prevented the rest of the team dying, if we'd been there."

She takes a step back and folds her arms across her chest. "It went wrong from the beginning with the man who gave the order. Have you looked into him? Why would he have wanted those girls dead?"

"He was a coward," I tell her. I've had time to think about this. "He panicked, Cat, which is the last thing someone running that kind of operation should do. The Navy must have agreed though I hadn't said a word. He was given a desk job back in the States." And a promotion that feels like a kick in my teeth.

"You've got girls rescued which lost your friend's life, that shouldn't have happened. A girl who tried to blow our troops up, and a kid missing. On top of that, your whole team died. Presumably they were witnesses to the girls' rescue…"

"Say that again," I growl.

She looks puzzled. "Except for you and the man who panicked, all who knew what happened that day are dead. If the terrorist activity was decreasing, who else would have wanted the story to have no chance of re-examination?"

"I don't have a fuckin' clue," I roar with more than a touch of anger. "Who? The other men in my unit? No fuckin' way. I'd have given my life for them all. The men on other teams? Fuck no. They're SEALs."

She presses her lips together. "So you returned leaving the girl missing?"

"What more could I have fuckin' done?" Her stubborn look intensifies. "What more, Cat? I'm one man. All the SEALs I was close to were gone. I searched for Marjan, it was like she'd disappeared off the face of the earth."

"Why?"

I frown and repeat, "Why?"

She rolls her eyes as though there's something I'm missing. "Seven years is a long time in a kid's life. What if she remembered something? This asshole who gave the command, he didn't want them rescued. Why?"

I throw up my hands. "I have no fuckin' idea." But she's sparked an idea off in my head. Smythe was simply a coward, wasn't he? He'd pressed the detonator as he thought the helicopter he was in was going to be shot down. He panicked. But what if there's more to it? I'd dismissed him. Could he have had a reason for setting off the explosion too soon?

She fully turns to face me and takes a step forward to put herself in my space. Her finger comes out and pokes me in the chest. "Who did you speak to about this? Who did you ask to help?"

"Who could I fuckin' tell when I didn't know who to trust?"

My words seem to echo around the kitchen.

Her finger prods me again. "You find someone, Finn. This is killing you from the inside. There must be someone who could help. Your club. Other SEALs—I have no idea how this works. There's a young girl out there all alone because you want to do everything yourself. You scream it from the rooftops. You get her some help. If you discover the reason, you might be able to give yourself a break."

"She's dead, Cat," I say, my tone softening, my eyes watering as I state what I believe is the truth. "Or will be if I make waves. I've got to believe that she's gone. If not dead, it's likely she's been trafficked." I hate telling her that. In her world, that sort of thing doesn't happen. But she's got me thinking. *What if Smythe wanted her dead from the beginning and she wasn't just collateral damage?* If she knew something, or there was a chance she could remember, that's a good reason for him wanting her to disappear.

"No." She contradicts me. "You start searching all over again. You say you're a computer expert. Money's normally at the bottom of everything. Check the finances of anyone who was around. See who's bought a house, a car, a yacht or a freaking tropical island. Money can be hidden, even I know that. You say your club are all information experts? Well, you ask them for help."

"That easy, huh?" I shake my head. "What do you think I've been doing?" Except asking for help. That's the only bit I left out. I turn away from her and start to pace. "I got sent out on my own as a nomad, representing my club but not being a true part of it. For the past three years I did everything I could to track traffickers down, following clues to see whether there was a link back to Afghanistan. The only plus is I took out some bad guys." Of course, at least two I should have left well alone. "Every trail I could find, I went down. I got zilch."

"Ask your club," she repeats. "If you've got resources, use them."

I snap, "You want me to go back to Utah? Sick of me already?"

Her face goes cold. "There's a thing called a telephone, you know. It can be useful."

"They'd drag me back."

"Then go."

"Okay." Steaks forgotten, I turn toward the stairs needing to go and pack as she no longer wants me here. "I hear you loud and clear," I throw over my shoulder. I'd been thinking how easy it was to discuss my problems with her, but all she'd heard was that I'd been a failure.

"Get back here now, Finn Palmer!" Her voice, so full of authority, stops me dead in my tracks.

"Why?" I toss back at her.

"Because I didn't take you for a quitter. Unless you're giving up on us already."

My hands form fists. I should go, leave her out of this mess. "What do you fuckin' suggest?"

"Let's put our heads together. Come at this from a different angle. Unless you don't want my help?"

Someone to bounce ideas off? She might not be able to make databases reveal their secrets to her, but she's not stupid by a long shot.

"On one condition," I capitulate. "You might be right. If I, *we,* decide bringing my club in is the answer and I need to go back, I want you to come with me."

Her eyes go huge and her mouth opens, then closes with a snap. She surprises the hell out of me when she asks, "What have I got here?"

She'd come with me?

The devil on my shoulder asks why the fuck I'd want to be tied down. Haven't I always run from responsibility? Hell, I've been happier even without men around. *Or have I been lying to myself?*

If she comes with me, I'll have to keep an eye on her. Could I keep her safe, let alone happy? But if she's with me, I wouldn't have to worry about her being alone.

Truth be told, I may not have known her long, but she's been the best thing that's ever happened to me. Maybe it's the way we met, and I saw her at her lowest point.

Most ladies I've met have been primped to the nines with full makeup on, doing everything they can to snag a biker or a SEAL of their own. Cat, well, she couldn't have been more natural. She attracted me when she was weak, now she's strong, she knocks my socks off.

Did she mean it? When push comes to shove, would she leave the memories here and throw in her lot with a biker who's uncertain of his future? I have to be honest with her.

"If I go back to the club, I'm not sure of my welcome."

She eyes me carefully. "Because you ran."

"I did." I think how to put it. There's no way to sugarcoat what I'd done. "My punishment for the betrayal is a beatdown, each member of the club taking a swing at me." I shrug off the horror in her eyes. "I deserve it, and hell, I can handle it. After that, I'll be busted down to prospect for six months. I'll be at their beck and call and may not have time to be the man you want."

Her hand covers mine. "I'll need to get a job, which shouldn't be too difficult. My skills are needed everywhere. I need a new start, Finn. I think you've shown me that. I've been surviving, not living. I don't want to go back to the city, there's nothing for me there. Moving somewhere new and starting over is something I'll need to do, whether you're with me or not."

I huff out a breath. "As a prospect, I might not be able to be with you, not all the time. They might want me to live at the club so I can be available at all hours."

"I'm likely to be on shift work. If you want it to, we'll be able to make it work." Her eyes widen, and she giggles. It's a lovely sound, Cat doesn't have much to laugh about. "Hey, your reverse psychology is working. I'm now trying to convince you."

Raising an eyebrow, I chuckle. "Good ploy, huh?" But she's made me think. What would it be like to return to Utah with someone on my side? Me, who's never depended on anyone.

"When do you have to make a decision?"

Growing serious, I consider her question. "Sooner rather than later. At the most, I've got a couple of months. There's no immediate rush, it suits no one's purpose if I can't control my temper any better than when I left. Pip…" No, Pip isn't the prez anymore, but he'll still have influence. "Pip, I'm sure would be on my side." But would Snatcher? He's so recently regained the Prez patch, he might make an example of me with Drummer and whenever I return, declare me out bad, though it said in the church minutes they're giving me time, he could have changed his mind.

"You wanted to take something back to them," she reminds me. "If you've got time, why not stay here and we'll put our heads together and come up with a plan? These things have been simmering for four years, there's no rush to solve them now." Her eyes soften. "You need to have answers. You're never going to move forward unless you stop looking back."

I chuckle again, but this time it's without mirth. "What if I can't?"

"I'll help. Look, I don't know anything about being a SEAL. I don't know how a computer works except by turning it on and off and getting frustrated when stuff doesn't work. But I'm a good listener, and I know what makes people tick."

I turn away, bowing my head and rubbing at my temples. Vaguely I'm aware Cat's resumed what she's doing to give me some time.

Finally, I have my thoughts in order. "The backstop if I can't come up with anything to take to the club is I could stay here. Start some sort of business." I shrug. "If they declare me out bad, it might be option B in any event." I raise my head, but not toward her. Instead I stare out of the window. "Two months, Cat. That's what I think we've got. Let's use them wisely." Now I turn directly to her and wink. "I'll give you my cock, and you give me your help."

"That, mister," she points a finger at me, "is a bargain I can't turn down."

I snort. "I'd best get those steaks grilling. Gotta feed my woman so she's got stamina tonight."

21

*C*at…

Even before Weston reappeared in my life, I'd known I was living here on borrowed time. The ghosts had such a tight hold on me that I couldn't see past keeping my family home. It had been built by my great-grandfather and now I was the last of the line. How could I turn my back on my heritage?

I had no choice, knew I'd have to move on eventually. Maybe I was just waiting for a man like Finn to enter my life, or at least something that would give me a proverbial kick in the ass.

I like Finn, a lot. I think I love him, though I try to tell myself it's too early for that. Daily, I'm learning more about him.

Our relationship is already comfortable, both in and out of bed. Even if this isn't forever, he might help me move on. Utah? I've never considered that state, but as I told him, a nurse could be a nurse anywhere, and all I'd need to get is a license for that state.

Finn's broken, I'm not blind to that. A therapist would say it went back to being abandoned by his mother and never having the real support of his dad. He doesn't trust anyone. Is it too late for him to learn?

If I abandon my home and go with him, am I setting myself up for a world of hurt? Or would it be the start of an adventure?

I may be the stupidest woman in the world, but I want to help him. Maybe it's because I haven't been subjected to what makes him Stormy, or maybe, I keep that side of him down.

He's promised to help me out by making the farmhouse an attractive property to sell, and in return I'll assist him in finding answers. While I may have doubts about my contribution, I can be a sounding board if nothing else.

It's not as if I'm rushing into anything. I can change my mind anytime.

Finn and I have already gotten into a kind of routine, and it's that we continue, the only difference being, we share the same bed. He does odd jobs around the farm while I sort out the horse and chickens, and start the slow process of going through all the stuff in the house. My chores take the longest, and I'm often to be found sitting staring at a photograph album or memento with tears flooding down my cheeks. More than once I've come back to myself with Finn's arms wrapped around me. He sits silent, saying nothing at all until I lay that particular ghost to rest.

Sometimes I feel guilty. I had a childhood that I can look back on with tears now, but which I know will bring me comfort in the future. Finn has none.

Steak is surprisingly not the limit to Finn's repertoire of food. Having fended for himself most of his life, he's no stranger in the kitchen, and while it can't be classed as gourmet food, it's more than edible. Despite my fears about a biker's misogynistic reputation, he doesn't expect me to wait on him hand and foot.

After we've eaten, Finn normally settles himself at the desk where my PC is set up, opening his laptop there too. It's then he disappears into his own world, sometimes not emerging for hours as he delves deeper into whatever database he's exploring next.

Another month has passed, almost without me noticing. I glance up from my book, seeing Finn's hands are raised in the air as he stretches. Standing, I cross over to him and rest my hands on his shoulders.

As I begin to give him a massage, I ask, "Getting anywhere?"

"Well, I've just found out that one of my old team members didn't die."

"What?"

He points to the screen. It shows a picture from the news of a team of six SEALs. "That's what I saw on the news report at the time, but it must have been an old photo, and the news got its wires crossed. Gun," he points to a photo, "well, he didn't sign up for the last tour. There was another man who died. I'd always assumed he was dead. But Gun, or Jeffrey Morgan, is very much alive."

"Suspicious?"

One of his hands covers mine. "I'm suspicious about everyone. But maybe in this case without basis. He'd done his time."

"Can you track him down?"

"That's what I've been doing. He's got a job in security, but whoever he's protecting now is classified."

"Hidden from you?"

Now he sits forward again. "Not for long. I doubt it's anything, but it's worth investigating. If anything, it would be useful to talk to him. He was around when everything went down."

Frowning, I ask, "Why didn't you know he hadn't died with the rest? Wouldn't he have gotten into contact with you?"

He shrugs. "Being a SEAL was all that I wanted from life. When I got kicked out, I didn't want any reminders of what I'd lost. Tailor, apart from Pooh, was the one I was closest to. He tried to keep in touch, but I blew him off. It was he who contacted me to tell me about Nazia." He thinks for a moment. "Even Tailor didn't know I'd joined the Satan's Devils, and didn't know where I was. All he had was my phone number. On my part, I didn't ask about the team, and he didn't tell me Gun hadn't re-signed up. I don't think Gun ever forgave me for getting Pooh killed, so he would never have contacted me himself."

The lines on my brow deepen. "I've listened to your story, Finn. You've told it a few times. But there's one thing I can't get straight."

"What?" As always, he turns, his eyes focused on me. It's one more thing I like about him—he never discounts I might have anything to add. Even, when most times, I don't. When he tells me why an idea doesn't have legs, that too appears useful, as it seems to help him get things straight in his head.

"Pooh was with you. He was there when you set the explosives." I try to put my thoughts into words. "Did he have a headset too? Could he hear what Smythe had to say?"

"Yes." As with any discussion about his friend's final hours, he turns away, as if not wanting to be reminded.

"In that case, wouldn't he have told you if he thought you were wrong? He helped you rescue those girls. Did he suggest for a moment that wasn't what you should be doing?" I move slightly so I can see his face.

Finn's mouth opens, closes, then opens again.

"Well?"

The words when they finally come seem to be forced out through gritted teeth. "Pooh acted as if it was the right thing to do. There was no way he was going to leave those girls."

My shoulders slump. It's a question that's been going around my mind, but will Finn accept the implications? "Pooh died as a hero, yet you were thrown out. Surely he was as equally guilty as you were found to be?"

He shakes his head. "You don't understand, I disobeyed a direct order."

"So did he." My words seem to bounce around us, echoing at

least in my head. Finn doesn't move, he doesn't even blink. I continue to press my case, softening my voice. "You're lucky to be alive, Finn. You might have been killed as well. Anyone setting off an explosion while not giving you time to get clear, well, the assumption might have been you both were killed."

He needs time, I give it to him. When the silence drags out too long, I ask, "Want a beer?" Without waiting to see if he does or does not, I move away. If it hasn't occurred to him before, he'll need time to process my point of view. What do I know about how SEALs work? As a civilian, I just can't help but feel something was wrong. Finn got punished for being alive. It was Smythe who killed Pooh, not him.

I take my time in the kitchen, pouring myself a glass of wine and taking a few sips before returning to the man who looks like he's barely moved. I place the beer down in front of him. When I do so, he grabs hold of my hand, holding onto it as though it's a lifeline.

"Pooh and I gravitated together as we both had the same type of minds. Smythe already hated us. He didn't have much time for any of the team, but me and Pooh, we had smarts that Smythe didn't have. One time, we didn't hold back pointing out a huge fuckin' hole in a plan, and Smythe had to backtrack. Pooh, I always thought was destined for promotion because of the way he thought outside the box." He pauses. "Both of us, well, we'd join dots together. He was into computers like myself, and it was almost a game to us to work through a mission, discussing what if this, and if that, then what."

"You were the thinkers."

He stares at nothing, thinking back. "Tailor, Gun, Slice and Buster, they weren't slouches, but they were more likely to look for the obvious, while Pooh and I would dig under that. Smythe hated us. In hindsight, probably more so than the rest of the men in the team."

"So it could have been deliberate."

Haunted eyes meet mine. "I wish you'd never suggested that. I thought it was a fuckup, accepted Smythe was a coward and out of his depth. Never dreamed it could have been premeditated." His hands push back the long hair which has flopped over his forehead. "Fuck, Cat."

The thought that Pooh could have been deliberately killed seems to have hit him hard. "Can you leave it now and come to bed?"

He ignores me. "At the time, we never knew who the girls were, or how they came to be there. They disappeared in all the confusion. I only knew their first names. What…" His words die off, he swallows, and begins again, this time more firmly. "What if they were innocent victims? What if the setup was to delay Pooh and I getting away?"

Suddenly on his wavelength, I realise what's so horrific for him. If the terrorists didn't plant the kids there, it must have been someone working with the SEALs. Someone who set up what was essentially murder.

His hands slam down on the table. "All the blame was put on me for keeping Pooh back. But you're right. It wasn't just me, it was he who agreed. Maybe tacitly, but he wasn't going to be able to leave Nazia and Marjan. I accepted the blame though I had no control or rank over him. I never fuckin' questioned it. I didn't defend myself—"

"You were in shock, Finn."

He grimaces, and then nods. "I wanted to be punished. Pooh had never seen his kid. Three lives torn apart, one literally, but his wife and child, how could they get over his loss? I didn't argue, didn't let my lawyer put up a defence, as I thought I had none." He purses his lips. "I could never have blamed a dead man."

"Neither of you are to blame," I tell him firmly.

His head moves to one side and back to the other. "I took it all on my shoulders. Even when they gave me the chance, I didn't even point the finger at Smythe. I didn't ask fuckin' questions, Cat. It didn't cross my mind."

He rolls back his chair and pats his lap. I'm more than happy to accept the invitation. Parking myself on his lap, I wrap my arms around him. He breathes in deeply, and for a moment, I let him take my strength.

"I couldn't understand," he starts after a moment. "It makes no sense. If the terrorists had planted the girls there, it was to raise an international incident. Fighting would have escalated, and more, not fewer, US forces would have been sent in. Us rescuing the girls meant there were no civilian deaths."

"You've said that before," I remind him.

"But if they were nobodies? Maybe no one would have cared, and me, and Pooh would be dead, and the death of the kids covered up."

"The girls had family, surely?"

He raises and lowers his chin. "They did. Fuck, Cat. All I'm doing is going around in circles."

22

───────

Stormy…

As the weeks have passed, I've become more and more comfortable living here with Cat. Since the talk a week or so back about whether I was wrong to take sole responsibility for Pooh's death, I've let go of some of my grief about his loss, and focused more on that night instead.

Cat had been right. Pooh was equally responsible, though it irks me to blame the man who paid with his death. But instead of pushing him to the back of my memory, I've resurrected him instead. Although I'm known as a loner, it was him I'd trusted to bounce ideas off. A position that's now been taken by a woman.

Cat might not have the background or experience that we had, but I've been impressed by her mental agility.

Clouds are starting to build overhead as I start my way down the ladder. Once on the ground, I take a few steps back. Looking up, I feel a sense of pride. The roof looks solid now, and I did it all by myself—with a few tips from YouTube videos of course.

Rubbing my palms, one against the other to brush the loose

mortar off, I turn and make my way back into the house. I'm heading to the bathroom to wash up when I hear Cat's voice.

"Yes, it was nice to catch up… No, I doubt I'll hear from him, but if I do… I'm sure he'll turn up… Bye."

Though she's entitled to talk to anyone she wants, so far, no friends have been in touch. Seems her childhood friends had moved on, and those from the city hadn't stayed in touch as she'd been gone for over a year. I raise my eyebrow in question.

She sighs and places her phone back on the side table, then pinches the bridge of her nose. After a moment, she looks up. "That was my aunt. Someone's been looking for Weston, and they're worried as he hasn't been in touch."

Well he wouldn't have been. Satan's Devils know their stuff. Weston is beyond the reach of anyone now, and not where anyone can find him.

"Who was asking for him?"

She shakes her head. "No one my aunt or uncle knows. I did ask." Worried eyes meet mine. "I may have done wrong. I told her he came here six or so weeks ago, but obviously didn't say anything else." I breathe in sharply, but before I can suggest whether she's done wrong or right, she carries on, "After all, we did go to Brook's Diner together. If they start circulating his picture saying he's missing, there was a girl I vaguely knew from school there and she might remember."

I immediately come down on the side of right. "You did good, Cat." Approaching her, I put my arms around her. "It's unlikely anyone will do much about Weston, but you were correct. If there's a chance of exposure, you minimise it."

She leans into my chest. "My aunt thought it strange he would come visit. If anything, it worried her more. It was out of character."

"What did you tell her?"

"I suggested he might have wanted to see whether there was a chance he could get money out of the house. But my parents didn't leave a will and the inheritance laws would be hard to challenge." She huffs. "It wasn't a reach for her to accept that excuse. She knows exactly what Weston is like." She pulls back a little, looking into my eyes. "There is a danger though. Before he went inside, Weston was a boxer. A good one as well. Though objectionable, he won fights. People might remember if she starts a search."

I know she'll think I'm changing the subject, but I'm not. "The roof is all fixed, Cat. Maybe it's time you approach a real estate agent and put this place on the market."

"And get away from any heat?" She catches on fast. "But are you ready to go back to Utah?"

That's the question I keep asking myself. Releasing her, I turn and start to pace, thinking aloud. "I wanted to find out more to take back, even if it was something I needed their help to solve, but as you know, I keep finding more questions than answers. The only headline is you're no risk to them anymore. They'll have already found that I fixed it so it looks like a fake account was set up to rent the fishing cabin, presumably by the perpetrators themselves. They won't be worrying about that."

"Will you ever be able to find something to justify you not just leaving, but staying gone?"

If Utah was a club full of men who loved their old ladies like Tucson, maybe I would and they'd understand. *Love?* That pulls me up. *Old lady?* Pressing my lips together, I get distracted for a moment, asking myself if I want to live a life with her in it, or returning to being my lonely self. As if a lightbulb has been switched on in my head, I realise not having her with me would be like losing part of myself. *I want to keep her.* Which means I need to build a future with her in it.

The world's my oyster, but what would I be without my brothers at my back? I thought I could do it, but as more time has passed, I feel a restlessness inside of me. I was never meant to be a civilian.

But how can I go back to the Devils?

Cat walks toward me, her hands reaching for my biceps, her fingers curling into the muscles. "What if you had an excuse for your behaviour?"

I snort. "I don't think there's any excuse for me being an ass."

"Yes, there is," she says, adamantly. "I think you and Pooh were set up. If you can find out why, that would explain why you felt so helpless and did what you did."

Me? Helpless? I bristle and straighten, ready to contradict what she's just said, but as I open my mouth, I wonder if she's right. I hadn't trusted anyone because I didn't understand how everything had got so fucked up.

Cat moves closer again, raising her hand to cup my face. "It's classic PTSD, you know? Pushing people away who can help. That might be enough of a sympathy card."

I don't have PTSD. I don't. "Is that your official diagnosis?"

"Yup. Something happened you had no control over, so you protected yourself by making sure it could never happen again. A therapist would suggest you look at what you can control and try to cope with what you cannot. In your own way, you tried to do that. You say your brothers served. They'd understand."

Damn it. She makes sense. But I'm not a man who runs crying to anyone else. But what if I discovered a reason for why it had all gone so wrong and returned to explain? It wouldn't stop the beatdown nor that I'd have to prospect for six months, but maybe I'd once again have brothers at my back and actually want them there.

"I need you, Cat," I tell her.

"I'll be right by your side." It's a promise.

"I'll start digging again. I'll go back to the beginning. See if I can find anything. Or at least get my thoughts in order."

"I'll begin to get the ball rolling here, starting with trying to find a good home for Star. There's a local farmer who'd take the chickens, he might take him as well."

"I'm sorry," I tell her, knowing how much she'll hate leaving her horse, particularly after she lost her dog. I know she still misses him.

It's her turn to straighten her back. "It is what it is, Finn. He can't move with us, and I can't stay here just to look after him in his retirement. If I find him a good home, I'll still be able to come back and visit."

And I'll make sure to scare the shit out of the person who takes him on. If that horse isn't properly cared for, they'll know they have me to answer to.

"Come here." I wrap my arms around her, leaning down to take her mouth. My cock, which always seems to harden around her, starts to swell. There's more than one benefit to living with Cat.

I'll never get fed up with her pussy. Never before have I wanted to go back, but having experienced hers, I know I have no need for another. As our encounter starts to become heated, and I call it a day and lead her to bed, I realise that I've changed since I've known her. For the better, I'd definitely say.

"Need me to do anything today?" I ask the next morning. Things I've thought about in the dead of night still going around my head.

"No, you go do your thing. I'll go get some groceries and call on Seamus to see whether he can take the animals for us."

"You okay doing that alone?"

Predictably, she rolls her eyes.

I grin. Of course she is. Cat is made of strong stuff and doesn't need me to always be behind her.

When she leaves, I note the healthier sound of the truck, now running much better since I serviced and tuned it. I make myself a coffee and take it over to the desk. Time to start digging.

Gun. Why did he get out before the rest of the team was taken out? When I first found out, I had no suspicions. Now I wonder whether I was wrong to discount the coincidence. I start to dig, and then dig deeper.

At one point I sit forward, my eyes blinking fast, trying to understand the information I'm reading.

Gun, or Jeffrey Morgan, had a half-brother. Unlike him, Ike hadn't followed a straight path. I get most of the information from a transcript of his trial when his felonies caught up with him. He'd been lucky to survive so long outside jail, but when he was sent down, he got twenty years having been caught moving product.

Did Gun know? Were they close? I can't remember him ever talking about a brother. But maybe he'd been in ignorance of how Ike earned his dollars. The court case was after I'd been kicked out.

Now that's interesting. Ike Morgan had been sent to the same pen as Saul Kincaid and Weston. But as far as I knew, their crimes were violent, but had nothing to do with drugs.

Drugs. Drugs. I tap my fingers against the desk. *Afghanistan is a huge producer of heroin.*

I start delving deeper, hacking into the database that keeps records of all military operations.

Interesting. At the time of Pooh's death, I'd already known our troops were being pulled back. After his death, they remained in the region. Another withdrawal had been planned, but again abandoned when Nazir tried to blow US soldiers up. Another coincidence? Rubbing my temples, I think maybe I'm making too much of troop movements in a volatile environment.

"I'm back," a voice calls out. Moments later I feel arms around me. I lean back into her touch. "Have you made any progress?"

"I'm not sure," I reply honestly. "I think I'm jumping at shadows right now." I just need to keep finding the dots, seeing how, or if, there's anyway to join them up. "How did you get on?"

"Good, actually. Seamus is more than happy to take Star. He said his granddaughter would love him. He showed me a paddock and an old stall he's going to do up. He's happy with the chickens too."

"That's great." I turn around, staring into her face. "You really happy with this, Cat?"

She gives a shrug. "I'd have had to do it anyway, Finn. I can't stay here, you know that. Oh, and I also went to see the real estate agent. He's coming out later to get the details to list this place."

"You've been busy," I tell her, surprised at how much she's achieved, before noting the digital numbers on the screen in front of me. She's literally had hours while I'd lost all sense of time.

The following days pass me by in the same kind of blur. Cat starts packing up the house, putting stuff aside to go into storage until we get our own place, and taking truckloads of other things to Goodwill. I offer to help, but she prefers to do it herself. In some ways I think it's cathartic. I lend my support when I catch her with tears in her eyes as she packs up her mom and dad's personal stuff.

The real estate agent thinks she can get a good price for the house—partly down to the repairs that I'd done.

As the house empties, it begins to echo around us, and I start to think we need to get out of here soon. It's like living in a coffin of memories. Apart from the bedroom furniture, the desk, sofa and her father's old chair, most of the items have been removed. I've promised her we'll start afresh with new, most of what was here was old-fashioned and well used.

I still haven't got answers, but I've started drawing a picture. I just need something to fall into place. While Cat's great to bounce ideas off of, I wonder whether I could do with some

more eyes on the problem. Bolt would be good, as would Rascal
—if they'd still give me the time of day, of course.

I've been gone two months.

I want to go back. I'm ready.

As long as I have Cat by my side.

23

——

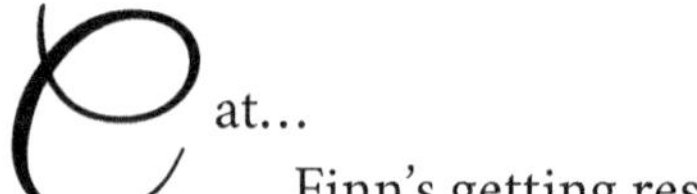

Cat…

Finn's getting restless. So am I.

If it was just a case of having to close up this house just so I could start a new lonely life, I'd have found it much harder. But along with being sad at the memories that keep coming back, I'm optimistic about the future.

I'm falling in love with Finn. I haven't told him that yet, but I suspect he knows. Our bodies do the talking each night when we're in bed, or, during the day when the impulse hits us. He hasn't told me what he feels for me either, but I hope he feels the same way. I'm more than happy to align my future with his, even though it's one that's uncertain.

If his club won't take him back, we'll still be together. If they do, for six months we might not have as much time to ourselves. I can survive on my own while it's necessary, I've done it long enough. I'll be able to keep busy, finding a new job and settling will be where I start, making a home for him to come back to when he regains his position with his club.

Of course, he might already be what he calls *out bad.* In that case, we'll make our own path.

"That's it." I walk into the lounge where Finn's staring at the screen of his laptop.

"Shit, babe. You alright?" Immediately he stands and enfolds me in his arms.

I've just seen Star loaded onto the horse trailer. I know he'll be spoiled and cared for by Seamus, who'd brought his granddaughter with him. I wipe away a tear. "It's the end of an era. He's been at the farm since I was a kid." Sniffing, I attempt a smile. "Georgia, the granddaughter, had a shine in her eyes much like I had when he first arrived here. He'll be fine."

"If we could have taken him—"

I place my fingers over his mouth. "We couldn't. I know that. I can't stay here, so this would have happened whether we were together or not."

He pulls me in closer, kissing the top of my head. "When we get a place, we'll get a dog."

I clutch at him. I know he's not had experience of animals, yet he knows that's what I want. It's on the tip of my tongue to tell him I love him, but I choke the words back. *Is it too early? What if he can't reciprocate?*

But I lose my chance when there's a knock at the door.

Sighing, I say, "I wonder if Seamus has come back?" I try to think if there was something or some instruction I'd forgotten to give him.

He pats my ass. "It probably is. You got this?"

I got this. I nod.

I walk to the front door without bothering to look and throw it open. "Whatcha forgot..." My words taper off. There's a man outside who I've never seen before.

Not only is he a stranger, but he's not particularly polite. He pushes me backward.

"Finn!" I scream out, and then again as the man spins me around, forcing my arms behind me, binding my wrists tight.

My eyes focus in front of me. Two other men are fighting

with Finn, they must have come in via the back door and have taken him by surprise.

"Finn!" I screech when he takes a hard blow to the chin.

"What the fuck?" The man pushing me into the room sounds angry. "What the fuck are you doing here?"

There's another man, which makes four in total. The one holding me pushes me into his arms. I fight, kicking back with my legs, but apart from a grunt, I do no damage.

"Stop fighting, bitch, or your man is dead." He nods toward the gun that's now trained on Finn.

"Her man?" the first intruder scoffs. "Stormy's never had a bitch in his life. But I'm mighty interested in what he's doing here." He cocks an eyebrow toward Finn and raises his gun in a threatening manner.

"Gun." Stormy's eyes flare.

"Boss? She seemed like she was expecting someone," the man holding me points out. "If someone's coming here, we better make this quick."

The man I now know is Gun, one of the SEALs who served beside Stormy unless I'm mistaken, slowly nods his head.

"That right?" he tosses to me over his shoulder.

"Yes," I confirm, hating that my voice sounds weak. "A local farmer who's picking some of my animals up." They've all gone now, but I'll think of something he could have left. Feed, perhaps? "Oh, and the real estate agent. He's coming to get the keys." We left those with him a day ago, planning to vacate in the next few days.

Gun's back stiffens. "Stormy being here complicates things."

"We taking them both?" one of the men holding Stormy asks. "Or just getting rid of him here?"

Gun looks around the room. When his face turns my way, he's wearing a satisfied grin. "Seems they've done all the work for us. There's a truck outside, we'll move all the boxes and put them in there, then move the truck into the barn. Anyone who comes calling will just assume they've moved out."

"What do you want here, Gun?" Stormy snaps.

"Well, I didn't want you," his former SEAL buddy says. Somehow, I don't think he's much of a friend now.

I wouldn't expect good vibes to be coming from anyone who'd invaded my house, but Gun's positively icy. If I were here on my own, I'd be a mess, but I'm staying strong because of Stormy.

"So, what are we going to do about him?"

I suck in a breath while internally screaming, *Don't hurt him, please.*

"Stormy's been a thorn in my fuckin' side for far too long. It would give me great pleasure to put a bullet through his head. But why's he here? That's what we need to find out." Gun steps forward getting right up into Stormy's face. "I've got an old friend who'd probably like to say hi, so you're coming with us."

All of a sudden I feel a prick in my neck and the world goes black.

I wake sometime later feeling groggy. When I try to move, my hands are tied, as are my feet. I'm curled up in a fetal position, with a strange vibration under me. My head pounds as though I've been on a drinking binge. I open my eyes, blinking hard until a shape by my side comes into focus.

I presume they'd given me a drug to knock me out. Finn looks like he's not been so lucky. His face is bloodied, one eye is swollen closed.

"Finn," I say, quietly, not knowing who's around me.

I get no reply. He's unconscious. *Oh God, Finn. What have they done to you?*

I flop like a fish as I try to move onto my back so I can look around. I presume I'm in a truck of some sort, but wherever we're going, the road is really smooth. The drone of the engine is loud though.

"Don't worry, Princess. We'll be there soon." The voice is that of Gun.

I glance up as best I can, and watch as he grabs a handful of Finn's hair, pulling up his head.

"Sleeping Beauty's still out, I see." He sounds satisfied as he lets Finn's head smash down with a bump. He sinks to his haunches and stares at me. "We'll be coming into land, shortly. I suggest you fasten your seat belt. Oh," he snorts a laugh, "you can't." He chuckles as if he's made a good joke. "Well, let's hope we have a safe landing."

I'm on a plane?

"Where, where are you taking us? And w-why?"

"I think you've got some answers for me. As for him," he shoots a look of hate toward Finn, "I find it very interesting that he was with you. Why was he?"

I don't want to be interrogated now. I want Finn awake and able to guide me. He knows Gun, he probably knows what I should or shouldn't say. Instead of answering, I groan instead.

"My head hurts. I feel sick."

He jumps back as though scalded. "Try not to puke," he instructs as he stands. "If you have to, vomit his way." He nods at Finn, then his eyes come back to me. "We'll be having that chat soon."

Almost as soon as he leaves, my ears begin to pop. The plane must have started to descend. I've no idea how long I've been out or where we're going to land. Or, even if I'm still in the United States.

Finn doesn't move as we bump down onto the runway, nor when Gun's men appear. He moans slightly as he's picked up in a fireman's lift, but his eyes stay firmly shut. *Is he faking?* Or hurt too badly to come around. I pray it's the former.

Me? Well, I'm subjected to the same treatment—carried ignominiously off the plane and dumped into the back of a truck alongside Finn. My brief glimpse of my surroundings gives nothing away, just distant trees and lush grass encircling what is probably a private runway.

This time the journey isn't so smooth, and I really do start to feel ill as a truck of some sort bumps the way along the road. Tied as I am, I can't protect my head, which slams down time and again. My headache gets worse. When I roll at a tight bend, my stomach churns and I can't prevent the vomit coming out of my mouth.

I'm scared, so very scared. I've been kidnapped and stolen away from my home and I can't imagine for what reason. The only thing that makes it bearable is that I'm not alone. *But will Finn ever wake up?*

Who knows? My gut twists, thinking I could never hear his voice again, or feel his arms around me. The very idea forces me to acknowledge how much he's come to mean to me in such a short time. I couldn't imagine moving on without him.

"I love you," I say softly, hoping somehow my words will filter through his head.

My headache hasn't improved at all by the time the truck takes a final set of nausea-causing turns and finally pulls to a stop. The back doors are rolled up. It's dark outside. *Just how long has it been since I was dragged from my home?*

"Get them inside."

The men don't hesitate to follow Gun's commands. The first man steps in, lifts Finn in the same way he carried him before, but the one coming for me hesitates, finally gingerly picking me up bridal style. I realise he's trying to avoid the vomit that's stained my front.

It's a shame I've already brought everything up, I'd love to puke all over him.

Even in the darkness I can make out we've been brought to a cabin, but I have no time to see much as I'm rushed into the house and taken to a room. There, I'm unceremoniously thrown down onto a single bed—well cot to be precise—there's nothing comfortable about it. At last, the ties that bind me are cut, and I can move my arms and legs, or at least I hope I will when I get some more feeling back.

I hurt. Every muscle is crying out from being kept immobile for so long. At first I can't move, but ignore that fact as I realise Finn's not here, and the man looks like he's going to leave without bringing him in.

"Where's Finn?" I cry out.

"Don't you worry about him. You just worry about yourself. And before you look to escape, there's no way out. You just sit here like a good little girl until we're ready for you."

Ready for me? For what? My mind conjures up possibilities which I don't want to imagine.

"Finn. He's hurt. Are you getting him medical attention?"

The man rolls his eyes. "What do you fucking think?" He leaves, slamming the door behind him.

I'd like to say I launch to my feet and throw myself at the door, but I'm far slower than that. I roll, groan, and when I finally get my feet on the floor, my legs give way under my weight making me clutch at the bed. My head swims, probably due to whatever drug they injected into me. Eventually I manage to make my way to the door, only to find it's locked.

Weakly I bang on it.

No one comes.

I sink to the floor, put my head in my hands, and cry, hating myself for being weak. But nothing has prepared me for this experience, even when Weston chained me up. There'd been a strange comfort in knowing I was in my own home, and with him being my cousin, I'd had hope that he'd return to release me.

Surely a former SEAL wouldn't hurt a woman like me?

But he already has. He's kidnapped me, flown me God knows where and is keeping me captive. I shudder, thinking there can be no good reason why he's brought me here. If he had questions he wanted me to answer, why not ask them at home?

Perhaps he would have done if he hadn't recognised Finn?

But he came with three other men. They must have managed to get in via the back door which I'm sure I'd locked. That's the only way they could have taken Finn by surprise.

Angry at myself, I swipe my tears away. Crying doesn't help.

Making a concerted effort, I get to my feet, stretching my aching legs and rubbing at the red rings on my wrists. Rolling my shoulders, I try to relieve the ache there and glance around. The only furniture in the room is the basic bed, but there is a window. Quickly I go to it, only to find it's been nailed shut. I pick at the gap, but it's tightly jammed. I lose two fingernails before I give up.

Christ, I'm sore, I think to myself as I take a step back, I stink of vomit—I'm a mess. Only now do I become conscious of another discomfort. My bladder is full. I've no idea how long it's been since I last relieved myself, but I suspect it's been more than a few hours.

This room doesn't come with an en suite, and my last resort would be to pee on the floor.

I go to the door and start to bang on it, calling out, "Hey, I need a bathroom."

For a while, my cries go unanswered. When I finally hear footsteps stomping on the wooden floor, I'm hopping from leg to leg, in desperate need of relief though also scared, regretting I needed to call for attention. But what else could I do? I'm so desperate, I could easily wet myself.

As the sound grows louder, I take a step back. It's Gun himself who opens the door.

"What you making this noise for?"

"I need a bathroom."

He shakes his head and rolls his eyes. "You fuckin' bitches

are all the same. Can't hold your piss. Well, come on. Best to get comfortable while you can."

It sounds ominous. He waves me out of the door in front of him. *Have I a chance to escape?* But what can I do? He's armed, and while visions of me headbutting him or kicking him where it hurts flit across my mind, I'm wary he's a man who's trained in unarmed combat. Perhaps for now it's best to act docile and hope a better chance to get free comes along.

He puts his hand on my shoulder when I come alongside a door. With his other, he reaches around me and opens it. Thank God it's a bathroom.

Stepping inside fast, I turn to shut the door behind me, but he keeps hold of it. "Leave it ajar."

Relieve my bladder while he's only just outside able to listen to me? The commode is a few steps away, I wouldn't be able to sit and make sure he didn't push the door open and watch me. My steps falter. I'm a private bathroom person, I always have been.

Pressure in my stomach reminds me I haven't got much choice.

Suck it up, I tell myself. Maybe when I'm feeling more comfortable, I'll be able to come up with a plan to get free.

The bathroom has only a small frosted window that I'd never be able to get out of, but surely some opportunity will present itself? Or, he'll let me go. There's no reason to kidnap me. I've no money and no one to pay a ransom.

Maybe Finn will have some ideas. *If he's still alive.*

I suppress the thought that he might be dead already. I have to hang on to the idea he's breathing and waiting to get me free.

With no option, I step forward. At least the bathroom is clean. I take down my pants and my underwear, and sit on the seat, willing my bladder to empty. Of course, even desperate, I'm all too aware of the open door.

When the flow doesn't start immediately, I hear Gun say, "Hurry the fuck up."

Of course, that does little to help me. But eventually, the damn breaks. I wipe, flush and wash my hands.

As soon as I've finished he steps in and takes hold of my arm. It's a firm grip, and one I can't evade. He all but drags me down the corridor. For a moment we emerge into the fresh air. I glance around, but there are no clues as to where the hell I could be. It's chilly in the morning air, a slight mist hovering over tree-covered mountains. Cooler than in Kentucky, but that could be altitude.

I don't have long to ponder before he takes me to a brick built shed. He puts a key in the lock and pushes me inside. The interior is dim, high cobweb covered windows stop much light coming in, but all thoughts of location flee from my head as through the gloom I see what's waiting for me. It's Finn, tied to a chair. One eye is closed, and his clothes are bloody.

"Finn!" I exclaim, but the hold on my hand stops me from running to him.

Two of the other men are already there. One offers a bone-chilling grin when I appear. I shudder.

Finn's eyes land on me, but then dispassionately look away. He stares up at Gun instead. "I wouldn't bother with her. She's got nothing to say."

He's cold. There's barely a flicker of recognition in his eyes. I thought he'd be spitting at Gun to let me go, but it's as if he doesn't care. It's like a kick in the gut, and my initial reaction is to beg him to give me reassurances—one that he'll get me out of there, and the other that when he'd shown love for me, it wasn't a ploy and he meant it.

The answer it hits me. *He's acting.* Perhaps Gun's trying to get him to talk by threatening me. If Finn pretends to care nothing for me, maybe the threats won't work. *That has to be it, doesn't it?*

Gun chuckles softly. "You were sharing her fuckin' bed, Stormy. Unlikely as it sounds, the bitch is yours."

"When have I ever had a bitch, Gun? She was an easy fuck. I needed a place to stay." As much as his injuries allow, Finn shrugs. His eyes find mine and hold them for a moment. "Sorry, doll, but that's all it was."

He's called me by my name and called me babe. Doll sounds odd falling from his lips. I'm sure it's a message that there's no meaning behind the words he just said.

"Yeah, she's fuckable, I'll give you that." Gun's voice chills me, especially when the fourth man who's just entered gives me an assessing leer. "Think we should have something pretty to look at while you and I are getting reacquainted." His next instruction is to me. "Take off your clothes."

What?

Gun steps away from me, and folds his arms, leaning against the door through which we've just entered. "You heard me. Get naked."

"I will not." I feel my eyes flash and my spine straightens.

He shrugs. "Either you do it yourself or my men will."

"Why?" I ask, but my most dire thoughts don't want him to put it into words. My clothes afford me some protection, little enough, but some. Without them, he and his men could do anything.

Again my eyes go to Finn, but he's only watching with mild interest as though he really doesn't care.

Gun swings me around to face him. Once again, his fingers bite into my arms so hard they'll leave bruises. The suddenness of his action makes me squeak.

"I said get naked," he snarls. "As for why, because you're covered in vomit and you fuckin' stink. Because it's cold up here in the mountains, and you'll be less likely to escape. There are animals out there. Barbed wire, brambles. You wouldn't get far.

And because, while I'm talking to Finn, I'd like something pleasant to look at."

If I get the opportunity, I'd prefer to take my chances with four-legged animals rather than the two-legged version in here.

As I still don't obey him, he beckons one of the men standing with Finn forward. "You haven't got a choice, darlin'. Either you take your clothes off or he'll do it for you. Can't say which I mind—a striptease or a stripping—but I doubt he'll be gentle."

My mind works fast. If I have a chance to escape, I might be able to find my clothes. The man who's approaching with a gleam in his eyes holds a knife in his hand. If they're cut off, they'll be no use.

I can't argue, I know that. Four armed men against one woman doesn't give me a chance.

I've been naked in front of only a few men. I don't wear skimpy clothes, and even in my own home, feel better when I'm totally covered. I feel audacious when I dispense with a bra under my top. To expose my body to these men? I'd do anything to avoid that.

Looking toward Finn, I seek a message, a sign of some sort. *Has he loosened his bindings? Will he suddenly leap forward like the big bad SEAL that he was and stop me?* But his expression is closed off. He's still staring at me, but as if only half-interested in whether I'm going to obey.

Another step taken by the man approaching me is the encouragement I need, I don't want him to touch me.

With shaking hands, I start to undo the buttons of my blouse, trying to convince myself I'll feel better once I'm no longer covered in puke.

It doesn't work.

24

———

Stormy…

I didn't come around until I woke up tied in this fucking chair. That blow to my head must have been hard, maybe cracked my skull from the way my head's pounding. The pain in my heart takes precedence though. *Cat.* Where is she? Is she hurt?

The thought that she might already be dead has me struggling against the ties that they've bound me with, but Gun knows what he's doing, of course he fucking does. I'm not going anywhere.

Why was he at the house? As if reviewing security footage, I think back, going over what he said. *He hadn't expected to find me there.* No, I was a bonus. So, what the fuck does he want with Cat?

It's got to be something to do with the connection I'd found between his half-brother and Saul Kincaid. If he was looking for Weston, his search might have led him to Cat. But why the fuck was a former SEAL who, unlike myself, retained his Trident, delving into a plot where Swift was kidnapped as a way to get to Pip?

Damn. Why did they hit my head so fucking hard? My eyes are finding it hard to focus, as is my brain, and I'm sure I've got a concussion. Something's niggling at me, but I can't quite hold onto it.

Saul Kincaid kidnapped Swift with the intention of Pip giving himself up. Pip had killed his twin brother, and his motive had been revenge. Or, so we had thought.

Pip. Who is he? He's a disavowed spy by his own account. He took over the Satan's Devils MC Utah chapter so he could continue to save at least some of the world his way. Admiral Hillier had known him, or at least of him, and had pointed me his way. Pip had his own methods of recruitment. I owe a debt to the man who'd given me back a reason to live.

Was there more to Kincaid's revenge than just killing the man who took out his brother?

Pip had buried his old identity, had had plastic surgery to change his looks. He'd been safe with the Satan's Devils for ten years or more, but was his past rearing its ugly head? Was Kincaid not the mastermind, was there someone else behind him pulling his strings? He'd had access to a computer expert to formulate the background that had fooled Dengra. Perhaps that's the lead we should have investigated.

Could Pip be a danger to someone, someone from his past who was still seeking retribution?

Just where the fuck does Gun fit in?

Fuck this headache. The pounding in my temples is making it hard for me to think. My brain normally works faster, but today the dots are just smudges on a piece of paper.

What does this mean for me, and for Cat? Sure, she's got a link between her and Tiny, but that's all there is. Does Gun know what I've been doing for the last few years? If he knows I'm a link to Pip and that's who he's after, I could be in trouble.

Whatever, I need more brains on it, more than the damaged ones now residing in my battered skull. I've got to get out of here and get back to the club. If I could land this problem in the lap of Swift, Honor or Duty, even Bolt or Piston, maybe they could find out more.

I tug at my bindings again, they're tight, but I'm a SEAL and they can't keep me trapped. I could get loose, should I get out of here now? But what happens to Cat? Is she here, or is she dead back at the house? Gun wouldn't have taken me and left her alive, he's far too careful for that. If she's here, why, and what are they going to do with her?

I think back to what I remember of Gun.

You get all sorts on a SEAL team, but what you can trust is that they've gone through the same training, and are willing to give their lives for the country they serve. I'd been closer to Tailor and Pooh. Gun had always been a little reserved. Like myself, he didn't talk much about his family. I never knew he had a half-brother. But who was I to criticise? I'd told no one about the way I'd grown up. It hadn't seemed important.

Unlike myself, Gun didn't openly criticise our lieutenant commander's orders. That didn't stop him being called to see Smythe a number of times, returning with a chip on his shoulder about being singled out. At the time I'd just thought I'd been cleverer, keeping my most traitorous thoughts to myself, or only voicing them to Pooh and Tailor.

Why had Gun left the SEAL team? Was it suspicious that if he hadn't, he'd have been dead? Just what kind of security had he been providing once he left?

I need answers, otherwise, I'm just going around in circles.

They've left me here, tied up. There's a camera up in the corner with a red light blinking, so someone's got me under surveillance. If I break out of here, they'll be on me, probably before I can get to the door.

If I sit here like a model prisoner, maybe I'll get answers. If I escape without knowing more, I'll probably get a bullet in the head.

So, I wait. It's up to Gun to make the first move.

I close my eyes, taking the time to try to let my head heal. When the door opens, I snap open my eyes. It's two of the thugs who'd accompanied Gun.

Jesus! He's sent them to work me over as they immediately start beating me again. Soon fresh blood leaks from my nose which I fear is broken, well, it's not the first time and won't be the last. My vision, that was already hazy, is now worse with one eye swollen closed. Having decided on my inaction, I stoically take what they hand out. When I make no protest, they seem to get bored.

They're disciplined, I'll give them that. They don't talk among themselves. I choke back the question *what are we waiting for?* The answer, I'm sure, would be for Gun.

When he eventually turns up, he's not alone.

At least Cat's alive and appears unharmed. The sight of her eases my soul. That she's told to dispense with her clothes makes me want to rage, but I'm sure Gun wants to taunt me. If I convince him she means nothing to me, maybe he'll let her go. Or, at least, be merciful when he kills her.

No!

I can't let it come to that. Not while I still have breath in my body. But I know how this torture will probably go, they'll use her to break me.

Hardening my heart and my expression, I look impassively through my one working eye, as if only mildly interested when that body that's mine is exposed. I bide my time thinking how painfully these four men are going to die. None of them will go easily.

She stands there, shaking, shivering with cold and fear. I want to tell her she's no need to worry, that I'll save her, but I keep silent.

"Good pair of tits on her," a nameless man behind me states.

Another, I can see out of the corner of my eye, is adjusting himself in his pants. *No, don't rape her. She's fucking mine, not yours.* But still I keep every expression off my face.

Gun looks at me, then back to her. "Hmm, I wonder which of you will break first?" He steps up to Cat and dares put a hand on her breast, twisting her nipple hard.

She shrieks and tries to dislodge his touch, but he backhands her across the face. His attention though is on me and not her.

"Not going to say anything, Stormy? Not when I'm touching your bitch?"

"I told you, she's nothing to me." My tone sounds weary, almost bored.

"Soften him up," Gun instructs.

While I was expecting it, I suffer through the attack, vaguely conscious of Cat screaming, begging for them to stop. The baseball bat they've chosen hits my ribs, my legs and my arms even though they're tied behind my back. I think my right leg has been broken, there's a worryingly sharp pain in my ribs, and my shoulder is pure agony as I lose the feeling in my right arm.

"Stop!" Cat screams again.

Gun laughs loudly. "Well, looks like this relationship is one sided." He turns to her, pushing her back hard against the rough brickwork. A small yelp of pain sounds from her mouth as her skin connects.

"How do you know Stormy?" he yells at her.

"I don't know him," she cries back. "My cousin tied me in the basement. Stormy found me. I've no idea how he got there."

Good girl. It's only the truth that can save her.

As Gun slaps her around the face, he demands, "Tell me more."

She continues, "It was a coincidence. He was looking for a place to stay. He found me, rescued me. I owed him a debt. I let him crash at my house." Her eyes narrow as they land on me. "I thought he liked me, obviously not. He was using me."

"Of course he was. I'll punish him, shall I?" Without giving her a chance to respond, Gun lets her go. As she stumbles trying to regain her balance, he takes out a knife and comes over to me. A flash of a blade and the knife descends sending more burning agony through me.

"Why did you choose her house?"

"I was riding past. It looked deserted." I gasp out, trying to force the pain down to a place I can keep it buried.

"I don't fuckin' believe you," Gun spits out. He rakes his hands through his hair, and I can almost read his thoughts. He won't believe me, but he's got nothing to go on. Even if I'm right and it's Pip he's after, he can't know my connection to him. Satan's Devils don't keep employment records, or not those which can be hacked into. Thank Christ he's into women and not men. If he got me naked, he'd see the tattoo on my back.

Cat's crying loudly, tears rolling down her face, snot coming out of her nose. The sight guts me, but I can't react, can't tell her I'm not worth her tears, and while they're beating on me, they're not hurting her. If that's my only win, I'll take it.

Gun starts on me himself. Maybe my head's already weakened, or perhaps it was a lucky shot, but my world soon goes black.

I wake, coming back to myself with a jolt. The first thing I notice is I'm not alone. Cat's here, naked, purpling on her skins shows her body already starting to bruise. She can't come to me, she's tied fast to another chair, and I can't go to her.

She's still weeping, or maybe she's started again.

"Cat?" I say, quietly. "Cat, you okay?"

Her answer is to sob harder, and my gut rolls. *Have they dared...?*

She struggles in vain against her bindings.

I want nothing more than to put my arms around her, to tell her that whatever's happened it doesn't matter. She's mine. I love her. But I'd left it too long to make my escape, my broken body won't cooperate. Once again, I've fucked up.

If I had gotten free earlier, I'd now have a bullet in the head. At least this way, I can talk to her.

"Cat, babe. Cat, look at me."

"They… they…" She can't put it into words.

Goddamnit, they've raped her.

"They're dead," I tell her. Then realise exacting revenge won't put her back to rights. "Cat, sweetheart, what they did…" But how can I tell her it's going to be alright?

I want to go to her, hold her, wrap her in my arms and tell her it doesn't matter to me. But I can't and even if I could, words would be unable to help.

She shudders, leans forward and is violently sick, retching until there's nothing more she can bring up.

"We'll get out of here, Cat. They'll never touch you again." I've just got to work out how to achieve my aim.

She turns to me, her eyes wide, horror written all over her face. "They didn't touch me."

They didn't?

Short-lived relief shoots through me. They might not yet, but they will. I'd seen the gleam in their eyes, the blatant approval of her womanly form. They'll be unable to resist her, just like me. The difference will be they won't treat her with the reverence and respect she deserves.

They did something though. My brow furrows. Her reaction, the way she was sick, I hope all they did was make threats toward me. I can take anything as long as she's safe.

"What did they say, Cat?" When she's slow to respond, I repeat with a growl to my voice, "What did Gun tell you?"

Her face turns to meet mine. There's no animation at all in her normally sparkling green eyes. From somewhere she seems to gather the strength to tell me. "They made me stand against a wall and…" she swallows hard, "photographed me. They were fucking joking about finding a buyer for me. Someone who doesn't mind a bit of extra weight."

A buyer? Fuck no. If that's their plan, they're not getting away with it. "That's not going to happen, Cat. I promise you." I'd willingly give up my life before they sell her as a fucking sex slave, which is clearly the implication.

I'm at a disadvantage. Fuck, I should have taken my chance before when most of my body still worked. *Have I got something to trade? Information to give to Gun?*

Betray my club?

My conscience pricks. Cat's worth the world to me, but can I balance her against honourable women and men? I can be clever, give Gun something. If, that is, I've anything he wants. *Give up Pip?*

Pip offered to sacrifice himself to save Swift. *He'd understand.*

I'll do anything. "I'm going to get you out of here, Cat." Even if it means giving up myself, and one of the men I respect most in the world.

My determined tone gets through to her. Her face rises and her eyes land on me, then she shakes her head. Her words are both mocking and sad. "You're hurt, Stormy." Fuck, her eyes are full of sympathy as she tells me the truth.

I'm hurt, badly, I know, and there's already far too much blood on the floor. But if there's a way that's humanely possible, I'll get us both out of this. Cat doesn't deserve this to happen to her.

Day turns to night, night turns to day. We sit, each restrained in our separate chairs. Cat drops off into an uneasy sleep, jerking awake quickly. I want to tell her I love her, tell her I'd go to the ends of the earth, deep into the depths of Hell itself to save her, but I don't want to give too much away. The camera's still on us, and I won't give Gun more ammunition. Putting us together was clearly a ploy, hoping we'd let something slip. Whatever I've got to use, I will. But it will be in my time, and when it's best to save her.

The next morning they return.

When Gun releases her, she drops to the floor. "Get up."

"Please, no."

We've got time, haven't we? They won't move her until they've got the truth out of me. Let her go, I scream inwardly.

Gun sighs, giving off a fake vibe he really doesn't want to do what he's about to instruct. "Hit him again."

It makes Cat cry out immediately. "No, I'll come!"

Don't. I'll take anything if it keeps you safe.

"Cat. No!" I try to scream, but it comes out more as a grunt.

It's too late for both of us. Meekly and stiffly, she drags herself to her feet and walks out without one look my way.

If her intention was to save me from further punishment, it doesn't work. As Cat is led out and I'm wondering whether I'll ever see her in this life again, Gun stays behind. He uses his fists, the baseball bat and his knife. I'm more dead than alive, but still conscious as he intended when at last he steps back.

"I'm going to take a little trip with your woman. When I get back, we'll finish this."

"Don't do this, Gun." Somehow I get the strength to push out the words. "This isn't you. You're a SEAL."

He shakes his head. "You never knew me at all, did you? Don't worry, I'm not letting you die. Yet. We've still got to have a conversation. And you will talk. You know as well as I do what I can use to encourage you."

He won't. I can withstand any torture.

But it's a promise for the future. Now the baseball bat comes into play again.

The world goes dark.

25
____

*S*wift…

I sit back on the couch, one hand holding tight to Road's while the other gently strokes App. It's good to be home and to have my man back with me.

He'd returned earlier than I, me only two hours ago. The time since, we have spent wrapped in each other's arms. I'm feeling content and satisfied now.

"Can't you two keep your hands off each other?" Bolt barks a laugh as he walks past. If I had a free hand, I'd show him my finger. Just one, I don't have the energy to move two right now. Yeah, my man's fucked me good. And I fucked him right back.

Road's already updated me that as expected, his mission went without a hitch. It was mine that had proved more interesting.

Taking a seat opposite, Cowboy asks, "So how was San Diego?"

But the prez interrupts, "If everyone's here we can move this into church. I was just waiting for Swift and Road to re-emerge. Bolt's ready and waiting for the debrief.

"Yeah, we had to wait until after you two fucked," the man in question calls out.

"Come on." Road moves forward putting his weight on his feet. I let him pull me up, but don't let go of his hand. I've missed him, and I'm going to make the most of being back.

Homecoming never felt so welcoming before I had him on my side. I only let him go when we move to different ends of the table.

Snatcher waits until everyone's seated before banging the gavel. "I know Swift and Road have business to attend to—"

"Think they've already done that, Prez." Thor barks a laugh.

Prez glares at his VP, turns back to the table and continues, "So this meeting will be quick. I'd just like to know how it went in San Diego."

Slipping into professional mode and sitting forward, I start, "You all know what Lost and his crew were up against, a particularly deviant pornography ring."

"Yeah, we did the leg work on that," Honor, sparing a nod toward Duty, interrupts. "Work is still progressing to bring it all down. Feds are grateful if bemused about where the information is coming from."

"Yeah, thanks for that." I give credit where credit's due.

"I was looking for more of your gut feel on how it was working with another club," Snatcher clarifies.

I purse my lips, trying to put my thoughts into words. "Better than I expected, to be honest. Oh, I got some shit at first due to the lack of a dick, but they overlooked that fast."

Bolt chuckles loudly. "I don't think they now see that as a drawback," he states, making me grin.

I raise my chin toward him, "I kind of thought we'd have to swoop in and take over their problems. I know you told us to work with them, Prez, but I'll be honest, I didn't think they'd have what it takes." I pause and glance around the table. "I have to say, I was wrong. I'd be happy to work with them in the future, and if the other chapters have half the calibre of men they have there, I'd not hesitate to do the same with them."

Bolt nods in confirmation. "San Diego has got some good brothers. I was impressed with their prez, and with Salem and Grumbler."

"Niran too," I add to Bolt's assessment.

"So it was a success?" Snatcher's mouth turns up. "May even help get Drummer off our backs. I know he's pleased that we got their problems sorted." His smile widens in satisfaction. "Speaking of our fearless leader, Drummer's passed a suggestion from San Diego on. They'd like to take advantage of Swift's knowledge and get her to set up a program for training enforcers in interrogation techniques."

Snorts go around the table, but I shrug.

Rascal sits forward, rolling a joint between his thumbs and fingers. When he finishes concentrating on his task, he raises his eyes to me ignoring the glare from Snatcher. He'll roll it here, but light it up later. "How do you feel about that, Swift? Sharing trade secrets?"

I shrug. "I don't mind. There's probably a lot I can teach them."

"Two way?" Piston asks. "Will you learn from them?"

I roll my eyes, thinking it's highly unlikely. Salem was a good brother, and I know Blade from Tucson has a lethal reputation. Getting together could have benefits for us all. Mace, from Colorado is to me an unknown, as is Twister from Vegas. But I doubt whether I could learn anything from them.

"Don't be too sure," Road remarks from his place down the table. "Ever scalped a man, Swift? Blade has."

"Yeah?" Leaning forward, my eyes land on my man. Now that sounds interesting and certainly isn't in my repertoire.

Road raises his chin. "Mouse taught him. It was quite an education." He chuckles. "He had two strung up. It was one way of getting the other man talking fast."

"You watched?"

"Sure. Turned my fuckin' stomach." Road doesn't seem the least put out to admit that he's squeamish.

So there might be something for me to learn. Maybe I was wrong to dismiss them so completely. Not one to miss an opportunity to tease my man, I wink at him. "Such a sensitive soul."

You love me, he mouths back.

"Fuck." Piston rolls his eyes dramatically.

"Could our cooperation get us off the hook with Drummer?" Pip asks seriously. "When he finds out Stormy's back and we've been hiding him?"

I raise my hand. "San Diego thinks we've got another week or so before we declare him out bad. I do think they accepted Stormy's fled out of the country or is dead in a ditch. Having met us, they don't think we're hiding him." I grimace. "I didn't like lying to them."

"I'm starting to think that was a mistake," Snatcher admits while rubbing at his temples. "From what Swift has said, we can trust them."

"But you didn't know whether he was alive or dead," Pip remarks. "Even now, we don't know if he'll ever regain consciousness."

"If he does, we can always say he just turned up," Honor puts in.

I'm about to say any lie would have to be well planned when my phone vibrates in my pocket. Unlike other chapters, since any of us could get a lead during church, we all keep our phones with us. I glance down at the screen and see it's a call from the doctor treating the man we're currently discussing.

"Speak of the devil." I turn to Snatcher. "It's the hospital."

"Answer."

I do, not expecting much. As I've been away 'on business' for a few days, I'm expecting the doctor's just checking in, or maybe telling me Stormy has lost the battle he's fighting. I place my finger to my lips, then put the phone on speaker.

"Doc?"

"Karen?"

"Yeah, you got her."

"I've got news. Jeremiah woke up. Only for a moment, but we've taken the ventilator out and he's breathing on his own. It's good news, and a sign that he might make it."

Snatcher points to the door.

"I'll come immediately. That's great, Doc."

A few more pleasantries and I end the call.

Pip starts to stand. "Mind company, Swift?"

Not at all. I nod at him. Road's the only one who I wouldn't want by my side. Not if I'm trying to kid the doctor I'm a halfway caring wife.

Pip and I waste no time. Leaving App with Road, I meet our ex-prez downstairs. He's already got the keys to one of the club's SUVs. I pass my cut into Igor's safekeeping as I pass the reception desk.

It's only a short drive to get to the hospital. Pip doesn't speak, and I don't try to make conversation. Inside, my thoughts are whirling. Will now be the time I get to find out what happened to Stormy? Of course, the main thing is discovering whether there's any danger heading toward the club. On a personal note, I'm hoping there's not. I can't wait for Road, App and myself to head back to our home. Staying at the club on lockdown as we've been for the past few weeks hasn't been terrible, but everyone knows our business, and seem to take special note of when we've been fucking. While it doesn't bother me them knowing, I've had enough of the leg pulling.

I can't ignore there's the issue that the club hid his re-emergence from Drummer, and I, by omission, lied to the San Diego club. If Stormy's betrayed us, maybe I should put him six feet under without anyone being the wiser. Outside of the club, no one would ever know what happened to him, and hopefully we'd retain our charter.

Pip parks and we both get out. A beep sounds as he locks the doors, and we walk to the building I've had a rest from the last few days. I take the same weary path as I've done many times previously.

The doctor appears to be waiting for me. He steps forward and opens the doors to ICU, allowing me and my companion inside. I start walking toward Stormy's room when he stops me.

"He hasn't said anything more. He woke up, said a few odd words, then became unconscious again. But he's no longer in a coma, it's a natural sleep. Maybe you can talk to him, and he'll wake again."

"What did he say?" Pip gets straight to the important stuff.

The doctor smiles. "I presume he's an animal lover. His words were, *I made my cat purr.*"

What? I exchange a look with Pip. As far as I know, Stormy doesn't have nor ever had any pets. *A cat person?* No, no way. I can't see that. Stormy might be up for pussy, but not of the meowing kind.

"Well, if he wakes, call a nurse, will you? He needs to be checked out." The doctor, oblivious to our non-verbal interaction, pauses and meets my eyes. "This is a good sign, Karen. I'm more optimistic at last. Now there could still be brain damage, and don't be surprised if he can't remember the crash. Often people have amnesia after a head injury such as his, if only for the last few minutes before they were injured."

Another pause, and a quirk of his lips. "Or injured for the last time in his case. Oh, and if you need to inform the cops, I'd like to assess him before they come in."

I'd tell him outright there'll be no cops involved if I could get away with it. Instead, I just smile.

Finally, at last, I'm allowed to enter my *husband's* room.

The changes are both subtle and enormous, the biggest one

being Stormy is breathing on his own now, steady breaths as indicated by the natural rise and fall of his chest. His face holds more colour, and his eyes twitch as though he's dreaming. His expression suggests his dreams are not pleasant.

I can't but hope that they're not. Stormy's disappearance could have lost the club its charter, his reappearance still might. If he's suffering, he deserves it.

As I watch, he twitches again, and his eyelids flutter. I move closer to him, pulling up the chair I've sat on so many times before.

"Stormy? Can you hear me?"

Pip clears his throat and nods toward the monitor. Stormy's heartbeat is increasing.

"Stormy," I hiss. "Wake the fuck up. You goddamn hear me, you motherfucker?"

Pip snorts.

It looks like he's fighting. His eyeballs are moving left to right behind his closed lids. His mouth opens, then shuts. His Adam's apple moves as though he's tentatively trying to swallow.

"Come on, man." Pip goes around the other side. "You've been sleeping too long. Wake up."

Stormy's chest starts to rise and fall more rapidly, his hand closest to me and not encased in a cast clenches. He appears to be fighting like crazy, and it seems natural to put my fingers around his.

"Come on, arsehole, wake up."

Pip catches my eye and his mouth quirks. I shrug. There was never any love lost between us. Stormy left an arse and I have no reason to suspect he's returned any different.

So fast it catches me out, his eyes open. He blinks rapidly as though trying to focus. He looks down at our linked hands, before squinting up at my face.

"Find Cat."

"Fuck the man. Trust him to wake up thinking of pussy."

I give a violent shake of my head toward Pip. That's not the impression I got. "Is Cat a person?"

"Cat…" Stormy's trying hard to get the words out.

"I'll call a nurse," Pip states, pressing the button. "His mouth is dry."

It obviously is, his lips are cracked, but Stormy doesn't stop focusing on me. "Cat," he tries again, blinking rapidly, "Catherine. Gun's got her."

26

tormy...

I can't move. Did Gun catch me again? Am I tied down?

I can't fucking get my limbs to work. I start to panic, in my head I'm thrashing, but everything stays still. My ears are full of a beep beeping, so monotonous I wish it would stop.

I've never felt so helpless in all my life. Maybe I'm dead. *I feel dead.*

No. Stop. Think. Open your eyes.

It's almost as much effort as running a marathon or emerging to the surface after a long dive with no air in my lungs. I concentrate, putting all I have into it, until suddenly, my eyes are open. My brain seems to function okay. *I'm in a hospital.*

My escape was a success. Swift and Pip are sitting by the bed. But that's no fucking use unless I can talk. Unable to work up saliva, I can't get words out of my too dry mouth.

I've got to save Cat. Now. Before she's been sold, before she disappears out of my life forever. *Cat. Hang on. I'm here. I'm coming for you...*

But first I've got to get out of this bed, and I'm too weak to do even that.

Machines go crazy as I struggle to speak. "Find Cat." I don't hear their response other than to realise they don't understand me. "Cat," I repeat. It's such a struggle just to do that.

A nurse rushes in. I allow him to check me over, only because he sponges my mouth, and gives me ice to suck, allowing me to work up some saliva. Enough, hopefully, that I'll be able to convince Pip to get me out of here.

At last the nurse seems satisfied with my vitals, and goes off, mumbling about fetching a doctor. Knowing I probably don't have much time before someone else comes to prod and poke me, I struggle to sit up.

I can't even do that.

Pip rolls his eyes. "You're half dead, Stormy. Take your time."

Time's not something I've got. My escape had worked, but how many hours ago was that? Cat needs help *now*. I rage inside, feeling so fucking weak and helpless. I swallow, swallow again, then with more determination form words and force them out of my mouth. "Cat. We've got to get to her. Get me my clothes and get me out of here." I try to raise my legs off the bed. This time one jerks, the other doesn't twitch.

"Whoa, you're not going anywhere." Swift places her hand on my left shoulder.

Now I've started, speech becomes easier. "You don't understand. Look, do what you want with me later. But Gun's got Cat, and he's going to sell her. We've got to find where he's taking her and stop him."

Pip and Swift exchange looks, and their expressions are neither what I'd like.

"Cat's an innocent. She's got caught up in something she shouldn't be part of. I don't fucking know what it's about. I've got to get out of here. I've got to save her. Kill me after, if that's what you want. I just need to find her. Gun took her earlier today…"

"Stormy!" Swift barks, her fingers biting into my shoulder. "Whoever this Cat is and wherever she is now, she wasn't taken today."

"She was!" I should fucking know. I was there.

Pip's face looms over me, bringing his features into view. His mouth twists when he tells me, "You've been in a coma for three fuckin' weeks."

"No," I refute. That can't be. No way. I'd know it. No way. Cat's only just been taken, there's time to stop them. There must be. "No."

I focus on sending the right instructions from my brain to my limbs. I have some success as Swift pins me to the bed. Making a concerted effort, I push myself up with my left arm, and immediately sway, feeling dizzy.

"Three weeks, Brother." It's the sympathy in Swift's eyes, the honesty in her voice, that lets me know I'm being told the truth.

My eyes leak, probably from weakness, but the roll of my gut is pure terror. "Three weeks?" I repeat.

"Who's Cat?" Pip asks.

But I have no time to answer. The doctor appears. He's a jovial man, or is now. Presumably he feels some success that his patient has woken up. After three fucking weeks, I suppose he's entitled.

"Welcome back, Mr Briggs. You caused us some worry. But you're on the mend now. I just need to go over some things with you—"

I cut him off. Any injuries I'll deal with myself when they make themselves known to me. I don't need him to catalogue them. "I want to discharge myself."

"I'm sorry, Mr Briggs. Or can I call you Jeremiah?" Without waiting for an answer to the question that makes my head spin, he continues, "As I've been telling your wife, even now you're back with us, you'll have a lot of recuperating to do before we can release you, and subsequently you'll more than likely be going to rehab."

My wife? Suddenly my heart leaps. *Cat's here?*

"Yes, I heard everything you said, Doc," Swift confirms from beside me. "You've explained everything to me."

Wait. What? Why is Swift talking about me? She's who he's calling my fucking wife? Fuck, I have died and now I'm in Hell. I must be.

"Yes, Karen. I know you understand. Now let's try and explain that to your husband."

She's using the first name that she hates? My head pounds as I try to make sense of everything.

One thing I know, I can't stay in this bed. I've got to get out and start searching for Cat. I don't care if it kills me. *Unless she's already dead.* In which case, I'll die with her—after I've dispatched Gun and his men to meet Satan.

Ignoring the doctor, I start pulling out the catheter in my arm, blood spurts staining the sheets.

"Mr Briggs!"

"I'm getting out of here."

"Doc," Pip says in a reasonable tone. "Can we have a moment alone with him?"

The doctor eyes the screens which are going crazy. When I pull the blood oxygen monitor off my finger, a single tone sounds. It's about right. Without Cat, I'm as good as dead.

"He's highly agitated. If you think you can calm him, I'll give you a few minutes. Otherwise, I'll need to sedate him." The doctor's smile has been completely wiped from his face. He looks flustered as though he's never had a man who's half dead argue with him before, or be prepared to totally ignore his expert advice.

When the door closes, Pip doesn't waste a moment. "Who's Cat?" he demands. "What is she to you?"

I don't hesitate. "I've claimed her. She's going to be my ol' lady."

Swift snorts. "Does she know?"

Though it hurts, I roll my head to the side so I can tell her straight to her face. "We were coming back. Together. Yes, she knows, Swift. She knows she's mine, and that, heaven help her, I'm hers."

"So this is fuckin' serious."

"You've got a fuckload of questions to answer." Swift glares at me and ignores the ex-prez.

Pip doesn't let her get away with it. "Swift," he says, sharply. "I can't argue with that, but whether or not Stormy's still club, the club would rescue a woman. It's what we do, you know that." He pauses and rubs a hand over his face. "Three fuckin' weeks. We have to know where to start."

"What are you proposing?" At least Swift now seems to be on board. Fuck knows, I'll be limited as to what I can do myself.

"I'm proposing I get a wheelchair and we bust him out of here."

I close my eyes and listen to them sorting the details out. At least Pip's on my side.

"He could die if he's not given proper treatment," Swift objects.

"I'll die if you leave me here." I snap my eyes open. "I'm begging you. Either you help me, or I'll crawl out of here by myself."

Pip's eyes land on my face. He stares intently, then abruptly stands. "He fucking would too. I'll go get the ball rolling. Oh, and I'll call Snatcher."

It takes time, of course it does. Every minute I suffer wondering where Cat is now and what she's going through. I don't let myself dwell on the possibility that I might never find her, or that she might not still be alive. Such would be the makings of a living nightmare.

Pip's exactly the right person to arrange my discharge. He knows how to speak to people in authority, and how to bow them to his will. Eventually the doctor washes his hands of me, glaring down as I ignore every piece of advice. I don't care if I risk death by leaving, Cat's more important to me than life itself. Sometime later, awkwardly, only able to use my left hand, I sign the form that releases the hospital from any responsibility should I keel over and die before I leave the parking lot. A likely outcome, in the doctor's view.

Armed with painkillers I have no intention of taking—I need to keep a clear head—I let Pip painfully assist me from the bed to the wheelchair. Still dressed in only a hospital gown, I'm taken down to the car park.

Every jolt, every bump, every movement is agony. Every hurt reminds me I'll go through anything for her.

Pip hadn't wasted time and had made good on his call to Snatcher. When we arrive at the clubhouse, a number of brothers are milling around. Seems they've all been called in and updated.

"Stormy." Snatcher greets me with just one word. He eyes the condition I've arrived in. "You discharged yourself and I'm making no allowances. I've convened church."

"Should he get some clothes on first?" Pip asks, eyeing my near-naked form. Sure, my ass is hanging out, or would be were it not for the chair, but fuck it, that's not important now.

"Can you dress yourself?" Prez challenges me.

I swallow my pride. "No. But I don't need...." *Clothes. I was going to say clothes.* Last time I saw Cat, she was naked. She had to cope, so can I. *Cat,* my mind screams. *For fuck's sake, Cat, hang on.*

"I got this." Fuck me, that's Bolt. If I had to have anyone, I would have expected a prospect would help me.

But it's Bolt who takes the handles of the appropriated wheelchair and rolls me into the elevator that I'm more than grateful for. I wouldn't be able to manage stairs. He's silent as we go to the upper floor where our rooms are located.

Fuck being helpless and in a wheelchair, I've no say in what happens to me. Knowing I need the club onside, I force down the anger that's rapidly coming to the surface, pushing it away and stating simply, "It didn't take long for everyone to get here."

"We've been on lockdown since you crashed into the clubhouse."

I crashed? What the fuck? I can't remember. "Did I do any damage?" I remember riding the bike then... Zilch.

"Wrote off that piece of crap you were riding. Okay now." He changes subject as he wheels me into my room using the master keycard he must have gotten from reception. "What are you going to wear?" He's asking himself as much as me.

With the cast on my leg, pants are beyond me, but Bolt pulls out a pair of workout shorts loose enough to pull over it.

"You've got a nice scar," he observes, helping me get my cast-covered arm into a t-shirt with surprising dexterity for a one-handed man—though his expensive prothesis seems just as good as a real one.

As I look down, I can see the amount of time that must have passed since Gun had stabbed me. The stitches have already been removed from the wound Gun had sliced into my stomach. *Three weeks,* I remember with a sharp pang of terror. Anything could have happened to her.

The roadmap of my body bears witness to how much punishment my body must have taken. I'm surprised I'm alive.

"You died twice," he remarks, coming to the front and staring down at me. I must have spoken my thoughts aloud. "Somehow they found your heart and managed to kickstart it beating."

Suddenly, before I go back to the first floor, I have to say something. "I was an ass, Bolt. And I'm sorry."

"Words are just words." He dismisses my comment—his

phrasing, his lack of the affectionate *brother*—showing I've a long way to go and that I'm only being tolerated because of my woman. I might never again have a place in this club, but that's the least of my worries. If I don't have Cat, I'll care about nothing. If I have her, that's all I need.

Clothed, I start to feel more like myself, and better able to mentally prepare as Bolt wastes no time wheeling me back to the elevator. My working hand rubs my temples. Now I've got to beg for help. The help from men I've shown I don't trust.

I'm not stupid. While I wish it was otherwise, I'm out of action, dependent on others to find the woman I love. As we near church, I tell myself I'll beg and grovel if I have to. Cat's the most important thing in my world. Nothing else makes sense if I don't have her.

I take a deep breath as I enter. Even Grinch, Mystic and Goofy are here, I notice, as Bolt wheels me to the space they've cleared. While eyeing the men, and Swift, all watching me silently, I realise there's no welcome here. No 'good to see yous' and not even a 'where the fuck have you been'?

When everyone's seated, Snatcher bangs the gavel, but instead of bringing it down, he points it at me. "Don't get used to sitting there." He lays the ground rules immediately. "You've no rights as a member."

My head is pounding. Sitting, rather than being stretched out horizontal for the last three weeks, or so I've been told, is fucking with my equilibrium. I push the weakness down, commenting only, "That's fair."

Piston whistles through his teeth and raises his eyebrow. A few murmurs go around, but for the most part, they all stare at me.

"Start speaking," Snatcher demands.

"Cat…"

"No. Not there. Start with why you ran, and why you didn't come back."

"Leaving your fuckin' cut," Preacher snarls. "Big disrespect."

He's spoken so loudly the words hit my aching head like a physical blow, but I refrain from rubbing at the pain. It's no time to show weakness. I don't want to waste time on the background, "That's not important. Finding Cat is."

Snatcher snarls, "That's for me to decide. Who she is, how you met her, is all part of the background we need to begin to track her down. You want us to find her? Start from the beginning. Now." The last word is barked, his expression is relentless.

I've no choice, so I summon up words to put my case succinctly.

"I left in a rage, on impulse. I rode, I didn't care where. I just wanted to put distance between us. At first I hated the club, but I soon calmed down. I knew I'd fucked up pretty quickly, and I wanted to come back home."

"Should have done just that," Thor remarks. "You scared of a fuckin' beatdown?"

My automatic reaction is to shake my head, but that only sends agony shooting through me. "I'm not scared. Not then, not now. I know that's coming." Whether they let me stay or kick me out, they'll do their worst.

"Yeah, you've got that coming. Once you've healed," Rascal promises, flexing his fingers as though relishing the prospect.

Expecting that, I ignore him. "I knew I disrespected the club. I wanted to come back but needed to return with something. Anything that would make amends. Remember the loose end with Kincaid's case, the woman? Well, I decided to track her down."

"The Airbnb records were fake," Honor states.

"Yeah, well, I might have modified those."

Snatcher bangs the table far too loudly. "You fuckin' what?" He's as angry as I've ever seen him. "And that was helping us, how?"

I breathe deep, not certain if I'm going to be able to get

through this without passing out. My hand shakes as I reach for the bottle of water in front of me. Bolt takes it from me, unscrewing the top before passing it back. When I've wet my still dry mouth, I get into the details. Quickly I tell them all about Tiny, and the state in which I'd found his cousin.

"And this is your Cat? So, the loose end led nowhere."

"She'd have died if I hadn't found her," I confirm. "Didn't think she needed you lot running after her. She was in a state." I raise my eyes. "Rats stole her food, almost made a meal of her."

"That would fuck with your mind." Preacher shudders.

My moveable shoulder shrugs. "I fixed her, got her well, and began to fix myself."

Swift's staring at me. "You needed fixing?"

Knowing I'm going to expose myself and also knowing I've no choice if I want them to help me find Cat, I'm in no state to rush anywhere and do anything, and the fog in my brain suggests I won't be much good digging for information. I'll probably miss more than I find, I need to bare my soul. So I do.

By the time I finish my story, bringing it up to date with Gun beating the fuck out of me, my suspicions about him and Kincaid, right up to Cat being taken to apparently be sold, I realise no one's spoken nor interrupted me.

"How did you get free?" Pip asks.

I'm tired, fighting to keep my eyes open. My leg and arm aches, my stomach is sore. My broken ribs throb, and I feel nauseous. But I keep going.

I eye Swift. "I used the chair."

"Fuck yes. I wondered when you were going to say that. Why didn't you earlier when you were still more than just half alive?"

"I thought I could get out of it using words. Gun had been a SEAL." I shrug as if that would explain it, and carry on, speaking. I visualise the scene.

Before he left me, Gun had stabbed me, dislocated my knees and my shoulder, and I had more than a couple of broken ribs, a broken nose, and a swollen jaw. Blood dripped on the floor around me. I could barely see, my ears were ringing.

I was dying. Or would be soon.

The one man he'd left to guard me taunted me by telling me a buyer had emerged for the 'fat girl' as he referred to Cat. That, above all else, made me see red. She's not fat, but after decent food for the last couple of months, she is deliciously curvy.

Without knowing whether it would work, I launched myself at him, head butting him first then immediately rolling and smashing the chair and ... fuck yeah... a shattered piece of wood is in my bound hands. Mentally photographing his position, in one fluid movement I turn, leaning forward and raising my tied wrists to pierce his neck. Then, I'd collapsed.

When I came to, I didn't know how much time remained until Gun returned. I managed to get my victim's knife, prop it between my ankles and slice through the bindings holding my wrists together, once that was completed, it was child's play to free my feet.

I crawled around that house. I tore sheets into bandages. Then...

I pause and raise my chin at Road. "I've watched you, Bro..." I correct myself, "Road. I popped my shoulder back first, I remembered the way I'd seen you put your knee back in. Fuck it's painful, and I had to do it twice. But I managed it. Next I strapped my knees up."

"Bad enough with one," Road acknowledges, his voice tinged with respect.

My wrist was broken, but if I could find a car, I could drive with one hand. As luck would have it, the only available vehicle had been a bike, not a model I'd have chosen, but transport at least.

"I immobilised my wrist and strapped my hand to the throttle."

Several heads shake and more than one pair of eyes look at me in admiration.

"I just knew I couldn't fail."

"Where the fuck were you?" My eyes go to Grinch and answer his question.

"I had no fucking idea. Would you believe the asshole's phone had smashed when I attacked him, and there was no form of communication in the house? No laptop, no nothing. So it was down to me to escape. At first, I just rode. When I joined a highway, I began to see signs. I was somewhere north of Flagstaff. All I did was focus on coming home."

"You made it," Snatcher says. "Fuck knows how, but you made it."

My eyes close. Once again, I feel water leaking from them. My head swims and I grow dizzy. It must be the effort of talking, of fighting the pain, but I fear I'm going to faint. *Keep it together. Cat's depending on you.*

Weakness? Pure fucking horror? All of a sudden I'm done as I wail, "And I spent three weeks in the hospital when Cat needed me. I failed you, I failed myself, and worst of all, I failed her."

I feel my head dropping.

27

*S*wift...

Stormy's passed out with his head resting on the table. Fuck, but I don't know how he made it so long. I'd even had a bet with Pip he wouldn't be able to make it through church, but fuck it, he did.

Snatcher's calling in Brute and Igor and instructing them to get Stormy back up to his room and into his bed and once he's there, to summon our on call doctor.

No one says much until the door closes behind the prospects and the wheelchair.

"Fuck." Snatcher smooths his hands down his cheeks. He takes a moment, then looks back up. "I've got three takeaways from that. First, we've got to find Stormy's woman. Next we find Gun and see whether Stormy's right and whether he was the mastermind behind the kidnap of Swift, and third, we decide what the fuck we do about Stormy."

Pip raises his hand. "I can only think it goes back to what happened when I offered a place in the Satan's Devils MC to Stormy."

Prez directs a hard stare down the table at his predecessor. "I suspect there were things you weren't telling me at the time, Pip. I was your good little VP who nodded in all the right places. Let's go back a step, remind me how you knew about Stormy. He was horrified when he found out what he was being invited into. The approach came from you."

"It did, didn't it?" Pip half smiles. "He wanted to run when he found out we were an MC." Seeing Snatcher's unrelenting gaze, he hurriedly continues. "I've got friends and contacts all over the military, one of them Admiral Hillier. I first heard about Stormy before he was kicked out. The Admiral didn't like the way the wind was blowing, and he ran the situation past me. I kind of got involved behind the scenes, and, well, it's down to me that Smythe was removed from the line of fire. He was offered a desk job in the US, even before Stormy's Admiral's Mast."

"And this Gun had been part of Smythe's team at the time?" Thor asks, picking at a tooth.

"He would have been, yeah. He served with Stormy."

"Do you think this could go up the chain? That Gun was working for someone?"

Pip sighs. "Undoubtably. Gun's not got resources to do this himself, or a reason, I've never come across him. I dismissed Smythe as an incompetent ass, now it seems I'll have to dig deeper. Perhaps I was wrong."

Road's eyes have been flitting between whoever's talking. I notice his face becoming set. It doesn't surprise me when he asks, "How are we going to find the woman? Isn't that our priority?"

"It is," Snatcher agrees. "But finding Gun, and who if anyone is behind him, could be the key."

Honor's frowning. He leans in and whispers to Duty, who nods. "Stormy said her photos were taken and obviously advertised to find a buyer. We're volunteering to try to tackle that angle first."

"And I'll look for Jeffrey Morgan, or Gun as he calls himself," Bolt offers. "Between us we should come up with something."

"Want someone to go try and find the place where he held Stormy?" Goofy asks.

"Nah. He'll know Stormy's gone and will think the place has been compromised," Thor dismisses the idea.

"I'll help wherever I'm needed," I put in.

Snatcher's been following the discussion closely. Again his eyes stare straight ahead. "Pip, you going to start with your contacts?"

"Sure, Prez. There seems to be a link between what happen to get Stormy kicked out of the SEALs, and Kincaid's attempt to get me. I'll start asking questions."

Snatcher raises and dips his head, then frowns. "I think it's time I put a call into Drummer." No one disagrees, but I doubt anyone envies him.

When he picks up the gavel to end the meeting, Mystic raises his hand. "I'll get the plane ready and fuelled, and Prez, it goes without saying. Whatever you want us to do," he glances one side to Grinch, then at his other to Goofy, "We'll be there."

Grinch butts in. "What are we going to do about Stormy?"

"Find his woman," I say sharply. "Take things from there."

Snatcher raises his chin toward me approvingly. "The woman comes first as always." When Bolt snorts he glares at him, and without missing a beat continues, "Just like in every mission. We concentrate on the victim." This time he does bang the gavel. "We've got work to do. Let's fuckin' get to it."

"Road?" I ask as he passes by my chair. "Could you check in on Stormy? See that he's okay?" I know it's a big ask. There was never any love lost between them, nor to be honest, between Stormy and me. But I'd picked up that Cat was a woman about whom he really cared. Maybe it's because I know how much loving Road has changed me, that I'm now feeling some sympathy toward the man.

"Sure." Without me saying a word, Road seems to under-stand. Briefly his hand cups my cheek. "Loving a woman can change a man."

And a woman. I'm not weaker by admitting how much Road means to me. It gives me hope that a new improved Stormy has come home—as long as we find his woman unharmed. If we don't, who knows what version of the ex-SEAL we'll end up with.

I go to the comms room, sit myself in front of my laptop and two monitors. Checking with Duty and Honor, I start delving into the horrors hidden in the depths of the internet ordinary people never venture into.

Some of our work is distressing. While Bolt and I had been out in the field in San Diego, Honor, Duty and Piston had spent their time watching paedophiles abusing children in order to track the users and photographers down. I've a strong stomach, but even mine often turns at some of the things we have to see.

Bolt shoots me the photo from Catherine Beeswick's driver's licence. I check where the others are searching, and start putting some feelers out of my own.

It's easy to lose track of time when you're delving into the dark web. One thread you're following may start to unravel, and you commence another with more expectation. I lose all sense of everything as I click my mouse and my fingers tap out commands.

"Hey." A voice sounds in my ear, and a familiar hand rests on my shoulder. Swinging around, I find Road standing there. He nods at the man I'd asked him to look after.

Stormy's precariously balanced on a stick I recognise, it's an old one of Road's that he's no longer got need for. Even with it Stormy seems unstable, his face pinched and white.

"Couldn't keep him locked down," Road tells me, loud enough for my companions to hear and for Stormy to shrug almost sheepishly.

"You should be resting," Honor tells him. "You aren't any help here. Road, what the hell are you thinking bringing him down?"

Road glares over the desk. "I was going crazy when Swift got taken. He needs to know what's going on."

"We're not exactly sitting with our thumbs up our asses." Duty glares at Stormy.

Instead of belligerence that I half expect, Stormy's voice holds more than a hint of pleading and a heap of distress. "I need to find her. I know there's not much I can do. But fuck, it's down to me Gun took her."

"How do you figure that?" I ask. "He went to visit her. He wasn't looking for you."

"Without me there, Gun would have probably questioned her, found out what I had about Tiny. That she'd booked the Airbnb but had no other involvement. That he took her was because of his suspicions about me, and to taunt me. I…" He swallows, and when he sways, Road grabs a spare chair and encourages him to take the weight off his one leg doing all the work. "I tried to deny she meant anything to me, but he didn't buy it."

It makes sense. "That you were there with her made her a person of interest. And there are not many men who'd stand by and let a woman be hurt. I've played poker with you Stormy, I doubt you gave anything away and made matters worse."

Honor eyes are narrowed and focused on Stormy. "You didn't fuck up and make Gun do anything he hadn't already planned, I'm certain of that, Storm. But Gun clearly didn't like you being there which is why Pip's trying to track back and find out how Gun could be involved, and whether that goes back to Afghanistan. Maybe you can help more by being his sounding board and filling in any gaps Pip's found?"

It's a good idea, logical. But Stormy doesn't seem impressed. "I, er, I want to be here. Trying to find her. My head is fucked, there are probably details I can't remember or use to put two and two together. Whether it's because of my injuries or that I'm so fuckin' scared of what's happening to her. I can't think straight to help, but I trust you." His eyes go to Honor, continue to Duty, then land on Bolt, Piston and finally myself. "I trust you. I know you'll move heaven and earth to get her back."

He trusts us. Words I didn't expect to come out of his mouth.

We'll find her if it's humanely possible, and if she's in the country. If she's already south of the border that will make our lives more difficult. Especially considering the time she's been missing. But I don't mention that. It wasn't Stormy's fault he'd stayed in a coma, though I'm certain he'll blame himself for being unconscious.

Honor sits back, putting his hands behind his head. "Seeing as you're here, tell me about Cat. Anything might help us to identify the person who has her."

It's not beyond how we normally work. Stormy places his left hand on the table and furrows his brow. "She's a natural redhead, gorgeous auburn hair and startling green eyes. She's freckled, pure white complexion with rosy cheeks."

"Her photograph shows that, Stormy, but what's she actually like? Is she sexually expressive, or shy? What kind of person would she appeal to?"

There's a flare in Stormy's eyes as if the question is intrusive, but soon the light dies. "She's shy. She's not had many sexual partners. She'd stand up for herself, but wouldn't be aggressive. She's..." he shrugs again, and adds inadequately, "she's nice. Normal. The girl-next-door type. She's the kind to give an asshole like me a chance."

It makes me wonder why they clicked. If I'd thought about it, I'd have imagined a person for Stormy would be active sexually, stunningly attractive, and probably more along a male line of himself. That he's fallen for someone who sounds his opposite is surprising. But maybe that's why it's worked. Maybe he needed normal.

For a moment the only sound is the clicking of keys as everyone gets back to work. Having been lying on my feet, App stands and repositions himself, trying to get comfortable.

"Who's that?" Stormy asks, as the movement catches his eye.

"Oh, it's App, my hearing dog."

I thought he'd scowl, see it as a weakness, but he surprises me when he nods responds with just one word.

"Cool."

"I've got a location for Gun," Bolt interjects suddenly, and all eyes go to him. "It's a place buried under several aliases, but I'm pretty certain it's the Jeffrey Morgan we're looking for.

"Local?" Honor asks, optimistically.

Bolt shakes his head. "Halfway between Flagstaff and Phoenix. About five hours riding from here."

Which would at least tally with the area where Stormy escaped from.

"Can we get our Tucson brothers to check it out?" They'd be much closer, and I have to say, after seeing how San Diego could handle themselves I'm fairly certain we could trust them to get the job done. Of course, if Drummer, Wraith, Blade or Peg got involved I wouldn't have any doubts.

"I'll go speak to Snatcher." Bolt stands.

"I'm coming with you." Stormy tries to push himself up but he hasn't got a handle on using the stick yet and if Road hadn't been there to catch him, he'd have crashed to the floor.

I'm surprised he's managing as well as he can, it must be his desire to see his woman safe that keeps him defying physical laws. He can't go on like this. I decide to take charge. Standing I round on him. "You sit yourself the fuck back down, or I'll take you back to the hospital myself and have you chained to the bloody bed. You're fucking lucky we're letting you sit in on this.

Just be honest, man. You can't even stand let alone ride a bike. This is one time you need to trust us to have your back."

It's like watching a tyre deflating as all the fight goes out of him. "I know," he says, and fuck me, but there are tears in his eyes.

Going over, I crouch down beside him and take his good hand in mine, just like I had for the past three weeks when I'd been with him in the hospital. "We've got this. We'll find her."

Road rests his hand on my shoulder. "You can depend on us," he tells him firmly. "It's what we do. You know that." He waves to indicate Honor and Bolt, and then down at me. "You've got the best in the business at your back."

The door opens and in walks Cowboy. He's carrying a tray laden with sandwiches, BLT if I'm not mistaken. He leaves them in the middle of the table. His eyes soften as they land on Stormy, he knows what it's like to lose someone close, and in his case, he's never recovered.

"Pip's going to need to talk to you," he tells him. "He's found out some shit that might have started all this."

"Pip the target?" Stormy asks.

Cowboy raises his chin. "Could be. Kincaid wanting revenge for personal reasons was one thing. Kincaid being used to get close to Pip to deliver him to someone else is another. That's Pip's thinking right now. He just doesn't know how the pieces fit together."

Road's phone suddenly appears in his hand. He reads a text, then touches Stormy's uninjured arm. "Snatcher wants to talk to you." Stretching out his hand he helps Stormy to his feet and waits until he's balanced. "I'll come with you to his office just so you don't fall the fuck down."

28

―――

$\mathcal{S}$tormy…

Feeling as weak as a kitten I accept Road's help. He opens the door to Snatcher's office, with a steadying hand on my arm. When I'm settled in a chair, he props the stick against the desk, and leaves with just one instruction.

"Give me a shout when you need to go anywhere."

His offer surprises me. *Before* he'd never have given me the time of day. I suppose his sympathy is because he knows what it's like to cope with injuries such as mine. I hadn't been that way with him, in fact I'd dismissed him as a waste of space. *Cat would be disappointed in me.* She might not be here, but she's taken up residence in my mind.

Belatedly I notice the phone sitting face up on the middle of the desk, but my attention is drawn to it when Snatcher speaks, not to me, but into the device.

"Stormy is with me now, Drummer."

Fuck. I'd hoped we'd find Cat and I'd get myself straight with Utah before having to talk to the mother chapter prez, or at least be feeling stronger. I'd expected Snatcher would ask for help in checking the Arizona address on the excuse we were tracking down an anonymous girl. But he's clearly come clean to Drummer.

"So the lost sheep has returned. I hear you're something of a miracle," Drummer remarks drily. "And that you've been hiding out with a girl." He chuckles softly. "There's always a fuckin' woman at the bottom of it."

"I shouldn't have left, Drummer." I dive straight in. "But I've been running on anger for many years now. It was when I met Cat and stopped for a moment, things became clearer."

"I get that," Drummer says. "First things first, we find your girl. You *were* a brother even if you're not one now, and family matters. I might have issues with you Stormy, shit that needs to be resolved, but I lost Sam once so I know how you feel. I've got Blade, Peg, Rock and Marvel heading north as we speak. It's only a ninety minute ride from us, so they should have something soon. Mouse is contacting Honor to see if there's anything he can do from our side."

Even if I had the strength to argue there's nothing I can object to. I might not be able to be there myself, but I've met Peg, the sergeant-at-arms and Blade, Tucson's enforcer and despite not showing it at the time, have a lot of respect for them.

"If Gun's not there, will you search the house? There may be paperwork, anything."

"Already asked my boys to do that," Drummer confirms, his tone making me suspect if I could see him he'd be rolling his eyes.

"Drummer, I…"

"As I said. We'll concentrate on finding your woman, anything else comes after that. I heard that you were unexpectedly delayed in reporting her missing. I'm sorry to hear about that."

Last time I'd seen Drummer he was spitting nails at me. Again, my eyes feel watery which must have something to do with me being so weak. Cat deserves their help, I don't deserve anything myself. As for his reference to me staying unconscious for three weeks, well I can't take pleasure in that. If Cat's not found alive, I would prefer that I'd died.

"I'll keep in touch, Snatcher. And let you know what Blade and the boys find." Drummer ends the call without uttering goodbye.

Snatcher eyes me for a moment. There's something in his expression that has me asking, "What?"

His mouth quirks. "The doctor warned Swift you might have brain damage. Seems like you have. You've come back with a personality transplant. I'm just wondering whether it will last."

I don't take offence. It's probably something that in his position, I would also query. "It's all Cat."

His brow furrows but he says nothing further. I guess he's wondering whether I'll revert to my previous form if we're unable to find her. I don't offer my thoughts, I think I'll be worse.

"Then we better find this woman of yours. Oh, Pip wanted to see you."

I reach for the stick, but it falls over. My eyes close and I count to ten, seems my impatience is hiding and not completely gone.

With a sigh, Snatcher gets up and comes around the desk. "Let me help."

I want to tell him I'm perfectly capable of getting up myself —if I can't, how am I going to rescue Cat when we get word of where she is? But I know I'm unable to. I mutter something like thank you when he hands me my stick and helps me to stand. But almost fall, forgetting I cannot put weight on my broken leg.

Damn it! I'm going to have to call Road for help. I refused to get back in the wheelchair earlier, preferring to get around by myself, but hell, I've got to swallow my pride and admit my body is still broken, though not beyond repair. I've just got to give myself time. *Time Cat hasn't got.*

"Let's get you to Pip," Snatcher says in a matter-of-fact voice.

He's helping me himself?

Pushing down my misplaced pride, I let him take my weight as we exit his office and move to the smaller one Pip had been assigned when he gave up his position to Snatcher.

Entering, Pip stands and comes to help me into a chair. Fuck, how I hate being so useless.

He raises his chin toward Snatcher. Once the prez has closed the door, addresses me. "You want anything, Stormy? Water?"

"Water, please."

He gets a bottle from the fridge, twists off the top and puts it on the desk in front of me. Then without asking questions about my health as he probably knows all he'd hear is a lie, he gets straight down to business.

I don't want to be here. I want to be out looking for Cat. Fuck knows, if Pip wants to pick my brain I've got nothing for him. All I can think of is finding the woman I love, hoping against hope I won't be too late. But the damage that Gun had done was more than enough to ensure that I was going nowhere.

Instead my nightmare had become my life. I'm depending on others to do what I should be doing myself.

The only difference being, is deep down I trust them. That's why I came back, that's why I apparently defied physical laws to do the impossible and ride a bike. Because there's only one team I need at my back, the Satan's Devils MC.

Why have I changed? It's not down to me, it's down to Cat. It all comes back to that one revelation of hers which I haven't been able to get out of my head. That I wasn't solely responsible for Pooh's death.

He could have persuaded me to leave the kids there. Perhaps he'd been the only man who could have done. But he'd not said a word.

"You said Gun didn't know you were part of the MC, hence there's no connection between he and I in your mind. So I've been thinking about why Gun was so interested in coming across you. The only link is Afghanistan, and what happened there," Pip says, "I'm presuming you had no contact with him since?" He notes the shake of my head, retakes his seat behind the desk, and rubs his temples thoughtfully. "You don't know this, but when I first learned about your case, I pulled strings and got Smythe chained behind his desk."

He did? No, I didn't know that. My brow furrows.

He's wrong, the timing doesn't fit. "He did a final tour after."

"I said *when I learned about your case*. That was before you and I ever met. When Hillier gave me the details, it was obvious Smythe was out of his depth. Sure, he had to do one more tour to finish up, but he knew then he would be Stateside when he returned."

"You think Smythe knows you were involved? You think he wants revenge?" I try to focus my thoughts. "He got a fuckin' promotion after Pooh died. He'd more likely thank you. I got discharged, he got made up, and a cushy desk job."

"Maybe." Pip doesn't disagree. "But I'm leaving no stone unturned. I wanted to ask you what you made of this." He turns his laptop toward me.

I wince, it's playing footage of Nazia's initial interrogation just after she tried to blow herself, and our troops up. With my head filled of Cat, at first I don't take it in, only idly paying scant attention as she replies in non-answers, not willing to explain her behaviour, or who she was working for.

My interest is caught. I pull the laptop toward me, and tap awkwardly at the keys with my left hand, playing back the last segment and watching it again. Pip passes me some notes, I check them, then watch a final time.

"You caught it, huh?"

My eyes rise to Pip's. I play the last few seconds again. "The transcript is wrong," I tell him.

"Yeah. I don't speak Dari, so I had the tape interpreted for myself."

I'd been told her words were, "I did it for Stormy," but unless my language skills have fled with those blows to the head, what she's actually saying is different. Not just the words, but the intonation. As far as I can make out, she's just said, "They made me do it for Stormy."

"Who's they?"

"I thought you'd pick up on that." Pip rubs his face again. "The reports say the military police were preparing to interrogate her again. What you just watched was the first of a series, and was more a case of asking the first questions, delving deeper after they considered her answers. That question would probably have been next, but someone got to her before they had a chance. The word was she killed herself because she'd failed, but the hit was clumsy, rushed. There was an attempt to cover it up, but it didn't quite work."

"But the MPs must have investigated."

"They did. But they were distracted by another incident, during which there was a fuck up. Her body was moved, the cell scrubbed clean, and lo-and-behold, surveillance tapes corrupted."

"Who was the last to see her?"

"Now that's where it gets interesting, particularly with what we now know. Your *friend*, Gun, had another prisoner located nearby. He was questioning him at the time."

I wince as I try to sit straighter. *Fuck these broken ribs of mine.* "Any proof he visited her?"

"None," Pip admits.

Dots, starting to form a pattern. But they're more like particles of dust I'm trying to catch in my hand.

"There's more," Pip says. "Nazia was strip searched." That's not unusual. Fuck, she'd been wearing a suicide bomb, no one would trust her. "During which," Pip continues, "it was noticed her body had been subjected to intensive abuse. Burns, scalds, some old, some healing. Evidence of previous broken bones. Her face was unmarked, but the rest of her had been brutalised."

Poor, poor girl. She obviously hadn't agreed to her task easily.

Suddenly Pip sits forward. "What if she agreed to doing what she did with the intention of speaking to you?"

"Me?" My head's working slowly. "But I'd long since been discharged."

Pip nods. "You rescued her and her sister. Saved them. What if you were the only man on the base who she could trust? She wouldn't have known you'd been discharged, how could she?"

"She didn't detonate the device," I muse out loud.

"Exactly. And from the reports I've read, she was acting suspiciously as though she wanted to get caught. Of course, the men stopping her all received commendations for their vigilance, but I'd place bets that if it had been her intention, she'd have carried out her task."

"If she'd been so abused, death might have come easy." But instead, if Pip's right, she'd let herself be caught. *To get to talk to me?* My brain starts to kick into gear. "Why the insurgents wanted to upset the uneasy peace has always confused me. The locals were trained and ready to take over for themselves. Our troops were withdrawing. These incidents made sure they stayed."

"That's been on my mind, too. And I've got an answer. Who would benefit from our troops being stationed there?"

He's obviously got more than me.

"Oh, Stormy," Pip sighs. "You were an honourable SEAL, however your career ended, no one can take that from you. Your world is black and white, good men served, the bad were the insurgents you were fighting. But what if some men weren't cut from the same cloth as yourself? What if some were reaping benefits by our presence in Afghanistan?"

Staying to eat a bullet, or die like my team had? I frown, not seeing many positives.

"It could have been drugs," Pip says, softly. "There's good money to be made." He waits for that to sink in. "I've lived in the underworld, Storm, nothing surprises me."

"How would it work? In this imperfect world of yours." He's sparked my interest, but not yet my belief.

"Getting the drugs out of the country? Come on, Stormy, you can't be that naïve. Where there's money, there's a way."

I narrow my eyes as the wheels turn in my head. "If equipment is being brought back to the States, it could be packed in the cases. As long as someone was on hand to remove it the other end. Enough money would grease wheels."

"And soldiers packs. Enlist men, either with money or threats over their heads. Smythe wrangled it for your team to use a dedicated pilot and plane."

He had, hadn't he? I used to think it was his connections. "This comes back to Gun, doesn't it?"

Pip sighs. "Maybe. If Gun was resourceful enough, he could have used the opportunity to develop a pipeline. But Gun would have no beef with me, unless the private plane was no longer available when I grounded Smythe, but that would point to Smythe being a major player. That Gun turned up and asked questions about Tiny, that there's a link between his half-brother Ike, and Kincaid, makes me think he was involved in Swift's kidnap, which was designed to bring me out of hiding. I had nothing to do with Gun, however, I'd had a hand in bringing down Smythe. Smythe might have stayed on the front line if it hadn't been for my interpretation of the situation which I'd given to Hillier."

I go still. "You think they were working together?"

"Is Gun a mastermind?"

The question rings in the air, and I take a moment to answer, thinking back to what I know of the man. "I think he's intelligent, but enough to pull such an enterprise together? I'd have to say no. But if asked, I'd say Smythe wasn't either."

Pip nods as if I've answered a question correctly. "Going back to the footage I showed you earlier. Why did the interpreter lie?"

I honestly don't know and tell him. Following it up with, "You know my go to excuse. Money."

"I've done an initial check of the financials of Gun and Smythe. Smythe comes from a good family, he's already loaded. Nothing immediately jumps out."

"Doesn't mean he doesn't want more." I frown. This is something I can do, okay it might be laborious tapping with just the fingers of one hand, but at least I'll be feeling useful while I'm waiting on others to do my job for me. "I'd like to look into it myself. See if I can find off-shore accounts."

"I've already asked Bolt to start digging."

Goddammit. Are they leaving nothing for me?

The door suddenly bursts open. "Pip, Stormy. Drummer's on the line in Snatcher's office. They've found something."

Pip doesn't have to be asked. As soon as the words are out of Gears' mouth, he's at my side, helping me to stand.

29

———————

Stormy…

Once again the phone is in the middle of the table, and once again Snatcher informs Drummer that I've entered the room. Pip hovers in the doorway, and he's waved to the seat next to myself.

"Your boys find something, Drummer?" Prez asks.

"Yeah. Your man Gun wasn't there, Stormy, but there's evidence people have been held in that location. Not going to pretty this up, but there were cages in the basement."

Jeez. No. I can't think of my Cat being caged. As for a basement, that would send her right back to the horror I rescued her from.

I swallow, not concerned when my voice sounds higher than normal. "You think she was held there?"

"Pretty certain. There was a picture of a cat scratched onto the brickwork."

"Drummer." I cough to clear my throat. "That's too close to how Tiny left her. She'll be freaking out."

"Hold on to the thought she's staying strong, Stormy." The mother chapter prez's voice bellows down the line.

"Was there anyone else there, Drummer?" Snatcher asks.

"There were six cages, from the dirt and dust left we think only three have been occupied recently. They found a PC set up and got Mouse to access it remotely. He'll give you the tech details if you want them. There's no way to put this sensitively, but there was a list of buyers. One for a submissive red head."

Yeah, Cat would probably be thought of as submissive, most of it being how she was raised. "Who?" I rasp out.

"A cartel down in Mexico. Run by El Bastardo Blanco, or that's the name he goes by."

A wail of despair comes out of my mouth. *She's over the border. How the fuck am I going to get her back?*

"Stormy!" Drummer barks into the phone. "Pip's not the only one with contacts. I have a score to settle with Devil as he played the fuckin' Utah chapter off against ours. He fuckin' owes me, and he knows it. He's familiar with the white bastard – he's apparently an Albino, that's how he got his name. He's on the case. If anyone can get Cat back, he can."

"I want to go," I say as firmly as possible. "I want to be there for any rescue."

"No can do, Storm," Snatcher says, his eyes softening. "You'd be a liability, you know that. You can't fuckin' stand up let alone walk."

Pip's voice sounds. "If Devil needs back up, I'll go."

"Pip?" Drummer asks.

"I'm here."

"Devil thought you might offer. He said to tell you to stand by. Stormy, Devil's not wasting any time, man. He's sorting out a plane and his mercenaries now. The only thing you can do is keep near a phone."

As if I'll be going anywhere without it.

"The White Bastard needs to be taken down, Drummer. This gives Devil the excuse he was looking for. He's a dealer, she might already have been moved on."

"Devil's well aware, Pip."

My face turns toward the man who'd been my prez for so long. His eyes have settled on me. "I trust Devil with my life. If it's humanely possible, he'll get Cat back."

I raise and dip my chin but the movement is automatic. I've never been so terrified in my life, imagining Devil storming El Bastardo Blanco's compound and Cat getting caught in the crossfire. She means so much to me, but nothing to them.

I've resisted putting my life into anyone's hands for so long it's completely unnatural now. I want to rage, shout, smash something, but Cat's voice seems to echo in my head calming me down. *You're not responsible for everything, Stormy. Sometimes you have to let someone help.*

"I'll call Devil," Snatcher suddenly butts in. "I'm not leaving it to him. Cat's Stormy's which makes her one of ours. I'll have a team ready to go. We'll be there. Preacher can fly us down."

"You work in the US," Drummer snaps back. "This is out of your territory."

"We have up to now. It will be volunteers only, Drum. But there'll be no shortage of those. Might not have fuckin' met her, but Cat is something to us now. She's club property and we're going to get her back."

Drummer's quiet for a second, then he chuckles softly. "I'll tell Devil to expect your call." As before, without a goodbye, the call ends.

It's like a whirlwind moving around me. Luckily someone sends a prospect back to give me a hand, otherwise I'd be crawling to wherever everyone else is going as Snatcher and Pip storm out seeming to have forgotten about me.

As Igor helps me into the clubroom, I see Snatcher hasn't wasted any time.

"So, I need volunteers."

I'm still trying to settle myself down but I pause to see who out of the brothers I disrespected are going to volunteer for a suicide mission to rescue a woman they don't even know. Half-fearing no one, fuck me, treacherous tears make me blink furiously as everyone raises their hand. Snatcher has to resort to picking names.

Swift's first and would have been my initial choice. She's trained in hostage extraction, and as for being able to keep a steady head on her shoulders, there's no one better. She's also female and Cat might relate to her. Preacher, obviously, as he'll be piloting the plane. Thor, no surprise there. Road? Well, a few months ago I'd have dismissed him, but clearly he's proved himself to Snatcher, and for once I know better than to question him. Cowboy, well, he understands the situation, and I know his past will want to make the present have a better result. Rascal and Piston are also going along, and it won't just be for the ride.

Honor and Duty are turned down, they'll stay here and sort out the flight details and where the plane will land. The final addition to the party who are going is Grinch, who'll be there as a mechanic on the plane. They don't want to be stranded in Mexico with an engine fault.

Pip walks in when Snatcher finishes choosing, it seems he's been the one to contact Devil.

"He's not happy," he announces. "But I persuaded him he needed the additional firepower. Preach, you got the weapons sorted?"

"Rascal?" Preacher, getting straight on it, asks, "You ready to help me load up some extra armoury?"

Of course, the answer's in the affirmative.

I sit, never in my life feeling so useless as I do now. I watch my brothers as they prepare to move out, wasting no time to go to get my woman for me.

Swift comes over, her eyes surprisingly soft. "We'll bring her back." Just four words, but there's such commitment in her eyes I will myself to try to believe.

"Hold on, Brother," Road offers, joining his woman.

"Not going to fail again," Cowboy tells me earnestly, being the next to stop by.

One by one they file past, each with a promise they'll bring her back to me. I'm surprised when Snatcher follows them. He's the fuckin' prez, he should be here, not on a mission to Mexico that might see them all dead.

"Snatcher," I hold out my left hand, and he takes it, "take me. I'll wait on the plane—"

Abruptly he shuts my plea off. "No can do. You need looking after, and that will detract from the mission. You've got to stay here."

"Shouldn't you?"

Snatcher looks after his men, and the woman, who've just exited the room, then back down at me. His mouth quirks. "Just trust we know what we're doing, okay?" With those parting words, he's gone.

Silence rings around the clubroom broken only by Brute behind the bar putting glasses away.

"Want to come to the comms room?"

I start and look over my shoulder. Honor has re-entered the room. "Duty's sorting out the flight plan and filing it. I want to look at what Mouse sent me. We're going to find a way to take Gun down. Revenge will be fuckin' sweet, I promise you."

Planning revenge won't stop me worrying about Cat, nor about the bulk of the club who've left on a mission solely for me.

Gun. The man I've come to hate with a passion. Things are starting to point to him being responsible for Pooh's death, and almost mine. I could imagine him in the helicopter egging Smythe on, even if the lieutenant commander wasn't in on it himself. He could have been the man to take Nazia's life, he was in the vicinity at the time. And it's not too much of a stretch to believe he had a hand in taking my old team out. And that's not forgetting half-killing me, and kidnapping Cat.

He's an evil man. While I settle beside Honor, I'm planning Gun's death in my mind.

He's going to die hard.

30

———

*S*tormy…

Twenty-four hours can be a fucking long time, going fast or slow depending on what you're doing. Hanging around waiting for the go ahead for a mission can make even minutes crawl by. Conversely, hours go flying by fast when you're doing something you enjoy.

Waiting for news about Cat, the time goes past just one minute at a time. Sixty long seconds when I have to remind myself to keep breathing.

Pip had given me the news they'd arrived and were scoping out the location. Finally, I'd got the update they were going in.

I can imagine they're proceeding with caution, and will be radio silent from now. But I'd prefer to know exactly what they are doing, and hate being kept in the dark. What's the compound like, how many guards? I wanted to be on hand to give advice.

All I can do is sit back and try to convince myself to believe what deep down I've always known. *I can trust the Satan's Devils.*

Without Cowboy here it's a matter of getting food for

ourselves, but I don't bother invading his domain, I've no appetite at all. If I suspend living for just a few hours, maybe that will bring Cat home. It's crazy, but that's the way my brain is thinking.

I've never been dependent on anyone, not like I am on her. She's as important as air to me. If I was a praying man, I'd send up a prayer right now, but all my life I've felt there's no omnipotent being watching over me, or if so, he'd been looking the other way too many times for my thinking. He'd never been there to halt my father's fists, or to stop my mother leaving. I wish I had faith now. Instead I can only trust in my flesh and blood brothers to find Cat and return her to me.

"Here. Made you some coffee. You want your painkillers?"

I thank Igor automatically and shake my head. No, I want as clear a head as possible, and these aching injuries? Well, those I'll suffer gladly as though by punishing myself I'll be saving her.

Honor and I had pulled an all-nighter. I think he wanted to sleep, but when he saw I wasn't giving in, he stayed up as well. Now he's coming in yawning, his hair wet from a shower.

He examines the results of a program that had kept running. "I reckon that's all of them now. All the haunts of Jeffrey Morgan. We should be able to close in on him."

I tap the screen I'm looking at. "I've found offshore accounts." The size of the figures make me grow cold. "Deposits started a few months before Pooh was killed and continue up to when Gun left the SEALs. Then there's a short gap, a huge payment, then more money rolling in."

"You think he had to lie low for a while?"

"Could be," I agree. "Maybe someone was getting too close?"

"Hmm." Honor looks thoughtful. "What happened to Marjan, Nazia's sister? Could she have been a threat to him? I think you're right, he killed Nazia himself."

"Maybe he got to her too. She was," I think back, "twelve or thirteen at the time. But kids grow up fast in that environment, they have to. Maybe Nazia told her something, and maybe he did kill her, or maybe she got away."

"If she had info, she would have come forward."

"Maybe not. I mean, how could she know who to trust?"

We both ponder that for a moment and are still deep in thought when the door bangs open.

"They've got her," Pip announces, sounding out of breath. "They're bringing her home."

Swinging around too fast, I make my head swim. "Say again?"

"Cat's safe, Stormy. They've got her. Went like clockwork according to Snatcher."

"*She's alive?*" I pull my stick toward me, wanting to stand up as though being seated isn't good enough for this momentous news. I don't get far, and slump back down again. "Is she okay? Is she hurt?"

Pip's eyes become hooded. "Physically, she seems uninjured. But mentally…" he shakes his head. "She had to be sedated as no one could get close."

I rest my head into my working hand, as pain of the emotional sort rushes through me.

"You got this Stormy." Pip comes closer, his fingers land on my shoulder and squeeze. "She's coming back to you. It might take time, she might be dealing with some bad shit, but you'll have her home. You've got this."

But have I? Christ, she'd been bad enough after being locked in her own cellar, but now? I can't run from the idea that she's been abused, subjected to things no woman should suffer. What do I know about making her right? What if I fuck up and say a well-intentioned equivalent of 'pull yourself together' or 'you'll be alright'? Have I got the backbone for this to be what she needs?

I only know I have to try, and just hope this isn't going to be another thing I'll fuck up.

It's not good news she had to be sedated. "Didn't Swift try and talk to her?"

Pip's lips press together. "She did, but she's not sure who Cat thought she was. Someone trying to trick her perhaps. In the end, they were worried she was going to hurt herself. That's all I've got, Stormy."

I suppose I've been dumb. I'd hoped once they'd got her free, I'd be talking to her on the phone, reassuring her and myself that everything was going to be fine. Cat's in a worse state than I had imagined.

"What do I do, Pip? What do I fuckin' do?" I plead for help.

Before he can answer, a knock sounds at the door. When it opens, it reveals a prospect and the club's doctor. Pip nod, clearly having summoned him.

"Come on, Storm. Let's go to my office."

The doc might be here to give me a lecture. Maybe I deserve one. I've been awake so long I'm running on fumes now. My body is one mess of agony, parts aching that I'm trying my best to ignore.

But I can't rest. Won't be able to close my eyes until Cat's here, and I see for myself that physically she's unharmed. Mentally? Christ, I don't even want to go there. I've never considered myself an emphatic man, how can I help her?

I focus on Pip, opening my mouth to tell him it's not me who needs medical help, but if he's here to work up a plan for Cat's treatment, I'll listen to him. I get no further than opening my mouth when I feel a prick in my neck.

My hand swings up to bat it away, but I'm too late. Already I feel my eyes closing.

When I awake my mouth feels dry and I'm disorientated. I open my eyes, noting I'm in my room, in my bed, and that I'm wearing only my boxers. I feel violated, I've been drugged against my will and someone, presumably a prospect, has undressed me.

Cat.

How long have I been out? Is she back? I sit up so fast the world spins around me, and my chest, arm and leg make their protests known as I ignore the pain of the still healing bones.

"Whoa. Take it easy."

I don't know that voice. The thought alarms me, and my eyes snap to the origin of the sound. It's a biker who's sitting in a chair next to me, but not one I've seen before. *Or have I?* In the scope of my rifle?

"Who the fuck are you?" I rasp, wondering if my eyes are playing tricks on me.

The man eyes me. "The name's Mace," he pronounces.

Mace? The only man of that name I know and who'd be wearing a cut is the enforcer of the Satan's Devils MC Colorado chapter. A man who could have little love for me, hatred, yes. I killed the man he wanted to torture himself. *I had seen him through my scope. Moments before I shifted my sights to Major.*

Still seated, I try to inch my hand toward the drawer of my bedside table when my firearm is normally stored.

Mace notices, the bastard. He shakes his head, and pulls out a gun of his own, holding it loosely in one hand. "I wondered what your reaction would be."

"How the fuck did you get in here?" Has the compound been breached? Is this to do with Drummer? Has his patience run out?

"You going to kill me?" Either gun or fists would succeed, I'm as weak as a kitten.

Mace barks a laugh. "There was a time when yeah, I'd have shot you dead soon as I had you in my sights. But I'll hold off on that for now."

"Torture me?"

"Christ. You're full of your own fuckin' importance, aren't you, Stormy? All you can think of is that I'm here for you. But I'm not."

It must be whatever sedative the doctor had given me, but my brain can't make sense of the words. My brow furrows. "Who are you fuckin' here for, Mace?"

He steeples his hands under his chin, and grimaces. "I'm here because I know about some of what you're going to go through. Drummer contacted my prez, Demon spoke to me. I had a chat with my ol' lady, and well, here I am."

It's a convoluted explanation that my injured brain's having difficulty following. Drummer, though, seems to be behind his presence.

Taking pity on me at last, Mace finds more explanative words. "My Shay was abused."

Bells ring, dots start moving into a line, but I don't understand why anyone would help me. But I remember he said he wasn't here for me. He intends to help her.

"No one's getting near my woman apart from me," I snarl.

Now he holds up his hands. "Too fuckin' right." He leans forward getting into my face. "Shay was fuckin' broken when I first met her. You know what that bastard Major did to her, no one could expect anyone to come out unscathed. I'm not forcing anyone to let me stay here, but Drummer suggested I might be able to help. Not your woman directly, but as someone who's been through it themselves, I might be able to give you some pointers." He pauses, sits back, and draws his hand down his face. "I've been there, Stormy. I know you just want to wrap her in your arms and tell her everything's going to be alright. That you love her, whatever. That just those words will make everything right."

They will, won't they? Of course, I'll have to convince her. Nothing that happened to her was any fault of hers. It's not as though she set out to cheat on me. I don't give a damn, she's mine. Nothing will effect that. But Mace has made me think.

"Isn't that what she needs to hear?"

Mace grimaces. "Hearing is one thing, believing it another. If she's like Shay, she'll feel unclean. Fuck, man, she might not even trust you."

"It was my fault," I tell him, looking down at my hands. "If I hadn't been there, Gun might not have taken her."

Now the Colorado enforcer nods. "Pip filled me in. Maybe, maybe not. But you were, and it's possible he took her to have leverage over you. Only, you got free before he could use it."

"Is there any more news?" I ask him, belatedly. "Is she back yet?"

He shakes his head. "They're in US airspace," he tells me. "She's safe, and nearly here. Preacher's ETA is in an hour."

I've got to get moving. It's a process that I need to take slow. Surprisingly, Mace goes about helping me without being asked. He goes to my drawers, asks what I need and gets it out.

"I don't understand," I tell him, as he holds the t-shirt so I can get my cast through it. "Don't you hate me for what I did?"

He sighs. "I did. At the time I was blinded by being robbed of the chance to torture Major. He didn't deserve a clean bullet to the head. Good fuckin' shot though that was." He winks at me. "But in the end, he's dead. I could spend time with Shayla, rather than spending hours in the basement torturing the fuck out of the man."

"Is she okay? Your ol' lady?"

Mace grins now. "Shay's fine. I won't say she doesn't still have nightmares at times, but I remind her she's safe and she's mine."

He's made me think. I'd assumed it was going to be easy. Get Cat here, tell her I'd never let anything hurt her again, hold her in my arms and everything will be right. Mace has shown me it might not be as easy, and that I'll need to be patient. Patience, though, is something I'm not known for.

When I'm ready, Mace brings over the wheelchair.

"I'll use the stick."

"Don't be a stubborn ass," he snaps. "You know why Pip called the doc? Because you were overdoing it. What good are you going to be with Cat if you don't look after yourself?"

After that, when he brings the wheelchair closer, I slide into it without further argument, but I stop the wheels with my working hand. Turning my head, I look at him over my shoulder.

"I appreciate this, Mace. I don't know what to say to thank you."

He shakes his head. "I'm just pleased to see you accepting help. Let us in, man. Then one day, perhaps, I'll be calling you brother."

Now it's back to waiting, so I take the chance to interrogate Mace, who's open enough to tell me how he made headway with his woman. I take mental notes, the circumstances weren't exactly the same, but some of his suggestions might work. The main result is that he's got shit straight in my head, my focus needs to be on my woman, and not on whatever relief I feel myself. Patience, kindness and understanding, that's what she needs. None of his pep talk lands on deaf ears.

When we get news that the plane has landed and Cat's only minutes away, Mace stands.

"I'll get back to my woman, leave you with yours. But Stormy, you want to pick my brain? I'm at the end of a phone, remember."

"Mace? Thank you. You came a long way."

He shrugs. "Didn't ride it man, I took a plane. Anyway," his expression changes and now he smirks, "it's given me the chance to see the man I'm going to be taking down, once you're fit again, of course." When my brow creases, he adds, innocently. "What? You surely didn't think I was letting you off the hook, did you?" With two fingers he points to his eyes, then my own. "You and I got unfinished business to deal with."

Great. So once I'm healed I'm facing a beatdown from my brothers, and now another from Mace. It's also unlikely that San Diego won't want in on the act.

31

———

*C*at…

    I keep my eyes closed tight, concentrating on making my breathing even, given away no sign that I'm starting to wake. Over the weeks I've learned waking never holds anything good for me, and the only escape I can get is when I'm asleep.

The bed feels different. There's a sheet and a blanket covering me, while I've become use to being allowed no dignity even when I'm alone. Kept naked at all times, and available for the time when my master needs me.

It's not only the bed that doesn't feel the same, I've woken without the aching to remind me how much I've been abused, and for once I'm not sore between my legs. At least today, I don't feel dirty and sticky.

Has there been a night when he hasn't come to me, or directed his men to use me? For the past two weeks since Gun had sold me, I've had no relief. It's not just been the night, but during every day. His one aim to break me.

I want to die.

I should fight. But I tried that, it got me nowhere, now any objection has been beaten out of me.

Am I alone? Listening hard, I can't hear anything. The room is light, not dark like the cell where I've been kept. And my back, well, that's not stuck to the sheets with blood as it had been.

I'd refused to call him Master. He'd whipped me.

There are other differences today. There's a scent in the room just reaching my nostrils, something tantalisingly out of reach but which seems familiar.

I'm dreaming that I'm awake. Or, maybe I'm already dead. I'd known it wouldn't be long before he went too far and killed me. If I'm dead, I'm not sure what I expected from the afterlife, but it's heaven lying covered in a comfortable bed.

My mind circles back to the last thing I remember. *Strangers.* Men, who the master would give me too, and a woman, hell, she was trying to trick me. I fought, I remember. Maybe that's what killed me? I should be covered in bruises, maybe broken bones, but my body doesn't feel sore, all the pain is in my head.

If this is death, it's better than being alive.

What do I do now? Maybe I should risk opening my eyes.

Cracking them open, I can see I'm in a bedroom of some sort. My first thought is that it's utilitarian, a closet, a desk, a chair in front of it. White painted walls. Well, white fits with the afterlife, doesn't it? Maybe I should stir myself and get out of bed. It's funny, I never believed in a hereafter.

Someone clears their throat beside me. My body freezes, but I manage to turn my head. When the figure comes into focus, I heave a sigh of relief, and a smile curves my lips. I'd never thought to see him again, but it's Finn. He's sitting beside it.

That confirms it. I know he's dead. Gun showed me his body. There must be a benevolent God, and now we'll spend eternity together.

Finn's hand touches mine. I jump, snatching my hand back. *It's Finn.* No. *It's a man.* It's my mind playing tricks.

"Cat, sweetheart, look at me."

I squeeze tight my eyes. Demons can change their shapes, can't they? This may be another ploy.

"Cat, darlin'," he pleads.

"You're dead." I state the obvious.

He snorts. "I'm very much alive, darlin'. Hey. Look at me."

"Gun showed me your body. He told me he'd killed you." The words come out on a monotone. I'd collapsed at the sight, I hadn't cared what had happened to me, seeing the man I loved beaten and bleeding, the limbs that used to go around me, broken and awry, a deep stab wound bleeding out. Gun had kicked him hard, and Finn hadn't flinched. There had been no doubt in my mind I'd lost him.

At that moment I hadn't cared what happened to me. It had been easy for Gun to take me away. I'd been compliant, thinking the worst had already happened to me. *I'd been wrong.*

"Cat," he pleads again. "Look at me."

When I do, my first thought is why I am feeling no pain after whatever punishment I'd taken to kill me, when he... His face is taut, stitches across his cheek and on his forehead. His nose is not the shape I remember. Continuing my assessment I notice one arm is in a cast, and he's not in a normal seat, he's in a wheelchair. As my eyes continue a downward journey, it's easy to see why. One of his legs is stretched out in front of him and covered with yet another cast.

Why heal me and not him? It doesn't make sense. Unless this is his purgatory.

The shorn side of his head is stubbly, it's a strange thing to note.

"I'm not dead, sweetheart."

But I am. I must be.

"Is she awake?"

This time my eyes snap open as the door opens and a stranger appears. The only thing I notice is that he's a man and that's all I need to know my slice of heaven has turned into hell. Screaming, I dig in my ankles and push myself back, holding out my hands to ward him off.

"Don't touch me," I beg.

"Cat." Finn's voice is firm. "Cat. It's alright."

But it's not.

"Cat, calm down, you're going to hurt yourself."

"Ms Beeswick, Catherine. You're safe," the stranger's voice says, but I barely hear him over my own keening.

This is another torture, making me think I'm safe, when it's a trick and he must be here to use me. Finn? Well, my subconscious must have summoned him up, if he's here, it's his spirit haunting me.

"Stormy, I'll need to sedate her again before she hurts herself."

Now there's more than one man holding me down, a prick in my arm, and darkness descends once again.

Next time I'm aware of anything, it's two people talking. It's Finn's voice, I'm sure. At least his ghost hasn't left me. But the other, speaking in clipped tones, in a British accent, is a voice I remember. *She was the devil who'd pretended she'd come to save me.*

Again, making no sign I'm awake, I listen carefully.

"I don't know what to do, Swift." He sounds agonised.

"She needs time, Stormy. Christ, that place where she was kept… I'm not going to lie to you, it was bad."

"She must have fought," Finn replies, his voice breaking.

The woman snorts. "You think? Yeah, the bruises on her face, the lash marks on her back. She didn't give in easily."

"Tell me he's dead, Swift."

"Already told you that."

"Tell me you cut off his dick and fed it to him."

The woman barks a soft laugh. "I would have, but we had no time for such pleasures. I gutted him, Stormy. Best I could do in the time frame."

"I should have been there."

"Maybe," Swift replies. "But she was in pain and terrified. She might have been the same with you. We had to sedate her, we'd have never got out otherwise."

Finn chuckles softly. "She do that?"

Swift again does that unladylike snort. "Yeah, she got a lick in. Maybe I should teach her some self-defence. She's certainly got the basics down."

She'd teach me to fight? That doesn't sound like anything the master would allow.

"She was still out of it when you got here. What the fuck did you give her?"

"We thought it would be better keeping her under until she was back. I was in communication with Doc, I knew what I was doing."

"She was out of it when she came around just now. She freaked when Doc came in."

"Give her time, Stormy. That's what she needs. It's a lot for her to process. She's been ripped away from her life, sold, abused, and now she's back. It will take a while for her to feel safe."

My face starts to throb whereas last time I awoke I felt no pain. My back feels sore. Can I believe the words I'm hearing? I'm a nurse, I know a sedative could have dulled the pain. Are my ears working properly? Am I really safe?

Chancing opening my eyes, I turn to the side so I can stare at Finn. He looks such a mess it's hard to believe he didn't die. Then, I turn the other way. I don't remember seeing her before, but the purple bruise on her cheek would suggest that I have if I can believe what I just heard.

Noticing me looking at her, she smiles. "Welcome back."

"Cat?" I feel the bed dip, and turning back see Finn's out of his wheelchair, bracing the arm that's not in a cast on the mattress and leaning over me. "Cat? It's me, Finn."

His hand hovers over my face, but I turn away.

"Cat, I'm so fuckin' sorry."

"It's not your fault." I turn back, swallowing. "This is because of what I did for Weston."

"Nah, sweetheart. It happened because Gun found me with you."

At last I realise I'm in the land of the living. And that Finn is too. I gaze at him in wonder. "I thought you were dead. He told me you were. He kicked you to prove it."

Finn winces, but it's Swift who answers. "Technically he did die, Cat. Twice. But nothing can keep his stubborn ass down."

He died?

I turn to look at him in time to see him scowl at Swift. "I'm here, now," he tells me, reaching again for my hand. But once again I pull it away, without even knowing why.

Could it be I blame him after all? But if I hadn't met him, I'd already be dead. *But not subjected to this living hell and memories I'll never be able to get out of my mind.* Or, is it because I feel so damn dirty? Or pre-empting his inevitable desire to walk away once he knows the kind of things that I'd done, more rightly what had been done to me.

His face hardens, and he glares at his hand before lifting it away from me once more.

I try to shift position, but wince.

Swift stands. "I'll go get the doctor. You may need more painkillers now."

"I'm okay," I say fast. I can't have a strange man in the room, not when I freaked earlier. And certainly not one who'd want to poke and prod me during an examination.

"Cat," Swift sits back down, her features softening, "Doc's asked a colleague of his to step in. He thought you'd be more comfortable with a woman. Can I go get her now?"

A short time ago I was imprisoned, without any control of my own. Then I truly believed I must have died. Now, it seems

I'm very much alive, and I appreciative for once, it appears I'm being given options.

"I'll see the doctor," I agree at last. My eyes follow Swift as she gets up and leaves the room.

"Don't worry," Finn says quietly. "I'll stay here with you, Cat. I'm not leaving you."

Widening my eyes, I violently shake my head. "No, Finn. I don't want you to hear what the doctor says." He can't stay. There's no way I want him to hear the questions I'm going to ask. He knows the headlines, that's enough for anyone to deal with. The detail is something I'll have to cope with by myself.

"You need me with you," he insists.

"In that case, send the doctor away. I'm not talking to her in front of you." Can I insist? I always thought I had control over my destiny until it was taken by three men. Weston, then Gun, then the man who introduced himself as my master.

I hadn't realised my voice had gone shrill, but Finn's backed away. "Hey, I don't mean to upset you. I just thought you'd like my support."

I force myself to be calm. "You'll support me better by not staying." I try to sound firm, hiding that inside I'm screaming like a little girl. It will break him to know what's happened to me, hell, I can barely deal with it myself. "Where am I?" I ask, suddenly realising something is amiss. If a doctor's on standby, should I be in a hospital? Not that I'm grateful I'm not, it suggests that my thoughts of a little while ago were way off the mark and I'm not in danger of dying.

"You're at the clubhouse." His lips press together. "We brought Doc to treat you here. But if he thinks you need a hospital, that's where you'll go."

"Are you alright, Finn?" I belatedly ask, waving at his broken body. "Will you heal?"

"Broken wrist, broken leg, cracked ribs and a fractured collarbone. I took a bump to the head and had a concussion, and

I've a few nice scars including on my stomach where Gun went to town with his knife, but I'll heal, babe. It's you I'm worried about."

Because his injuries are all on the outside.

An awkward silence comes over us.

The door opens and Swift comes back in. "This is Doctor Mason."

"Do you want Swift to stay?" Finn asks.

I shake my head. Swift goes to Finn's wheelchair and pushes him away. I feel like a part of me has left the door with him.

But now I've got to pull up my big girl panties. Before the doctor can ask anything, I get in first.

"Doctor Mason, can I be tested for STDs, and…" I swallow hard, feeling tears fill my eyes. "Can I have a test to see if I'm pregnant?"

32

---

*S*tormy…

I hate not being there while the doctor is talking to Cat. How can I know how to help her when I can only guess at what she's been through? I hate relying on imagination which is bad enough, I'd prefer to deal in hard facts.

At my direction, Swift silently pushes me to the comms room, and I take it from there, Wheeling myself over to a free workstation.

What I'm going to do next is child's play. Unfortunately, it doesn't go unnoticed.

"You sure you want to do that?" Swift, holding a cup of her preferred tea is standing behind me.

Normally I don't try to justify myself, or explain my actions to anyone else. My modus operandi is to do whatever I fucking want, and what I want now is to get the information that I can't do without. But that talk with Mace is going around my head on repeat. I have no idea how to deal with Cat, all I know is I want her in my life, and have no greater desire but to help heal her. How can I start without any idea what the bastards put her through?

"I have to." I pause the cursor on the screen, hovering over the club doctor's medical report. "She won't tell me, Swift. I know she won't. She'll keep it bottled up as if it's only her that has to deal with it. How can I help her and how the fuck can I move forward myself, without knowing her triggers?"

"How's it going to affect you, Storm?" She pulls up a chair and sits next to me. "You love her, don't you?"

A simple nod suffices, while thinking how bizarre this is. A conversation about emotions was not one I'd ever have expected to have with Swift.

"Well, fuck." She gives a small smile. "You're different since you came back."

"She grounds me," I reply, simply. "It's for her that I came back to the club. Not just to ask for help in her rescue, the decision had already been made. We were all packed up." And thank Christ for that. Her beloved animals are being well cared for. "Cat made me see it was because I couldn't make sense of anything that I cut everyone out. It was letting her in, admitting I needed her, that made me realise I needed you too."

"I presume you're talking about the club, not me." She winks.

Despite the circumstances I smirk. "Even you, Swift."

"Loving Road has changed me," she admits. The previous me would have scoffed, would have accused her of being weak. How can I now? When I understand only too well.

"You're softer, Swift. More approachable." When she bristles, I add, "And just as fuckin' dangerous."

"Threaten my man and you're dead," she confirms, voicing how I feel about the woman I love. "Which is why when we find Gun, I'll make him wish he'd never been born."

I don't tell her I want to do that myself. How could I, given my current physical limitations?

"Waterboarding?" I might have picked up on some of the discussions about what she'd got up to in San Diego.

"Oh, I can think of worse," she promises earnestly. "This

time it won't matter if I leave marks." She jerks her chin toward the monitor, returning to our previous topic. "You do this, you can't take it back. Whatever you find, she might be hurt you invaded her privacy."

I hear what she says. "I'm out of my depth, Swift. We've rescued women before, but handed them over to the experts."

"Perhaps you ought to do that."

Maybe I'm not as changed as I'd like to think. Cat's mine, and I want to be the one she leans on, not leave her to talk to an anonymous person. I need facts to formulate a plan of attack, even if the enemy is all in her head.

Leaving the decision to me, Swift pats my shoulder, then gets up to leave.

"Want a coffee, Storm?" Honor offers as he gets a beverage for himself.

The mouse is still hovering over her file, but Swift is right. If I do this, there's no going back, for a moment, I hesitate.

So I accept his offer, and ask, "Got anything?" When he places the cup near my left hand, I reach for it, picking it up.

"Would you believe communications between Smythe and Jeffrey Morgan?"

I still, replacing the cup, my coffee forgotten. "Recent?"

Honor looks self-satisfied as well he might. "Did you know Pip had a hand in getting Smythe away from the front line?"

I give a sharp nod. "Pip told me, and that it happened before I met him."

The man I'd love to again be able to call brother shrugs. "Pip and your Admiral go way back."

And the admiral gave me Pip's card, I kind of guessed it had to be something like that. "Have you evidence Smythe knew about Pip's involvement?"

"I think he does."

My eyes sharpen. "Was Smythe behind Swift's kidnap? Was it him who wanted revenge on Pip rather than it being down to

Kincaid?" If so, it seems flimsy, and I let Honor know why. Shaking my head dismissively I explain, "Too much time has passed. And Smythe wasn't demoted, why the fuck should he care? He's safer to himself and us working from behind a desk. I never felt he was comfortable in an active role." Pausing a second for effect, I add with emphasis, and a barely suppressed shudder, "*Gun* hated me, Honor. He wanted to inflict maximum pain. I tried to hide what I felt about Cat, but he fuckin' saw it."

"I think it's safe to say you were supposed to die along with Pooh. You lived longer than he'd expected. Once he had a chance, he tried to rectify that."

"If he wanted me dead, why not come after me immediately?" I grimace. "I was in a bad place, Honor. There were easy ways to set something up to make it look like I swallowed a bullet."

Honor's brow creases. "Back then, when you were kicked out, even if you knew something, Storm, how much would the word of a disgraced SEAL count for? It would have been put down to sour grapes. I'd venture that it was your presence in Cat's house that made him presume you had something to do with his failure to take down Pip. That would have caused alarm bells to start ringing." He gives a cold mirthless chuckle. "I'd also say you were lucky he hated you. Otherwise it would have been a simple headshot. Him wanting you to suffer kept you alive."

Gun had wanted me permanently out of the picture. But why? What threat was I then, and what threat am I now? Is there something I know of which I hadn't realised the significance? Maybe just the suspicion I do would have been enough to justify in Gun's eyes, a death sentence. One in which Cat was an innocent pawn, her only crime being caught up in my life, which lays her horrors firmly at my door.

Honor takes pity on my damaged brain trying to work things out, my fingers rubbing at my temples gives away that my head's aching. "I'll keep looking, and I'll let you know immediately if I find anything concrete." Before he retakes his seat, Honor's eyes soften. "I heard what Swift said, but I think you're right. Cat will find it hard to open up. I don't think you should tell her anything you find out, let her tell you herself. But as you said, being aware of her triggers could help you avoid them."

I place my left hand over the mouse, and move the cursor back to the file, hesitating only because I know once I open Pandora's box I won't be able to put the contents back.

Clicking, I seal my fate.

The doctor's notes are succinct, short and to the point. As I read, I'm grateful Cat was sedated at the time he examined her. Vaginal tearing I kind of expected but it's still hard to read. Bruising, that's no shock either, but shit, the pain my woman must have felt. The next bit is harder, there's anal damage as well, nothing that won't heal, but even I had never taken her virgin ass. She'd been raped, repeatedly and violently. She'd been whipped, some gashes so deep they'd had to be stitched.

I should have known it would come with the territory, but it's the cold brief notes about testing for STDs and pregnancy that have me stumbling out of the wheelchair, grabbing the stick and somehow propelling myself out of the room to the nearest john. I only hold my vomit until I get there.

"Brother," Honor says hesitantly from behind me. "You had to have expected you wouldn't be reading a fuckin' fairy tale."

I flush, wipe my mouth on paper, and stand with the support of the wall. "I knew, but hadn't accepted it. That's why I needed to see it, Honor. She might be pregnant. I never thought of that."

"Is that what's bothering you?"

"It's the whole fuckin' thing, everything she's having to deal with. I fuckin' thought getting her back would be the end of it, but it's just the beginning. I hate it all, Honor. I hate that she was raped, that she might have an STD. She doesn't deserve this."

He stares at me for a moment. "You need to fuckin' calm yourself before you see her. It's not about you, Storm. I'd tell you to take a long ride on your bike to get your head on straight, but…" He doesn't need to complete his sentence. I'm in no state to ride even if I had my bike here, which I don't.

My bike's still back in Kentucky, or is if it hasn't been stolen, along with everything Cat owns. The plan had been to move down here and find a house, renting to start with if we couldn't find anything we wanted to buy immediately. Would that still even be in the cards? Or, will Cat want to hide and lick her wounds in private, and without me? Fuck, I hope not. If I'm right and her suffering was all down to me, how could she ever forgive me?

"Stormy. Doctor Mason has gone."

I acknowledge Swift who seems to find nothing wrong in that she's just invaded the men's bathroom. "I've got to go see how she is."

"Here, let me." Swift has helpfully brought the wheelchair along. She helps me into it, then takes the handles. She pushes me to the elevator and, having taken the keycard from her cut, slides it in and out of the slot. As the elevator begins to rise and the music I'm normally so accustomed to that I usually no longer notice plays. This time it irritates the fuck out of me.

At last the doors open and Swift starts wheeling me along the corridor, stopping outside my door. "You got yourself under control?"

I take a breath, appreciating the few seconds to calm myself. *It's Cat who's important, not me.* When I nod at Swift, she leaves.

Leaning forward, I knock, listening out for permission to enter, but instead it's opened. Cat's standing there, whether she knows it or not, she's wearing one of my t-shirts and a pair of my sweatpants which drown her. I try to ignore the possessive feelings her attire raises within me.

My eyes narrow. "Should you be up and about?"

"The doctor said there's nothing physically wrong with me

that bed rest wouldn't cure." She's holding onto the door, as if reluctant to let me in.

I wave at what she's wearing, unable to resist. "The clothes suit you."

The look she gives me is all suspicion. "I don't know who these belong to. I helped myself to stuff I found in the drawer."

"I don't mind."

"Oh shit. Is this *your* room?" When I nod, she doesn't seem so confident as she had a moment before, and takes a step back from the door.

I could tell her I'd go away if she wants to be alone, but I don't, I think being left to dwell on everything by herself is the last thing she needs.

"Er, is there somewhere else that I can go?"

I fix my eyes on hers, wishing like hell I was whole. I rise to my feet, well, one foot, and that awkwardly and with having to hold onto the chair. "This is where you're meant to be, Cat. Okay, so we pre-empted the move to Utah, but we planned to come together. It might not be the home we intended, but for now, my room is yours."

"That was before…"

"Before?" I suck at this. Suck at trying to find the words to convey all the meaning I want to. "Cat, I love you. You're mine, and I'm yours." I want to touch her, hold her, but it's far too soon. "Nothing's changed."

"Nothing's changed?" she throws back, with a touch of the flare of her temper. I don't mind, it's better to see some animation in her face. "Nothing's fucking changed?" She turns her back to me and wraps her arms around her. "Three weeks and two days, Finn. And fuck, everything's different. I'm not the same woman, and you? You're not the same man."

"I will be," I tell her, entering properly and closing the door behind me. "My bones will heal. And nothing's changed, you're still my woman."

"I can't be." Pushing the wheelchair for support, I hop close enough to see tears streaming from her eyes. "I'll never be the same. They stole something from me."

"Okay, Cat, I get that." On my part I know how devastating it was to lose her. How driven I was to get her back. "But different doesn't mean worse."

"Three weeks and two days," she repeats. "If you were alive, why didn't you come for me sooner?" she wails.

"Cat, I was in a coma," I remind her patiently.

She turns away, well aware of that. I know she's trying to find somewhere to put the blame. Reminding her she wouldn't have suffered if it weren't for me, won't help right now. I force down my guilt and instead place it on the culprit instead.

"Gun did this to you. And sweetheart, I promise, he's going to pay."

"But it won't make it better." She shudders and I know it's in an effort to stop her tears. She straightens her shoulders. "If you're staying here, is there somewhere else I can go?"

She'll be going nowhere. She'll be sleeping in my bed whether I'm there or not.

"Cat—" I open my mouth to tell her.

"I don't want you here, Finn. I need to get my head straight. I was, I was thinking of going home."

"Not while Gun's still in the wind." I hate having to remind her. "If that's what you want, just stay until I'm healed and I'll come with you."

"I don't want you!" she cries. "Can't you see it's over?"

My gut rolls, and I pray she doesn't mean it. My voice though, is patient. "No. Nothing's changed my feelings toward you. Cat, you've dealt with things no woman should ever have to, but you survived. I'm fuckin' sorry I couldn't get to you sooner…"

"You died, Finn. That's what Swift said. You fucking *died*. It was pure luck Gun didn't actually kill you. As for me, if it hadn't been you, Gun may not have taken me. I'd have told him about Weston, and he'd have left me to get on with my life."

I have no defence for that. We're going around in circles and my leg is aching now. I sit on the bed and rest my chin on my hand. "If you want me to give you some space, I'll go, Cat. On my part, I'd rather we work this through together."

She remains standing, her body rigid. "I may have an STD, Finn. I may be pregnant. My treatment, what I do, is up to me to decide."

"We're a team, Cat," I tell her softly. "It's not just the good we share. It's also the bad. If you need ongoing treatment, I'll be there beside you. If you're pregnant, whatever happens, that's a decision only you can make."

"Is it?" she asks, equally quietly, but hers is deceptive. And fuck, her hand starts beating her stomach rhythmically. "If there's something growing in me, I want it gone. Would you be happy with that? Or what if I decided to keep it?"

"That's up to you." I inject strength into my voice. "I'll be whatever you want me to be. A partner, husband, father, if that's what you want."

"How could I have a baby fathered by one of my abusers? How could I look into its face and not see the man who sired it? How, Finn? Tell me how?" She's screaming now.

I'm fucking this up. I should be calming her down. Struggling upright again, I risk laying my hand on her arm. "You don't have to decide now. We take one fuckin' day at a time. If you want me to sleep elsewhere, I will. If you want me to hold you through the night, I'll do that. When we know what we're dealing with and you know what you want, I'll be there, supporting you. With you. Because you're still my woman, and no one can ever come between us. Not even those abusing fucks."

33

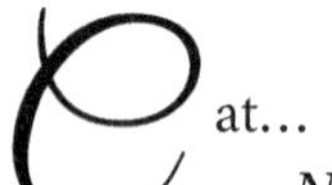 at…

No one can come between us.

Those words from Finn ring in the air. My eyes widen as I realise he just doesn't get it. Someone already has.

I'd let my mind drift while the doctor was examining me, but it hadn't gone anywhere good. Though her touch had been gentle and professional, it still made me freeze up. The thought of a man, even Finn, touching me intimately makes me feel physically ill.

After she'd left, I'd tried. Fuck, I'd really tried to summon up how Finn could make me wet simply walking into the room, with a cock of his eyebrow raised in suggestion, or even the sight of his bare skin. The feeling of his dick pressing into me was one that I previously thought I'd never get tired of.

I've come to the realisation that I'd never again look at him the same way. It isn't fair leading him on. He might think he'll wait for me, but he'll be waiting forever. My house is still mine, though I'd arranged for it to be sold, I'm not aware I've been asked to sign anything. I'll go back, be comforted by the ghosts and fill my house with pets who I'll lavish all my affection on.

If I avoid men, maybe I'll be able to forget this episode. I know I'll never move past it. Shuddering, I think how much I don't want to be near a man's dick again, even Finn's. However long he thinks he'll wait for me, it won't be long enough.

What if I'm pregnant? What if I'm left with an STD that can't be totally cured?

It wouldn't be fair to drag Finn down with me.

I want to go home.

According to Finn, I might not be safe there. What if Gun knows I'm free and comes after me again? He'll be after Finn, the one who got away, and how better to get to him than to use me.

"I don't want to stay here." Here being the clubhouse, here, being in his room.

"You can't leave," Finn speaks patiently. "You know the risks. Until we catch up with Gun and discover what's behind this, it would be crazy for you to go. You must know that, Cat. Here, we can protect you." He glances down, shakes his head, then looks up with new resolve. "Well, the club can. If it's me upsetting you, I'll go. The club will look after you, whether I'm here or not."

The thought horrifies me. "But that would mean you'll be in danger. Gun will want to finish what he started with you. You're in no state to take him on."

A mirthless snort comes from his mouth. "So, you can't leave, and I can't go. Seems we're both stuck."

My sore muscles make themselves known as I pace the room, trying to make myself think rationally. Being kidnapped and sold once was bad enough, but I wouldn't survive a second time. And that's if Gun wanted to take me alive. While my first impulse is to put as much distance between myself and Finn as I can, how could I survive looking over my shoulder all the time? Even Finn who's had training was still caught out when his former teammate came knocking at my door.

It's safer for my body to stay.

But not for my heart. Even now I can't bear to look at Finn. Deep down I know it's because I love him so much, but I can't see how I could lead him on. I'll never be the same woman again.

"Stay, Cat," he pleads. "Or, at least, before you make up your mind, give the club a chance."

"How do you know what your club will do?" My mood swings and I want to hurt him now. "They might kick you out, and what will happen to me?"

"You're right, they might. But you don't know the brothers like I do, Cat. Be assured even if they turn me loose, they'll do everything in their power to keep you safe. They'll never turn their backs on a woman in trouble."

I eye his room. It's bare, no personal effects. But I remember he'd been a long time on the road, *nomad* he'd called it. I suppose he hasn't really got a home, though he fitted into mine. I stifle a sob as I remember our dreams, a home, maybe even a family in time. A man to be at my side, when maybe I was born to be alone.

"So what do you propose? I stay here?" I gesture around. "You don't even have a television, Finn."

"I can get you anything you need, but first, I asked you to give the club a chance. Get to know them, you might like them if you let them in. You won't need to stay locked up in this room."

"You don't trust your brothers," I remind him.

Suddenly he wobbles, his need to sit again, makes my heart wrench. "Well, I do now. I was wrong, Cat, I admit that. I was wrong to shut them out."

"Maybe you're wrong about us." I spit at him, "Maybe you always were."

My words ring as I circle the argument back to where we'd started.

Finn moves his head side to side, and sighs. "Come with me, I'll show you around. Introduce you, then maybe that will make up your mind."

"Introduce me as what?" I blurt out. "The woman who was sold, used in every way a man can? They already know that."

"Introduce you as a woman who's fuckin' strong. A woman who can hold up her head when nothing she did was wrong." He pauses and settles an intense stare on me. "Yes, they know. Yes, they'd cut you slack if you wanted to bury yourself in here and hide. No, they won't pretend nothing's happened to you. But fuck, woman, I'm asking you to give them a chance. You can't hide for the rest of your life."

"Why not?" I scream at him. "When that's exactly what I want to do?"

His eyes soften. "Because that's not the Cat I know. My Cat has an inner strength, and soon that's going to show."

"I'm not yours." And I'm not strong. Not at all. I have to disavow him of that deceit. "After I was punished the first time, I didn't fight, Finn. I could have bitten off the cock that was shoved into my mouth. I didn't. I could have tried to kick his balls, I didn't."

He gestures toward the stick leaning against the wall. Interpreting his request, I get it for him. *He's going to leave now he knows I just gave up.* Finn would never give up, he'd have died fighting. I must disgust him.

When he pulls himself up and gets himself balanced, I step back, biting back tears, waiting for him to go. But when he takes a step, it brings him closer to me, not further away, not touching, but near enough so I feel the warmth emanating from him.

"Is that what's worrying you?" His nearness is too much, my foot moves back. Undeterred, he continues, "You did what you had to do to survive. Cat, I don't mind that you didn't fight. I'm fuckin' grateful. If you had, I seriously doubt you'd be here now. Your survival instinct kicked in, and it was right."

"Someone like Swift would have fought." I'm just me, and I don't measure up.

"Yeah?" He regains the space he'd lost. "Swift would have analysed the odds. Sure, she's got a better chance of fighting her way out than you had, but if she was outnumbered, she'd have played the same card. Survival," he repeats the words, "that's what's important. And Cat, you're hurting right now. You're trying to make sense of what happened, it will take time, forever perhaps to fully come to terms with what went down. But you're no helpless victim. You're a fuckin' survivor, and I fuckin' admire you for that."

I'm grateful when he moves back, but his face is still fixed on mine. "Speak to Swift. She was trapped, as helpless as yourself. I heard her story, Cat, but don't take it from me, hear it from her. As for me? Gun taunted me with what he was doing to you, and I was unable to do fuck about it."

"You got away." My tone is almost accusing. "I needed help to escape."

He barks a laugh. "Yeah, so did Swift as it happens. And you tell Swift you and she were at a disadvantage because you were women." His head shakes as if he can imagine the reaction I'd get.

"I was raped," I shout. "You've got a cock, that wouldn't have happened to you."

"You think?" His eyes have opened wide. "Babe, sometimes I forget how innocent you are. If that was what it would have taken to break me, Gun would have tried that. But I escaped, yes. And you know why?"

"Because you could," I reply stubbornly.

"Because of you. I had to get out. I had to save you. Christ, Cat. If I hadn't had that fuckin' desire to stop you being harmed, I might have not had tried."

Afterwards I'll wonder whether our voices have become

raised and our conversation had been overheard, but a knock on the door stops us going around in circles.

Finn awkwardly hops, balancing on his stick as he goes to open it and nods at the man standing there.

"Cowboy's cooking again. Thought you might want to come down for dinner."

I'm not hungry, I couldn't eat a bite. But Finn answers for me anyway. "Yeah, we'll be right down."

"Oh, and Road got you these. Thought they might help." Whoever the stranger is, passes over some crutches.

As Finn takes them, closes the door, and tries his new acquisitions out, I huff. "I'll stay here." I fold my arms over my chest to show that I'm serious, giving off the vibes of a confidence I don't feel. I do notice he uses the crutches competently, as if he's used them before. As well he might have done, he must be used to a life full of danger and injury. Unlike me, and when I was tested, I'd failed.

"There's no need to be scared." Finn shows I've not fooled him at all. But if you stay, I'll stay here too. A prospect can bring us something up."

He confuses me, overwhelms me. Maybe if I go with him, it will dilute his presence. Again, he shows how he can read me, as he examines my face, then, giving a sharp nod, he goes to the door, opens it, stepping back and waiting for me to precede him out.

I walk alongside him, seeing he's adept at using the crutches. They give him more stability than the stick, allowing him to keep his cast off the ground, while staying upright.

I haven't seen anything of the clubhouse outside his room before. Despite the nightmare of the past few weeks replaying on a loop in my head, I look around, the fact this is nothing like I expected catches my attention. I could be walking along a hotel corridor—it's nothing like any MC clubhouse I've read about or seen on television. When we come to an elevator and step inside, I laugh shortly with shock. Now this type of music I've heard before, but more often in a shopping mall. And when the very feminine voice announces we've arrived on the first floor, I raise my eyebrows.

"Honor and Duty's little joke," Finn explains.

The doors open onto another hallway, this one looking like it could be found in a modern office block. I follow Finn as he clomps and swings his way down the corridor which leads into a cafeteria, again, something that seem incongruent against the backdrop of the members of the MC. It's full, and I immediately halt.

"It's alright," Finn whispers into my ear. "Cowboy runs a tight ship. If the brothers aren't here on time, they don't get fed."

I thought I had no appetite at all, but the aromas coming from the kitchen area make my mouth water. *Bikers eat like this?* It's not what I expected for sure.

"Cat!" Swift spies me and stands, waving me over. "Come sit with us." She's pointing to a single empty chair, making me wonder whether Finn's invited or not.

Finn looks at me, nods and gives me a rueful smile.

I suppose anyone with a vagina is expected to sit together, and at least it will give me respite from Finn for a short while.

Knowing my hands are shaking, I fix my eyes on Swift, and make my way across the room, praying I won't be stopped or touched. Unimpeded, I find my way to her.

One man already sitting at the table nudges his companion. "Looks like we're going to be listening to girl talk."

Swift makes a V sign with two of her fingers. "Fuck off, Duty. If Cat wants to talk makeup and nails, she's out of luck. Unless Honor joins in the conversation?"

Presumably it's Honor who snorts. "What you going to talk about? How fast you can strip down a Glock and put it back together?"

"Glock?" Swift shakes her head and winks at me. "An FN Minimi perhaps."

"Christ woman, do machine guns get you wet?"

"Probably as much as handcuffs get you hard, Duty."

As a few more good-natured jokes go around, I find myself relaxing. Enough that eventually I enter the conversation. I hold out my hands. "I'm not much of a nail girl myself." All mine are bitten down to the quick.

"What do you do, Cat?" a man sitting opposite me asks. "I'm Bolt, by the way." He holds out his hand to me.

A man's hand. I stare at it, feeling panic, suddenly realising it's not so much how they're going to treat me, it's how I'm able to treat them. I no longer feel comfortable doing everyday normal things. *I can do this,* my internal voice lectures me, worried about making an example of myself. I reach out, tentatively take it, but let go almost immediately. My eyes at first widen, then narrow. It felt almost real, but cold.

"I'm a nurse," I answer him. "And I'm sorry, but is that prosthetic?"

"Yup," he replies without candour.

"A nurse?" Honor tilts his head to one side. "So, what's your weapon of choice?"

Weapon? Oh, he must be referring to Swift and her perchance for machine guns. I think for a moment, then say, "I have been known to use an anal thermometer."

"Hey, Duty," Bolt exclaims, thumping his *non-prosthetic* hand on the table. "She sounds just right for you."

I notice Honor and Duty are sitting close together, closer than most other men. *Are they a couple?* It makes me wonder. But good on them, if so, and on their friends as it doesn't seem to bother them. Bolt just gets a good-natured finger from the man he named.

"Grub's up," Swift observes, and stands. To me she instructs, "Just stay here."

"Yeah, stay and keep me company. Being one-handed, I'm sure someone will wait on me."

"Fuck off, Bolt. We paid a fuckin' fortune for that hand. If you can't pick up a plate with it, we should demand our money back."

But Bolt stays seated, as does Duty. After a moment, Swift returns carefully balancing three plates. She places one in front of Bolt, one she hands to me, then sets down the third for herself. Honor returns with one for Duty.

"You're not vegetarian, are you?"

Shaking my head, I stare down. It's so not what I expected. "What is it?" I ask, gingerly.

"Roasted breast of pigeon with confit leg and beetroot spaghetti," she informs me, as if they eat this every day. Grinning she betrays herself when adding, "Or that's what Cowboy informed me."

Gingerly, I peck at the dish, surprised when after a few moments it's completely clean.

Conversation picks up again, all kept lighthearted. I realise after the main course has been served, a fish dish with some delicious sauce, that they're purposefully avoiding certain subjects: what's happened to me, Finn's place in the club, and what they're doing to find the man who kidnapped and sold me.

After a meringue, cream and fruit dessert which I again enjoy despite the circumstances, I broach the topic myself. "Have you found any sign of Gun, yet?"

Swift settles her eyes on me. "Not yet, but we're closing in. I can feel it."

"Got some things which we might be able to tie together." Honor, his face now serious, confirms.

"We'll get there, Cat. This is what we do." Bolt's sincerity has me believing him. "All you've got to do is hunker down until we get him out of your way."

"I want to leave," I tell them, honestly.

Swift shakes her head. "We need you to stay. Stormy seems to have pulled himself together right now, but if you went away? Hell, he'd be uncontrollable."

I stare down at my now empty plate. He'll survive. He had before me, and he will again. He won't want long term with a woman as damaged as me.

34

Stormy…

The dining area was crowded as it so often is when Cowboy's in the midst of his depression, so if I was going to eat, I'd had to take the only space open. That was on a table alongside Grinch, Mystic and Goofy.

"You got your head out of your ass?" Grinch starts on me as soon as I sit down and while he's helping me place the crutches on the floor by my side.

Three months ago I would have exploded, now I make the first of what will probably be a hundred apologies. Or as much as I'm capable of. "Yeah."

"You trust your brothers now?"

I grimace at Mystic. "I never stopped. Trouble seemed to follow me. I was better off out of it."

"You think we wouldn't have had your back come what may?" Goofy snorts.

"It was the 'come what may' that had bothered me." I admit. Things had happened with no reason, how could I have stopped the same happening again?

Grinch leans back, staring at the pigeon that the prospect

had brought over to him. "Fuck this. When's Cowboy going to cook a decent fried chicken steak?"

"You needn't have come, Brother," Mystic reminds him. "Could have gone to a KFC or something."

"Fuckin' KFC." Grinch picks up a knife and fork and starts dissecting the tiny bird on the plate in front of him.

"Two mouthfuls and it's gone," Goofy observes. "Fuckin' gourmet food isn't worth eating."

I've been toying with mine. When Mystic looks over hopefully, I pass the remainder to him. It only takes him a chew and a swallow to finish it up.

"I spent the day checking the plane. It's refuelled and ready," he assures me. "Whenever you need to go get Gun, just say the word."

The next course is served. I wonder how these old-timers have got the prospects running after them while the other brothers get up to help themselves. But I don't say a word, just accept when a new plate is placed in front of me, appreciating their special status as carrying a plate while hopping on crutches is probably beyond me. As I dig my fork into a plate that looks good but seems completely tasteless, I wonder whether I'll be on the Satan's Devils plane when it heads out after we've got Gun's location.

I also wonder, watching the prospects helping Cowboy, whether I'll be a kitchen hand next time I'm in here. As far as I know, I'll be joining their ranks for six months. And that's the best I can hope for.

"Anything to avoid, Stormy?"

Grinch snaps me out of my reverie, but I don't understand his question.

He takes pity on me. "When we give you a beatdown."

"His head, probably," Goofy says, knowingly. "Unless we want to beat the sense back out of him."

Mystic flexes his fists making his knuckles crack. "Oh, I do love a good beatdown. How about you, Storm?"

"Depends which end I'm on." My statement makes them crack up. I don't doubt they're looking forward to it. A beatdown just short of death serves two purposes, one a punishment for the man being beaten, and hell, I can't deny I've wronged the club badly. The second? Well, once a man's used his fists, all crimes are forgiven. I'll be starting again with a clean slate, albeit sporting a prospect rocker on the back of my cut and a few additional bruises. Idly I wonder whether it will be my original cut, or did they destroy it when I'd walked out?

That's if that's even on the cards. I find myself hoping they are going to beat the hell out of me, it will mean I'm back in the club. Snatcher's given me no indication whether the sentence will be carried out, of if once everything's sorted, we'll part company, and next time I won't be welcomed back.

Brute swings by the table and leans down. "She's eaten everything but drunk no alcohol."

That doesn't surprise me. Cowboy goes all out, his meals would tempt the dead to rise from their graves, though I admit, it hadn't had that effect on me. I risk a glance over at her, pleased to see her smiling. While I hate being apart from her, I know she could do with some space. During our altercation it was obvious her mind was all over the place.

Dessert has come and gone, most of mine devoured by the ever-hungry Mystic when I notice Honor and Duty rise and leave the table. I eye the spaces they've left behind, wondering whether I can go and join Cat. I'm still deliberating when Igor starts making the rounds.

"Church in fifteen," he says, approaching our table.

"Us too?"

Goofy, Grinch and Mystic live at our old clubhouse and maintain a typical MC front for the club, and aren't required when the discussion is about the business side of the club. But as Igor nods and Grinch groans, seems tonight they don't get a pass.

As brothers finish up, taking dirty plates to be stacked on the counter, I stay where I am. I've no position here, and while it hurts, I know won't be invited into church. My sense of loss abates when I decide I'll take my chance to talk to Cat again. Maybe I'll take her up to the clubroom and show her around, see if I can play pool one legged and one-handed. Leaving her on her own to stew and think about things wouldn't be good for her to my mind.

"Whatcha doing?" Snatcher stops by my side. He's frowning at me.

"Waiting for the room to clear, then I thought I'd take Cat upstairs." I stare over at the woman who I'm still treating as mine.

"Need your ass in church." His tone is gruff.

Yeah? That takes me by surprise. My initial enthusiasm fades. "I can't leave Cat, not here with the prospects."

"Take her up to the clubroom and switch on the TV. I'll speak to Brute and make sure he looks after her."

Brute might scare her. "Either that or she can wait in my room." It's not ideal. I don't want her to be alone. It seems I don't have a choice.

Gears is manning the front desk, so I first go to him, explaining under no circumstance is he to let Cat leave. Next I swing my way back into the cafeteria where Cat's now sitting alone, watching Brute and Igor rinse then stack the dirty plates into the dishwasher.

She turns as she hears the clack of my crutches on the floor.

"I've got to get into church," I tell her. "If you want, you can go to the clubroom. Brute or Gears will keep you company, and you can watch TV."

"I'm tired, Finn. Can I go back to the room?"

It's an excuse, but it's easy to understand why she's wary of spending time with strange men. I lead the way, and unlock my door. "Stay here, okay? I'll be back as soon as I can."

"I'll just go to bed early, Finn."

I don't bother to tell her I'll be with her anyway. Sitting on the chair if I have to. There's no way in hell I'll leave her to her nightmares tonight.

I'm the only man walking into church who isn't wearing a cut. I feel naked, excluded, as if there's no place for me anymore. Also telling is how they scramble to bring in an extra chair, then all move up one until there's space to place it. It puts me next to Road. Without being asked he takes the crutches and props them up against the wall behind.

Snatcher bangs the gavel and the room goes quiet. For a moment he doesn't speak. When he does, I'm not surprised the topic is me.

"Your woman coped with her introduction to us."

"She did. But she's wary."

"She needs time," Swift says softly. "I like her for you, Stormy.

"We've got decisions to make about you, Stormy." Snatcher seems impatient to move this along.

I hold out my non-cast-covered hand in supplication. "You've heard what I have to say, even I know I can't justify myself. I knew I'd made a mistake the moment I took off my cut. But I couldn't turn around and come back." I take a breath and remind them, "Even before Cat was taken, I decided to return to the fold, prepared to take the beatdown or worse and to prospect for the club."

"Or worse?" Thor parrots. "You think we'd put you down like a rabid dog?"

I shrug. "If that fits. But in that case, I want a promise you'll make sure Cat is safe."

Out of the corner of my eye I notice Honor tapping the table impatiently, making me recall it was after he'd received a call that we'd convened. I start to doubt my future is the reason for this meeting.

Snatcher confirms. "Words are words, Stormy. We," he moves his gaze around the table, "will abide by the terms originally set. You are at this meeting as a courtesy only. From the moment you leave this room, you'll be a prospect. Thor?"

The VP shoots something down the table toward me. It's a prospect rocker. What can I do but pick it up and give a respectful nod toward the man I can once again call Prez? I knew I couldn't come back as a full member, and hey, it's better than being out of the club. The sympathy vote for my injuries was one I had no right to expect.

"I won't let you down, Prez."

As Snatcher looks dubious at my comment, Preacher narrows his eyes. "Your beatdown's coming, Stormy."

Again, I just nod. I know what to expect.

"Honor?" Snatcher changes the subject.

The brother addressed wastes no time. "Gun's reared his head. I've got a ping on his location. The fucker's in San Diego."

"We calling on Lost to pick him up?" Swift asks.

Prez shakes his head. "Not happy bringing another chapter into this when it's not their fight."

"We work as a team," Preacher states. "Each of us knows our part. Strangers might not help us. We can't blow this, we've got one chance when he's got careless, so we go in heavy and make no mistakes."

"He slipped up," Duty informs the table. "He's clever, and Preacher's right, I doubt he'll do that again. It was pure luck on our part, the door closed immediately after we got the location ping. Hopefully he'll think it was too fast for anyone to get a handle on it."

I consider myself one of the best in the business, yet even I'd once slipped up, forgetting momentarily to cloak where I was.

It's not beyond the realm of possibility that Gun also fucked up. Even so, I can't keep quiet.

"It could be a trap."

I'm not the only one to think it, but as the discussion flows, the brothers, the patched members who'll make the decisions, seem to believe it's worth checking out. Preacher's need for going in heavy is explained, mindful it could be as I'd suggested, a trap, They need to be prepared for anything.

"I want to go," I state. Surely I've got a right? It's down to Gun that I'm next to useless, and I may have lost the only woman I want in my life. As for Cat? She's got to live with what's happened to her. I have to do what little I can to make things right.

"You're staying here, Prospect. First, you'd be a liability in any fight. And second, you've got a woman who needs you here."

I open my mouth and shut it. Much as I hate it, he's right.

"We'll leave the old-timers here at the clubhouse. You do whatever the fuck they say, Stormy. Grinch will be in charge."

And doesn't that burn in my gut? Again, though, what option have I got but to raise and dip my head in resigned agreement? This could be a test. One sign I'm not toeing the line, and I won't be a prospect anymore.

"Preacher?" Snatcher prompts the sergeant-at-arms.

"Flight time's two hours. I want to hit hard, fast and under-cover of darkness. Wheels up in an hour."

I'm torn. I wish I was going, wish I could have input at least. I want to know whether the intention is to take Gun alive and bring him back so we can get answers. But being a prospect means I won't be involved, I'm only at this meeting on sufferance. Gun's punishment won't be at my hands, I may not even know about it.

Fuck, being a prospect is hard. I have to trust these men to do what I'm not allowed. There's no point appealing to

Snatcher, I signed up for this when I walked out, leaving my cut without a backward glance.

Cat. *Focus on Cat.* She's what's important.

As the full members waste no time, standing, pushing chairs back under the table and walking out, I turn and reach for my crutches. Getting them under my arms, I lever myself up.

Pip's hanging back as though waiting for me.

"Six months, Stormy. That will go fast."

At least I've a chance to be a member again if I don't act in character and fuck this up. Pip, with his prosthetic legs, has no such chance. For the first time I wonder whether the loss of his cut hit him hard.

"You going to San Diego?"

He shakes his head, "No. I'll be supporting from this end."

I want to ask whether I can help him, but can only resolve to do anything I'm asked. I'm just a prospect, excluded from everything.

35

*E*at...

Whether it had been Swift's presence at the table, knowing she'd take no shit from anyone, or just that the conversation had been kept lighthearted, I'd relaxed at dinner, and surprisingly eaten everything on my plate.

While I'd been captive they'd not treated me like a human, food was scarce and unappetising when or if it appeared. That the gourmet plates were tasty but tiny probably helped. I'd eaten more than I had at any point during the past three weeks. The consequence being, when I returned to Finn's room, I couldn't stop yawning.

I didn't mean to fall asleep, but I did.

I was back there. The Master was pinning me down, forcing himself on me. I screamed, and as I'd done the first time, before he beat me so badly, I fought. I got free, but it was like running in treacle, he was catching up with me.

I cried for help until my voice was hoarse, begged for mercy, for him to let me go.

He kept on coming, closer and closer, I could feel his warmth, smell his fetid breath, and all the time I knew he'd beat me so cruelly...

"Cat. Cat, babe. Wake up."

He grabbed hold of my shoulder... Not again! Summoning up all the strength I have, I throw him off.

"Oomph."

Something about the voice breaks into my subconscious. I open my eyes to see Finn lying like an overturned turtle on his back on the floor by the side of the bed.

"Finn!" My emotions might be all over the place as far as he is concerned, but he's injured, and I've just knocked him over. I slide off the bed full of regret. "Finn, are you alright?"

His eyes examine me, then he gives a half-smile. "Not the first time you've knocked me off my feet, Cat."

"I didn't mean to, I…"

"You were having a nightmare. I should have been more fuckin' careful about how I woke you up. But fuck, Cat, I didn't want you back there."

If anyone knows how to wake me from bad dreams, it should be him. Only this time, he can't do it with a gentle touch or by pulling me into his arms. My stupid mind equates a man's touch with *his*.

Gingerly I reach out a shaking hand to help him up, but he does it himself, pushing his weight against his one working hand until he's sitting up. "He's dead, Cat. He can't hurt you anymore."

"But Gun can," I admit. "What if Gun finds out where I am?"

He stares at me. "I suppose I shouldn't be telling you this, but all the brothers have gone. They've got Gun's location. Within hours, Cat, Gun will be dead or captured, and you won't have to worry anymore."

My voice drops to a whisper. "Are you sure?"

"I trust them, Cat. They're the best."

I know him too well. "Why didn't you go with them?" Even hurt as he is, I know he'd have wanted to be there.

"Because I'm just a prospect, Cat." He reaches in his pocket and pulls out a patch, showing it to me. "I'll be honest, at first the thought of staying behind was almost more than I could take. But I saw you having that nightmare and knew you were more important to me. This is my place. You're more important to me than revenge."

"I want him dead," I tell him seriously. "He let me believe you had died. That hurt me so fucking much."

"I want him taken alive," Finn replies, quickly adding his reasoning. "The crimes against us are the tip of the iceberg. I want to know what more he's got to hide. I'm not arrogant enough to think it all comes back to me, or is about something that happened years ago."

She thinks on that for a moment. "When will we know if they've caught him?"

"They'll be boarding the plane now and should be landing in San Diego in a couple of hours. I don't know how long it will take to get where he's holed up. But hopefully, by morning we'll know whether they've been successful or not."

I sigh. "It's going to be a long night just waiting." I don't think I'll be able to go back to sleep.

Finn's brow creases. "Mystic will stay at the airfield waiting for the plane to come back. Apart from Grinch, Goofy and the prospects, we've got the place to ourselves. Why don't I show you around? You still haven't seen the clubroom yet."

It's better than staying here in this room. Time is going to hang heavy on our hands. Could it really be that by dawn I'll no longer have a threat hanging over my head? It won't wipe out the recent past, but it may help me to move on. If I still want to, there'd be nothing stopping me going home.

For an answer I collect his crutches from where they've fallen and pass them to him, then stand back and let him get himself sorted. Wondering what I'm heading into, I follow him out.

The clubroom is situated on the floor beneath where the

accommodation is housed. It's a big space, a bar down one side, a pool table, games machines, and a dartboard. There are sofas, tables and chairs. Like the cafeteria downstairs it's spotless. When I comment on its cleanliness, Finn grimaces, and reminds me, keeping it so will fall to him now.

"Want a drink?"

I shake my head, no. I want to keep a clear head. I've had enough of being sedated and drugged.

"You play pool?"

I did, when I was a trainee nurse. My first inclination is to refuse to play, but what can I do instead except brood? "A bit." I doubt if I'm in his league.

I'm right. Three games later I'm losing to a man balancing on one leg and playing with not even his dominant hand, needing to use his cast to steady the cue stick. Finn tries to help me line up shots, but as he abstains from physically touching me, I find his instructions hard to follow. I can't keep my eyes from watching the clock, but the minutes seem to tick by so slow.

Finn's phone buzzes in his pocket. Taking it out, he rolls his eyes. He taps something back. And gets a reply.

"Brute needs me in reception." He's frowning.

"What for?"

"Probably wants me to take over from him and man the front desk. I'm one of the prospects now, guess he's going to play on it."

"Prospect duty?"

Finn shrugs. "I knew this was coming."

"Can he order you around? He's a prospect himself, isn't he?"

"He can't. But all prospects help each other out. Maybe he just needs a piss. Whatever, I've got to go down. Do you want to—"

"I'll come." I don't want to stay here by myself. A prospect's manning the bar, but I don't know him. Even if I did, I doubt right now I could trust anyone.

In no hurry, Finn gets his crutches under him again and does that swing hop thing over to the elevator.

"I wish I could turn back time." I muse aloud. "I wish we could start over, Finn. But once Gun's not a threat, I am going home. Alone."

"Cat…"

"I don't belong in your world."

"You want me to leave the club?" He moves so he can face me. "If that's what you want, I'll do it. I'll do anything for you."

The elevator, which seems slow, at last arrives, and the doors slide open. He gestures for me to enter first.

As he presses the button to take us down, I know I can't give him false hope. "I need to find myself again, Finn. I'm sorry, but as soon as I can, I'm going to go."

"You're being hasty," he tells me, as the doors meet once again. "You need time. I'll give you some space, Cat, but I'm never going to give up."

The downward journey ends. Stepping out of the elevator, I round on him. "I need control," I wail. "I need to take back my life. I need to do this on my own and on my terms. I want to go home. Alone."

Pain fills his eyes, but this isn't about him now. It's about me, and what I want. He starts to move toward the front of the building, and I follow. He stops so fast, I crash into his back.

"What the fuck?" he exclaims.

Peering around him I can see why he's stopped. Brute's on his feet, a gun pointed toward one of the older bikers, one of those Finn was sitting with during our meal. He looks rough around the edges and more like you'd expect as a member of a motorcycle club. But, over his cut he's wearing some kind of device covered in wires. Even a civilian like me can guess what it is.

"Goofy?" Finn asks, and rather than moving back, steps

closer at the same time pushing me behind him. "Brute! Put the fuckin' gun down."

"They've got the place surrounded," Goofy replies, his voice sounding pissed rather than scared as he glances disdainfully down at the bomb strapped to his chest. "They've got Grinch and Gears. Fuckin' jumped us where we went out for a smoke."

Finn waves toward the device and says very calmly. "What are they waiting for?"

"For Pip to give himself up. They said, if he does, they'll let the rest of us go."

Finn hops back, motioning Goofy to step forward. I realise he's moving him out of sight of the front window. He turns to Brute. "Get me the toolkit from under the desk, then go warn Pip. But tell him to stay put." He starts talking again, this time it seems like it's to himself. "It's Gun, isn't it? He wants Pip alive. Which means we've got time before this blows. Else he risks him going up with everyone else."

Brute snaps to obey Finn while I wonder at the dynamic. He doesn't object being given an instruction from another prospect, but there's something about Finn's voice, a new confidence. He sounds like a man completely in control. Me? I'm terrified. I haven't come through what I have only to die now. As Brute gets the toolkit I notice looped around his wrist is a lead, and connected to that, a handsome black spaniel. My eyes widen, then shutter. *Don't let his dog die.*

"I'm sorry," Goofy says. "We didn't have a fuckin' chance. It was Gun, I recognised him from the photos. Honor was showing around. Before we knew they were there, they surrounded us." He sounds so calm, standing stock still while I'm shaking.

"SEALs have a habit of doing that," Finn observes calmly, walking around Goofy now, his eyes moving, missing nothing. "I thought San Diego might be a trap, though I didn't expect it to be a decoy. Nothing you could have done, Brother. Don't blame yourself."

"Is that a bomb?" I ask, shakily, while knowing it can't be anything else.

"Yeah," Finn says, distracted by his inspection. "Booby trapped, I expect."

"He told me I couldn't take it off."

"I'll just have to disarm it." Finn states, confidently, moving to the toolkit which Brute had placed close.

"He said no one could. Any tampering and it will blow." Now I notice a slight tremor in Goofy's voice, he's clearly trying to keep a brave face. "You should go, Stormy. Get the girl out of here and the others."

"Nowhere we can go if he's got the place surrounded, Goof. You know that. And Pip's not giving himself up. The saferoom won't hold everyone."

Will it hurt, I wonder? Will I feel my body blown into smithereens, or will there be no warning just darkness? A welcome relief from the nightmare in my head, or a missed chance at a new life?

Suddenly I know, I want to live, I don't want to give up.

"Stormy?" A stunned sounding voice asks.

"Get back into your office, Pip. Take Cat. Both of you will be safe in the saferoom. Take App with you."

App? Who the hell's App?

"Fuck that. If there's a chance I'm going to take it. Grinch is out there." Pip stands his ground. "I'll give myself up."

Finn rounds on him, no, that's wrong. This isn't my gentle Finn, this is Stormy. More used to barking orders than taking them. "Gun's not going to leave any of us alive, Pip. But he doesn't want you dead. We've got time as long as you keep your fuckin' head down. Brute? Make sure Pip stays and keep him safe."

"I'll get him into the saferoom." Brute agrees. "Come on, Pip.

Stormy's right. You're more useful to everyone inside and alive. And someone's got to look after Cat and the dog. Swift would have my balls if anything happens to him."

"No."

"Fuckin' go, Pip. You too, Cat,"

"I'm staying," I tell Finn stubbornly. "You said we'd should stay together. Well, I'm not leaving you now."

Finn's growl makes me jump, and Pip glares. "Get him out of here, Brute. Igor?" He motions to the other prospect who must have realised something's wrong. "You fuckin' help him." Pip tries to stare Finn down, but apparently his prosthetics make him no match for the two burly prospects who take him by the arms and none too gently leads him away, one still holding the lead of the dog who's tail is wagging like it's some kind of adventure.

Finn's eyes meet mine. "You will be joining him, Cat. I won't be able to do anything without knowing you're safe. But for now, I need your help. I can't do this one-handed."

Me help? I squeak, swallow, then notice Goofy's eyes on me.

"He's got this," Goofy says, his husky tone belying his confidence. "If anyone can disarm this, Stormy can."

Finn isn't going to give me a choice. "Cat, come around here. See these wires? Very, very gently, slip your hand under them." When I do, he gives praise. "Good girl. You've got small hands which will help. Try to keep them steady."

I notice he's got some wire cutters in his hand. "Do you know which to cut?" I'm praying he says yes, a snip and the danger will be over.

"I wish it was that easy. First, I've got to try to trace them."

I swallow. Hard. "Couldn't he detonate it any moment? Will he suspect what you're doing?"

He's staring at something intently and moving to the left slowly. "Gun doesn't know I'm part of the Satan's Devils, he won't expect me to be here. I was in the hospital under a fake identity."

"He knows all the tech experts of the club are on their way to California," Goofy reinforces what Finn's saying. "Motherfucker was talking when he was trussing me like a fuckin' Thanksgiving turkey. I doubt he thinks one of the prospects is a bomb disposal expert."

"You're right, this is booby trapped, in a number of ways," Finn states, almost in admiration. "Wires leading nowhere, the colours misleading. Anyone who didn't know exactly what they were doing would have a problem with it."

"And you do?" I bite my lip as I ask, willing my hand to be steady. It's the only part of me not shaking.

"Ease your hand down, Cat. No sudden movements. There'll be pressure senses."

So much could go wrong. It puts my ordeal over the last three weeks into perspective. If this is my last few minutes on earth, I don't want to leave without telling Finn the truth.

It's probably not the best time to tell a man how you feel for him when he's in the middle of disarming a bomb. "I love you, Finn. I never stopped."

He doesn't even look at me, but his lips curve slightly. "Babe, I love you too. We're going to move past everything, okay? Now, give me a second…." He lifts a wire. "Hold this, will you?"

I watch him close his eyes briefly, his lips move as he closes the blades of the cutter together around the wire that's draped over my finger, in the deadly silence the snick of them meeting is deafening.

But no explosion.

"Stay still," he warns Goofy. "That's one, but knowing Gun, he'll have a failsafe."

Goofy doesn't move, he doesn't speak. If he wasn't still standing I'd wonder whether he'd stopped breathing. "Cat, put your hand here. I need you to pull on this wire."

I do so, gingerly.

"Harder."

Holding my breath, I tug it, it comes loose, and Finn fast has his hand on a switch underneath and is pushing on it.

"You see the yellow and green wire? Take the cutters and cut through it."

"Me?" My voice has gone up an octave.

"Yeah, I can't let this go, and I can't use my right hand."

I gulp, swallow, and stare into steady eyes that gaze back into mine. His are full of emotion, leaving me in no doubt he'd not just parroted my words. He really loves me. How did I ever think I could live without him?

Taking the cutters from his pocket, I concentrate, and do what he's asked me.

Nothing. No explosion. Suddenly there's a knife in Finn's hand and he's slicing through the straps that bind the explosives to Goofy's chest.

As Goofy struggles out, getting the device off himself, he turns to Finn and hugs him warmly. "What do we do now?"

"Now we get Grinch and Gears," Finn says seriously. "How many outside, Brother?"

"Ten that I saw."

"Gun will be getting impatient. He'll make a move soon if he wants Pip alive, maybe kill one of ours. We've no time to waste, let's get tooled up."

Goofy doesn't have to be told twice, he heads down the corridor with Finn on crutches after him. When they come to a cupboard Finn enters a key code and it opens to reveal an armoury. The two men take out a variety of weapons, and a pile of Kevlar vests, one of which Finn passes to me.

I slide into the awkward garment, take the gun Finn hands to me, but without a clue how to use it.

He notices my unease. "Just point and pull the trigger."

36

Stormy…

I run through what I know of the men at my disposal. Yeah, I've put myself in charge. Pip's an intelligence man, not military, though he'll be able to use a handgun. Igor is ex-Army, Brute a former Marine. Goofy's been brought up in the school of hard knocks, and Cat might be new to this, but as long as she doesn't aim at our team, the spray of bullets from the semi I've handed her could come in useful. We might be outnumbered, but I'm confident in my small army. I have to be.

We convene in Pip's office. Despite my instruction, he hasn't gone into the safe room. When we appear, Brute passes App into Cat's surprised safekeeping, with the explanation he's Swift's hearing dog and that he wouldn't like to be her if she doesn't keep App safe. I'm grateful she's got something else to focus on, maybe I can use her love of animals to protect him, if not herself.

"We've got the element of surprise," I tell them. "But only if we move fast. I'd like to take Gun alive. Which means taking the other men out."

"If all fails, put a bullet in his head." Pip catches my eye and tilts his head toward Cat. Yeah, I know what I'm protecting.

My modus operandi, up to now, is what's got me into trouble. "Last resort," I tell Pip. We want answers.

Quickly I sketch a drawing, pointing to the parts of the building where each of us should go. Heads bowed around me, everyone stares and listens. No one interrupts, they just nod.

"You going to be able to aim, Brother?" Goofy asks once I've explained my hastily thought up plan.

"Yeah, Goof." As long as I can steady my rifle, my left hand can pull the trigger.

I point to the rough sketch again. "I'll be up on the roof and take who's holding Grinch first. Igor, when it's time, you kill the outside lights, Brute, you get out the back, they'll be surrounding us. Shoot first, ask questions after." The prospect, I'm pleased to notice, has equipped himself with three guns fitted with silencers.

Cat's green eyes flare, then fill with worry, but she stays silent. I'm guilty that as is usual for a sniper I'll be in a position of relative safety, except… But what can I do? I'm handicapped with an arm and a leg out of use. I can't creep up on anyone unawares, not balanced on crutches. The best I can contribute is keeping my head down and picking them off. At least this building is sturdy, or so I hope. I've got the easy job.

"You got this Pip?"

"I got this." He tells me with a sharp nod. "I know what to do."

"Cat, you'll be okay in the safe room, it's built like a fuckin' tank. As soon as Pip's back with you, the door will be closed."

"I want to be with you." Her voice trembles.

"No fuckin' way." I take the chance of curling my hand around the back of her neck, pulling her forehead into mine. "I can't be distracted, Cat. I need to know you're safe and not be worrying about you. If someone gets the door open, you've got the gun. It's set to automatic fire. You just put your finger on the trigger and hold it there. And take care of App. He'll be frightened, okay?"

She throws herself at me. "I can't lose you, Finn. What I said before was wrong."

There's no time for discussion. "Be the strong woman you are," I say against her ear. "You don't get rid of me that easily. I told you, you're mine and you're not getting out of that. Be strong for me, Cat. All you've got to do is wait for me."

"Why don't you just kill Gun? Won't that mean it will be over?" She bites her lip, asking for assurances I can't give.

Pip comes nearer, his face full of sympathy. "I'm convinced Gun's another foot soldier. He's got no personal beef with me. I don't know who's pulling his strings, but I'm sure someone is. If so, those men out there will continue to fight for their paymaster."

I agree with him. Gun's the immediate superior, but taking him out will give them pause, but not move them from the objective.

Making myself pull away, I move Cat toward the safe room. "It's time, Cat. Promise me you'll do what we've agreed. This won't work unless I know you're doing exactly what I told you."

Pip looks at her. "Every soldier must play his part," he says, gently, giving a soft push to encourage her to move."

"Finn..." I hate to, but I have to ignore her pleas. No words will change this. We're outnumbered. It's the only way.

I should give her more time to get over her ordeal, but if I'm going to die, I want to go with her taste on my mouth. She's halfway into the safe room but I pull her back. When I lower my lips, hers come up to greet mine. Tangling my hands in her hair, I pull her to me, thrusting my tongue into her mouth. Then, before I'm ready, I pull back.

"Go, Cat. Be safe. I love you."

I don't watch her all the way into the safe room. Instead, I exit as fast as I can, making my way clumsily to the elevator, not thinking how I'll be getting down later. With a final word to Pip, nods directed at Goofy, Igor and Brute, I take my lonely journey up to my perch, wedging myself between the parapet and an air-conditioning unit.

Wasting no time, I pull down my night goggles allowing me to find Gun. Grinch is being held by another man and has a gun trained on his head. The man holding him looks military from the way he's standing. Whether Grinch knows what to do or not, his body isn't directly aligned with the man holding the weapon. I've got a clear headshot. Gears is further back, he's short and stocky, and luckily being held by someone taller.

We're avoiding communication devices, knowing Gun might have hacked in and be listening, I wouldn't put anything past him. So I use the old-fashioned method, watching the second hand of my watch tick round to the minute.

I steady myself, at five seconds I inhale and hold it, the lights go out and simultaneously my finger tightens…

At the same time as the second bullet leaves the barrel my world explodes.

My optimism was misplaced, this building wasn't built to a high spec code, or the explosion of the bomb in the foyer was badly placed, or was far more powerful than I had anticipated. As the roof starts shifting beneath my feet, I throw myself clear of the air-conditioning unit, knowing its weight will drag me down.

I lose my weapon as I try to hold on to anything that appears relatively stable around me as blocks of the three-storey building start falling.

The creaks, groans, crashes which signal the death throes of the clubhouse are punctuated with the sharp sounds of gunfire. All I can do is hope that we're on the winning side. At least Cat will be safe, the reinforced steel room she's in was at least built to survive a full force explosion.

I start to slide. My right hand tries to work, scrambling for purchase, but the cast around my fingers is too tight for them to be much help. My left shoulder screams in agony as I grab strands of wire and hold tight to them.

Christ! Something hit my head. Hard. I shake it to clear the moment of fogginess. *All I've got to do is hold on...*

I'm at the front, right over reception, right where the building is slowly collapsing. I try to move back toward the rear of the building, but gravity is now against me.

I'm hanging over a precipice, a yawning three-storey gap beneath me. I'm losing my grip…

I grab at something, it's an air-conditioning duct, swinging in the breeze, but at an angle. My cast covered leg almost gets stuck as I slide myself onto it, using it as a slide to get lower.

One floor down.

The duct twists, throwing me out, tossing me against the falling building. *So close yet too far.* A blown out window, I hold the frame, feeling the bricks crumble beneath. My hand's sliced by glass, but I've more than that to worry about as the whole frame tilts and I'm falling again.

Another floor down far too fast.

Knowing this is going to hurt like hell if not kill me, I let go, tucking my body as though I was landing from a parachute. I hit the ground, jarring my legs, but automatically roll until I come to a stop on hands and knees.

I'm fucking alive.

For a moment I don't believe it.

A man runs up to me. Shaking my head and blinking my eyes to clear the dust from my sight, I tense, knowing I'm unarmed, *enemy or foe?*

Igor stops in front of me. "You okay?"

Though I haven't tested it out, I think I am, or at least, not in danger of dying. While I'm not sure I can move, I can snap orders. "Status report."

"Nine dead, all theirs. Gun is injured but still alive. Gears took a bullet, but he's breathing."

"Cat?"

"Cat and Pip are fine. The safe room was intact, just difficult to open."

We did it. But it's too soon for elation. And that fucking explosion will have garnered attention. "Prospects on clean up. We've got to get the bodies out of here fast."

"Already on it." Igor half turns. "You need help?"

"Yeah." I admit, allowing him to pull me to my feet.

I forget my non-weight-bearing leg and stagger which isn't surprising, my good one's hurting just as much. He offers me his shoulder to lean on and leads me to the truck which is already laden with bodies and bits I barely recognise as human.

"Finn!"

"Whoa!" I try to catch a sobbing and crying Cat before she knocks me over, and App, the brat that he is, nearly finishes the job wrapping his lead around me. I wait while she untangles him.

"I'm okay," I try to impress on her, once she's got me free. "I'm okay."

"I was so worried. I saw…" *She saw me fall.* "I thought Igor would come back and tell me you were dead. How the hell did you survive?"

Having no idea myself, so I can't tell her. I try to minimise the risk I was in. "I was a SEAL, Cat. We're survivors."

Whatever she's going to say next, she's interrupted.

"All loaded!" shouts Brute. "I'm out of here!"

"Can't pick up all the bullet casings," Grinch moans.

"Leave it to me." Pip gives me a nod, and from somewhere summons up a grin. "I'll deal with the cops. Fuck knows they won't be too concerned about someone blowing up an MC, or evidence from our target practice."

It's then I realise someone's missing. "Gears?" I snap. Igor had told me he was shot.

"Gears took a bullet to his leg. He'll live, but he's gone with Brute." Pip shakes his head and pulls out his phone. "I better get in touch with Snatcher now comms are safe to use. Oh, and Stormy? Gun's shot but cursing up a storm. Thought you'd like to know."

That cheers me up.

"Grinch okay?

"Singing your fuckin' praises. Do you even have to ask?"

Nah. I don't. Even one-handed, I'm a fucking good sniper. But I'd had to make sure, the building exploded before I saw that the bullets had hit their intended targets, the men holding Grinch and Gears.

As Pip walks away to deal with Snatcher, I can hear sirens in the distance. With an expert eye I look around. Sure, behind us what remains of the building is burning, destroying everything we own. But we're alive, and anything can be replaced. Our equipment might be gone, but our intelligence isn't bound by servers and computers, it's all stored in the cloud. We can rebuild.

"I found this in the safe room. I hung onto it." Cat's holding something to her. I bark a laugh when I see what it is. It's my fucking cut. Pip must have stored it there. "Do you want to put it on?"

"Nah, not until I've changed the rocker. Hold onto it for me, will you?" I'm pleased to see it, having expected it to have been destroyed, if not by the Devils then by the explosion.

"What do we do now?"

"Wait for the cops." I tell her.

"In the state you're in?" Pip's eyes widen. "Fuck that. Nah, you get out of here, Storm. Take your woman and the dog and get back to the old clubhouse. I'll be there as soon as we can.

You've done enough for tonight." He throws me the keys to one of the club's SUVs.

Giving him my thanks with just a raise of my chin, I hop with one hand on her shoulder around to the rear of the clubhouse, and slide into the passenger seat, taking App's leading and giving it a small tug so he jumps in with me. "You drive," I tell her, pointing to the rear exit to the compound. Going that way we should avoid the cops speeding our way. Thank goodness we're right on the outskirts of the city, and none of the other units are occupied this time of night.

"Where do I go?"

I give her directions, and soon we're drawing up behind the old Utah chapter clubhouse. Surprisingly, it's like coming home, though I've never been based here, and only before have visited when attending club parties.

I assess it fast. There are bedrooms enough for most of the club, though as they've only been used as crash or fuck rooms after a party for years and probably won't be up to much. But better than turning up bloodied and bruised at a hotel. Though Cat deserves more, we'll make the best of it.

When we go inside, again, with me having to lean on her, her holding App's lead and the spaniel traipsing along behind, we're not the only ones here. Doc is already sewing up Gears' leg. Gears, is swigging from a bottle while he does.

Doc turns when I enter, his eyebrows rise making his eyes widen. "I presume you're next."

"Nah, I got off lightly." I catch sight of myself in the mirror above the bar and snort. I can see why he was worried. My features are barely visible through the amount of dust on my face, and my forehead and cheeks are bloodied."

"Finn!" Cat exclaims, getting her first proper look at me in good light.

"All superficial, babe." Though fuck knows how. Someone was on my side tonight. *The second time I've escaped death in an explosion.* I vow not to try my luck and hope to avoid a third time. "I just need a shower. You okay Gears?"

"Through and through." Moving closer I bump my left fist against his. We're both survivors.

I turn as Cat exclaims. "I don't get you men. Gears was shot, you've been blown up and fell from the roof, the club's lost everything, your home, your work. Yet you're both *fine.*" She huffs, and places her hands on her hips. "What does it take to faze you?"

"Nothing if I've got you," I tell her truthfully, lowering my voice so Doc remains oblivious of our conversation. "Nothing's lost which can't be replaced. Gun's alive and Swift will be in her element getting answers. At last we'll find who's been targeting Pip, then the club will be safe."

Gears winks at me. He might not have heard the words, but he's read the sentiment.

"I'm going up to get a shower. Hey," I grimace, "The accommodations aren't much here, Cat, but we'll make do for now, okay? You coming?"

"Leave App with me, if you like?" Gears calls out.

As Cat passes off Swift's hearing dog, I use the bannister to haul my ass up the stairs, and turn into the closest room. There's a bed and that's about all I can say, and a bathroom which could probably do with a scrub, though it will need one again once I've finished, so I'm not bothered.

I can't get a read on Cat, I muse, as I wonder whether to strip off in the bedroom or try to manoeuvre with my awkward casts in the tiny bathroom. I decide it will have to be the latter as I don't want to traumatise her. While, for now, she seems more like her old self, she's probably running on adrenaline. When she crashes, I'll have to be prepared for her to come down hard. She's had one shock after another, and my literal fall from grace as I slid from the building can't have helped her.

She's followed me into the bedroom and is looking around in disgust, her nose wrinkling.

I feel embarrassed. "Look, it's not much. We'll go to a hotel tomorrow."

She gives a quick shake of her head. "A few days ago, I'd have looked on this as paradise, Finn. I'm just trying to process that I'm here, and so are you. I thought I'd lost you again tonight."

I go to her side fast, risking placing my hand on her chin. "You can't get rid of me that easily. It's over, Cat. All we've got to do is move on. And we can do that. Tonight you can say we're both survivors."

She sobs, and for a moment I hold her against me, well, lean on her really, but just let her cry it out. I'm proud she's held it together as long as she has. For a moment I thought I was a goner, knowing she'd seen that, well, fuck.

I'd taken risks, while I never doubted I'd disarm the bomb, she hadn't known my confidence nor my level of skill. It dawns on me she must have thought she was going to be blown to smithereens.

"That bomb, Cat. You weren't in danger."

"I know," she says through another sob. "I trusted you, Finn. But, why did it explode later?"

"That was me, I rigged it to cause a diversion." It had worked better than I had expected. I didn't expect the whole damn clubhouse to go up.

"Next time, could you give me some warning?"

I can't help it, I laugh. "I'm fuckin' hoping there won't be a next time."

She pulls away, but only so she can rub away her tears which have mingled with the dust that covers me from head to toe. Her face might be lined with streaks, but she's never looked more beautiful to me.

When she glances at her hands, she notices they're filthy,

then her eyes narrow on me. "You need to shower. Do you want me to help?"

I didn't realise how tense I was, how scared of saying, doing, the right thing until she said those words. Fuck yes, is my answer.

"I have to get out of these clothes. I shower naked," I make it plain. "Though, don't expect much. I think I might have broken my dick on the way down." I certainly hadn't done it any favours.

"I'm not exactly in working order," she tells me with a shudder and her eyes become hooded at her own reminder.

My lips purse. "We'll get through this." I promise her again.

37

*C*at…

Back in Kentucky, when Finn first spoke about the Utah Satan's Devils' clubhouse, I'd imagined something much like the place I've come to now, and nothing like the modern office block where I'd woken up—hell, was it just yesterday? So much has happened it seems a lifetime ago.

This is more rustic, basic. A long two storey building with an auto-shop attached, a compound surrounded by chain link fencing, and a huge sign proclaiming it's the home of the Satan's Devils MC. The clubroom has nicotine stained walls and ceiling, and the bar top is smooth, polished by thousands of elbows that must have rested there over the years and ringed from numerous drinks. The air is tainted by the scent of stale beer and cigarette smoke.

The kitchen, well, from my quick sneak look is nothing like that which I saw when I'd glanced behind the counter during dinner last night. The thought of Cowboy cooking a gourmet meal in there is laughable. The grease on the stove is half an inch thick, it looks like no one's ever cleaned it.

The bedrooms, well to say they could do with a good clean is an understatement, they could probably do with fumigating as well.

I know why Finn didn't take me to a hotel, our appearance would have caused questions, but his concern this place would make me cut and run isn't right either. It's old, but lived in and used. Surprisingly, even given the state of the furniture and decoration, it feels more like a home than the building that was so recently destroyed.

A new mattress, fresh lick of paint, a good polish and a gallon of disinfectant, and I'll be quite happy to stay here.

The near loss of Finn had put everything into perspective.

I knew Finn was going to the roof, I'd heard that part of the plan. But what I hadn't picked up was that he was going to blow the place sky-high with him on top of it. If I'd known that, well —could I have stopped him? I doubt it. It's probably best I knew nothing about it.

Thank heavens for Pip who'd kept me company in the safe room. Barely had he shut the door when there was that deafening explosion, the safe room had rocked, moved, making me stagger and knock into the side. The panic of not knowing what was going to happen outweighed the fear when Pip took me into his arms, using his body to save me from injury.

Even when the initial movement had ceased, the crashes, bangs and agonised shrieks of steel beams thundered around us, were amplified by the steel cage we were in. App, well even as well trained as he is, added to the cacophony by barking. I'd picked him up and had held him.

"You're safe," Pip had told me, firmly. "We're going to survive. This room is fireproof, and sturdy."

I didn't care about myself, didn't have it in me to care about anyone else, not even the dog I was holding. Suddenly it came into focus, the way Finn had left me, a goodbye in his eyes as he ascended to the roof. What do I know about buildings? Had

Finn been aware he was putting his life on the line and saying goodbye for a final time?

"Finn!" I cried out.

Pip's arms had tightened around me, and such was my fear for Finn, I barely noticed. "Finn did what he had to do, what only he could."

"He's dead, isn't he?" He has to be, it sounds like the whole building is coming down.

"Don't think like that," Pip snaps. "Finn's resourceful."

I know he is, he was a SEAL for fuck's sake. But his wings have been clipped. Even whole he'd have difficulty coming down from the roof.

A particularly loud crash had me startling. In the light of Pip's flashlight I catch sight of his wince.

He answers my unspoken question, "That was the elevator, I think."

And Finn has difficulty on stairs.

Time seems to stop, the sounds begin to die off, a rattle here, a shudder there, another loud bang as something else crashes into the box we're in.

"They'll come for us as soon as it's safe," Pip reassures me.

"Can't we get out?"

"Not letting you go anywhere until we get the all clear."

I didn't voice my fears, but that hadn't stopped me thinking them. What if the plan hadn't worked? What if our side is dead? What if Gun's still free? Who exactly would be opening the safe room up when the building finally settled?

We waited, in silence. I'd been kidnapped, sold to a man who kept me captive and who abused me. I'd thought I'd never be able to move past that, but the loss of Finn? That I know I won't survive.

It's like being trapped in the cellar all over again. If I was on my own, I'd go crazy. As it is, the walls feel like they're closing in.

"Can't we communicate? Maybe they don't know we're alive in

here?" Surely men as resourceful as this club would have a method of getting a message to the outside world?

"They know. And we don't know if our comms have been compromised. It's radio silence until someone comes and opens the door up."

It was probably not as long as I felt it had been in my mind and my terror about Finn, but eventually we hear different noises outside. Pip unbolts the door from the inside, then steps back fast, a gun appearing in his hand. He picks up the one Finn had given me and pushes it at me.

"If you don't recognise them, pull the trigger," he'd said, tersely.

I might not have shot anyone in my life, but if Finn's dead, I'll have no reluctance killing his murderers.

In the end, it's Pip who forces the barrel of my gun down when the door opened to reveal Grinch and Goofy. Quickly they'd ushered us out.

God, the next few moments were hard. My memory replays them as I look around the clubhouse, seeing my rescuers at the bar having a well-deserved drink. Our side had won, but Finn? I shudder at the memory.

I'd counted every one. Gears was injured but walking under his own steam. One by one I crossed off everyone, except for Finn. Finn. Where was he? The building was half destroyed, and the half that wasn't was on fire, the building my man was on top off with no way down given his injuries.

"There!"

With my heart in my mouth, I looked where Grinch had pointed. Not daring to breathe, I watched Finn slide and fall his way down what barely resembled a building at all, making a vow that if he survived, I'd hold onto him, and never leave him. It seemed impossible. What had taken moments seemed to stretch out forever.

Until he hit the ground.

Pip had held me back while Igor had rushed over...

Now I'm here, in the clubroom, standing next to the man I thought I'd lost forever. It's still sinking in.

"I'm going to get a beer." The voice of the man I'm thinking about comes into my ear. I turn to face him. He's clean and wearing borrowed clothes. Apart from the cuts now scabbing over on his face, he's as handsome as I've ever seen him.

"Don't leave me," I cry, sinking into his chest. "I thought you were dead."

He kisses the top of my head. "Never. You'll never get rid of me."

Grinch saunters across, his beer raised in salute. "To the man of the hour."

Finn snorts. "I played my part, that's all. It was a fuckin' good team effort. Hey, Cat. You can probably let App off in here. He won't go anywhere."

But something makes me keep holding onto his leash. Gears had given him back to me when I'd come back downstairs. Like me, he'd had one hell of a shock tonight, and I don't want him running off.

"Good to hear the words team effort from your mouth, Stormy." We both swing around.

"How the hell did you get back so fast?" Finn's mouth is open in surprise.

Snatcher's face sours. "We knew we were conned as soon as we arrived. The place was booby trapped, but we figured that out. Turned on our heels and came back immediately. When Pip's call came, we were already in the air."

Around me more men are walking in, but instead the crowd building up concerning me, I count them off in my mind, pleased to see them all alive and breathing. There's Swift and Road—when Swift spies App she comes running over, snatching the leash out of my hand, lifting him up and cuddling him to her.

"Thank you for keeping him safe. I was so bloody worried." I wave her off, I think App saved me as much as I did him, at least he was something to think about.

Honor and Duty walk in, then, after a few others I only know by sight, there's Bolt, another of my dinner companions.

The clubhouse might be gone, but everything that's important, the people, had survived.

Snatcher whispers something in Finn's ear. Finn jerks his head up and down in response. As his prez walks off, he turns to Grinch. "Got any clean bed linen around here?"

"Sure. There's a closet in the hall upstairs. Hell, we'd have made the place spick and span if we'd known we were having visitors." Grinch yells across the room, "Prospects. C'mere."

As Brute and Igor run over, and Gears limps along behind them, Grinch issues his instructions. "Got beds to be stripped and made."

I feel Finn's sigh as much as hear it. "I'll be back later, babe. You going to be alright here?"

Grinch's eyes open wide. "Stormy?"

"I'm a prospect, aren't I? Best start as I mean to go on."

Now it's Thor who approaches. "Like you can make a fuckin' bed with one leg and one arm, let alone after you fell from the roof of the fuckin' building. You get a pass. *This time.*" The brawny man winks at me. "How about you and your woman get your own room sorted first? Then," his eyes narrow and his face becomes fierce, "you can explain why you blew up our fuckin' clubhouse and I'm not going to be sleeping in my own fuckin' bed tonight."

As Thor and Grinch move away, I bite my lip. "Are you going to get into trouble for that?"

Finn chuckles softly. "Nah, but I'll get my chain yanked. Brothers are going to get some good mileage from it. Come on, let's do what he said. Let's get our room sorted."

Our room. A few hours ago I'd have run from a possessive like that. Now, I don't want Finn out of my sight.

Again, he uses me as a crutch as we go upstairs to where the prospects are already hustling and bustling around, doors bang open and dirty laundry is chucked out as they try to get some order into the chaos. Gears seems to be limping more heavily now.

Finn notices as he's handed some fresh linen from a rack. "Don't overdo it, man. You took a bullet for the club tonight."

Gears rolls his eyes, and shoots Finn a frustrated look. "They were getting impatient. They said they'd shoot the 'little fuck' first to hurry you up. I had minutes man, I knew death was coming, but you took that fuckin' shot. I owe you."

Finn shrugs the obvious thanks off clearly embarrassed. But he deserves it, Gears might have had doubts about his own future, but a shiver runs through me remembering how I'd thought the worst had happened to Finn. Never, ever, do I want to watch my man seemingly fall to his death again.

What's happened since my rescue has put things into perspective. I don't know how, but I know I can't leave Finn. It will take time, I will need help, but having almost lost him, I'll do anything to hang onto him now.

As I take his weight again, he needs me to be a strong Cat now, not one the wind is likely to blow over. Slowly—he's a big man—I help him back to the room he'd labelled as ours. The pronoun that had seemed so wrong yesterday means the world to me now.

"Sit before you fall down," I instruct, noticing him rubbing his temple. "I can do this."

Falling off a building will take it out of you, I think to myself, the last few hours seem to be catching up with him as he obeys without argument. He sits on the chair, leaning back his head, and closing his eyes for a moment. I leave him be as I strip the bed while wishing I was wearing rubber gloves, then, after washing my hands, remake it. I avoid looking at the mattress as I do.

But as I'd told him, where I was kept just two nights ago had been far worse. Well, quite a lot anyway. Even with clean sheets, I'll be sleeping fully covered tonight.

"Finn?" Once I'm finished, I crouch at his side, taking his left hand in mine. "Are you alright?"

"What?" He comes to, giving himself a little shake. That he's feeling bad is clear, when he grimaces. "My head aches. Everything aches."

It's no wonder, given what he's been through.

"Lie down for a bit." I pull at his hand.

Again, there's no argument as once more he leans heavily on me as he moves from the chair to the bed. It's apparent from the careful way he lies down that he's hurting, a lot. Once again, his eyes close.

I watch his chest rise and fall, the motion strong, but slow. *He's asleep.*

When a knock comes at the door, I go and open it. Seeing it's Swift, I ease out into the corridor, putting my finger to my lips. "He's asleep."

"He's a crazy bastard." Her eyes roll, but I can see admiration there as well. "I came to see how you were doing, Cat. I know this isn't great, and we're all doubling up, hell, three in some rooms. But if you prefer, Road can stay here, and you can sleep in my room."

The thought I'd be anywhere but with Finn tonight hadn't crossed my mind. "I need to be here."

Her eyes soften and I see admiration. "Good. He needs someone with him. He probably hit his head again today, you know about concussion watch?"

"I'm a nurse," I scoff. The thought had already occurred to me. Especially once he'd mentioned a headache.

"How's Stormy?" It's Preacher coming along up the stairs now.

"Sleeping," I tell him, or he was before the sergeant-at-arms just barked.

Preacher looks at Swift who raises her eyebrows and shrugs. "Can't wait for him, Preach. He's just a prospect. He'll understand."

I don't know what they're talking about but am thankful when they both move off.

Finn hasn't been woken, he's lying on his side. I check he's comfortable, then go to sit in the chair, leaning my chin on my hand and just watching him.

Finn's always described himself as an asshole, and sure, there are things about him that can't make me argue with that. But there's more to him, he's an honourable man.

He'd never force me. Even if I wanted to jump his bones right now, I wouldn't be able to. Not until I know that I'm in the clear. But I know he'll be patient with me.

My main fear isn't that I won't make it back to some semblance of the woman I was before. No, what scares me most is that the bastards left something inside me. An STD which can't be cured, or, heaven forbid, a pregnancy.

Unbidden tears start rolling down my cheeks. I didn't deserve what had happened to me.

But if Finn hadn't come into my life, I'd have died when Weston hadn't returned to release me.

My hands clench as I hang onto that Finn's not to blame for what Gun did to me. I owe my life to my man.

We'll get through this.

Finn seemed so sure.

Wiping away the wetness from my eyes, I stand, go over to him and wake him. He grumbles and growls but is compliant when I check his eyes.

"Fuckin' nurses," he objects, but he winks at me.

38

———————

Stormy…

During the night Cat wakes me regularly. My complaints are automatic, fuck knows my body needs rest. Her actions show how much she cares.

They also serve another purpose.

Not normally one to dwell on anything, tonight my brain taunts me. I'm plagued by nightmares in which I'm falling, dropping without anything to hold on to, everything happening in slow motion. Each time as I drop through the air, I see Cat with a gun to her head. I'm screaming in my head, knowing I won't be able to get to her. Then, thank fuck, she's put on the light and is staring into my eyes.

When I fall back asleep, the dream plays on repeat. Each fucking time I'm too late to save her. Each time I'm soothed back to sleep with dulcet tones and a warm hand caressing my forehead.

I wake, refreshed with a woman in my arms. Not any woman, but Cat. Still caught in the vestiges of my dreams I check her for injuries then the events of last night come flooding back.

Fuck. That had been close. I'd thought my number was up.

"You're awake," she murmurs softly. "How are you feeling? How's your head?"

At her mention of it, I raise my hand and massage a bump on my skull. "Better than it was." Fucking fantastic actually. She's in my arms when there were moments I'd thought she'd never be there again. I refrain from asking her how she's feeling, I'll leave her to just do what comes to her naturally.

I hadn't lied, I'm far from in working order. Even if I wasn't, she needs time to heal. My nose starts to twitch, I sniff the air. "What's that smell?"

"Brute brought some breakfast up for us. Coffee and an egg and bacon muffin if you're up for it?" She chuckles softly. "They ordered in. You could hear Cowboy from up here when they asked him to cook. *That kitchen* and *over my dead body*, as well as a few *fuckin' rats* were phrases repeated quite a lot."

And I slept through that? It's unlike me not to keep one eye half open at night. Still, after falling off a roof, I might have needed it.

I groan as I replay her words and think of the implications. "Prospects are going to have to clean that shit up."

"Count me out if there are rats." She shudders. "I've had enough of them to last a lifetime." She has, both of the animal and human kind.

As I gingerly ease myself up, *yeah, the headache is all but gone,* and reach for the muffin, I realise there's a hell of a lot of noise coming up from downstairs. Voices that I don't immediately recognise.

"What's going on?"

"Visitors, I think. Snatcher poked his head around the door and said you're to go down when you're ready."

I'm surprised he didn't insist on waking me up. If visitors have descended, prospects will be run ragged and I was deemed one of their number yesterday. Even disabled as I am, I'm determined not to be found wanting. Who could they be? Colorado, belatedly come to help us? That's our nearest chapter.

If so they're far too late. From the fire I saw burning yesterday, there won't be much left of the other clubhouse.

I need to get a move on, have a question for her first. "How are you, Cat?" I don't refer to that fact I just woke up with her arms around me.

"Better now you've woken up. I was worried about you."

"Babe, I've survived worse than a little concussion."

She huffs. "You've already had one concussion too many. You've got to be careful about your head."

Chuckling, I can't help pointing out. "I didn't exactly plan for the building to collapse."

But it's too soon for joking, as her disgusted glance suggests. I suppose I was lucky, I only had time to react and do my best to survive. She had to fucking watch me. I reach for her hand and squeeze it. "I'm so fuckin' sorry. I'll do better okay?" Or I'll try. Even inadvertently I never want to hurt her. Another worry hits me. We've got Gun, there's no danger to her now. "You're staying, aren't you? Not running off to Kentucky?" Please let her say yes. I don't want space between us. I can't let her go.

She sighs. "I meant what I said, Finn. I love you. Maybe it took nearly losing you to show me, and I want to get back to the woman I was. I'll stay, but you'll have to be patient. I'm going to try, but it's going to take time."

She'll get there. She might not realise but she's no longer flinching from my touch. Small steps, in one way, huge in another.

"We've all the time in the world," I tell her. I lift the cup placed within reach of my good hand, and down the life-giving coffee. "You going to be okay while I take care of business?"

Her mood lightens. "Apart from the kitchen which I'm not going near, I spoke to Snatcher earlier. He's assigned the prospects to me, and we're going to clean up the place and make it habitable. Brute's already arranging to pick up new mattresses and couches." She giggles softly. "I don't know that Snatcher considered his wisdom of putting a nurse in charge of sanitising."

I chuckle with her, then her words hit me. "You've been downstairs?" My eyes widen.

"Well, you have been asleep for hours. I kept checking in on you."

I don't mind her leaving me. I'm pleased as hell she's confident enough to go down to the clubroom without me.

"So we're staying here for a while," I surmise from her comments. I suppose it makes sense, though this old clubhouse isn't really what I had in mind for starting our new life together.

"Apparently so. Snatcher thinks it just needs a woman's touch." She rolls her eyes, and giggles. "Swift told him rather firmly to count her out."

Swift would, but as for Cat, I think Snatcher's right. Left to us men, we'd pretend not to notice the squalor around us.

I sit up, realising I've no fresh clothes to change into. But I won't be the only one. I'm still wearing Grinch's oversized-for-me sweats and t-shirt, I notice as I start to get to my feet.

"Here." Cat jumps up and brings new crutches to me. "Someone went out first thing and replaced them."

Someone needs my grateful thanks. It had been hell without them.

Now ambulatory again, I go to the bathroom, piss for what feels like hours, happy there's no sign of blood, then splash my face with water.

"Hey." I grin as I return to the bedroom, a thought having hit me. I give her a mock salute. "I'm a prospect, so you'll be bossing me around. Yes, ma'am, no ma'am and all that."

"I will, won't I?" Her face lights up.

I growl. "Make the most of it."

I'm not looking forward to this, but hey, I agreed. I said I'll take my punishment and I won't take that back though the joke isn't lost on me. Yesterday it was a sniper rifle, today I'll be armed with a sponge or a duster. But I'm alive, and Cat's promised to stay with me. What man could ask more than that?

Downstairs the room is full but a quick glance at Cat shows she doesn't seem uncomfortable. Giving her a task to focus on probably helped with that.

Oh fuck. I hear him before I see him. It's Drummer, the mother chapter prez, his voice bellowing out even though he's probably speaking normally. For a second I wonder if I can escape back to the room and plead concussion or something. But knowing I may be many things but I'm no coward, I clump my way down the stairs, the crutches and my uneven gait giving me away immediately.

"It's a fuckin' corpse walking!" Someone, I think it's Blade, the mother chapter's enforcer calls out.

Drummer swings around to face me and barks a laugh. "What does it take to kill you, Stormy?"

Snatcher answers drily, "Well if two explosions, being beaten half dead, crashing a motorcycle and a fall from a three-storey building didn't do it, I think we can safely say even Satan doesn't want him."

The words make me smirk. Sure, there's probably some truth in that. Hopefully, though, in six months, even if Satan still doesn't, his Devils might. I eye Brute and Igor, and start to make my way over to them.

"Where the fuck you going?" Thor stops my progress.

"To join the other prospects." I shrug.

"Nah. Debrief. That's why Drummer's here. He wants you here."

"Church?"

Thor's eyes go up and back down again. "The old fuckin' meeting room's being used as a storeroom, and the table was moved to our now defunct clubhouse and all that's left are charred matchsticks. Drummer said we might as well have the meeting here."

Now I notice men are beginning to move tables aside and arranging the chairs in a circle. Cat's already in conversation with Gears, who's waving a piece of paper.

"Hey!" Bolt shouts. "Make sure the jeans you buy have extra room in the crotch area." He mimics jerking off a cock that's at least a foot long.

"And no jokey slogans on the shirts," Piston yells.

"What's going on?" I must have missed something.

Thor replies, "They're off to get clothes and necessities for everyone. I told them just to buy out the store, it's probably easier."

I notice Cat's got a gleam in her eyes, and it seems she's viewing the forthcoming shopping trip with pleasure. I raise my chin as the four disappear out of the door, suppressing my momentary panic that she'll be out of my sight. I trust my fellow prospects to watch over her. All three proved their worth last night.

"Gears okay?"

The VP nods. "Yeah. Like you, he's using a stick." His face scrunches up but there's a twinkle in his eye as he adds, "Think we should rewrite the regulations and demand prospects have two working legs."

My finger rises automatically. He barks a laugh.

Once the prospects and my woman have disappeared, Drummer bangs a glass loudly on the bar then glares at it as though it's the poor inanimate object's fault it's not a gavel. "Sit the fuck down. Let's have church."

I'd prefer not to draw to myself, but the clack of the crutches is loud, and my slow progress and necessity of arranging of my cast covered leg means I'm the last to sit down.

Drummer's, "Nice of you to join us," causes a burst of snorts and laughter. It's a required release of tension after the events of the day before.

In the absence of a gavel or table to bang it on, Drummer stamps his foot for silence.

"First order of business. Stormy."

I wish there was a table for me to slide under. Yesterday I hadn't liked the floor literally opening up beneath me, but I'd do anything for that to happen now. Snatcher said I could prospect, but is Drummer going to take that back?

"Snatcher's told me you returned to the club three weeks ago. Yet I wasn't informed." He raises his eyebrow at Snatcher.

Snatcher's face twists, and for some reason he glances at Pip. "Stormy was more dead than alive. It was a toss-up whether he'd make it. Wasn't much point informing you until we knew whether he was a corpse or not. Then, well, the imperative was to rescue his woman once we knew about her."

"You fucked up again, Snatcher. Dead or alive, or anywhere in-between, I had a right to know."

"I suggested—"

"Shut it, Pip." Drummer's steely eyes settle on the man who I doubt has often been told to zip his mouth. "Snatcher's the one in the president's chair. You should have no influence over the running of the club, if things have changed—"

"They haven't." Snatcher glares at Pip, then his focus moves back to Drummer. "I take full responsibility." His mouth twists. "We didn't know who'd beaten him, and we couldn't rule anything out. Wanted to see if we had a chance to speak to him before I informed you. You could say it was a technicality, he wasn't actually back at the club, just in the vicinity—"

"Fuck that, Snatcher," Drummer roars. "What you're saying is you don't trust the other chapters. You think one of them came across him."

"Er, Drum?" Blade's twirling a knife in his hands. "If he'd been seen in Tucson, we could well have given him a beating."

"Yes, but…" Drummer's voice trails off and he grimaces. "Okay, most of the chapters would have wanted their pound of flesh but wouldn't have half-killed him."

"I wanted to know what we were dealing with."

Snatcher's got Drummer's full focus. A full minute passes before the mother chapter prez speaks again. I, and I think everyone else is holding their breath.

Instead of addressing Snatcher again, he turns back to me, his hard eyes softening. "No woman should go through something like yours did." When I dip my head in agreement, he sighs deeply, and moves his head slowly left to right, then repeats the action before he brings it back to centre. "And just when I think it can't get any worse, you fuckin' blow up a Satan's Devils' clubhouse."

I smirk. It's wrong, but I can't help it. "It was a good distraction. In my defence, I didn't know how much C4 Gun had been used. He'd found some lethal stuff from somewhere."

"Lethal in—fuckin'—deed." Goofy rubs his chest.

Drummer spares him a glance of sympathy, then his face tightens again. "Utah's a pain in my fuckin' side. But you proved useful in that business with San Diego—though Lost might have something to say about Swift and Bolt hiding the truth from him." He pauses and shakes his head as though he'd gotten off track. "Snatcher, you've been prez of this chapter since I took over this club and continued to play that role even when Pip came in and took over. I never doubted you were a strong prez. You always showed support for other chapters, and you lost Thumper just a couple of years back. Otherwise, you kept yourselves to yourselves, and I didn't push that. You didn't cause trouble but didn't offer much either. Maybe I gave you too much rope, which I certainly won't be doing in future."

"Too bloody right," Wraith says, his own eyes narrowing.

"Maybe we all need to prove we can work together and build trust between us," Drummer continues. "I don't want to lose a charter, and I don't to break in a new prez. On my part, I agreed Stormy had three months to pull himself together. We're just inside that. So, if you promise to play nicely with others, I'll let you keep your charter, Snatch."

A wave of relief crosses over Snatcher's face. I'm relieved as fuck. Maybe we got the sympathy vote as we're now down a clubhouse.

Drummer leaves his place by the bar and walks so he's standing right to my front. His eyes view me. His expression is unreadable. "Snatcher's brought you back in as a prospect. I'm sorry, Stormy. It's too late for that."

The club won't be punished for my misdemeanours, no, all that's going to land on my head. I deserve it, words, even deeds, won't make them trust me again. All I can pray is that they leave me alive to make a new life with Cat. Back in Kentucky, perhaps. But hell, it hurts.

I left not wanting a team behind me. I've returned wanting nothing less. Now it's all going to be taken from me.

I glance down to where my left hand's cradling the cast on my right, wishing I could close off my ears and not hear the pronouncement I've no place in the club anymore. I knew I should have returned earlier, but even knowing that I'd do it all over again as being with Cat had got my mind back straight, I'm also aware I deserve everything thrown at me.

Drummer's been quiet for a moment. When he starts speaking next, there's no doubt he's making a president's announcement, as *the* president, presiding over all our clubs.

"You can take the cut off the man, but you can't take the Devil out of him. As president of the mother chapter, I propose to vote for Stormy being reinstated as a full member. He's quick thinking, proved himself as a team player, fuck, a team leader yesterday. We gave him space to get his head out of his ass, and he seems to have done that. Of, course," I feel his eyes burning into me, and he waits until mine come up to reach his, "that's what a good woman will do for you." I just nod, it's the truth. But I'll be fucked if Drummer doesn't continue. "If Utah doesn't want him, he can transfer to Tucson. Always have a use for good fuckin' brothers."

Wait...

"Oh, Prez. I kinda like our clubhouse," Blade interrupts.

"Over my fuckin' dead body," Snatcher growls. "He's a member for Utah."

What?

My eyes go to Snatcher, then to Drummer, then back. My mouth drops open. I don't trust myself to speak in case my ears aren't working.

"Brother's fuckin' naked," Wraith observes.

"Got his cut right here." Preacher stands up.

He's holding the familiar leather which I'd left upstairs as left-handed there was no way I could sew on the prospect insignia. Now the sergeant-at-arms comes over to me and helps me put the cast and my good hand through the arm holes. As it settles on my shoulders, I shake my head.

I'm choked with emotion and it's hard to get any words out. "I won't let you down again," I finally say earnestly.

"You sure you won't consider a transfer?" Blade asks. I notice he's now picking his teeth with the stiletto.

I open and shut my mouth, considering he might well have an ulterior motive and have no qualms refusing the offer. "I'm good here, *Brother.*"

"Hey," Grinch calls out, his brow furrowed. "What about the fuckin' beatdown? We're still doing that, aren't we?"

The laughs and general uproar drown out the actual answer, and I can only guess at what it is.

By now Drummer's back at the bar and banging the glass again, once, then twice more. When the room finally quiets, he says, "Moving on. I've been asked to hand over to Pip right now." His mouth twists in distaste as he turns to face our ex-prez. "What have you got to say for yourself?"

Pip stands and starts to pace. He doesn't look as sure of himself as he usually does. "Last night," he begins, rubbing his hands through his hair, "we questioned our prisoner, Gun." He turns to me. "I'm sorry, Stormy. I, er—"

"It was too important to get answers," Snatcher interrupts without remorse. "At the time, Stormy was just a prospect."

The old me would have been irate. The new me remembers waking up with Cat. I wave it off knowing which I'd prefer. "What did you get out of him?"

"A fuckin' lot." Swift smirks. "He thought he could resist seeing that he was a former SEAL."

I grin. He'd clearly met his match with a woman who qualified for the British SAS.

Pip's glances at Swift, then back to myself. "What we learned is that I fucked up, Brother. I made mistakes."

He's got my attention, and everyone else's. His eyes now alight on Drummer. "I was arrogant. Maybe I shouldn't have taken over the club. Maybe I should have helped Snatcher out of his mess with the mafia, then stepped back. But I saw a use for the men, and a way to use the chapter. I changed my name, changed my appearance, but in order to obtain contracts, I had to maintain some contacts. One of those was with Admiral Hillier."

As Drummer growls at Pip's admission, I shake my head. "Hillier's straight," I say. Nothing would convince me otherwise.

"Damn right he is," Pip confirms. "But there are leaks everywhere. You asked me once, Stormy, why the insurgents in Afghanistan wanted to maintain a US presence. Why when it seemed we were preparing to pull troops out, something always happened which led to our soldiers staying there?"

"I thought we'd come up with the reason. The drug trade." That had made some sort of sense.

"And we weren't wrong. Drugs, yes. Women too." Pip inclines his chin toward Swift. "Once the enforcer started to ply the tricks of her trade, Gun gave everything up. A fuckin' tale of intrigue and betrayal."

"Spit it out," Drummer growls.

"Equipment." Pip lets the word hang in the air for a moment. "Arming insurgents by taking in extra weaponry and selling it to them."

I stiffen. That's worse than running drugs or women. That's… "Treason."

"Exactly. And I didn't fuckin' consider it. I thought of things coming out, but not going in. And, at first, I considered someone like Jeffrey Morgan, Gun as you know him, running it. It took me a while to realise it went higher than him, and that there was only one person it could be Smythe. Sure, Smythe's in it up to his neck. And Gun wasn't the only man working for him."

That doesn't make sense. "Smythe doesn't know how to find his asshole," I scoff. "He's no mastermind."

"That's where you're wrong. He's not a combat man, but put him in charge of logistics, and he's a fuckin' genius. So what did I do? I put two and two together, and ended up with a negative number. I got him Stateside and into a desk job, which provided him with everything he needed to keep his scam going. Gun was one of his men on the ground, making sure, even at the expense of sacrificing his team, that the US maintained a base in the area."

Smythe?

"They got rid of the team?" Fuck, Tailor, Buster, Slice and the new team members, they hadn't deserved that. Dying a hero in a foreign land is accepted, being culled by your own side because you were inconvenient. Fuck that. "Gun dead?" I snarl, hoping he isn't. Hoping I'd have my chance with him.

"I made sure he died screaming." Swift raises her head. The coldness in her eyes shows she's telling me the truth.

But fuck it. That was my kill. I push my rage back down, proud that my voice sounds calm when I get back to questioning Pip. "Does it stop with Smythe, or does it go higher?" Just how big is this nest of vipers?

"Smythe. And you might like to know something else." Pip turns to Honor, who passes him a photograph. He hands it to me. "This is Smythe's wife."

Automatically I take the picture and stare at it. There's something familiar about it. She's very young, not Caucasian, her skin is darker, her eyes almost black. Her lips, her cheeks, something about the shape of her nose... it looks familiar. I narrow my eyes. Nah, unfortunately people of the same race tend to look the similar, and people of colour would say that about white people. That must be what it is, but it's almost like I'm looking at a younger Nazia.

"It can't be Nazia," I tell him. "She's dead."

He raises an eyebrow. Suddenly dots fall into place. *"Marjan?"* At his nod, I swear loudly. "Fuck that. She's only, what, sixteen?"

"They've been married four years. He went out on one of his visits—about the time you were last there, Stormy. That's why Nazia did what she did, to try to save Marjan. That's why she was killed before she could be questioned. She needed to do something, and hoped she'd get your attention. She wanted to speak to you, thought you might help."

"Why the fuck would Smythe want an underage kid for a wife?" Except for the obvious, that he's twisted, it makes no fucking sense.

Pip grimaces. "It's a convoluted story. Nazia and Marjan were daughters of an influential Afghan leader, one who hadn't been on our radar, a powerful man who'd stayed behind the scenes. He even acted a part as a member of our friendly forces.

Smythe's original plan was to kill them to ensure a major escalation in hostilities. Instead, you saved them. Smythe, proving he was clever, took the credit for them being alive. Working behind the scenes, Gun discovered the girls' father was responsible for distributing the weapons they were supplying. To say Smythe isn't a trusting man is an understatement. He needed something to hold over the father, something that if he was captured, would keep him quiet. So, he took his daughter. To make it legit, he married her."

"She was, *is*, just a kid." I say horrified. No wonder Nazia did something to try to get attention.

"I'm sorry, Stormy. I put Smythe in the position that allowed him to do all this. I should have looked deeper. But like you, I saw a man who couldn't hack it at the front line so removed him, then forgot about him."

"He's dead," I say, coldly. I'm going to make it my life's mission to find him, kill him, and give Marjan back her life. I hadn't been able to save Nazia, but I could save her sister.

"He will be." Pip states in a voice full of promise. He stops pacing and retakes his chair.

His hand waves toward Swift as though giving her permission to speak. She takes advantage. "Pip asked why Gun orchestrated my kidnapping. We all know it was to bring Pip out into the open, but not why." She throws what can be interpreted as a look of disgust at the man who so recently we all called Prez.

"Spit it out, Pip." Drummer voice drips with impatience.

"I'm a spy, or was. It's not something I can switch off. When Stormy went on his break, I knew it had nothing to do with his mom. I tried to track him but lost him. I wondered whether he'd received new information, or whether after all these years, he wanted revenge for the death of the SEAL. I put feelers out to watch Smythe. If Stormy was stupid enough to take out a serving officer, my aim was to intercept him and bring him back." He clasps his hands together and rubs them both against his nose. "I cancelled the op when Stormy reappeared, but a trace was still there. Eventually, one of Smythe's aides picked up there were eyes on him. To cut a long story short, when my name came up, Smythe wanted to smoke me out to discover just what I was doing. He played the long game, and eventually found me."

He wipes his hands down his face, and looks straight at Drummer, then at me and finally at Snatcher. "As I said, I fucked up. So I'm leaving the club."

"What? No." Snatcher's on his feet now. "Look, man. We all make mistakes. We can take Smythe down…"

I growl. It's my call. I've a lot of vengeance to seek.

"This barrel is full of fuckin' bad apples," Pip snarls. "It's not just one man. It's his whole operation." He calms slightly. "You've got things to be doing here, rebuilding your clubhouse and your lives for a start, and continuing with the business we've built up. I need to focus on righting these wrongs, and that means me coming out of retirement."

Pip can't do that. "They'll kill you," I state. "We all know what will happen if you show your face."

"Maybe," Pip says. "Maybe not. It's a risk I'll take. But this is huge, Stormy. It's national security. I'm going to be working with Devil and Grade A Security, using his government contacts. Sure, you can take Smythe out, rescue Marjan, if as I believe, she needs rescuing, but the size of the operation is more than one club can handle. Stopping the weapons trade has to be the focus."

Pip's face is set. I haven't known the man for seven years not to be able to read him. I'm not the only one.

Snatcher's eyes close briefly, then reopen. "Can we dissuade you?"

"No." Pip shakes his head. "The wheels are already in motion. During the last few hours, thing have moved fast. I still have some contacts at the Pentagon. Undercover agents are already being briefed to go in and rout out the players Smythe's got in place. For now, he's untouchable." He raises his eyes to me. "Got to ask you, Stormy, to hold off. Can't have you going rogue with your sniper rifle. We need to give him enough rope to hang himself."

"I'll come work with you, I'll—"

"You've got Cat!" Pip rounds on me. "You going to give her up, man?"

It's hard. I see Drummer's eyes on me. Hardly anyone is breathing as they wait for me to make the decision. I'm being asked to leave this to someone else, to trust others to seek the revenge for me.

Three months back, I'd have laughed in his face.

Three months back, I hadn't met the woman that I love.

"You can fuckin' trust me, Stormy. I *need* to make this right."

"Stormy?" Snatcher raises an eyebrow at me. He seems to be letting me know this is my choice. That whatever I decide, he'll have my back.

Cat. For once in my life I have someone who needs me. She gives me a reason to keep breathing. She keeps me from sliding back to the stone-cold-hearted asshole I once was. If I throw in my lot with Pip, it would set me right back. Instead of her, revenge would be my priority.

I can't do that.

I find myself drawing in a deep breath. "Just promise me you'll end this, Pip."

Drummer jumps in. "Never liked you, Pip. Never liked that you deceived me. Always felt you were using the Utah club for your own ends. I never warmed to you. You're not one of us. So I'll give you a deadline. If this Smythe's not taken out in six months, then Stormy has my blessing, and the backing of the Satan's Devils to take him out."

Pip nods sharply. "Six months is enough." He stands and looks around. "Enough, but not long. So I'll leave now." Giving a twisted grin, he adds, "It's not as if I've got much to pack anyway." He pauses again. "I'm not one for long goodbyes. See you around, *brothers*."

With a wave of his hand, he steps out of the circle of chairs, makes his way to the door and exits while leaving us all sitting open mouthed wondering what the fuck just happened.

Drummer clears his throat. "You've got this, Snatcher," he states firmly, in a voice that brooks no argument.

Snatcher shakes his head, draws his hands down his cheeks, then he looks around, his eyes settling on each of the Utah members.

"We've got this," he confirms.

Drummer bangs the glass again. "Moving on…"

A burst of nervous laughter greets him. How the hell do you move on from the desertion of your ex-president? But I suppose on that topic, there's little more to be discussed.

"Are you going to rebuild?"

"No." It's our VP who answers the mother chapter prez. He stretches out his legs and links his hands behind his head. "I never fuckin' liked that fuckin' music. Or that I was living in a hotel."

Stomps of feet, laughs and hollers come from all around.

"I much prefer the old place myself," Snatcher agrees.

"Speak for your fuckin' selves," Cowboy complains.

I hadn't thought about Cowboy. Now I think about it, I half wonder whether he'd go with Pip. Now I let the thought into my head, I wonder if Pip had already spoken to him.

Cowboy seems to read my mind. He sits forward. "Joking aside, it was right for Pip to move on, and time. Not one hundred percent about the reason, but he needs to put things right. If you're wondering about me, I'm a fuckin' Devil. Not going to give up the patch on my back. But…" he glances behind him and his face twists, "it's fuckin' takeout until I get a new kitchen."

"I can get Viper's crew here to help you rebuild," Drummer offers, and Snatcher gives him a grateful nod. "You need more rooms at least. Complete overhaul, and I doubt the electrical is up to standard."

"Goofy's handy with dry walling." Grinch puts up his hand. Goofy nudges Grinch hard in the ribs, reminding him, "You're not too shoddy yourself."

"Do we need to vote?" Snatcher asks. "All in favour of making this our home, say Aye." Ayes come from all directions. When he asks for nays, there are none. He shakes his head. "I thought it would be harder than that."

"Put it this way," Rascal calls out. "Stormy won't have so far to fall next time he's up on the roof."

While it's a welcome release of tension and brothers might be laughing too hard, I'm just hoping there won't be a next time, certainly not like the last. I raise my middle finger toward Rascal.

"Only thinking of you, Brother," he retorts.

Brother. I think I've been permanently smiling since they recommenced calling me that.

Stormy...

Cat's driving as we head away from the clubhouse while I'm in the passenger seat chuckling to myself.

"What?" She takes her eyes off the road for a second and throws me a suspicious look.

I move my head side to side as I tell her, "I can't believe you persuaded them to get chickens."

She giggles. "Cowboy's on board. His eyes lit up at the thought of fresh eggs."

Yeah, and some of the brothers have been talking about fried chicken, but I won't remind her of that. Hopefully they'll get enough that we can swap them out and not have her examining her meals too closely. I know how much Cat has missed having livestock around, even if it's just of the feathered sort. At least once I'd gotten her a new phone and hooked her up with her old number, she'd received a slew of updates from Seamus, all with photos of Star, her old pony, being spoiled rotten by his grandkid. That had certainly put a smile on her face.

Behind the old clubhouse, well, just the clubhouse now I

suppose, is a large expanse of wasteland. Cowboy decided to plant a vegetable and herb garden so we can have fresh food. His new venture makes me fuckin' glad I didn't have to sew on that prospect patch. Working the land is not something I need on my résumé.

Viper and his crew descended a couple of weeks back. Some of the brothers have moved out while the building work, to make the place habitable to cater for the number of us and the expansion that's required, is ongoing, but Cat and I have stayed. She's thrown herself in to supervising the decorating, and even Cowboy's taken to consulting her on things like countertops. Me? I've split my time between advising on the construction of the gym and equipment, and working with Swift, Honor and Duty on the provision of a new comms room. It's exciting, most of our equipment was a year or so old, and in the age of technology, state of the art changes all the time. For now, we're making do with a few laptops hurriedly purchased, and can't wait to get a proper set up again. To say over the past four weeks we've been busy is an understatement.

One thing our business has made us is comfortably well off, so money's no object, or hasn't become so yet. For now, Rascal's still smiling and signing off purchases which I take as a sign we haven't gone overboard.

Cat drives to the hospital without direction, having started to learn the city's roads. Once there, she expertly parks the truck. When she applies the handbrake, she turns to me. "You sure you don't want me to come in with you?"

I wink at her. "I'm a big boy, I think I can handle it. And you've got your own appointment."

Her face falls. "Yeah."

"I can put mine off." I reach for her hand.

She squeezes mine before releasing it. "We've already talked about this. I'd rather go by myself." Her eyes glaze slightly, and I know she thinks she needs time to process alone whatever she might be told.

I don't try and persuade her, even though I'd give anything to be by her side. Cat's got an independent streak, and while at times I don't like it, I've learned arguing with her once she's got something set in her mind causes a flare of her temper. I'll be there, though, after. I'll know if there's something wrong by the expression on her face. I think I'm prepared for anything, as I've told her more than once, we're stronger together, and we can face anything. "Whatever happens, we'll deal with it, okay?"

I hate that she sniffs, as if she's pre-empting her results and fearing the worst, but I keep silent as she visibly pulls herself together and puts on a strong front. "You better get inside, or else you'll miss your appointment. I know you're itching to get back on your bike. You've been staring at it ever since the prospects trailered it back from Kentucky."

I can't deny that she's right, I have. What's a biker without his motorcycle and working limbs to ride it? Gears and Igor had brought it to Utah along with all our stuff we had packed up. The furniture and shit stayed in storage. Someday, when the clubhouse is finished, I'm hoping Cat and I will look for a place of our own. *Before* they start culling the chickens, hopefully.

I'm not the only one to miss my bike. Luckily most of the brothers had ridden their bikes to the airport that fateful night, but Grinch's, Goofy's and the prospects' had been lost. New models have been arriving, another club purchase, but some miss the rides they've spent time personalising. With all the expense though, it's a wonder that the treasurer is still in a good mood.

I ease myself out of the truck, and get the crutches in position, hopefully for the last time. When she comes around my side, I lean forward and kiss her. I don't wish her good luck, preferring to avoid the reference it could be otherwise.

"I'll text you if I can't find you." Then, muttering my unspoken desires for a positive outcome under my breath, I swing and hop away, leaving her.

My appointment doesn't take long. I don't even need my practised arguments of why I'm good to have the casts taken off. The doctor just looks at the x-rays, tells me my bones have mended and gets those darn things off.

Did I expect to be able to walk normally? Yeah, I suppose I did. But my wrist and leg are weak, and I take on board the exercises he suggests, and the list of physiotherapy appointments he sets up.

When I go to find my woman, the only drawback is I'm still favouring my leg. But hell, it's fucking fantastic to put two feet to the ground.

It doesn't take long to find her. She's waiting outside for me.

"Well?" I ask, impatiently, suspecting the results from the smile on her face.

"I'm clear of almost everything. He did suggest using a condom to be sure for a while."

"How long's a while?" My eyes narrow.

She bites her lip. "Syphilis can take twenty years to show up, and some forms of Hepatitis up to four months. HPV, maybe ten years."

"Fuck that," I growl. I'll take my chances. I want her pregnant long before a decade has passed. That's if…

"And?"

Her eyes light up. "I dodged a bullet. I'm not pregnant."

As relief floods through me, I pull her to me, glad she doesn't have to cope with decisions that would have to be made if she was, but can't help adding, "Yet."

"Yet?"

"Yeah. You're already my woman, now I'm going to marry you and give you babies."

"Yeah?" Her breathing speeds up. "To do that, we'll have to fuck."

"Make love," I correct her, then take a deep breath. "Well, when you're ready for that."

We've slept in the same bed since the night of Gun's attack, neither of us could bear to be parted. It's only in the past couple of weeks we've started to touch each other. Only days since I first put my mouth on her as I slowly reacclimatise her with my touch. Baby steps. I'm being so fucking careful, too much too soon will send her straight back to her nightmare.

"I'm ready." She gestures at my leg. "It's time, isn't it? With your casts off and my results, Gun no longer has any control over us. It's time to move on."

Curling my hand around her neck, I exhale. "Are you sure?"

Green eyes, now with a spark, stare up into mine. "I think I am."

"I'll drive." I snatch the keys from her hand and move toward the truck faster than I've done for weeks. Laughing loudly, she follows.

Fuck, every time she makes that sound, I appreciate it. There had been a time when I thought I'd never hear that again. Almost losing her, almost dying myself, has made me realise my life might have had a fucked up beginning but because of her, it's definitely become worth living for.

Driving for the first time in weeks, I go faster than she had done, and get back to the clubhouse in record time with just one thing on my mind.

"Hey, Brother!" Piston calls out as I enter. He comes to a stop and nods appreciatively as he notices my casts are off. "This came for you in the mail."

It's an envelope which feels like it's got documents inside. There's no return address. After examining it carefully I find nothing about it to raise my suspicions, so I slide it open.

"What is it?" Cat asks.

"I don't know…" A photograph drops into my hand. It's a picture of my mother and that must be me as a toddler. I didn't know any existed having thought, if there were any, that my dad had destroyed them. *Who the fuck sent it to me, and why?* I tap out the documents, starting with a press cutting. The headline itself reveals all.

Drunk Driver Kills Young Mother

Natalie Palmer (26) was killed when she was crossing the road yesterday. A man's been arrested and charged with driving under the influence. She leaves behind a husband and six-year-old son.

That's all there is. In the scheme of things, it seems Natalie Palmer wasn't important. To me, she was, her supposed abandonment had fucked up my life, but to anyone else she was irrelevant, only worth a few lines. I read it once, again, then for a third time. As the implications hit, I stagger, needing to balance myself against the bar.

Why had my father lied?

My whole fucking time on earth had been shaped by the belief she walked out on me, a six-year-old unlovable kid that she had no problem leaving behind. I'd found it hard to trust as I'd been left by the one person who should have loved me unconditionally, instead being raised by a man who hated me.

She hadn't left of her own accord.

I let the papers drop out of my hand and as fast as my weak leg will take me, head up to our room, wanting time and space to process what this means. My whole life has been a lie.

"Finn?"

Flung face down on the bed I'm aware she's entered and closed the door. Unmanly tears seep from my eyes as I mourn for a woman whose life was cut short and the boy she inadvertently left behind.

I know she'll have read the article, who wouldn't? "Why did he lie to me?"

The bed dips as she sits on it. "Who knows, Finn? Maybe he thought it was easier on a child. He lost her too."

"I believed him. I never questioned she'd just walked out. Christ, Cat, I envisaged her living a whole new life with a new family. He made me hate her." And in doing so, I grew up hating myself. I should have looked for her, but instead I'd tried to wipe her from my mind.

Her arms come around me and gently she rocks me. "Did you notice who the letter came from?" When my head provides a negative response, she tells me, "There was a note from Pip. He said he hoped this would make sense of the past and told you to remember you can trust him. He said *soon,* whatever that may mean."

He means it will be soon that he takes Smythe down.

"I spent my life never letting anyone get close, Cat. And it all goes back to that fuckin' lie you hold in your hands."

"But you let me get close, lover." She leans into me, sits up and with gentle prodding gets me to roll over onto my back. Then, fuck me, she straddles me. "The past is behind us, both yours and mine. It has no power to hurt us anymore."

My eyes flick to hers fast. Her words were a message for me and for her.

Gently she moves her hips back and forth, her movements having a predictable effect on my cock. When she notices my growing hardness, she grins.

"Hmm. I think you promised me some action when we got back."

I move my hands under my head and rest back on the pillow. "I'm all yours. Take me."

It will work better like this. Me giving her control.

"Yeah?" Her hands trace my now throbbing denim covered dick. "Is this mine?"

"All yours. But, woman, it's been fuckin' weeks. Don't play too long."

"Ooh, on edge, are we?"

I cock an eyebrow at her. "You could say that."

I thought the first time we actually got down to fuck she'd be nervous. I love this playful side of her. *It's different.* I'm not taking like that bastard did. Although it goes against my nature, I'm leaving everything up to her.

Her teeth dig into her bottom lip as her hands fiddle with the button on the shorts I wore for the last time over my cast today. My hands itch to help, but apart from tightening my stomach to give her more room to work, I stick to my resolve.

Relieved I'm not wearing button up shorts, this torture is more than only a strong-willed man could stand, I hold my breath as she finally pushes it through the hole, and starts to move my zipper down.

She's careful, though. I've not gone commando today, she still eases it down making sure to keep it well away from my dick. Her fingers though, they brush my shaft, even that gentle touch makes me suck in air through my teeth. If she doesn't watch out, I could blow.

Is she going to jerk me off? Fuck, I'd prefer to be inside her when I come, I've been waiting for this moment for two months.

But no, Cat obviously wants me naked. Torturously slowly she starts to pull down my underwear and shorts. Again, I offer assistance by raising my hips. She giggles softly when she realises I'm still in my boots. Once those have been discarded, my legs and ass are bare, and my clothes are on the floor.

Her eyes focus on my cock for a moment as I fail to hide how much I want her. She licks her lips and instructs, "Take off your shirt."

I obey, curling my abs to sit up and rip that fucker over my head. It's actually hot that I'm now completely naked, and she's still clothed. I can't fucking wait for whatever striptease she has planned, fast or slow, I just need her revealed to my eyes.

Her brow furrowed in concentration, she leans forward and wipes the pearly drop of precum off the tip of my cock. Just the gentle touch of her finger makes me gasp. But she's hesitant, almost fighting against herself. While I'd love my dick in her mouth, she's not ready.

"Touch yourself, Cat," I instruct.

40

———

$\mathcal{C}$at…

I hadn't known how much I'd been poised for bad news, what I'd heard instead hadn't been a complete clean sheet of results, but the most I could hope for under the circumstances. I knew the doctor was only being cautious, the chances of having a disease that would only show itself many years in the future was simply covering their backs.

The news I wasn't pregnant was the best I could receive.

Now there's nothing holding me back. I knew I was eager to make love with Finn.

That he was blindsided by the letter meant I'd had to take the lead.

I know Finn thinks he's helping, giving me control. But the truth is, I want my man to take me. I want to feel him inside, I want to forget anyone else was ever there. I don't want Finn to pretend to be something he's not.

He'd told me to touch myself when I feel robbed that he's not touching me. Instead of his eager cock upright and begging arousing me, the fact he's not driving is doing the opposite to arousing me.

How can I make him see what I need?

Lowering my body, I put my lips on his. He kisses me back, but doesn't entangle his fingers in my hair, or even put his arms around me.

Frustrated as hell, I pull back, punching his shoulder lightly. "This isn't what I want."

"Babe." His hands slide out from under his head, his brow furrows, and his eyes half close. "Cat, no worries if you're not ready yet."

If I'm not ready now, I'll never be. My eyes flash sparks and my temper flares. Now my hands beat at his chest. "I'm more than fucking ready, Finn. Can't you see it's you I want? I want my man, not a toy. If I wanted something to just lie there, I'd have gotten a blow-up doll."

A frown covers his face.

"Finn, for the love of God, just fuck me." Seething, I spit the words at him.

Still, he holds back. He swallows making his Adam's apple bob, and the lightning tattoo on his neck flex. "Cat, if you give me control, I won't be gentle. I can't. It's been too fuckin' long."

"I don't want gentle, I just want you." How can I make him see? What Gun did had robbed me of something, and now he's in danger of succeeding in taking my man from me. "You're still treating me like a victim."

He stills. One beat, two. When I feel a third beat of my heart, he suddenly turns the tables on me. Impressively using his abdominal muscles to pull himself up, one moment I'm sitting astride him, and the next I'm on my back and he's looming over me.

Oh, thank God. Now he's kissing me in the way he hasn't done for weeks. Pouring all his emotion into the caress as his tongue invades, and his teeth nip my lips.

We're both breathing fast by the time he pulls away, he stares at me for a moment, then starts to move down my body.

The only memories he brings back are all about him and how right he's making me feel, as he lavishes his attention on my breasts. His fingers descend to my clit, and finally his mouth is there.

My head slams back, my shoulders push into the bed as he makes me feel so good. Using hands and mouth expertly he brings me fast to the peak and I scream.

While my muscles still quiver, he rears back, reaching to the bedside table and extracting a condom.

Forcing my eyes open I watch as he smooths it down the cock which is jutting out proudly from his body.

I think he's going to hesitate, so I give him no choice. "Fuck me, Finn. Make me yours."

"You're fuckin' mine, and you're going to know it," he growls, then wastes no time pushing into me, filling completely.

It's amazing, it's wonderful. It's all that I hoped and expected it to be. As I flex my hips, he rotates his. Raising my legs I wrap them around him, giving him even greater access.

There's no room for anyone else here, all I know is him. All I breathe in is his scent. All I can see when I open my eyes is the face of the man that I love. The only taste is of our combined flavours as again he kisses me.

Nothing exists except us.

He pumps like a man possessed, I wail as I reach for relief. I come, again, for a second I see stars as he roars and grunts out his own release.

Moments later I'm in his arms.

"I fuckin' love you, Cat." His chest vibrates as he chuckles. "I fuckin' love hearing you purr."

"Oh, I think you just got the full meow."

He pushes himself up on an elbow and leans down to look at me. "Want you on the back of my bike, babe. I want you to wear my property patch, I want us to buy a house. I want you to be my old lady, and I want to get married. I want, *need*, to tie you to me in all the ways I can. And when you're ready, I want my babies to grow in there." He places his hand on my stomach, caressing it so lovingly.

"Do I get any say?"

He snorts. "You hold the keys to my heart, babe."

I'm not going to argue, everything he wants aligns with my own desires.

"Thank you for saving me." He's brought me back from the brink twice now. Once by physically being there, and then by just give me his unerring support.

But he shrugs off my comment. "You saved me right back, babe."

EPILOGUE

tormy…

"Yeah?"

"Stormy, it's Pip."

My eyes widen, the call was from an unknown number. "How the fuck are you, man? It's been months."

"Fancy taking a trip and bringing your rifle along?"

"Smythe?" I hold my breath. Gun didn't die at my hands, but Smythe is the man that I want.

"Yeah. They've got everything out of him he's ever going to give up. He's a waste of space now. Just so happens he'll be transferred to a high security prison, and I've got a time and place where a man of your skills would be able to take him down."

I want it so fucking much I can already savour the sweet taste of revenge. But, I can't risk losing everything now. Another unauthorised execution may dissolve the trust I've slowly built back up. "I'll need to clear it with Snatcher."

Pip snorts. "You've changed a lot."

I have. I've got a woman who wears my patch and a club at

my back with members who I trust and would die for. I'm not going to be going rogue or taking off solo anymore.

"Seems like your ol' lady's stolen your thunder."

"Nah, Pip. She's given me it back." I know I'm more of a man with her. My eyes find the woman in question, she's over the other side of the clubroom speaking to Piston, her hand lying on the stomach where only the two of us currently know our baby is incubating.

Kill Smythe? Yeah, I want that. But I'm not risking everything that now takes precedence in my life.

"I'll speak to Prez and let you know. Can I reach you on this number?"

"Yeah. The transfer takes place a week from now. Let me know if you're going to be there. If you're not, I'll make other arrangements. One way or another, Smythe's days are numbered. He's not worth the cost of feeding him during a long imprisonment.

"You sure you don't need him alive?" Not that him dead isn't what I'd prefer.

"No need. Devil and I have been helping to dismantle his operation. His dominos have already fallen. He taints everyone who breathes the same air. I've had the go ahead to take him out with extreme prejudice."

And he came to me.

"I'll let you know," I repeat, and end the call.

I don't have to wait long, tonight's our regular church. As I walk into the now cleared meeting room restored to its original glory, I take my seat, deep in thought and staring down at the new table we've had commissioned. In similar vein to much of the furniture in the clubhouse which has fast become home, the table was made by a local carpenter. Engraved in the middle is our emblem, Lucifer carrying his scythe and looming over three devils.

It's a far cry from the previous clubhouse. I don't think any of us feel less comfortable here.

I wait for the appropriate 'any other business' slot, then raise my hand. In a concise few words I update my brothers about the call from Pip.

"You're asking fuckin' permission?" Thor shakes his head and raises his eyes to me.

"You could really walk away?" Preacher seems surprised.

Snatcher just lifts his eyebrows.

"Smythe will be taken care of," I emphasise. "It doesn't need to be by my hand. I'm not saying I wouldn't enjoy taking him out, but there's more that matters to me. My club, my family, and my woman."

"Just goes to show some knocks on the head have lasting effects." Goofy grins. In true Stormy fashion, I show him my finger, but it's half-hearted. Since the time I disarmed the bomb he'd been wearing, I and the old man have become close.

"I think you should do it," Prez states, his lips pursing. "This is club business. Smythe was behind the attack that lost us the clubhouse. Anyone disagree?"

No one does. One raised hand surprises me, or not so much the action, but the words that accompany it.

"Not going to let a brother ride on his own. I'll go along." Swift raises her chin toward me.

I couldn't ask for better than that. "I'd be glad to fuckin' have you," I reply, sincerely. Oh, it's not all roses between us, I remain determined to one day beat her ass in the gym. So far, she's always bested me. But asshole that I am, I keep trying.

A quick vote is taken, and it's quickly decided. I'm going, and Swift is coming with me.

A week later, I'm sitting on top of a roof, watching as a prison truck comes into view half a mile away to rendezvous with the jail transport that's waiting. I take in a deep breath, hold it, steady my hand and wait.

Nonchalantly, Smythe steps out acting as if he's no care in

the world. His attitude makes me wonder if he's still expecting to somehow find a way out.

No chance. You end today. This is for you, Pooh. And for you, Tailor, Buster and Slice.

I pull the trigger, taking the relatively easy shot that doesn't come close to my longest distance.

A single bullet to the forehead and he drops down dead, slaughtered like the animal he is.

Swift chuckles beside me as I start to pack up. "That's all there is to it? Fuck, Brother. That's too fuckin' easy. You don't even get your hands dirty."

As we retrace our steps and go to our motorcycles parked next to the SUV, I nudge her. "Yeah, fuckin' coward that's what I am." I pass my equipment over to Brute, who immediately drives away.

"Well, you can keep that. I prefer seeing the whites of their eyes."

"Each to their—" My phone rings, cutting me off. "Pip?"

"It's over, Stormy. Thought you'd like to know Marjan's safe."

"Fuck. Is the kid okay?"

"She will be," he says grimly. "She provided a lot of the evidence that put him where you could get to him today."

"She in danger?"

"Don't worry about that. We're getting her somewhere safe."

I end the call feeling lighter than I think I ever have.

As Swift points to some shrubs, like a gentleman I turn away, letting her take her piss in private. It's over, I muse, swinging my leg over the seat and waiting for her. Soon we'll be on our way, heading back to Utah and the woman who's waiting for me. All the loose ends have been tied and all the ramifications of my fuckups in the past have been erased.

A breeze blows the hair into my face, air tinged with the smell of cordite and gun oil, the distinctive aroma left after an assault weapon has been fired. It brings back a memory of Pooh and I as we cleared an area of insurgents, as if he is here with me today. Suddenly, a bird shoots up from the undergrowth beside me, a young hawk flying away. *Was that a sign, Pooh?*

"Promise me one thing, Storm," Swift calls out as she walks back. "You won't be pulling that trick of crashing into the clubhouse today."

I snort.

"I promise you." Placing her hand on her hips she winks. "If you try and show me your finger, I'll fucking break it off."

Now that, I wouldn't put past her.

Two bikes ride off. Two *brothers*, friends and comrades in arms. Twisting the throttle, I toss back my head, letting the wind carry my laughter away.

Throttle

Born into the club, I'm a Satan's Devil to my core.

I suppose, given that my mom is a firefighter and my dad the ex-sergeant-at arms, I grew up with the need to protect running through my veins, and was the logical choice to become the enforcer when the vacancy emerged.

I may be young, but I'm strong and dependable, and always in control. I love my life and want no other.

But I was knocked off kilter when things started happening that I couldn't understand. Suddenly, I was plunged into a world I couldn't direct. Unable to fulfil the expectations people had of me, I began to flounder.

How could I balance my own desires with the duty that was being thrust on me?

I didn't want a woman of my own. I didn't want to be a husband. I had years before I thought I'd be settling down.

But fate, it seems, has other ideas.

And it terrifies me.

ACKNOWLEDGMENTS & AUTHOR'S NOTE

From the moment Stormy introduced himself to me I knew he had a story to tell. Unfortunately, he decided to keep that to himself for a while, but once he started speaking, it was worth listening.

I did wonder whether he'd be able to redeem himself, but in the end, I think he did. I loved revisiting Swift and the other members of the Utah chapter.

As I'm writing this, 2020 is coming to a close, and what a hell of a year it has been. It has been distracting and difficult to write at times, but my new year's resolution is to try harder next year.

We will be revisiting Utah at some point, but the next book will be the third in the second-generation series. We'll be catching up with the San Diego chapter, as well as, by popular demand, starting our ride with Red in Vegas. Lots of stories to tell.

I've relied on beta readers a lot this year as they've managed to point out a lot of inconsistencies in the plots and helped me get everything straight. Sheri and Danena have been brilliant yet again, and thanks also go to Tami, Alex, Nicole, Terra, and Zoe. As usual all comments have been helpful.

This is another book edited by Maggie Kern and I really can't think of anything to say that I haven't said before. I love working with you and I can't recommend you enough as an editor.

Thanks to Melanie Darrow for the proofreading of Stormy's Thunder. Thank you so much for your timely responses and suggestions.

The cover image was provided by Golden Czermak of Furious Fotog. As before, he had the perfect model, Nick Bennett, who was a perfect muse for Stormy. The cover was again brought to life by Dar Dixon of Wicked Smart Designs. Thank you all.

Finally, last as always, but definitely not least, thanks to all of you, my wonderful readers who've taken a chance on this book. If it wasn't for your encouragement, I wouldn't keep writing. I have recently received messages and emails telling me how much you like my books, and I love reading every one. A positive message inspires me to write more.

This book, like all of my works, has been to beta readers, through editing twice, to a proofreader and then to ARC readers, but there could still be the odd typo that's crept through. Please message me if you've found anything so I have a chance to correct the book. I love to hear from readers, even if you're pointing out something I've gotten wrong.

If you've enjoyed this book, please consider writing a review. Reviews are essential to us authors, and I appreciate and read them all.

This book may be done, but don't worry. There'll be another Satan's Devil coming along very soon.

STAY IN TOUCH

Email: manda@mandamellett.com

Website: www.mandamellett.com

Sign up for my newsletter to hear about new releases in the Satan's Devils and Blood Brothers series.

Facebook reader group: https://www.facebook.com/groups/mandasbadboys/

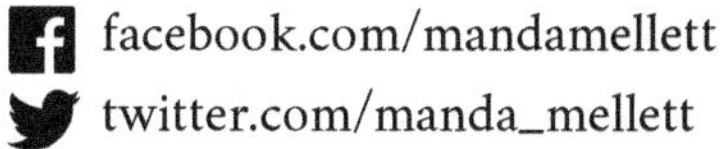

facebook.com/mandamellett

twitter.com/manda_mellett

ABOUT THE AUTHOR

Manda's life's always seemed a bit weird, starting with a childhood that even today she's still trying to make sense of, then losing her parents in the late teens. Going from the tragic to the bizarre, who else could be unlucky enough to have had two car accidents, neither her fault, one involving a nun, and another involving a police woman?

There isn't enough space to list everything that's happened to Manda, or what she's learned from it. But by using the rich fabric of her personal life, psychology degree, varied work experiences, and amazing characters she's met, Manda is able to populate her books with believable in-depth characters and enjoys pitting them against situations which challenge them. Her books are full of suspense, twists and turns and the unexpected.

Manda lives in the beautiful countryside of Essex in the UK, the area's claim to fame being the Wilkin's Jam Factory at nearby Tiptree. She can usually find jars of jam which remind her of home wherever she goes. As well as writing books and reading, Manda loves walking her dogs and keeping fit. She lives with her husband of over 30 years, who, along with her son, is her greatest fan and supporter.

Manda is thankful that one of the more unusual, and at the time unpleasant, turns her life took, now enables her to spend her time writing. Confirming, in her view, every cloud has a silver lining.

Photo by Carmel Jane Photography

www.ingramcontent.com/pod-product-compliance
Lightning Source LLC
Chambersburg PA
CBHW072007180726

48291CB00001BA/169